# A MURDEROUS RELATION

# A
# MURDEROUS
# RELATION

## A VERONICA SPEEDWELL
## MYSTERY

# Deanna Raybourn

BERKLEY
NEW YORK

BERKLEY
An imprint of Penguin Random House LLC
penguinrandomhouse.com

Copyright © 2020 by Raybourn Creative LLC

Library of Congress Cataloging-in-Publication Data

Names: Raybourn, Deanna, author.
Title: A murderous relation / Deanna Raybourn.
Description: First edition. | New York: Berkley, 2020. |
Series: A Veronica Speedwell mystery
Identifiers: LCCN 2019043282 (print) | LCCN 2019043283 (ebook) |
ISBN 9780451490742 (hardcover) | ISBN 9780451490766 (ebook)
Subjects: GSAFD: Mystery fiction.
Classification: LCC PS3618.A983 M87 2020 (print) |
LCC PS3618.A983 (ebook) | DDC 813/.6—dc23
LC record available at https://lccn.loc.gov/2019043282
LC ebook record available at https://lccn.loc.gov/2019043283

First Edition: March 2020

Printed in the United States of America
1   3   5   7   9   10   8   6   4   2

Cover art and design by Leo Nickolls
Book design by Kristin del Rosario

*In memory of Mary Ann, Annie, Elizabeth, Catherine, and Mary Jane. We will not forget.*

# A MURDEROUS RELATION

# CHAPTER

# 1

London, October 1888

W hat in the name of flaming Hades do you mean his lordship wants me to officiate at the wedding of a tortoise?" Stoker demanded.

He appeared properly outraged—an excellent look for him, as it caused his blue eyes to brighten, his muscles to tauten distractingly as he folded his arms over his chest. I dragged my gaze from the set of his shoulders and attempted to explain our employer's request again.

"His lordship wishes Patricia to be married and asks if you will do the honors," I told him. The fact that the Earl of Rosemorran had made such a request shouldn't have given Stoker a moment's pause; it was by far not the most outrageous of the things we had done since coming to live at Bishop's Folly, his lordship's Marylebone estate. We were in the process of cataloging and preparing the Rosemorran Collection—amassed thanks to a few hundred years of genteel avarice on the part of previous earls—in hopes of making it a proper museum. With our occasional forays into sleuthing out murderers and the odd blackmailer, we were a bit behind, and his lordship's latest scheme was not calculated to improve matters.

"Veronica," Stoker said with exaggerated patience, "Patricia is a Galápagos tortoise. She does not require the benefit of clergy."

"I realize that. And even if she did, you are not clergy. The point is that Patricia has been quite agitated of late and his lordship has taken advice on the matter. Apparently, she requires a husband."

Patricia had been a gift from Charles Darwin to the present earl's grandfather, a souvenir of his travels to the Galápagos, and she occupied herself with eating lettuces and frightening visitors as she lumbered about with a disdainful expression on her face. She was as like a boulder as it was possible for a living creature to be, and the only moments of real interest were when she managed to upend herself, a situation that required at least three grown persons to rectify. But lately she had taken to hiding in the shrubbery, moaning mournfully, until the earl consulted a zoologist who suggested she was, as the earl related to me with significant blushes, tired of being a maiden tortoise.

I explained this to Stoker, adding, "So his lordship has ordered a suitable mate and has every expectation that when Patricia is properly mated, she will be right as rain."

Stoker's expression was pained. "But why a *wedding*? Tortoises are not precisely religious."

I resisted the urge to roll my eyes. "Of course they aren't. But Lady Rose is home just now and overheard her father discussing Patricia's new mate." I started to elaborate but Stoker held up a quelling hand. The mention of the earl's youngest and most precocious child was sufficient.

"I understand. But why am I supposed to perform the ceremony? Why can't his lordship?"

"Because the earl is giving away the bride."

Stoker's mouth twitched, but he maintained a serious expression.

"Very well. But whilst I am marrying two tortoises, what will you be doing?"

"Me?" I smiled graciously. "Why, I am to be a bridesmaid."

I would like to say that a tortoise wedding was the most eccentric of the tasks to which we applied ourselves during our time in his lordship's employ; however, I have vowed to be truthful within these pages. Even as I persuaded Stoker to officiate at reptile nuptials, I was keenly aware that we were perched on the precipice of a new and most dangerous investigation. Our previous forays into amateur detection had been largely accidental, the result of insatiable curiosity on my part and an unwillingness to let well enough alone on Stoker's. (He claims to involve himself in murderous endeavors solely for the benefit of my safety, but as I have saved his life on at least one occasion, his argument is as specious as Lamarck's Theory of Inheritance.)

We had just emerged from a harrowing ordeal at the hands of a murderer in Cornwall* when we were summoned back to London by Lady Wellingtonia Beauclerk, Lord Rosemorran's elderly great-aunt and éminence grise behind the throne. For the better part of the nineteenth century, she and her father had made it their mission to protect the royal family—not least from themselves. Lady Wellie meddled strategically, and no one save the royal family and a handful of very highly placed people of influence knew of her power. She dined twice a month with the Archbishop of Canterbury and regularly summoned the Foreign Secretary to tea, and the head of Scotland Yard's Special Branch held himself at her beck and call. This last, Sir Hugo Montgomerie, was my sometime ally, albeit grudgingly on his part. He knew, as

---

* *A Dangerous Collaboration*

did Lady Wellie, that my natural father was the Prince of Wales. I was unacknowledged by the prince, which suited me perfectly, but my very existence was dangerous. My father had undergone a form of marriage with my mother—entirely illegal, as she was an Irishwoman of the Roman Catholic faith and he was forbidden by law to wed without the permission of his august mother, Queen Victoria.

"Bertie always was a romantic," Lady Wellie once told me with a fond sigh.

"There are other words for it," had been my dry response. Lady Wellie did not appreciate levity where her favorites were concerned, and my father occupied a particularly cozy spot in her affections. For that reason, perhaps, she was sometimes indulgent with me, turning a blind eye to my unconventional occupation as a lepidopterist. Butterfly hunting was a perfectly genteel activity for ladies, so long as one was properly chaperoned and never perspired. But I had made a comfortable living from my net, traveling the world in search of the most glorious specimens to sell to private collectors. Even if my parents' union had been a conventional one, sanctioned by both church and state, the fact that I frequently combined business with pleasure—using my expeditions to exercise my healthy libido—would have made it impossible for the prince to recognize me officially as his child. That Lady Wellie had, in the days of her robust youth, indulged regularly in refreshing bouts of physical congress no doubt influenced her attitude of bland acceptance to my discreet activities.

In fact, she had encouraged them on more than one occasion, at least as far as Stoker was concerned. In spite of his numerous attractions—and the fact that we were both more than a little in love with one another—we had hitherto resisted the more primitive blood urges. Stoker frequently swam in whatever available pond or river provided a chilly respite, and I submerged my yearnings in rigorous scientific study and the odd evening spent sampling the collection of robust phallic artifacts I had been sent by a grateful gentleman who had escaped the noose thanks to our efforts on his behalf.*

But in the course of our most recent adventure, Stoker and I had cast off our reticence at last, acknowledging that the curious mental and emotional bond we shared seemed to comprise a physical element as well. At least that was how I liked to phrase it. The truth, dear reader, is that I was as ready for him as any filly ready for the stud. My blood thrummed whenever he came near, the air crackling between us like one of Galvani's electrical experiments. It was a mercy that we had not been alone in our train compartment on the journey back to London; otherwise, I suspect the urgent swaying of the conveyance would have proven too much for my increasingly limited self-control.

Stoker, as it happens, was possessed of more decorum. Lady Wellie would have pronounced him a romantic as well, for he insisted that our inaugural congress must be properly celebrated—to wit, in a bed. A *comfortable* bed, he added firmly, with a wide mattress and a sturdy frame and a headboard that would bear some abuse. I blinked at this last, but agreed, realizing that time and privacy would be required to fully sate us both.

The result was that we arrived back in London in a fever of anticipation, bickering happily about which of our lodgings should provide the better setting for our genteel debaucheries. Lord Rosemorran housed us in two of the follies on his estate, Stoker in a Chinese pagoda, and me in a miniature Gothic chapel.

"Mine has a wider bed," I pointed out.

"Mine is nearer the Roman temple baths," he reminded me. I fell

---

* *A Perilous Undertaking*

into a reverie, distracted at the notion of a very wet, very imperfectly clothed Stoker and the hot, heavy air of the baths with their vast pools of heated water and comfortable sofas.

"Excellent point," I managed.

But we returned to find that the plumbing in the Roman baths had exploded modestly, damaging the temple and Stoker's adjacent pagoda.

"No worries," Lord Rosemorran told him, unaware of our predicament and therefore jovially oblivious to our dismay. "I have had Lumley move your things into the house. You can sleep upstairs. There is a very nice guest room next door to the night nursery."

I spent the better part of that day trying to decide whether Stoker should break out of the house that night or whether I should break *in*, but in the end, the matter was decided for me. Preparations for the upcoming tortoise nuptials had set the household at sixes and sevens, and amidst the chaos, Lady Wellie sent for us. We had been summoned back to London at her insistence. The audacious killer known as Jack the Ripper had begun a murderous rampage, slaughtering his victims so brutally that it had caught the nation's attention—and Lady Wellie's. We knew the villain had struck again, two victims in the same night, and it was this heinous double crime that caused her to dispatch a telegram insisting upon our return and ending our Cornish adventure.

After the bracing air of Cornwall, London was a contrast of sooty fogs and afternoon lamps lit against the early October gloom. Lady Wellie awaited us in her private rooms, her dark gaze alert. A clock on the mantel ticked softly, and in the corner stood a large gilded cage in which two lovebirds chattered companionably. Lady Wellie flicked a significant glance towards the clock.

"It is about time," she said by way of greeting.

Stoker bent to brush a kiss to her withered cheek. She did not simper as she usually did, but her expression softened a little.

"I do apologize," I told her. "His lordship waylaid us on the way in with news of alterations in our lodgings, and then we were sorting the details for a tortoise wedding. Patricia is to be a bride."

Lady Wellie's clawlike hand curved over the top of her walking stick. "I know. I was asked to provide her with a bit of Honiton lace for a veil," she replied. "But I have not summoned you here to discuss the latest family foray into madness. I need your help."

Lady Wellie was plainspoken by habit but seldom quite so forthright. Stoker shot me a glance.

"The East End murderer," he supplied. "We read the latest newspapers on the train this morning. He has a penchant for prostitutes, this fellow."

"Not prostitutes," she corrected swiftly. "The newspapers know what sells, but the most one can say definitively of these unfortunates is they are women who possibly turn to the trade in moments of necessity. None of them has been a true professional."

"Does it make a difference?" I put in.

"I imagine it does to them," she replied. Her hand flexed on the walking stick, and I noticed she did not offer us refreshment. Lady Wellie kept one eye on the ormolu clock upon the mantel as she spoke. For the first time, I was aware of a taut stillness in the room, something expectant, stretched on tiptoe. Even the lovebirds fell silent.

She went on. "It is still early days in the investigation, but it seems each of them had a regular occupation—flower seller, hop picker. If they sold themselves, it was only to make the price of a bed at night or a pint of gin. When they had need of ready cash and nothing left to pawn, they exploited the only asset in their possession."

"Poor devils," Stoker said softly. We lived in luxury thanks to his lordship's largesse, but we had seen such women often enough in our travels about the city. Haggard and worn by worry and poor nutrition, they were old before their time, their flesh their only commodity.

Whether they used their bodies to labor in a field or up against the rough brick of an alley wall, every ha'penny they collected was purchased at a dreadful cost.

Lady Wellie cleared her throat. "Yes, well. As you can imagine, the newspapers cannot contain themselves. They are utterly hysterical on the subject, whipping up the capital into a fever of terror and speculation. I do not like the mood at present. Anything is possible."

She narrowed her eyes, and I filled in the rest. "You mean republicanism is on the rise again."

"There is agitation in every quarter. These *journalists*"—her voice dripped scorn upon the word—"are taking this opportunity to stoke resentment against immigrants, against the Jews, and against the wealthy."

"Not groups that ordinarily fall in for resentment from the same quarter," Stoker observed.

"They do now. The middle class is perfectly poised to hate in both directions. They think the lower orders criminal and they fear them even as they look down upon them. And they resent the rich for not taking better care of the situation, policing the poor and the indigent."

I thought back to the tent city that had occupied Trafalgar Square for the better part of the year, row upon row of temporary structures sheltering those who had no other place to go. For months, the indigent had slept rough, washing themselves as best they could in the fountains, passing under the gaze of the Barbary lions. There were not enough soup kitchens and shelters and doss-houses to keep everyone fed and warm, and it was all too easy to step over some slumbering wretch upon the pavement and dismiss it as someone else's trouble to solve.

"The mood, at present, is dangerous," she went on. "The goodwill from last year's Jubilee seems to have evaporated." Queen Victoria, desolate in her widowhood, had withdrawn from public life, immuring herself in stony silence at Windsor Castle.

But it had been two and a half decades since Prince Albert's death, and the queen's unwillingness to show herself to her people had bred annoyance, which had turned to outright debate about whether a monarchy was even relevant in modern times. The previous year's Jubilee had seen the queen out and about, a rotund little figure swathed in black silk and larded with diamonds, nodding and waving to the cheers that resounded as her extended royal clan trotted obediently in her wake in a glorious and glittering panoply. But a year was a long time in public memory, and over the winter—the hardest in decades—privation and want had grown so terrible that all of the warm feeling of patriotism and bonhomie towards the royal family had melted like ice on a summer's day.

Lady Wellie clasped her walking stick more tightly. "It is the very worst time for any sort of scandal to break." She paused, and I saw her gaze sharpen as she looked from me to Stoker and back again. Suddenly I understood that feeling of taut expectation.

"Which one of them?" I asked.

"You will see soon enough," she replied grimly.

Just then, the clock struck the hour and there came a low scratching noise behind the paneling next to the fireplace. Lady Wellie looked to Stoker.

"Open it. You will find the mechanism behind the china shepherdess on the mantel," she instructed.

Stoker did as he was bade, pressing a hidden button on the mantel. The paneling next to the fireplace swung open on silent hinges, and for a moment all I could see was Stoker snapping to attention and making a low bow as Lady Wellie struggled slowly to her feet, then sank into a deep curtsy. A tall, slender figure swathed in heavy black veils entered. I found myself standing with no conscious intention of rising. She had that effect upon people.

"Your Royal Highness," said Lady Wellie. "Miss Veronica Speedwell and Mr. Revelstoke Templeton-Vane, the younger brother of Viscount Templeton-Vane. Veronica, Stoker, Her Royal Highness, the Princess of Wales."

# CHAPTER

## 2

The princess threw back her veils. Even without Lady Wellie's introduction, I knew that face. It had stared out at me from countless shop windows, graced innumerable newspapers and fashion magazines. Our future queen, Alexandra of Denmark, wife to the Prince of Wales, and my stepmother.

Another figure stood behind her in the shadows and I gave a cry of astonishment. "Inspector Archibond!"

The inspector was not a particular friend of mine. Stoker and I had made his acquaintance briefly during a previous investigation,* and none of us had been terribly impressed. He thought us meddle-some and willful and we thought him distinctly humorless and brittle.

He still looked well-groomed and nondescript; nothing about him would make an impression of any duration, but it suddenly occurred to me what a useful quality that might prove in a policeman.

He gave a nod, acknowledging my greeting, but said nothing, look-ing instead to the princess. It had been a breach of etiquette for any of

---

* *A Treacherous Curse*

us to speak or acknowledge one another before she did, but there was no trace of irritation in her manner. She took a seat and signed for the rest of us to resume ours. The gesture—like everything she did—was graceful. Her expression was composed, but faint purple smudges shadowed her eyes. She sat slightly forwards in her chair, and I remembered that she was a little deaf. She gave me a gentle smile.

"Miss Speedwell, I regret we are meeting under such unusual circumstances."

I flicked a glance to Lady Wellie before looking again to my stepmother. The princess was modestly dressed in a sober, simple skirt and jacket of navy blue with only the collar and cuffs of a crisp white shirtwaist peeking from the edges. It was, at first glance, the sort of austerity one might expect of any well-bred lady of some forty-odd years. But the skirt was beautifully draped by the hand of a master dressmaker, the hems delicately pinked to resemble petals. Her jewels were discreet, only a heavy locket and her wedding ring, with an enameled watch pinned to her lapel and the gleam of pearls beneath her cuffs. Her hat was a little broader than fashionable, with its thick black veil to conceal her still-beautiful face. It was a face I might have been happy to see at another time and in another place.

"Not at all, Your Royal Highness," I said tightly. "This is not the first time I have been summoned by a princess who wished to preserve her incognita," I told her, harking back to a fateful meeting with my father's younger sister that had ended in bloodshed.*

The princess did not flinch. "Louise," she murmured. "Yes, she and Lady Wellie have been eloquent on the subject of your abilities."

I bowed my head but said nothing. After a moment, the princess went on.

---

* *A Perilous Undertaking*

"It is on Lady Wellie's advice that I asked to see you, Miss Speed-well," she told me. "And you, Mr. Templeton-Vane," she added with a glance to Stoker. "I know what you have been able to accomplish in the past, and it is my hope that you will be able to help me now."

"Help you? With what, ma'am?" Stoker asked kindly.

She paused and looked to Lady Wellie, who gave her a firm nod, as if to stiffen her resolve. Inspector Archibond had taken a chair a little distance apart, tucked discreetly in the shadows. Presumably, he had attended in order to preserve the princess's safety during her incognita in the streets of London. But I knew he was attentive, listening to every word we exchanged.

The princess drew a deep breath. "It is my son, my eldest, Prince Albert Victor. We call him Eddy in the family." She reached up and unclasped the golden locket, passing it to me as she touched a narrow button on the side. It sprang open to reveal a photograph.

I knew that face as well. Images of the eldest son of the Prince of Wales sold newspapers. He was our future king, after all. He had our father's heavy-lidded Hanoverian eyes, but his face, long and slender, belonged to his mother. His dark hair waved over his brow, and a pair of elegant moustaches turned up at the ends over a full, sensuous mouth. He might have been handsome but for his chin. It receded slightly, giving him a mildly feckless look, the sort of face that belonged to a man one might not be able to depend upon in times of trouble. But the eyes were kind and the mouth sweet.

I handed the locket back and the princess held it, looking down fondly. Still I did not speak.

"What is the difficulty, ma'am?" Stoker asked.

"Eddy, like most young men, has sown a few wild oats," she said, her expression a little embarrassed.

"I am the product of a wild oat myself, ma'am," I told her. "I think we all know what you mean."

"Veronica," Lady Wellie murmured. I did not know if Archibond had been made aware of my paternity, but Lady Wellie and the princess would understand my inference.

The princess flushed, a sweep of warm rose heightening the color in her cheeks. A lesser woman might have flounced away at such a provocation. But Alexandra of Denmark was a future queen and empress, and I saw then that she was made of sterner stuff. Her posture stiffened and she regarded me down the length of her nose.

"Miss Speedwell, it does not escape me that the circumstances of our meeting are extraordinary. I hope we may at least be civil to one another, and let it begin with me. I offer you my heartfelt apologies."

I blinked at her. "For what, ma'am?"

"For the cavalier manner in which you have been treated. You have demonstrated loyalty and honor in your dealings with the family, and for that you should be commended. I regret that you have not been dealt with more kindly."

I thought of the promises, made and broken and made again. I had never asked for, never *wanted* anything more than a moment of my father's time. I did not crave recognition or money or anything other than the bare acknowledgment from this man that he had taken part in my creation, that he had loved my mother and that I had been born of that love.

Instead, I had endangered myself, risking my own life and Stoker's on more than one occasion on their behalf. And for no greater reward than a series of hidden meetings conducted in shadows and secrecy. When my own uncle had plotted to overthrow the monarchy on my behalf in a plot of breathtaking melodrama, I had chosen the family that would not own me, without hesitation and without regret. My uncle had offered me a throne, and I had refused it—as much for the sake of my blood family as for the sake of my own inclinations. But still there was no direct word from my father.

A hot streak of anger simmered always, just below the surface, but I did not give vent to it.

"What do you want of us, ma'am?" I asked.

Realizing that an emotional appeal would not serve, she clasped the locket safely back around her neck, snapping the golden door closed upon my half-brother's face.

"Eddy is in trouble, I think. With a woman." She broke off and gave an anguished look to Wellie, who supplied the details.

"Her Royal Highness has had a discreet communication from her jeweler. It seems that the prince may have commissioned a jewel for a lady."

"A jewel?" I inquired. "What sort of jewel?"

"A diamond star. You are too young to remember, but there was a fashion for them in the sixties. All the rage, they were. Empress Eugénie had a particularly lovely collection."

"Winterhalter liked to paint them," the princess put in, a small nostalgic smile touching her lips. "Empress Elisabeth of Austria used to fancy them as well."

"Indeed. I had rather a fine set myself," Lady Wellie said. "And Her Royal Highness has the most extensive collection in Europe, most notably a set by Garrard. It is they who have contacted her about the prince's purchase."

I recognized the name of one of the most esteemed and fashionable jewelers in London. From time to time a member of some royal family or other would be married, and it was traditional to shower the bride with jewels. Sketches of her parures would be published in the newspapers and invariably the name "Garrard" made an appearance, usually attached to the most lavish and extravagant illustrations.

The princess picked up the thread of the narrative. "Because they were fashionable for so long and because so many women have them, it is difficult to tell them apart at first glance. Mine are all marked with an engraving on the back of the Prince of Wales feathers." She reached into her reticule and withdrew a small velvet pouch. When she opened her palm, it was as if she had offered a handful of light, the faceted diamonds catching the glow of the gaslights and flinging them back again. Wordlessly, she turned it over, showing the back, where the feathers were sharply incised.

The badge of the three white ostrich plumes was recognizable anywhere. Princes of Wales had been engraving, embroidering, painting, gilding, and jewelling the image on anything that belonged to them for the better part of five centuries. I was only surprised none of them had managed to tattoo it upon his person yet.

"From what I am told, the prince commissioned a star patterned upon this one, save for the badge on the reverse. It was embellished only with his initials. AVCE. Albert Victor Christian Edward." She turned it over again, dazzling us with the dancing light before putting it away, almost reverently.

She took a deep breath. "The jewel can be traced to him. It is imperative that it be retrieved before that happens."

"Why?" I asked, canting my head.

Her expression softened. "My son is in love, deeply, and the match is a good one."

"His cousin," Lady Wellie supplied. "Princess Alix of Hesse and by Rhine."

I had never heard of her, but that was not surprising. The queen had dozens of grandchildren scattered across the courts of Europe like so much thistledown. I flicked Lady Wellie a glance and she explained.

"The queen's second daughter, Princess Alice, married the Grand Duke of Hesse. Poor Alice has been dead a decade now from the diphtheria," she said, the corners of her mouth pulling down. She had been overseeing the royal family with unswerving devotion and all the fury of an avenging angel for the better part of seven decades. I wondered how many losses she had counted in her time.

"Princess Alix is Alice's youngest daughter. She is sixteen," the Princess of Wales put in. "She is shy and too young for marriage at present. But my son cherishes the hope that in time she will come to love him as he does her."

"And you believe his gift of this jewel to another woman would prove an impediment?" Stoker suggested.

The princess's smile was thin. "No woman likes to know she is not the first in her husband's affections." She did not look at me when she spoke, but I felt the thrust of her remark just the same. My father had loved my mother enough to risk an empire for her. The fact that he had given way to his destiny was a testament to the weakness of his character, not the strength of his love.

"Besides," she went on, "Alix is a devout Lutheran. She has been strictly brought up in a small and conservative court. If she were to discover that my son has conducted himself with anything less than perfect propriety and discretion, she might never entertain him as a suitor."

"Perhaps she shouldn't," I pointed out. "If she does not know the truth, she cannot know his character. She might accept him based upon an imperfect understanding of him, and that never bodes well for a marriage."

The princess's expression was pained. "My son is not a bad man, Miss Speedwell. He is twenty-four years old. His character is yet incompletely formed."

I resisted the urge to look at Stoker. His character had been graven in stone by the time he had run away from home at the age of twelve. He had ever been as he was, solid as the earth and master of his own fate. The fact that the princess still clearly viewed her son as a child would be the least of Alix of Hesse's worries if she chose to marry him, I reflected.

"What did His Royal Highness say when you questioned him?" I asked.

Her expression was aghast. "I would never discuss this with Eddy."

"Then, forgive me, ma'am," Stoker said gently, "how do you know what he did with it?"

Inspector Archibond roused himself from the shadows. "Her Royal Highness asked me to make a few discreet inquiries, but I have reached the limits of my abilities in this matter." He gave a half shake of the head, as if to warn by the gesture and his clipped tone that he would not provide further details in the presence of the princess.

"The prince is in Scotland at present," she told us. "This is the perfect opportunity to retrieve the jewel before matters get out of hand."

I blinked at her. "You want us to *steal* the star?"

To her credit, she did not flinch. "That is not a word I would have used, Miss Speedwell, but I will not quibble over syntax. I want the jewel retrieved so that a small mistake made by my son in a moment of youthful impetuosity will not ruin his chances for future happiness."

Blood rushed to my head, pounding in my ears like a war drum. "Yes, it would be a pity if a prince had to accept the consequences of his actions," I said softly.

There was a sharp intake of breath from Lady Wellie, and the two men watched us warily. The princess gave me a level look. "I did not come to spar with you. I hoped you would be sympathetic to my cause. Eddy is not like other boys," she said, her maternal affection softening her tone. "He is gentle and easily led. He is not, by nature, suited to the difficult decisions that kingship will bring to him. He is far more my child than his father's," she added with a rueful smile. "No, Miss Speedwell, I am not blind to my son's faults, for all that I am an indulgent mother. I know Eddy's flaws, and if he were a private gentleman, they would touch no one but him. But it is his destiny to become king. And his choice of wife will be the most important decision of his life. She must be stronger than he is, more resilient. She must prop him up when he requires it, give him loan of her strength when he has not enough of his own. She must draw forth his courage and his principles. He has sweetness and devotion, and with the proper wife to inspire him, he will do great things. But not without her."

"And you think Alix of Hesse can do all of that?" Stoker put in. "You said she is only sixteen."

"But her character is formed," the princess insisted. "When she is ready to marry, she will bring strength of purpose and focus to her husband. I want that husband to be Eddy."

"What of the recipient of the star?" I asked. "Won't she complain to the prince when it is taken from her?"

"Eddy will understand that I have retrieved it and there will be no need for discussion on the matter. I do not like scenes. All will be as it was."

I did not glance at Stoker, but I knew his thoughts. He would be as skeptical as I under the circumstances, but he was a gentleman to his marrow. He would not voice the doubt we shared as to the princess's objectivity with regard to her son. She was clearly besotted with her firstborn and willing to overlook considerable faults while relying on the skills of a mere child to shape him into the king he ought to become.

Suddenly, I hated the lot of them.

"I presume the prince's inamorata is a woman of questionable virtue?" I asked pleasantly.

The princess gave Archibond an oblique look, prompting him to speak.

"I can provide the details for you later," he said hastily. "I have learnt enough to get you started, but there is no call for Her Royal Highness to be party to such a discussion."

"Let us discuss it now," I said with a deliberately pleasant tone. "His lady must be of questionable virtue. Does she have private lodgings or a place of business to conduct her *affaires*?"

Lady Wellie thumped her walking stick and the lovebirds in the corner stopped their wittering, stuttering to a sudden silence. "Enough, Veronica."

Stoker spoke. "It is a difficult subject, but I think in light of what you are asking of us, we have a right to know. What sort of place are you expecting us to go?"

The princess pressed her lips together, sealing her silence. Lady Wellie gave us a withering stare, and it was left to Archibond to speak. "Private lodgings," he said at last. "A sort of club, as it were."

Stoker's response was swift. "No respectable lady would enter such a place."

"But I am not respectable," I said with a smile at both Lady Wellie and her royal guest. I nodded to Archibond still sitting quietly in the corner. "That is the point, is it not? You might have asked Special Branch to attend to this particularly nasty piece of business. It is their purview to protect the royal family, after all. I daresay they might have enlisted the aid of a willing female to assist them."

"Special Branch can do nothing," Archibond interjected quickly. "Every man is devoted to the Whitechapel murders just now. Even I can spare only minutes to help Her Royal Highness. The princess is adamant upon the point of secrecy. And the fewer who know of this, the better."

"Not even His Royal Highness, the prince's father?" I asked.

The princess clasped her hands together tightly. "Not even he."

"You surprise me, ma'am. I have been given to understand the Prince of Wales is a loving and indulgent father."

I held her gaze level with my own and felt a rush of triumph when she looked away first. She was silent a long moment, but when she spoke, it was without the dignity of a princess or a queen-in-waiting. She spoke as a mother.

"Please, Miss Speedwell. I will pay whatever fee you deem suitable. He is my son," she said simply.

"And I am nothing to you," I told her, rising to my feet. Archibond sprang silently to his feet in the corner. Stoker stood also, at my back. "I must refuse. You may rely upon my discretion in this matter to speak nothing of it. But my assistance will go no further."

She gripped the arms of her chair, her lips thin and pale. Lady Wellie thrust herself to stand, her gnarled knuckles white upon the walking stick she held in her hand.

"Veronica—"

I put up a hand. "Nothing you can say will change my mind, Lady Wellingtonia. I am sorry to disappoint you, but I have made my decision."

She appealed to Stoker. "Will you say nothing to change her mind?"

He roused himself. "I would not attempt it, my lady." He bowed to the princess as she stood, slowly, as if in defeat.

"I should have guessed this would be futile," she said to Lady Wellie. She turned to me. "Good day to you, Miss Speedwell. It has been an illuminating encounter."

She drew her veil over her features, shadowing them from view. Archibond went to the door, holding it for the princess. He gave me a long, inscrutable look, then disappeared into the darkness.

The princess covered Lady Wellie's hand briefly with her own before descending the stairs after the inspector. She went without a backwards glance. Lady Wellie closed the door after her, securing the piece of paneling so that it fitted flush against the fireplace wall.

Her silence was pointed as she resumed her chair.

"I meant what I said," I told her. "I will not speak of this to anyone. The prince's elegant little debauchery is his own affair."

"It exposes him to blackmail should his lady friend take it in her head to do him harm. The prince's disgrace will be on the front page of the *Times* if I cannot find a way to stop this," she retorted.

Her expression was fretful and Stoker went to put a consoling hand to her shoulder. "The Prince of Wales has had any number of skeletons rattling around his cupboards, most of them salacious," he reminded her. "He has even been subject to subpoena in divorce proceedings as a witness to a wife's infidelity. No one seriously believes that a bit of untidiness in his personal life should disqualify him from being king. Prince Eddy is no different. If the scandal breaks, it will be a tempest in a teacup."

Lady Wellie said nothing, but her lips were working furiously. It was unlike her to be so reticent. Or so agitated. It was said she had once faced down a Slav anarchist bomber with nothing more than an umbrella. But now she seemed ill at ease—or perhaps just ill? There was a color I did not like, a whiteness at the lips that struck me as unhealthy. The rest of her complexion was high, and tiny beads of perspiration pearled her hairline.

"Lady Wellie, perhaps you would like to rest," I suggested.

"Rest?" Her lips tightened. "I think not. There is too much at stake."

"Very well." I sighed. "But Stoker is quite right. A jewel given to a courtesan will hardly raise an eyebrow in most circles. I cannot imagine the bishops will be terribly pleased, but I am certain you can handle any opprobrium from that quarter."

She shook her head slowly. "It is not the jewel that concerns me."

"What, then?" Stoker asked, his voice gentle.

She hesitated, saying nothing for a long moment. She had slipped into a reverie of sorts, her expression faraway. I sat forwards in my chair. "Your telegram mentioned the Whitechapel murders. You said it was a matter of life and death," I reminded her.

She shook her head almost angrily. "I cannot think why," she muttered.

Stoker darted me a glance, alarmed at her sudden confusion, but when he spoke his voice was soothing. "Lady Wellie, I think Veronica is right. Rest now. We can talk in the morning—"

"I wish I knew what to do!" she exclaimed. She put out her hands, heavily ringed with filthy diamonds. Stoker took them, and she squeezed hard. I could see his fingers whitening in her grip.

"You must help," she insisted, her voice a rasp of pain. Suddenly, she pitched forwards, and would have landed on the floor had Stoker not leapt. He caught her, cradling her to his chest as her head lolled back, her eyes rolling white.

"Lady Wellie!" I dropped to my knees, but Stoker had already taken charge of the situation. His time as a surgeon in Her Majesty's Navy meant that he was extremely effective in a crisis. He wrenched open the fichu pinned to her neckline as he put his head to her chest.

"She breathes," he pronounced. He rose in one motion, sweeping her stout form up into his arms. He carried her through to the bedchamber where her maid, Weatherby, had just entered with an armful of clean linen.

One look at her prostrate mistress sent her into hysterics, and it took me a sound slap and the better part of a minute to bring her around. When she was in command of herself once more, I sent her to fetch his lordship and Lady Wellie's regular physician.

"What else?" I asked Stoker.

He was keeping careful watch upon her pulse. "When Weatherby returns, have her change Lady Wellie into a nightdress and bring hot bricks to keep her from a chill. She needs a stimulant. Bring brandy," he instructed.

I did as I was told, haring swiftly down to his lordship's sideboard for a bottle. Stoker ladled a spoonful down her throat. She sputtered and swallowed but remained insensible. He turned to me. "It is not strong enough. Her pulse is thready. I fear we are losing her. There is a preparation of foxglove on the washstand. Fetch it."

I found it, a small green bottle marked with a skull and crossbones on a label from the local chemist. He wrenched out the cork and dosed her, holding her mouth closed with one hand until she swallowed involuntarily. His expression was tortured but determined, and I knew it cost him something to force her to take the medicine.

After a moment, her breathing seemed to ease slightly, and he slumped a little.

"There is nothing else to be done until her physician arrives," he told me soberly.

"What is it?"

"Angina, most likely. Possibly apoplexy."

My hand crept into his and he gripped it tightly. "How bad?"

He shook his head and said nothing. He would not guess. We kept her comfortable during the long, agonizing wait for her physician. Lord Rosemorran appeared with Weatherby, weeping quietly into her sleeve. She started to make noise but I fixed her with a quelling eye and she subsided once more into silence, wiping her eyes as she aired a nightdress.

"If the gentlemen will withdraw, I will help you," I told her. They did not have to be told twice. They waited outside the door as Weatherby and I carefully undressed her mistress and wrapped her in her nightdress. We tucked her into the warmed bed just as the physician arrived, huffing a little. He had the flushed-pink nose of a devoted port drinker and the assurance of a successful Harley Street practitioner. He listened gravely to Stoker's quick summary of the events and shooed us from the room to make his examination.

Lord Rosemorran seemed at a loss as we stood outside. "I hardly know what to think," he managed at last. "She has always been there. Ever since I was a child, I thought of her as immovable, fixed."

"You make her sound like the Rock of Gibraltar," I said with a smile.

He smiled in return. "Exactly that. She is our rock."

Hours passed, slowly. Lumley, the butler, brought chairs for us, and from time to time a frightened maid peeped around the corner, then whisked away to report that there was no news. We, none of us, had an appetite for dinner. Lord Rosemorran's sister, Lady Cordelia, took charge of the children and sent food up, but we sent it back untasted. She came to sit with us after putting the children to bed. We said little more until the physician emerged, his expression somber.

"I will not pretend her condition is not serious, my lord," he began. "She has indeed suffered a severe attack of angina. The worst of the crisis is past, but it remains to be seen if she will return to consciousness or how great—if any—damage the heart has sustained." He looked to Stoker. "You said you dosed her with foxglove?"

"I did."

He gave a sharp nod. "Likely saved her life with that. It's a dangerous proposition but in cases like these it is the only possible chance."

Stoker's relief was unspoken but palpable.

"May I see her?" Lord Rosemorran asked.

The physician shook his head. "She is resting now with that girl. I've had a stern word with her about keeping watch. If there are any changes, she will alert you. I will return in the morning to look in on her and assess her condition further. If she shows signs of distress, send for me at once."

His lordship walked the physician downstairs as Lady Cordelia rose, smoothing out her skirts. "I will sit with her. Weatherby is loyal but she is flighty as a hummingbird in a crisis."

"You will fatigue yourself," I protested.

She waved it off. "It will give me something useful to do." There was a slight bitterness to her mouth, a new resentment I had not seen before. Lady Cordelia was by far the most intelligent member of the family, but her talents were often wasted in domestic trivialities. She seemed to be floundering of late, not least because she had endured a painful trial of her own only a few months past.

"You will send for me if you have need?" I asked.

She gave me a grateful nod. Stoker stepped in. "I will walk Veronica to her lodgings and return to sleep in the China Bedroom. Wake me if there is anything I can do," he urged.

She accepted with thanks and bade us good night before slipping into Lady Wellie's room. The door closed with an air of finality and Stoker took my hand, leading me down through the quiet, slumbering house. Lord Rosemorran had taken himself to his study; a slim band of golden light shone under the door. We passed through the side door and into the cool air of the night.

The grounds were quiet, sleeping under stars that were mere pinpricks within the city. Stone paths meandered between manicured hedges, leading from one part of the estate to another. We reached the door of my little Gothic chapel and Stoker turned, his eyes glittering in the darkness.

His hands were heavy on my shoulders. "Tonight—" he began.

"Is not the night for us," I finished.

"Still, I cannot rest," he said, his nerves obviously strung as tightly as mine. He tipped his head. "I think we should have an outing. It is not too late."

# CHAPTER

## 3

To my very great surprise, within a short period of time, we were bound for Hampstead Heath in one of his lordship's carriages, a stout wooden crate following in a cart. I asked no questions. It was oddly restful to be simply carried along, like a cork in a river current. The evening was cool, brisk even, but without dampness for once, and as we climbed out of the metropolis and into the clearer air of the heath, I found my spirits rising.

Stoker directed the driver to a secluded house, a Queen Anne villa nestled on significant grounds. It was thickly—if unimaginatively—bordered by shrubbery, tangled and overgrown. The house itself was in good enough repair, although here and there the pointing wanted freshening. Wood smoke poured from the chimneys. An old-fashioned house, I thought with pleasure. I hated the throat-thickening clouds of coal soot that blanketed the city. An honest wood fire was a joy too little encountered, I reflected.

Stoker directed the porters who had come with the cart as he lifted a hand to the door knocker, a tarnished brass affair fashioned into the shape of a dolphin.

The door was thrown back almost instantly by a small man who peered nearsightedly through a pair of smudged spectacles. His hair stood out like spun sugar, a great airy tuft at each temple, with an expanse of bare pink scalp in between. His brows were lavish and expressive, and beneath them twinkled a pair of bright dark eyes.

"Mr. Templeton-Vane!" he cried. "This is an unexpected pleasure! And you have brought *her*!"

I made a modest little bob of the head, but he was staring past me, towards the crate that was being unloaded from the cart. "Oh, my good fellows, do be careful, I beg you!" he called.

"Mr. Pennybaker," Stoker said gently, recalling his attention. "May I present my associate, Miss Speedwell? Veronica, this is Mr. Pennybaker, a collector of natural history."

The little fellow, slight as an elf, blinked furiously as he looked up at me through his spectacles. "Veronica Speedwell? What a delightful name. A great joke of the botanical variety," he said, nodding in agreement with his own observation. "A great joke *indeed*."

I smiled in spite of myself. It was not the first time my name had provided amusement to the botanically inclined, and I knew it would not be the last. We shook hands, or rather he took mine and pumped it furiously. He turned, tailcoat flapping as he gestured for the men to bring his trophy into the house. "Come along, come along!" he urged, leading the way through a series of corridors and into a gallery of sorts. Every corner was crammed with taxidermied specimens, some of them quite good, most tolerable, and one or two frankly appalling.

The men maneuvered the crate into the center of the room, where Mr. Pennybaker was fairly dancing on the balls of his feet in anticipation. He rummaged in his pockets for coins. "A shilling each," he crowed. "Go and have a pint or two with my thanks," he told them. They exchanged glances at the munificence of the tip, tugging their forelocks in gratitude.

Stoker unfolded a series of canvas tarpaulins to protect the carpet while I surveyed the specimen nearest to me. The glass case was misty, spiderwebbed with cracks, and so occluded I could hardly determine what was inside.

"I see you are admiring my kittens' coronation," Mr. Pennybaker said waggishly.

"I beg your pardon?" I blinked at him.

He removed the cover and exposed the diorama in all its repellent glory. Inside the vast case, on a worn piece of Axminster, two dozen stuffed kittens had been arranged. Stoker usually insisted upon the more accurate term of "mounted" but I could clearly see the sawdust oozing out of their tiny seams. Every kitten had been fashioned into a different character to play a role in the tableau. There was a plump tabby bishop holding a small golden crown in his diminutive paws. Sitting before him on a miniature copy of the Coronation Chair from Westminster Abbey was a black and tawny striped kitten dressed in a gown of satin, once white, I thought, but now discolored by age to an unappetizing shade of yellow. Maids of honor perched near the throne, and courtier cats had been dressed in knee britches and the odd uniform of the army or navy. Behind them all, little banners had been sewn with heraldic badges and a pair of marmalade trumpeters held tiny brass instruments to their mouths.

"How extraordinary," I murmured. It was utterly appalling, and I had little doubt Stoker hated it as much as I did. He had strong feelings about the dignity of dead things, and there could be few things less dignified for a dead kitten than this display of sentimentality.

Mr. Pennybaker turned away suddenly.

"Oh, it begins!" he said, clasping his hands in excitement. Stoker had taken up a pry bar and was applying himself to opening the crate.

"What is it?" I inquired, catching a little of Mr. Pennybaker's enthusiasm.

"The king's ass!" he said in a delighted whisper.

"Indeed?" I managed.

He nodded, his spectacles bobbing on his face, the tufts of hair waving madly. "The king's painted African ass!" he exclaimed.

Stoker wrenched the last board free and there it was. It was unlike any animal I had ever encountered. I peered at its plain hindquarters, its sturdy equine bones, the flourish of stripes upon its forequarters. "That is almost a zebra," I observed.

Stoker smiled. "Almost."

"It is a quagga," Mr. Pennybaker pronounced in tones of rapture. His brows trembled a little, perhaps in ecstasy, I reflected.

"*Equus quagga quagga,*" Stoker said to me. "Related to but not precisely a zebra. From the plains of the southern part of Africa. The first in this country belonged to George III."

"You see," Mr. Pennybaker explained, "the king and his queen, Charlotte, were quite interested in natural history. The queen received as a wedding present her own painted ass, but that was a full zebra, a she-ass. The poor thing's mate died en route from Africa," he said mournfully. "Otherwise, we might have bred them here."

"It was attempted," Stoker told me. "The queen's zebra was crossed with a donkey and something quite similar to a quagga was produced. But the king was given a proper quagga. It eventually died, and its remains were thought lost for decades."

"Until I found them!" crowed Mr. Pennybaker. He moved around his specimen, peering into its eyes. "I do not know what to say, my good fellow. I look into his eyes and I would think she lives again," he marveled.

Stoker said nothing, but I could feel the surge of satisfaction within him. He took tremendous gratification in his work, and this specimen was something of which he could be rightfully proud.

"What state was it in when you found it?" I asked Mr. Pennybaker.

His expression was aghast. "A ruin, my dear lady. A *ruin*. I cannot think how Mr. Templeton-Vane has resurrected him, but he is a veritable magician. I had only a hide to give him, and that a moth-eaten relic. Not a single bone, not an eyelash remained! And from that he has given me . . . this." He broke off, admiring his trophy again.

I turned to Stoker. "When did you do this?"

He shrugged. "It was my primary commission whilst you were in Madeira. I took apart a few zebras and donkeys to assess the skeletal structures and build an armature. Then I sculpted the body, mounted it, and made the necessary repairs in the hide," he said, as if it were as simple as making a cup of tea. "There was nothing left to do by the time you returned except finish the eyes." One of the most interesting—and gruesome—parts of Stoker's job was the creation of the eyeballs for his mounts. He trusted no one else with their painting, preferring to take a fine sable brush and finish the task himself. This particular specimen looked out with a watchful expression, her gaze fixed on a distant point on the horizon, as careful as one would expect a herd animal to be upon the grassy waves of the African plains.

"It is a marvel," I told him.

"A marvel?" Mr. Pennybaker said, blinking furiously. "It is a miracle! My dear lady, do you realize that this creature is now extinct?"

"Is it really?"

Stoker shrugged. "There may be a few left in the African interior, but none in European captivity. The last one died a few years ago and the remains were not saved."

"A tragedy!" Mr. Pennybaker said, his brows waving furiously, like the antennae of an angry beetle. "A crime!"

"Well, at least you have this one," I soothed.

He nodded, turning once more to his prize. "This is far in excess of my imaginings," he said solemnly. "And it calls for a celebration—a toast!"

.  .  .

When Mr. Pennybaker proposed marking the occasion of the quagga's arrival with a toast, I expected a glass of sherry, sticky and sickly sweet, poured from a dusty bottle and offered up in a cordial glass of some antiquity.

Instead there was French champagne of a decidedly extravagant vintage, poured into the finest crystal and—at one point—my shoe. I will admit that Mr. Pennybaker's high spirits were infectious, and although Stoker enjoyed a glass or two of the refreshing beverage, the rest of the bottles were consumed by Mr. Pennybaker and myself with giddy enthusiasm. We talked long into the night about the state of natural history, opera, the burgeoning threat of a unified Germany, and shoes.

"It takes a woman of great distinction to wear a shoe such as this," he pronounced as he slid the black kidskin slipper from my foot. "It is nunlike in its simplicity. But note here the delicate curve of the heel, the austerity of the little strap across the instep. It is poetry! A sonnet in shoe leather," he said, tipping the last of the champagne into it. He sipped and smacked his lips.

Stoker sighed, rising. "I think it is time we said good night," he suggested. It took another two glasses before Mr. Pennybaker and I agreed, and we exchanged Continental kisses on both cheeks as we parted.

"What a darling little man!" I murmured into Stoker's chest as we settled into the carriage for the ride home. "Pity about his stuffed kittens, though."

Stoker's chest rumbled under my cheek and it was a moment before I realized he was laughing. "Go to sleep, Veronica. I will wake you when we are home."

. . .

In point of fact, he did *not* wake me when we arrived home. I woke alone and dressed in the clothes from the night before with a pounding headache and a taste in my mouth like a decaying wolverine. Having not reached my bed until the small hours of the morning, I rose much later than was my custom. I washed and dressed and made my way to the Belvedere, the enormous freestanding ballroom where the Rosemorran Collection was housed. It was both workspace and refuge for Stoker and for me. Amongst its riot of paintings, statues, specimens, and artifacts, we found occupation and joy. How happy I was to lose myself once more amid the splendid chaos! It was as if someone had looted a particularly erudite and accomplished city and carried home the spoils for us to explore. (Which, if I am honest, is not far from the facts. The previous Earls of Rosemorran had been devoted to the notions of empire and colonialism, which we must now find repugnant. It is a tribute to my own hypocrisy that I could simultaneously appreciate the collections and deplore the method of their assembly.)

It is my earnest belief that much physical affliction may be overcome by studiously ignoring it, and so—in spite of my headache and slightly sour stomach—I ate. As was my habit at breakfast, I took the meal at my desk. Food had been carried down by one of the maids and left atop a moldering sarcophagus—an imperfect specimen of the Greco-Roman period of Egyptian occupation. I consumed a hearty plate of the now tepid offerings and the morning edition of the *Daily Harbinger*. It was not the most elevated of London periodicals, to be sure. From its lurid headlines to its unnecessarily graphic illustrations, it was designed to appeal to the lowest of impulses. But I had good reason for reading it. The newspaper frequently displayed the byline of one J. J. Butterworth, a gifted and audacious reporter who had crossed our path during a particularly challenging investigation into an Egyptological curse.* I would have deplored Butterworth's penchant for the purplest of prose, but I could not deny the arch wit, the unparalleled grasp of facts, and the ability to convey them in sharp, succinct fashion. The fact that Butterworth was a woman attempting to carve a career for herself in a distinctly masculine world appealed to me; I, too, had often published under my initials in order to preserve the incognita of my sex. My natural sympathies lay with her—so long as she kept her knife away from me and mine.

But she had more impressive game to hunt, I reflected as I studied her latest piece. They had not given her the front page; that honor was reserved for more senior writers bent on howling outrage against the Jews, the poor, the Catholics, the immigrants, and anyone else they thought might possibly be behind the appalling crimes in Whitechapel. They castigated Sir Charles Warren, the captain of Scotland Yard, with obvious glee, calling for his resignation in the face of his failure to apprehend the culprit. They speculated wildly on methods of investigation, and an entire column was devoted to letters from vulturelike members of the reading public urging ever more outrageous solutions. And page after page featured descriptions of the hideous mutilations inflicted upon the victims in stomach-churning detail.

J. J. Butterworth's article stood out amid this orgy of sensationalism. Rather than focus on the crimes or the perpetrator, she had instead turned her pen to the subject of the victims. She named them, repeatedly, and described the lives they had led. She made them not faceless drabs who got no better than they deserved, as so many be-

---

* *A Treacherous Curse*

lieved them to be. She told their stories, painting portraits of grinding poverty relieved only by the temporary respite to be found in a bottle of gin. She described the few options available to women who had been let down by society, by their families, by their menfolk. She talked of pathetic attempts at dignity and self-respect, the desperate cobbling together of an income by way of picking hops or making silk flowers, and how these uncertain wages must so often be augmented by the selling of the only commodity such women could command—their own bodies. Butterworth called out the evils of a class system that did not offer opportunities to women such as these; she condemned the church and the government and every other institution that regularly looked past these women as though they did not exist. It was a brutal and scathing indictment of those who held the power to amend but did nothing with that authority.

That J. J. Butterworth was such a firebrand was no surprise; that the *Daily Harbinger* chose to publish such a diatribe, albeit buried far towards the back, did give me a moment's reflection. The proprietors prided themselves on stoking the fires of sensationalism, generating public debate about the most polarizing topics of the day. They attacked anyone they could rouse to reaction and thus sold more newspapers than many of the more sedate journals. But they were scandalmongers, not ideologues. They might champion the poor and downtrodden this week against the wealthy, but next week they would be just as likely to call for the expulsion of the Chinese from Limehouse on the grounds that they trafficked in human beings and opium. (The engagement of the Chinese in either of those practices was greatly exaggerated. There were far more native-born English selling their own kind into the basest of trades, and the only opium house I ever personally entered was maintained by a schoolmaster in Bloomsbury.)

I moved on from Butterworth's piece to a lengthy article about the rising threat of anarchists, the tragic death of a famous lady mountaineer, and a detailed description of the monument to George Washington presently to open in the city bearing his name. It was a singularly odd-looking edifice, an obelisk of faintly Egyptian design.

"But with not a single hieroglyph," I sniffed just as Stoker appeared, eyes heavily shadowed and a fresh growth of morning whiskers upon his jaw. Trotting after him were the dogs, Lord Rosemorran's Caucasian shepherd, Betony, Stoker's bulldog, Huxley, and his newest acquisition, a pretty Egyptian hound called Nut. Huxley and Bet had already produced a litter of extremely questionable attractiveness and were devoted to one another. But they had admitted Nut with good grace, and she was a dainty, unobtrusive creature given to displays of adoration where Stoker was concerned. He tossed sausages to each of the dogs, then reached for a piece of toast and dunked it directly into the pot of honey.

"How is Lady Wellie?" I asked.

"Resting," he said. "I looked in on her a few times in the night. She roused once towards dawn and took a little brandy with an egg beaten into it, then slipped into sleep again." I started to open my mouth again, but he shook his head. "It is too soon to know what sort of permanent effect this will have upon her health."

He finished his toast and reached for another piece. "What are you reading?"

I did not mention the monument—Stoker had very strong opinions on architecture—but acquainted him with the latest on anarchists and deceased lady mountaineers before giving him the highlights of J. J. Butterworth's article. He lifted a hand halfway through.

"Don't, I beg you. It is too much to bear this early in the morning."

The clock in the Belvedere was a singularly unattractive thing, enormous and held in the paws of a slightly cross-eyed sphinx. I gave it a meaningful look. "It is not morning. It has just gone noon."

He groaned and reached for the teapot, pouring himself a large cup of tepid, muddy brew. As he sipped, I thought of what Lady Wellie had been trying to communicate when she had fallen ill.

"Do you think she was simply confused?" I asked. "She asks us to return because of the Whitechapel murders, says it is a matter of life and death, and then asks us instead to retrieve a jewel on the prince's behalf. It makes no sense."

Stoker shrugged. "It must have, at least to her. Somehow those things must be connected in her mind."

"But what connection could there possibly be between a prince of the realm and those dreadful murders?" I demanded.

"Good morning, all!" came a cheerful voice from the doorway. The dogs roused themselves, welcoming our visitor with an enthusiasm that bordered on the ridiculous. Huxley sniffed him eagerly whilst Betony made a gurgling noise of pleasure deep in her throat and Nut applied herself to rolling ecstatically upon her back in front of him.

"Mornaday!" I exclaimed with mingled pleasure. Stoker was far less keen.

"Mornaday," he said curtly.

Sir Hugo's junior at Special Branch, Mornaday had been, upon occasion, both adversary and ally. We had encountered Mornaday during our first adventure in detection, and while I liked him—he boasted a pair of merry dark eyes and an endearing charm that could coax birds from the trees—Stoker found him decidedly less amiable. The pair of them raised one another's hackles and they usually spent most of their time circling one another like feral cats. They tallied their grudges against one another with maddening accuracy and held them close, nurturing them with care.

"Well, if you are not a sight for the sorest of eyes," Mornaday said, stepping neatly over Nut to kiss my hand. "Far too long, it's been." His gaze held the faintest touch of reproach. "Do I have to marry you myself to prevent you from haring off for parts unknown?" he demanded.

"I sent you picture postcards," I reminded him.

"You did?" Stoker raised a brow and Mornaday beamed at him, settling comfortably onto a camel saddle with the air of a man well pleased with himself.

"She did indeed. What's the matter, Templeton-Vane? No letters from across the azure sea?" he teased.

Stoker stuffed the last piece of toast into his mouth and rose. "I am going to polish my eyeballs," he informed me. He strode off to his workbench, where he retrieved a tray of glass eyes, each of them glittering balefully in the light.

Mornaday shuddered. "He is a cold-blooded one, he is."

"You are terribly squeamish for a policeman," I observed mildly.

He made no apologies. "I have a gentle heart," he said, laying a solemn hand upon that organ. "But jesting aside, I am glad to see you again."

I grinned. "Likewise." I poured myself a second cup of tea and one for Mornaday. He took it, cradling the china in his palm. I pointed to the newspaper. "I was just reading the latest piece from the pen of J. J. Butterworth," I said blandly.

His rosy complexion blazed to life, reddening to the tips of his ears. "Have you, then?"

"I have. She is most eloquent upon the subject of the Ripper victims. Very moving."

"Well, she is a talented writer," he said.

"Only a man head over heels in love would affect a tone so casual," I told him.

He blushed further. "I have no idea what you are talking about." He took a long sip of his tea, evading my gaze.

"Yes, you do. Or have you forgot the evening you drank too much of my very effective aguardiente and confessed your unrequited passion for Miss Butterworth?"

"I remember," he replied, a trifle sullenly.

"What is the matter? Does she still hold you at arm's length?"

His small smile was mirthless. "Arm's length, leg's length, and half a mile beyond. She is so committed to making a name for herself as a journalist, she cannot be bothered with matters of the heart."

"Have you seen her?"

He shrugged. "She spends a good deal of time scuttling about the Yard, sniffing for clues about the Ripper."

"I meant in a social capacity."

"I invited her to accompany me tonight to the Savoy. The new Gilbert and Sullivan is to debut—*The Yeoman of the Guard*." He drew a pair of tickets from his waistcoat pocket and thrust them at me. I studied the squares of coral pasteboard and admired the tiny butterfly embellishment above the legend, FIRST CIRCLE.

"A promising choice," I said by way of encouragement. I tried to pass them back, but he waved me off.

"She says she is otherwise engaged," he told me sourly. "You may as well use them yourself."

"But surely you could invite someone else," I began.

He rose, putting his cup down abruptly. "I haven't the heart. Besides, it is probably for the best she refused me. I bought the tickets some weeks back and circumstances have changed. It is all hands to the tiller until the Ripper is apprehended. Sir Hugo would have my guts for garters if I left the Yard for more than half an hour. If he learns I've come here, I'll be in the blackest of books," he added with a pleading look.

"He shall never learn it from me," I promised. "Is there no fresh new line of inquiry that might lead to this monster's apprehension?"

He spread his hands. "I wish there were. He is a fiend, the likes of which I have never seen. You can read in the newspapers what he has done to them, but I will never speak of it."

"You needn't fear my sensibilities," I assured him. "I am of strong mettle."

"I am not," he retorted. "I had to attend one of the autopsies and I sicked up my breakfast."

I was not surprised. The ferocity of the crimes was appalling, and I found it endearing that a London policeman who had seen his share of atrocities was still gentle enough to be affected by the humanity of the victims.

I tapped the tickets. "You must allow me to repay you."

He waved. "No need between friends." He jerked his head towards Stoker's workbench. "Promise you will take him."

I smiled. "I am surprised you are so eager to give Stoker the pleasure of an evening at the theatre."

His answering smile was thin. "Oh, it isn't a pleasure for him," he reminded me. "That's why I gave you the tickets."

He touched his brow and inclined his head. "Until we meet again, my dearest Miss Speedwell."

"Good-bye, Mornaday."

The dogs trotted after him as he left, sniffing eagerly and inelegantly at the crotch of his trousers.

"Those dogs have the most appalling manners," I told Stoker as he left his eyeballs and came to sit.

"I hope they bite where they sniff," Stoker said. "What did he want?"

I brandished the tickets. "To give us these."

"Theatre tickets? For tonight?" He swore softly. "The bastard does know how to torment me. If there is one thing I cannot abide, it is harnessing myself into evening dress to listen to three hours of patter songs and caterwauling." He gave me a narrow look. "I suppose you want to go?"

"Not with you," I told him in my sweetest voice. "I am very happy to ask Tiberius. I know how much he enjoys the theatre."

Stoker snatched the tickets out of my hand. "Be ready by seven."

"I planned to."

# CHAPTER

# 4

We worked comfortably for the next few hours, Stoker at his latest large-scale mount—a hippopotamus that had been badly handled and was shedding ears and long, wiry hairs as well as emitting a fragrance that can best be described as insalubrious—and I at my correspondence. I had just finished penning a rousing rebuttal to a criticism of my latest contribution to *The Lepidopterist's Quarterly Guide to South American Butterflies and Greater Moths* when another visitor appeared, also unannounced. Stoker and I had worked through luncheon, taking only sandwiches and cold tea for our refreshment, and I was nibbling the last egg and tomato sandwich when Inspector Archibond popped his head around the door.

"Good day, Miss Speedwell," he began.

I beckoned to him, dusting the crumbs from my hands. "Inspector Archibond," I said, coming forwards to welcome him. "What brings you here?"

His smile was weary. "I wanted to look in on Lady Wellie."

"She is holding steady," Stoker said, emerging from his hippopotamus. As ever, he had discarded his shirt in the process of his labors. He was sweat streaked and filthy, covered in sawdust and cobwebs and other unimaginable horrors. But nothing could conceal the splendor of his musculature, and I gave him a lingering and appreciative look before primly removing my gaze to the inspector.

Archibond spoke. "I am glad to hear it. I did not want to disturb the household, so I thought it best to come here."

"You are most welcome," I assured him. "Stoker, do wipe off the worst of that filth and put on a shirt for the inspector. We will have something to drink."

The inspector held up a hand. "No tea for me," he said.

"I was thinking of something rather more interesting," I assured him. I retrieved my flask of aguardiente and poured out a thimbleful for each of us. He took one sip and his eyes went wide, his color harsh.

"My God," he managed hoarsely. It took him some minutes to recover, but when he did, he gave a nod. "I do not generally indulge in spirits before nightfall, but I thank you, Miss Speedwell. These are unusual times, and a stiffener is most welcome."

I made to pour him another but he thrust his hand over the top of his glass. Stoker joined us, having performed a minimal toilette, and settled himself in his customary chair. "What else brings you to our lair, Inspector?" he inquired.

The inspector's smile was sudden and oddly charming. He had a tiny dimple in his cheek that I had never had cause to notice before. He settled himself gingerly on the camel saddle, his manner confiding.

"Instinct, I suppose, although a policeman is supposed to be guided by logic. But logic is of no use to me when matters are so clouded." He paused. "I wondered if you knew what was troubling Lady Wellie, if she had confided in you before she collapsed."

"What makes you think there was something troubling her?" I asked carefully.

"I have known her for some time. She has not been herself these past few days. I saw her once or twice in this matter of the prince and she was preoccupied, vague."

"The Prince of Wales is one of her favorites," Stoker told him. "Surely the threat of a scandal touching his eldest son is enough to preoccupy and distress her."

"I wish I could believe that is all that ails her, but I am convinced there is something more."

I flicked a glance to Stoker, a warning look that I knew he would interpret correctly. Until we understood Lady Wellie's fears with regard to the prince and any possible connection to the murders, I would not betray her secrets, not even to Archibond, her confidant.

"If she were distressed about something else, I am sure she would share her concerns with Special Branch," I said.

Archibond's expression was grave. "I do not think I can adequately communicate to you the atmosphere at Scotland Yard at present, Miss Speedwell. There is always a sense of urgency, of duty, that the security and peace of the capital depends upon us. But now . . ." He spread his hands. "It is a snake pit. Man against man, department against department. Everyone wants to be the first to bring the Ripper to justice, so there is no proper cooperation. We talk and we theorize, but there is only superficial sharing of information. Everyone wants to develop the hypothesis that will bring this monster's reign of terror to an end. I am afraid it has led to a mood of great distrust within the department—and beyond."

"Lady Wellie no longer trusts her contacts at the Yard?" Stoker asked, incredulous.

"She would always trust Sir Hugo," Archibond assured us. "But Sir Hugo is in the fight of his life, merely trying to survive. Every day, there are calls in the newspapers for the resignation of any of the superior officers attached to the investigation. He has no men and no heart to spare for anything except the Whitechapel case."

"And that is where you have come in?" I asked.

"It is. I did not realize the scope of Lady Wellie's influence when I first arrived at the Yard," he admitted. "But I quickly learnt her worth. She is invaluable to the Metropolitan Police, and to this country. In the past months, I have come to know her better, and I can say truthfully, there is no one I admire more."

This was a change, I reflected. When we first encountered Archibond, he was ambitious and stern, determined to ascend the ladder at Scotland Yard and reach the pinnacle of Special Branch. But six months was a long time to be mired in the shifting sands of the politics of the Metropolitan Police. I had been in Madeira for most of the year, and Stoker had been occupied with his own work, notably, his quagga. We had neither of us kept up with Lady Wellie as we ought, and with Sir Hugo growing increasingly busy—as well as occasionally ailing—it was no surprise that she had begun to cultivate his successor.

Stoker opened a tin of honeycomb, rummaging through the sticky layers for a sizeable piece. He appeared to be munching contentedly on his sweet, but I saw the watchful gleam in his eye. He did not yet trust Archibond; however, it occurred to me that with Lady Wellie incapacitated, she would not be able to vouch for the man. It would be up to us to determine how far she had taken him into her confidence.

"You were no doubt surprised to see Her Royal Highness appeal to Stoker and me for assistance," I began, dangling the baited hook.

He bit, smiling gently. The expression warmed his features, making him almost attractive. "I was not, actually. I know in what esteem Lady Wellie holds the pair of you, and of course, your own position, Miss Speedwell, makes you unique." It was the perfect response, just pointed enough to reveal that he knew exactly who I was without the indiscretion of speaking it aloud. Archibond, I decided, was a careful man.

He went on. "I understand why you refused her. I have learnt something of your previous help, both of you," he added quickly, gathering Stoker with a glance. "It must be difficult to accomplish so much and never be properly thanked for it."

I lifted my chin. "I do not do it for gratitude. I do it for the sake of what is right."

He shifted on the camel saddle—not a particularly comfortable perch at the best of times, but I fancied he was choosing his words carefully. "And never for your own purposes?"

Stoker's nostrils whitened at the edges, the only perceptible sign of his irritation, but I could tell he was spoiling for a fight. I shoved another piece of honeycomb at him. "Eat, I beg you, before you say something all of us will regret." I turned to Archibond. "We have an uneasy relationship with Special Branch, at best, Inspector. We have frequently been at odds with Sir Hugo, and do not even speak the name 'Mornaday' in Stoker's presence unless you wish to see him lather at the mouth like a rabid dog."

Archibond's slender mouth quirked up into a smile. "Then we have that in common, sir. I have long wanted to thrash the fellow myself."

The fact that Mornaday had—with great cheer and little hesitation—ordered him comprehensively searched when Stoker was mildly arrested had done nothing to repair their strained relationship. Archibond's antipathy was equally fervid but for a completely different reason. Mornaday, as Sir Hugo's right-hand man of long standing, posed a threat to Archibond's ambitions in spite of his own superior rank. (Mornaday, when deeply in his cups, mourned the fact that Archibond had secured a plum position by dint of his dogged application to duty and rigid adherence to the rules and regulations of Special Branch as well as a few strings discreetly tugged by his godfather, the Home Secretary. I consoled Mornaday with a dose of strong spirits and sympathy, which prompted him to offer me an obligatory kiss. I politely declined and he took no offense.) Still, the brawls at Special Branch were none of our concern, and we could certainly be cordial to both of them even as they plotted to have each other's livers and lights.

"The enemy of my enemy is my friend?" Stoker said lightly.

"Something like that," Archibond agreed.

"You are both speaking nonsense," I told them, rather more harshly than the conversation merited. "Mornaday is no enemy to either of you, and he has, upon occasion, been an extremely good friend." I gave Stoker a lowering look and he rolled his eyes heavenwards.

"How many times has he proposed marriage to you?" he asked.

I primmed my mouth. "I have forgot, and that is beside the point. He is never serious and his affections lie elsewhere, I assure you. Let us return to the topic at hand, Inspector. You were, I suspect, attempting to bait us into some course of action, perhaps by means of guilt after accusing me of acting in self-interest, a tactic doomed to failure," I warned.

He held up his hands in mock surrender. "You mistake me, Miss Speedwell! I do not charge you with any crime of which I myself am innocent. I find myself here because . . ." He hesitated, coloring deeply. "Because my own guilt is almost more than I can bear and I hoped to find a kindred spirit."

"Why should you feel guilt where Lady Wellie is concerned?" I asked.

"Because I did not listen," he said heavily. He ran his hands through his hair, disordering it slightly. "A few days ago, the day she wired you in Cornwall, I was here. I had called upon her to speak with her about the latest developments in the Whitechapel investigation—unofficially, of course. There are still plenty of people at Scotland Yard who do not know of her influence." He paused, seemingly searching for the right words. "Her mood was distracted, distressed. She said she had sent for you both, and I was glad of it. I thought having you here might soothe her mind, but she would not settle. She wandered a little in her mind and it alarmed me. It is the first true sign of age I have seen upon her," he said with a rueful look.

"She does seem to go on like England itself," I agreed.

"In the very best way. She is what England used to be, I think. What it might be again. Every virtue to which I have ever aspired, she has mastered." He broke off, coloring a little, clearly embarrassed at his burst of sentimentality. He cleared his throat and resumed his narrative. "I pressed her for why she was so upset, but she kept muttering about Prince Eddy."

"Well, discovering that the future King of England has been handing out diamonds like boiled sweets to his light-o'-loves is a trifle unsettling," Stoker put in.

"Indeed," was Archibond's dry reply. "But it was more than that. Whilst we were talking, she asked me to fetch a magnifying glass from her desk. Her eyes have been giving her trouble of late. While I looked for it, I saw a number of papers lying loose, clearly something she had been working at before my arrival. When she noticed they were still on the desk, she swept them into a drawer with her diary and locked it, clearly distressed that I might have noticed the nature of the papers." He shifted again, clearly uncomfortable. "I would not compromise her privacy, but had I known she would so soon be incapacitated, I would have pressed her. I think whatever she was working at was connected with this thing that has been troubling her, but I have no notion of what it is."

"Occam's razor would suggest that the simplest and therefore likeliest explanation is that she was concerned about the prince's peccadillo," I offered.

"Of course," Archibond agreed. "It may indeed be nothing we do not already know, and that affair is certainly worth some concern."

"What do you know of the lady involved?" I asked suddenly.

Archibond shrugged. "At the edge of Bloomsbury, there is a private house known as the Club de l'Étoile."

"The Club of the Star," I observed. "How fitting for an establishment of nocturnal entertainment."

"Indeed. It is a very discreet club for ladies and gentlemen of means and certain habits," he said with delicacy.

"A brothel," I said brutally.

"A club," he corrected firmly. "There are no regular employees save the domestic staff, and it is located in a private home. Everyone is of the appropriate age and there are no permanent professionals on the premises in the strictest sense of the word. The club caters to many tastes and there are entertainments given, themed parties, that sort of thing. It is beautifully furnished, luxurious in every detail, with exquisite food and drink, a veritable palace for debauchery."

"And His Royal Highness is an habitué of this place," Stoker finished. To his credit, there was not the slightest hint of judgment in his tone. But as Stoker had spent years living in a much less grand establishment in Brazil, he had precious few stones to throw.

"He is," Archibond supplied. "It is run by a Frenchwoman of some notoriety. She has gone by many names in the past. Now she calls herself Madame Aurore after the goddess of the dawn. She was a courtesan in Paris for some years, I am told. She is terribly discreet. Her guests are never troubled by the police or journalists, and she has arranged for several entrances and exits from the property so that her callers will not be noticed either arriving or leaving. She does nothing illegal and therefore we can do nothing about her activities. She maintains perfect silence about her callers."

"You seem to know a great deal about her," Stoker remarked with studied blandness.

Archibond shrugged. "It is our duty to keep a weather eye upon all such places frequented by the great and good. One must be ever vigilant where the possibility of blackmail exists."

"I suppose if His Royal Highness must exercise his libido, he could hardly find a more suitable spot," I mused.

"You have a Continental mind, Miss Speedwell," Archibond said in a tone that was somewhere between aspersion and admiration. "As you say, if the prince were going to indulge himself—and what young man does not?—he could hardly do better than a quiet establishment where everyone knows the rules and no one dare break them. Unfortunately, this particular club is quite expensive."

"How expensive?" Stoker inquired.

"Ten thousand guineas to join," Archibond replied.

I sucked in my breath. "Ten thousand guineas. Do you know what I earn for one specimen of a *Papilio amynthor*? Three guineas. Three guineas for a perfect specimen of one of the most beautiful creatures in the world. And you are telling us that this place charges its members the worth of *thousands* of such creatures just so people can debauch themselves in private?"

"The world, my dear Miss Speedwell, is an unjust place," he said with a shrug. "But I suspect you knew that already." He went on. "In addition to her *nom d'amour*, the proprietress, Madame Aurore, always appears robed as the dawn goddess. She wears a sort of tiara given her by Napoléon III, a galaxy of diamonds. It is a custom of the club that when someone has enjoyed her personal favors, they present her with a diamond star, the more lavish, the better."

"And who could make one more lavish than Garrard's?" Stoker put in.

"Precisely. And one that is patterned after the prince's own mother's jewels? Can you imagine the newspapers?" Archibond shuddered visibly. "If they get their teeth into this, they will harry it to the death, running down every sordid detail."

"And you are certain that it is this Madame Aurore who has the jewel?" I asked.

"Oh yes, quite," Archibond said. "The princess approached me in some distress a fortnight or so ago. She confided that her lady-in-waiting had had a curious communication from Garrard. It seems the jewelers were keen to alert the princess to a possible mésalliance on the part of the prince."

"A bit above and beyond the purview of one's jeweler," I observed.

"The princess is a very good client," Archibond said with a shrug. "They would do almost anything to avoid losing the future Queen of England as a client." He went on. "She was naturally anxious to avoid troubling the Prince of Wales, so she came to Lady Wellie and asked for her help. Lady Wellie tasked me with discovering what I could about the prince's purchase of the star and its whereabouts. I had precious little time to devote to the matter, but luckily for me, His Royal Highness is not terribly devious," he said with an indulgent smile. "His notion of discretion is having his driver take a turn around the block before going inside."

"He wore no disguise?" I asked.

Archibond sighed. "Not only did he fail to wear a disguise, he took one of the Prince of Wales' coaches."

"Oh dear," I murmured.

The three of us exchanged glances, our lips twitching in suppressed mirth.

"Heaven help us," Stoker said, shaking his head. "The future King of England is a simpleton."

"He is not quite so hopeless as that," Archibond said with a fond expression warming his features, "but I will admit he is considerably less adroit than his father in managing his affairs." He retrieved the thread of his narrative. "We had known for some time that the prince frequented this establishment and that knowledge—coupled with Madame Aurore's penchant for diamond stars—made it easy enough to guess who was in possession of the jewel. I reported my findings to the princess and Lady Wellie, and only then did I discover why Her Royal Highness was so keen to retrieve the star."

"That poor child," I said, "Princess Alix of Hesse."

Archibond spread his hands. "No one will force her to marry him," he assured me. "But she is a princess. She will marry from a very small, very exclusive circle of dolts and simpletons. At least if she chooses to throw her lot in with Prince Eddy, she will be most tenderly loved. He is capable of great affection, if not great intellect."

"She is sixteen," I reminded him. "How can she know what she wants?"

"She might not," he agreed. "But whoever he marries, his mother is quite correct—she will be the making of him. He wants a strong character beside him."

"A rather tall order for a young girl," Stoker said.

"Show me an aristocratic girl who doesn't know she's meant for such things from the cradle," Archibond replied. "But this one may be what he needs. If she demands he refine his character to her standards, then he will be worthy of her."

"I begin to think you are a romantic," I teased.

"My greatest secret is that I am an idealist who will never relinquish my ideals," he said simply.

I ventured a question. "Out of curiosity, how did you expect us to even retrieve this jewel? Presumably it is secured in a bank vault."

"Oh no," he said quickly. "That is part of her mystique, this Madame Aurore. She wears her collection of stars several times in the course of a month. Every Wednesday, she holds a sort of masquerade where her regular guests are permitted to bring visitors in hopes of attracting newcomers. One need only know when and where and one can easily gain admittance."

The inspector's gaze suddenly fell upon the tickets to the Savoy. *"The Yeoman of the Guard!"* he exclaimed. "I do love Gilbert and Sullivan, but I fear it is to be quite some time before I can spare an evening for this. Enjoy yourselves," he said, rising to his feet. "Do send for me if Lady Wellie takes a turn," he urged.

I promised that we would and Stoker rose, shaking hands with him. The inspector turned to me. "I am glad to know you a little better, Miss Speedwell. Lady Wellie thinks very highly of you, very highly indeed. I begin to see why."

# CHAPTER

# 5

His departure left a heavy silence as Stoker occupied himself with finding a sausage to break up for the dogs.

"Shall we quarrel now or later?" I asked pleasantly.

He gave a heavy sigh and pitched a bit of herbed pork to Huxley. "We shall not quarrel at all."

I blinked. "I beg your pardon?"

"Veronica, you might give me a little credit for knowing you as well as I do. We might argue back and forth about this ridiculous endeavor and it will end with you haring off into danger and me trotting obediently after like your very own mastiff."

"Not a mastiff," I protested. "A partner."

"A sidekick, as you have informed me upon occasion," he reminded me.

"Yes, well, I was wrong to say so. We are equal partners in these enterprises. We have both benefited from them, both been harmed by them. We have undertaken them at your instigation and at mine. We are both of us worthy of the blame and the credit."

"Exactly. And I do not much feel like quarreling with you at present," he said, his eyes bright with meaning.

"Oh," I told him, feeling suddenly breathless. "I would rather do otherwise as well."

I took a step forwards, but he moved quickly, putting the sarcophagus between us. "That is not a good idea."

"What isn't?"

"Proximity," he said through gritted teeth. "I have spent the last years in strictest control of my baser instincts, but when I am with you, I find myself rather less able to keep my mind on loftier matters."

I swallowed hard. "I understand. I share your difficulties," I reminded him. "And there is no need to fight such impulses any longer. We have decided upon that."

"Veronica," he said flatly, "I am not going to take you on top of a moldy sarcophagus. I do not require love poems and fireworks, but kindly grant me a better audience than a stuffed wildebeest and a pack of sausage-breathed hounds." (For accuracy's sake, I should note that he did have a fondness for Keats, and the hounds did have sausage breath, but the wildebeest was, in point of fact, a gnu.)

I nodded. "Yes, quite. A quick tumble amidst the collections is hardly fitting. Besides, we have other matters to attend to at present."

"Yes," he said heavily. "Like breaking into Lady Wellie's desk to see what she was concealing from the inspector."

I blew him a kiss and he retrieved his lockpicks. He treated me to a discourse on the ethical conundrum of burgling the private correspondence of a friend.

"It is not *burgling*," I told him in a tone of indignation. "We shall not remove anything. We only wish to see it. Besides, what if we learn something of significance? What if we are able to piece together what worried her and provide some sort of resolution? She might very well awaken to discover that we have relieved her of that burden."

He grunted by way of response, but neither of us needed to speak further. We both knew the real reason we were undertaking this bit of sleuthery. My denial of her last request had been both swift and severe. If I had the means to undo it, I would. Breaking into her desk and uncovering her puzzle to solve it for her was not for my own excitement. It was expiation.

It was a simple enough matter to gain access to Lady Wellie's sitting room. A private woman, she never permitted the housemaids to clean her rooms unattended, insisting instead that Weatherby attend to the dusting and the scattering of damp tea leaves to brush the dust from the carpets. The austere lady's maid stood guard over the footman who came to black the grate and lay the fire each morning, and if she were not at hand, he was instructed to wait until she was. And woe betide the bootboy who tried to collect her shoes for cleaning without Weatherby's presence. She was also instructed to burn all of the blotting papers herself on the hearth, changing them hourly for fresh and destroying any correspondence that Lady Wellie directed be burnt. She was paid a handsome bonus for her additional duties, but I suspect she would have happily engaged in them without. I have never yet met a lady's maid who did not enjoy a bit of intrigue, and who could blame them? Washing another woman's corsets for a living was a shiversome prospect, I decided, and the occasional bit of skullduggery would certainly relieve the tedium. She was, mercifully, absent when we slipped into the room, although the lovebirds set up a fuss, wittering fluently as we worked.

Stoker bent to his task, fitting the lockpicks to the elaborate inlaid desk as I stood watch and soothed the lovebirds by crooning a soft tune.

"Veronica, for the love of Lucifer, stop singing to those bloody birds," he ordered in a harsh whisper. He had eased open the lock and was pulling the center drawer open with careful fingers.

"Her diary," I suggested. He drew out a large volume of dark blue kid stamped in gold with her initials and the year. He flicked through the pages until the book fell open to a place marked with a scarlet silk ribbon. Several loose items had been tucked between the leaves of the diary, and he skimmed them quickly.

"Well?" I prodded. It seemed wildly unfair that he had proverbial first crack at searching her things when the whole idea had been mine to begin with. And all because he was the one who knew how to break into things, I reflected bitterly, making a mental note to apply myself to learning the illicit arts of lockpickery.

Suddenly, he snapped the book closed and shoved it under his arm. He closed the drawer silently and locked it up again without a word. I opened my mouth to speak but he cut me off with a single sharp shake of the head. We slipped out of the room as quietly as we had come, and it was not until we were back in the Belvedere that he spoke.

"I know what was distressing her," he told me. He opened the diary to the marked page and handed it over along with the collection of loose pages.

"Newspaper cuttings?" I asked. I thumbed through them. Each was from the Court Circular, a daily announcement of the whereabouts of the members of the royal family, everything from investitures to ribbon cuttings. There were those who made a habit of following along, but these were usually the folk who could be relied upon to buy commemorative plates bearing pictures of the royal family and to drape bunting from the lampposts. People sometimes made use of the circular for their own purposes—presenting informal petitions or the odd attempt at assassination—but they were by far in the minority. Every cutting was dated in the margins, each noted in her elegantly sprawling hand. I flipped through them again, narrowing my gaze.

"How very peculiar. They go right back through August, and she has scored under Prince Eddy's name in every one of them, as if she were making notes on his movements and whereabouts on particular dates."

"Keep going," Stoker said grimly. Beneath the Court Circulars were a series of cuttings taken from the *Daily Harbinger*. Each of these had been dated as well, but in a different hand, the numbers thick and black, slashing at the page.

"Each is a précis of the Ripper murders," I noted. "And not from the *Times*. Lady Wellie would never read the *Harbinger*."

"She didn't," he told me, nodding towards the collection again. At the bottom was a single piece of cheap paper, marked with the same strong black handwriting, a few simple words in capitals. *WHERE WAS PRINCE EDDY?*

I looked from the dates marked on the cuttings to those of the Court Circulars, then lifted my gaze to Stoker. "The dates of the Whitechapel murders. Someone sent her this note and the Ripper cuttings to—"

"To suggest that dear dolt Eddy might be responsible for the most heinous crimes of the century," he finished.

I tamped the pages together almost angrily. "Stoker, it is absurd. She could not believe him capable of such an atrocity."

"Of course not," he agreed. We fell silent a long moment, lost in our own thoughts.

"Unless she did," I ventured finally. "She *was* cross-referencing his whereabouts on the nights in question."

"It is the logical place to begin," he agreed. "If there were the slightest possibility that he had some involvement, however tangential, establishing an alibi for him would be the first step."

I looked at the cuttings again. "He has one. He is at Balmoral at present, which puts him quite out of the running for the murders on

September 30." The night that had driven Lady Wellie to send for us had been the setting of an obscene double event. Two victims, Elizabeth Stride and Catherine Eddowes, had fallen to the Ripper's knife, and hysteria had gripped the capital—not just at the murderer's ongoing reign of terror but at the notion that he seemed to be falling even further into butchery.

"Trains run to Scotland," Stoker pointed out.

I frowned. "He is with the queen. I should think she would notice if he went missing."

Stoker canted his head. "You are protective of him."

I opened my mouth, then snapped it shut again. I counted to twenty in Mandarin, then spoke calmly. "I am not. I am merely pointing out the flaws in the case against him."

His voice was gentle. "It would be nothing to marvel at if you did feel as though you ought to defend him. He is your little brother."

I cleared my throat. "The merest accident of birth, I assure you. Besides, you know I do not subscribe to the belief that blood is thicker than water. One has only to observe you for ten minutes with any of your brothers to understand the fallaciousness of that philosophy. Now, whoever intended to set the cat amongst the pigeons, they must have worked quite quickly to have got this in the post to her that morning."

He shrugged. "Perhaps they had the scheme laid out and close at hand, waiting for the next outrage to implicate the prince."

The notion of a poison pen writer carefully assembling a hoard of cuttings, marking them and tucking them neatly away until it was time to send them, was faintly horrifying. To do evil suddenly, to kill or harass when provoked beyond endurance, when life or safety was threatened, that I could understand. It was the plotting and planning of it that I could not comprehend.

"If Lady Wellie did believe Eddy had anything to do with the crimes, she would never cover over his involvement. She loves England too dearly for that," I told him.

"I agree," said Stoker. "But she did not yet have proof one way or another. I think at that moment it was only a notion, a hideous one, almost too terrible to contemplate. So she put together the dates to see for herself if it was even possible."

"It is not," I told him flatly.

He shrugged. "I daresay there are plenty of servants and visitors at Balmoral who could vouch for him, either because he was actually there or because they are loyal."

"You just agreed she would not countenance his involvement in the crimes," I reminded him.

"But why send for us if she even entertained the possibility of his connection to the murders? The telegram made reference to the crimes in Whitechapel. She said it was a matter of life and death," he said to me. "The recovery of the diamond star is hardly a matter of such grave importance."

"Unless she was not thinking of the diamond star when she sent for us," I began, working it out as I spoke. "It is too great a coincidence that he should be implicated in *two* scandals at once. What if she feared the star might be somehow connected with this?" I asked, brandishing the flurry of cuttings. "What if she wanted us to retrieve the star not because—as the princess fears—it might be used to scupper his marriage plans by proving him to be unchaste but because it might be used to implicate him in something much, much worse?"

"I think that is the sort of sensationalist nonsense J. J. Butterworth only wishes she could imagine," he began, but a note of doubt crept into his tone.

I waited and he finally gave a gusty sigh. "Very well. It is *possible*," he conceded.

"Better than possible," I said with conviction. "I am certain of it. Lady Wellie would never dare raise such a possibility in front of the princess. Her Royal Highness is already quite distraught at the idea of her son's dalliance with a courtesan becoming public knowledge. What sort of hysterics might she be prey to if she suspected he was being spoke of in relation to the most vicious crimes in London?"

"Lady Wellie could very easily have told us if she feared such a plot," he pointed out.

"Feathers!" I retorted. "Lady Wellie would never speak to anyone of such a thing until and unless it were confirmed. She plays her cards well close to the vest," I reminded him. "Far simpler to commission us to retrieve the jewel, using the princess's influence to persuade us."

"But it did not," he returned evenly.

"She was not to know that!" I strove for patience, but my exasperation was growing. I could see it all so clearly, the devoted retainer determined to preserve her future king's reputation, her future queen's serenity. She would take no one into her confidence until necessity required it.

"She must have been on the verge of telling us when she collapsed," I mused.

"Well, we cannot do anything until Lady Wellie recovers," he began.

"But what if she does not?" I challenged. "I know we do not want to consider such a possibility, but we cannot deny that while she might have passed the crisis, the future is uncertain. She might have suffered damage of some sort to her mental capacity, mightn't she?"

Stoker gave a grudging nod. "Yes. It is far too soon to ascertain any type of permanent infirmity."

"And damage to her memory or faculties might mean she is never able to retrieve her thoughts, her intentions with regard to this matter," I went on. "And only we know of it."

I paused then, letting the weight of my words settle between us before going on. "We are the only ones who know of Lady Wellie's suspicions. We can examine the facts and ascertain the truth."

"And then?" he inquired. "What if we discover that the author of that vicious little note is correct? What if Eddy is involved?"

"You said he had alibis for the nights in question," I reminded him.

"And I said witnesses can be bribed. Documents can be forged. Truth can be molded into whatever the powerful want it to be. They have been doing it for centuries."

I took a deep breath. "Then we will decide together what must be done."

"Even if what must be done is exposing the Prince of Wales' eldest son as a vicious murderer?" Stoker demanded. "You sail dangerous waters, Veronica. You are asking us to possibly destroy the monarchy."

"Or am I asking us to save it?" I said softly. "If we do nothing and this villain spreads his poison further afield, it could do as much damage as if Eddy held the Ripper's knife himself. Think of it, Stoker. These murders are hideous, vicious crimes that have set the country aflame, fanned the sparks of hysteria." I pointed to the copy of the *Daily Harbinger* I had discarded that morning.

"Look at the headlines! There is a fresh crop every day, encouraging every segment of society to turn on the others. It is setting Christian against Jew, native-born Englishman against immigrant, rich against poor. And what if into this maelstrom, someone—one of these devilish newspaper proprietors, perhaps—suggests that our future king is responsible? The very possibility of such a thing would be incendiary. We have had riots this year. Can you imagine how much worse they would be if people believed even the merest possibility that a senior member of the royal family were involved in these crimes?"

"Anarchy," Stoker said succinctly.

"Precisely. England would go down in flames, everything destroyed."

"It is a far cry from patronizing an establishment like the Club de l'Étoile to ripping up innocent women in the streets of Whitechapel," Stoker objected.

"Not in the minds of the British public," I told him. "We are a nation of priggish shopkeepers and you know it. Give the upright middle class a crumb of scandal and they will make a banquet of it, as you know to your cost," I said. He made a low growl of acknowledgment. Stoker's own divorce—itself something of a novelty in semi-aristocratic circles—had lit the fires of gossip for months, the flames fanned by the salacious details of his wife's abandonment of him in an Amazonian jungle while he lay waiting for death. His subsequent debaucheries in the brothels of Brazil had not helped. But the thrust had gone home, and I pressed my advantage.

"We know the star is at the club," I said. "And it is as good a place as any to start our investigation. Perhaps there is someone there who might think to use the prince's presence in such an establishment as a means of whipping up opposition to the royal family itself with an eye to political change."

"Is such a thing even possible?" Stoker asked.

"Marie Antoinette did nothing worse than play at being a milkmaid and the French called her Messalina," I reminded him. "It is not the reality that matters, it is the perception." I smiled. "And today is Wednesday— the night each week when Madame Aurore welcomes prospective members to her masquerades. We have only to present ourselves as interested clients and we will be welcomed, I have no doubt."

Stoker stirred. "You realize you are suggesting we take ourselves to a club devoted to the most sophisticated and elaborate debaucheries," he said.

"I have survived murder attempts, shipwrecks, abductions, and the eruption of Krakatoa. I do not think I will falter at a little exuberant nudity."

He sighed heavily. "We would need costumes. And we must learn whatever we can about the Club de l'Étoile and Madame Aurore before we hurl ourselves into this endeavor."

"And I know exactly where we can go to remedy both of those deficiencies," I informed him as I pinned on my favorite hat. "Tiberius."

# CHAPTER

# 6

"ood God, I have only just got rid of the pair of you," his lordship grumbled. But he said it with a flicker of a smile, and I knew he was rather glad to see us. Well, one of us.

"Good day to you too, Tiberius," I said with a grin. Stoker's eldest brother, Viscount Templeton-Vane, had been engaged in a lazy afternoon at home with a pot of chocolate and a mildly pornographic French novel. He wore a dark dressing gown over his trousers and shirt, and his chin was freshly barbered.

"Veronica, my dear, I am always delighted to see you, but I have had my fill of Stoker for the present. Perhaps you might come alone next time," he suggested, his eyes alight with mischief.

Stoker swore a little under his breath, but it was a distinct improvement on their last disagreement, which had ended with a light stabbing. They had made up after a particularly harrowing and almost fatal experience, but it was apparent that their rapprochement was going to be of the oceanic variety; it would ebb and flow with their moods.

But Tiberius had come to think of me as a confidante and friend—more than family, he had assured me—and I hurried to explain to him the barest essentials of what we required. He listened intently, and as I finished, he tipped his head towards his brother.

"Let me understand you correctly, Stoker," the viscount said silkily. "You require costume pieces and information because you mean to escort Veronica to one of the most notorious sex clubs in London?"

"Those are the broad strokes," Stoker affirmed.

The viscount crossed one leg over the other and sat back in his chair.

"And why, precisely, are the pair of you embarked upon this bacchanal? One can only presume you are venturing once more into the mysterious and dangerous realms of detection."

"Something like that," I told him. "But we cannot share the details. You understand the necessity for discretion."

"Better than most," he said with a rueful expression. His own peccadilloes had come to light more than once in the course of our investigations. "But it is not convenient. I am in the process of shutting up the house," he told us with an airy wave towards the ceiling. From above there was the racket of shutters being fitted into place.

"You're going away?" I ventured.

His smile was humorless. "I thought a change of scene was in order after our latest little adventure."

Tiberius had a talent for understatement. The "little adventure" had nearly cost us our lives and had handed him a devastating revelation.* It would take him time to recover, I had no doubt, but it was decidedly inconvenient that he had chosen this moment to leave town.

Still, how often had I used travel as a means of escaping my troubles? An untidy love affair, a thwarted professional commission, a dis-

---

* *A Dangerous Collaboration*

appointment of any sort—these had frequently provided the impetus for a fresh journey. How the spirits lifted with every embarkation! The sound of a steam engine roaring to life, the full-bellied sway of canvas sails, the sharp tang of hot metal rails or salt-scented sea. There was nothing more promising than the first stage of a new expedition. Everything was possible in that moment; there was no past, no future, only that hollow in time when everything paused.

But while I understood Tiberius' desire to escape, Stoker was less sympathetic.

"You owe us, Tiberius. I saved your bloody life," he began.

Tiberius held up an elegant hand. "After you endangered it, my dear boy. I rather think, under the circumstances, that you owe *me*."

They stared each other down for a long moment, so alike in some respects, so different in others. They had inherited their mother's bone structure, beautifully sculpted with a refinement any artist would envy. But while his lordship had chestnut hair and dark, flashing eyes, Stoker bore the coloring of his natural father, the black hair and bright blue eyes of the Welsh painter who had entertained the late viscountess for a short period of time during her unhappy marriage to Tiberius' more conventional father. Watching them square off never failed to rouse distinctly primitive instincts, particularly as their battles occasionally deteriorated into fisticuffs. Stoker's stitches were almost healed from their last such encounter, but the viscount's face still bore the slightest violet traces of bruising from Stoker's handiwork.

As I scrutinized them, I smelt a proper quarrel brewing and rose to stand between them, adopting my most governessy tone. "Boys, that is enough. Stoker, you should know by now that the gleam in Tiberius' eye means he is amusing himself at your expense. He enjoys watching you fly into a temper. Do not oblige him. As for you, Tiberius," I added with a repressive look, "stop torturing your brother. You know everyone in London, and I daresay you can tell us all that we wish to know in less time than it will take Collins to pack your collar studs. Don't be difficult."

"Collins, in point of fact, is on a leave of absence due to his lumbago—yet another reason for shutting up the house," his lordship informed me. Then he smiled. "But as ever, my dear Veronica, I am putty in your capable hands." He paired the remark with a courtly gesture, reaching out to clasp the hands in question before bringing them to his lips. "You are right, of course. Now let me get on with costumes. We haven't much time."

He paused to regard his brother's physique. "The most obvious choice is a buccaneer, and if he means to be a pirate, he ought to at least look a successful one. I have a few things that will be suitable, although I daresay his thighs and shoulders will split the seams," he added with a moue of distaste. "He has the muscular development of a peasant."

Stoker snorted. "Says the man who never lifts anything heavier than a hand of cards."

I intervened again. "You are both very attractive in your own way," I temporized. While the viscount's lean elegance would turn any woman's head, I had a keen personal appreciation for Stoker's more obvious musculature. "But Stoker's physique is not peasantlike," I corrected loyally. "His proportions are Praxitelean."

Tiberius gave a little snort and turned his attention to me, scrutinizing my figure with the eye of a practiced connoisseur. "Boadicea," he said in a tone that brooked no argument. "I quite like the idea of you, hair unbound, short tunic revealing shapely legs . . ." His voice trailed off suggestively. "Very tempting."

"I would be very happy to go as the Queen of the Iceni," I said.

"She likes it because it means she can carry weapons," Stoker informed him.

Tiberius laughed, his peculiar sharp fox's bark of a laugh. "I have no doubt. Well, I always did say Stoker ought to have a bodyguard. Do you mean to haul a spear around all night? I only ask because it might get in the way of your more intimate activities."

"There are not going to *be* any intimate activities," Stoker said. "We are going there to work, not to participate in an orgy."

Tiberius lifted his brows. "My dear boy, if you only 'participate' in an orgy, you are doing it incorrectly. One must join such endeavors with enthusiasm or not at all."

Stoker ignored the jibe. "It occurs to me that the Vane parure might be suitable."

"The Vane parure?" I asked.

Tiberius sprang to his feet. "Splendid notion! Oh, my sweet Veronica, it seems my benighted brother has been touched by genius. Come along."

He led the way to his dressing room, a distinctly masculine room with dark wallpaper figured in green vines and a thick carpet. The room smelt of leather and whisky and vetiver. I sniffed appreciatively as Tiberius went to the portrait hanging over the narrow fireplace. It was a particularly good copy of a Boucher—or perhaps it was not a copy. The Templeton-Vanes had enjoyed a good deal of money for a good deal of time. This was brought home to me when Tiberius swung the painting aside to reveal a wall safe fitted neatly behind. He spun the dial and worked a swift series of numbers to open it. Inside were a number of leather portfolios—legal documents and deeds, no doubt. He pushed these aside and began to extract a succession of boxes, leather, kid, morocco, suede. Each was stamped with the name of a prominent jeweler from London or Paris. He sorted through them until he gave a little exclamation of satisfaction.

"Here," he pronounced in triumph. "I have it."

He came forwards bearing a case of red morocco, embossed on

the top with the Templeton-Vane coat of arms. He held it out to me with a flourish.

"For me to borrow?" I asked, hesitating.

"Of course," Tiberius assured me. "It is precisely what Boadicea requires."

He flicked the golden clasp of the box and, pausing just a moment with all the instinctive timing of a master showman, he lifted the lid.

I caught my breath and stared into the case. Nested on a bed of black velvet was the most astonishing jewel I had ever seen. It was a tiara of considerable size and obvious expense, set with rubies. It was unique and old and clearly valuable.

It was also the ugliest thing I had ever seen. I poked it with a reluctant finger. "What on earth is it made of?" I asked.

"Foxes' teeth," Tiberius informed me, grinning. "There is only one other in the British Isles, and ours is far more expensive."

"I have never seen anything like it," I told him truthfully. I darted a look to where Stoker was standing, a small smile playing about his mouth.

I bent to examine the tiara more closely. A series of foxes' teeth— many, *many* foxes' teeth—formed the circular base in crisscrossing motifs, rising to a height of some three inches. The tip of each tooth was studded with a small ruby, drops of blood captured in jewel form.

"Why on earth was such a thing commissioned?" I demanded.

Tiberius gave me its history. "Our grandmother Vane was an heiress, more money than the Rothschilds, and our Templeton grandfather, in spite of his very old title, was poor as the proverbial church mouse. He needed her pots of cash. Unfortunately for him, every other regency buck was in pursuit of her, writing her sonnets and sending her pretty baubles."

Stoker picked up the tale. "But Grandmama did not care for titles or poetry or jewels. She lived to hunt. Grandfather sold everything he could get his hands on to buy her a gift to persuade her to marry him."

"And he bought her *this*?" I asked, incredulous.

"Good God, no," Tiberius corrected. "He bought her the best hunter in Ireland, an enormous brute of a horse called Tewkesbury. No one in that country could ride him, but he was fast as the wind and beautiful to boot. Grandmama sent back every other gift but that hunter and she eloped with Grandfather to Gretna on that very mount. But a viscountess must have a tiara, so Grandfather thought he would commemorate her favorite sport. He commissioned this monstrosity with her money and had it set with the teeth of every fox she had run to earth as well as the last of the Templeton rubies."

He lifted it from its velvet nest and set it on my head. "Have a look, my dear," he urged. I went to the looking glass perched over his washstand. The tiara was formidable, gruesome, teeth grinning even as the rubies winked in the lamplight.

"Frightful, isn't it?" Tiberius asked with a smile.

"It is the most dreadful thing I have ever seen," I told him truthfully. "I both loathe and adore it."

"I thought you might," Stoker told me. He glanced at Tiberius. "The armillae too, don't you think?"

Tiberius nodded. "Yes, there is something quite savage about them." He rummaged in the boxes until he unearthed a pair of armillae. Wide cuffs of gold, they were heavily figured in a triple spiral pattern, the triskelion, an ancient and feminine symbol of power. He fitted them over my sleeves, just above the elbows. "You will want to wear these on bare arms, of course. But they will do nicely."

I tipped my head. "You seem terribly certain. Have you been to the Club de l'Étoile?"

Tiberius shrugged. "Upon occasion. I have been approached a

number of times by the lady who runs the establishment, offered membership as it were. I have yet to accept, but she has left the invitation open."

"I suppose it would be a feather in her cap to secure the presence of the Viscount Templeton-Vane," Stoker said blandly.

"My dear boy, you have no idea," his brother said with an arch smile. "Among certain circles, I am famous."

"Not so much circles as pits," Stoker said.

To my astonishment, the viscount laughed.

"Don't be churlish, Stoker," I chastened. "This is not the first time Tiberius' interesting proclivities have been of use to us."

"And I bloody well hope it is the last," Stoker put in with fervor.

The viscount and I ignored him. "What should we expect?" I inquired.

Tiberius gave it some thought. "It is a refined establishment. Most of these places are so draped in frills and furbelows, one can hardly tell where the upholstery leaves off. But Madame Aurore has exquisite taste, as one would expect from a lady with her history."

I propped my chin on my hands and widened my eyes, doing my best impression of a schoolgirl. "Do tell, Uncle Tiberius. And don't leave anything out."

"Cheeky wench," he said with a fond smile. "Very well. I suspect nothing will shock you, but if Stoker falls about blushing, do not say I failed to warn you." He settled back into his chair, lacing his fingers over his slim waist. "No one knows where she came from. There are a thousand different myths, but she confirms none of them. She sprang, like Athena, fully formed on the stage of the Opéra, warbling out a passable Cherubino. It was not the quality of her voice which enthralled, you understand. It was the shapeliness of her calves in her costume as a footman."

"Naturally," I said.

"Her form attracted attention, as she no doubt intended it should. Her voice, as I say, was only passable. But she played a longer game, going into the keeping of a gentleman of wealth and renown. He polished her up, burnishing her to a brilliant shine. She left him within months for a prince of the blood. Then was an industrialist, an American, I believe. She had been, for eight months, the talk of Paris. And then the Prussians came."

I shivered. No one who had heard the stories of the siege could forget them, the proud city, bombarded by the Prussians until the Parisians were so assailed by hardship and privation they turned to eating rats and domestic pets. Seventeen years had passed since the siege of Paris, but there were survivors of that time who still shuddered every time they saw a rabbit on a plate because of its unfortunate resemblance to cooked cat.

"Why did Madame Aurore not leave? If she had an American lover, surely he could have got her away? America was neutral during that war."

He shrugged. "No one knows what held her in France, but she stayed. And because she stayed, she became a legend, suffering with her people. The lady never sang again. She put it out that starvation had ruined her voice, and all of Paris exalted her for her sacrifice. When the city was freed and life went back to what passed for normal, she found new lovers, a string of them, and devoted herself to becoming the continent's most beloved courtesan. It was a title she held for a decade."

"Then what?" Stoker roused himself to ask.

"Then, for reasons that are—like much in the lady's life—shrouded in mystery, she left the Continent and established herself in London. Some said it was to renew an acquaintance with the French emperor in his exile, some say it was to escape the memories of a city that had grown too thick with ghosts. In any event, she made a success of herself because she is careful and discreet here. Her house is equipped with multiple entrances and exits so that one may enter and leave unobserved. She keeps no formal membership list, no records."

I flicked a glance to Stoker and back again as I pondered Eddy's vulnerability. In giving a costly proof of his affections to such a woman, he had put himself squarely in her power. "Then she would not be likely to blackmail one of her guests?"

"My dear Veronica, that would be entirely contrary to her own best interests. Talk about killing the goose that laid the golden egg! She makes thousands out of her clientele. If there were the slightest whisper of indiscretion, she would have to close her doors instantly. And, given the number of extremely notable government figures who have graced her doors, I daresay the lady would find herself on the receiving end of a lengthy prison sentence to boot."

Before I could ask any further questions, Tiberius rose, rubbing his hands together briskly. "Come along, then. We haven't much time to make Stoker look like a respectable gentleman of means, and God only knows how long that will take."

# CHAPTER

## 7

In the end, it took the better part of three hours before we assembled an appropriate wardrobe for Stoker. He objected to anything flamboyant of Tiberius', and since the viscount had a flair for beautiful fabrics with dramatic cuts, the battles were many and heated.

"I look like a bloody magician's assistant," he protested at one point as he flicked the ruffle at the cuff of a particularly elegant ensemble.

"You are a magician," I reminded him.

"Never professionally," he retorted. "And I do not see the need for *lace*."

Tiberius' expression was pained. "That is Alençon, you philistine, and it was created for an exclusive fancy dress party given by the Queen of Bohemia." The viscount stepped back, assessing him. "How do you do it?" he murmured. "You make the most exquisite tailoring look like something from the dressing-up box."

"I feel ridiculous," Stoker put in.

The viscount sighed. "You cannot carry it off, my boy. You haven't the aplomb. Very well, a pirate you shall be. Your own trousers will have to do. I have a shirt with appropriately Elizabethan sleeves, and here, take this shawl of India paisley to wear as a sash to hold your cutlass and pistols."

Stoker rolled his eyes heavenwards. "I am not wearing a cutlass and pistols."

"The more fool you," Tiberius told him. "I daresay Veronica will be armed to her pretty teeth."

The viscount thrust the garments at Stoker and beckoned me into the sitting room next door.

"We can have a coze while that Neanderthal is defiling my tailoring," he said, pouring out a tiny glass of violet liqueur.

"Tell me what you think of this." He presented it with a flourish and I took a sip, relishing the lush floral headiness that burst over my tongue.

"Crème de violette!" I exclaimed. "I recognize it. This is the handiwork of Julien d'Orlande."

Julien was a Frenchman of Caribbean extraction, rigorously schooled in the traditions of the finest patisserie. Thanks to Stoker's efforts, he had secured a position at the Allerdale Hotel and a reputation as one of London's rising stars.

"I didn't realize you were acquainted with him," I told Tiberius after another decadent sip.

"Stoker introduced us and Julien has catered a number of private entertainments," he told me. I thought he might say something more, but his lordship fell silent, a shadow over his eyes.

"Tiberius?" I said softly.

His mouth quirked into a mocking smile. "Ah, she wishes to play Florence Nightingale, to take the temperature of my soul and assess the state of my mind's health. Tell me, Nurse, what is the prognosis? Shall I live? Give me your expert diagnosis of my ailment."

"Heartbreak," I said.

"Succinct and accurate," he told me, downing the full measure of his violet liqueur and smacking his lips delicately. "I taste hay, fresh green hay, in that. Do you?"

"Tiberius," I said again.

He put his glass aside and gave a deep sigh. "Veronica, do not ask me to drop the mask, not even for you."

"Is it so terrible to be honest with one another? What do you fear?"

He rolled the dainty glass between his palms. "That if I let loose of the mask, I shall never find it again."

"That would not be a catastrophe," I told him. "You have played the part of the devil-may-care roué for long enough, don't you think?"

The brow rose again. "My darling Veronica, if I am not he, then who am I?"

I covered his hand with my own. "A man who deserves to be seen for himself."

He stared at our hands where they touched. "Bless you, sweet child."

"You talk as though you were Methuselah. Shall I fetch your walking stick and slippers, Grandpapa?"

"I was right to call you a cheeky wench," he said. He slipped his hand out from under mine. "I am fond of you, Veronica. Fonder than I have ever been of any woman I have not bedded. Do not make me question that."

I had pressed him too far, but given all that we had endured together, I felt justified. I tipped back my head and drained the rest of the glorious purple concoction.

"Very well. Take refuge in your masquerade, if it gives you comfort. But when it fails you—and make no mistake, one dark, lonesome night, it *will* fail you—we will be here."

"I could almost regret my decision to leave," he told me as we rose.

"You needn't go. You could stay and help. Stoker and I could use you."

He smiled, a wicked grin that betrayed the good humor he so often hid under a pose of languor. "If Stoker cannot deduce what to do with you in a house full of beds, he does not deserve you."

He dropped a kiss to my temple just as Stoker appeared in the doorway, a wrathful expression on his face. "Do not make me bruise you again, brother."

Tiberius turned to examine his efforts. "He looks more a gentleman than I thought him capable," he said. "Don't you agree, Veronica?"

"I agree," I said simply. The trousers were his own, fitting him snugly through thighs and elsewhere. The shirtfront was white as a virgin's sheet, soft and flowing into lavish sleeves and opened at the throat. The paisley shawl was slung low upon his hips, knotted at the side, the fringes rippling over the solid length of his legs. His hair was tumbled and far too long—he had obviously not borrowed Tiberius' hairbrush—and gold rings gleamed at his lobes, remnants of his past as a naval surgeon. But his tattoos were covered by the best of British tailoring and the scar that traveled a slim silver line from his temple to his cheek kept his appearance from bandbox perfection. He had donned his black eye patch, a square of silk meant to rest the eye that had once been damaged by a jaguar's claws and which still tired easily. Draped over one shoulder was the wing of a heavy black cloak. The effect was one of extremely successful piracy.

"You hardly look like yourself," I managed, although this was not strictly true. He looked as much Stoker as he ever had, only more polished and aristocratic. His mother's blood was blue, after all, I reflected, and a thousand years of breeding does sometimes tell—no doubt due to the advantages of a healthy diet and good medical care, I noted.

"It will do," Tiberius said at last.

"High praise indeed," Stoker mocked.

Tiberius rolled his eyes heavenwards. "Sit down in front of the fire.

Collins' replacement will bring you sandwiches and tea. Consume them and for God's sake, do not get butter or crumbs upon my garments or I will hang you from the nearest lamppost." He turned to me. "Come, Cinderella. I have to play faery godmother and there isn't much time."

Tiberius took his role as costumier seriously. It took hours for him to achieve the effect he desired. To begin with, he instructed a footman to go immediately to a costume house and hire suitable apparel.

"A short tunic," the viscount insisted. "Tights to match the color of Miss Speedwell's dainty flesh and some very simple flat slippers with ribbons to the knee."

"Tiberius," I said repressively, "no woman has ever led an army in slippers that lace to the knee. I shall look like a chorus dancer."

He gave me a stern look. "I am not creating a warrior, I am creating the *fantasy* of a warrior, and if you do not understand that, the least you can do is be quiet and sit very still until I am satisfied."

I obeyed, occupying myself with reading the latest adventures of Arcadia Brown, Lady Detective, as he conjured his magic. When he was finished, I hardly recognized myself. He had unbound my black hair, shaking it free until it waved loose almost to my waist. From each temple he had gathered a lock to braid, weaving it back and into the other. A few more braids here and there were worked into my coiffure, each spotted with a tiny ruby bead borrowed from the Vane collection. Atop this he sat the fox-tooth tiara, the jewels in it glittering savagely in the lamplight. The armillae gleamed from my bare arms, just glints of gold beneath an enormous scarlet cloak topped with a leopard-skin cape.

The hired tunic was shorter than I would have liked, although it is no false pride to say my legs could bear the scrutiny. A wide belt at my waist was the perfect place to secure a short, sharp dagger borrowed from its usual place on his desk, where it functioned as letter opener. I was pleased to find the tunic had a pocket, and when Tiberius was busy searching out his supply of greasepaints, I quickly transferred my tiny good luck charm, a grey velvet mouse named Chester. The little fellow had been my constant companion as long as I could remember, nestling in my pocket through all of my travels and bringing comfort with just a touch of my fingertip to his soft fabric. He had even survived a near-fatal drowning, thanks to Stoker, who had mended him with careful stitches and replaced his black bead eyes with new ones of bright blue. He was all the dearer to me for his tribulations, and I gave him a reassuring pat as I tucked him into my pocket for one more grand adventure just as Tiberius reappeared.

The viscount rummaged in his case of greasepaints—kept specially for his frequent attendance at masquerade balls and other less wholesome entertainments—and touched my lids with a bit of silvery salve to make them glisten. A similar concoction with a ruby hue was applied to my lips. He took a stick of kohl and outlined my eyes, making them huge and dramatic, ringed with smoke from a watch fire.

"There," he pronounced. "I have made a Briton queen of you, my dear."

He led me to a looking glass and I peered at my reflection.

"Tiberius, no one has ever looked less like a Briton queen. To begin with, I have no spear or short sword. I have no blue woad for my face. My tunic should be ankle length for this climate, and I will not even begin to discuss the impracticality of leaving one's hair loose for battle."

"You look perfect," said a low voice from the doorway.

Stoker stood motionless, wearing an expression I had never seen before.

Tiberius gave a smile of satisfaction. "And that is my work done."

The viscount took up the greatcoat that lay over his chair. "I am taking my leave, children. Behave yourselves."

He shook hands with Stoker and kissed me again. "I do not know when I will return."

"Will you write?" I asked.

"Probably not. The pen is a demanding mistress. I take delight in thwarting her expectations."

"Go already," Stoker told him. But there was an anxious line in his brow, and I realized that in spite of their brawls, some new common ground had been found between them thanks to our shared adventure. Our experiences in Cornwall had wounded Tiberius deeply, exposing old heartbreak and inflicting unimaginable pain that would take years to ease. I could only hope that his travels would mend his wounds as they so often had mine.

"Godspeed, Tiberius," I told him.

He took his leave in a swirl of black greatcoat, like a pantomime demon disappearing through the smoke. Stoker breathed a sigh of relief or sadness, I could not tell. He grinned and slipped a hand into his pocket. He retrieved a paper twist of honey drops and popped one into his mouth, crunching hard with his lovely white teeth.

"Some things do not change," he assured me.

I returned the grin. "Shall we embark upon our next adventure, then?"

He linked his arm through mine. "Excelsior!"


Tiberius had given us the use of his town carriage for the evening on the grounds that it might be difficult for Boadicea, Queen of the Iceni, and her pirate companion to hail a cab. We settled against the squabs—bottle green velvet discreetly stamped with Tiberius' arms in silver—and fell into silence. We had left in good spirits, but a whiff of constraint hung in the air. Was it proximity, I wondered, our nearness in the dark, close space of the carriage? I could smell him, warm flesh, lightened with leather and honey and a touch of brandy. It was a heady combination. The seat was luxuriously plush and generously proportioned. It would be an easy matter to tell the driver to make his way slowly around the park a time or two before moving on. What things might we get up to in the velvet shadows of that intimate darkness?

My fingers crept near his across the expanse of the seat, but just before they would have touched, he raised his hand and scratched his cheek. He was turned to face the window, in profile to me, a black and inscrutable silhouette against the glass.

I glanced out and saw an elderly woman, leaning upon her walking stick, and was instantly put in mind of Lady Wellie. I dropped my hand into my lap. This was not the time for erotic pursuits, I told myself severely. We had a mystery to solve and would need all of our wits about us. There would be ample opportunity later for the amatory arts.

There was little traffic and the pace was brisk, the lights a streaming blur as we drove smartly from the refined elegance of Mayfair through the stolid respectability of Westminster to the more subtle charms of Bloomsbury. We crossed this neighborhood, almost to the edge of Clerkenwell. This part of London offered endless variety, from placid streets snug in their quiet prosperity to livelier roads that offered more rustic entertainments. One could turn a corner and move from silken security to homespun hardship. Here and there, small, tidy green squares were tucked away, remnants of the days when the great aristocratic families owned huge swathes of the land beyond the gates of the City proper. These had all been broken up and sold, developed into shops and houses, schools and offices, but the odd pocket of verdure remained, and the most expensive houses always stood clustered around them, protective of their privilege. They might be residences or private clubs, offering seclusion within the urban surroundings and more anonymity than one might enjoy in a similarly situated property in Mayfair—and certainly at less expense.

It was a superb choice for Madame Aurore's establishment, near enough to the great and good that they could make an easy evening of it, and yet sufficiently far to ensure the casual bystander would not recognize those who wished to enjoy their pleasures unobtrusively.

"Interesting that Madame Aurore has opened her club to ladies for membership," I remarked to Stoker. "I suppose that sets her apart from other such entrepreneurs. She provides complete discretion for those who wish to disport themselves, male or female."

"How very modern of her."

"Indeed. And clever of her not to tie herself to one man," I observed.

He turned his head swiftly, blinking at me in the dim light. "What do you mean?"

"Limiting herself to her first protector nearly got her killed in the siege of Paris. It was wise of her to diversify her interests."

"You have got cynical in your old age," he said.

"Don't be testy," I ordered. "Have you eaten recently? You are always so frightfully prickly when you are hungry."

He said nothing but retrieved the paper twist of honey drops from his pocket and crunched a few as I went on. "She seems to have pursued Tiberius as a member of her club. I wonder if she ever entertained your father."

"I wonder if she ever entertained yours."

"Oh, you are in a nasty mood," I said in a tone of mild reproach. But he was correct. If there was a crumb of salaciousness to be had, the Prince of Wales could usually be found with a seat at the table. I sighed. "But you are not wrong. The more I hear of him, the less I understand how the princess bears him."

"Because it is what wives have done for centuries," he reminded me. "They turn a blind eye and take up needlework. Or découpage. Or flower arranging. Or they throw themselves into their children as Her Royal Highness has done. It is not healthy."

"You don't think a mother ought to be devoted to her children?"

"Prince Albert Victor is almost five and twenty years of age. He is a fully grown man. Why should he order trinkets for his ladylove from his mother's jeweler? He had to have known she would get wind of it and be upset by his indiscretion. And whilst we are on the subject, why should she have to clear up his mess? Why doesn't she just order him outright to retrieve the jewel himself?"

"She explained. It would be awkward for her to raise such a subject with him. Besides, it seems perfectly apparent that she indulges him," I replied.

"And why should that be? She has other children who are still in the schoolroom and no doubt have need of her. She oughtn't be sweeping up after him. She is the future queen."

He was almost angry in his defense of her, and I was silent a moment, considering. The princess was slender and beautiful still—she was only forty-four, after all. There was a cool elegance about her, a remoteness that dissolved when she looked at you with those steady grey-blue eyes. "Saints preserve us," I murmured, "you have a tendresse for the princess."

"I may admire a woman without it going further than that," he said coldly. I knew that tone. It was like the striking of a stag's hoof to the ground, a warning to be wary. Of course, I usually interpreted it as a signal to push him further solely because there were few pleasures more enchanting than watching him rise ferociously to a choice bit of bait. But there was something vulnerable in his tenderness for the princess. I thought of his mother, likewise beautiful and neglected, locked in a marriage with a man she did not love, consoled only by her handsome, loyal sons. She had been unable to protect them from the wrath of her husband. Stoker, her cuckoo in the nest, had been the product of her only rebellion, her fleeting grasp at a joy that would prove elusive. And I could not mock him for admiring a woman so very like her.

My throat was tight and I said nothing for a long moment, turning my face away so that it was my turn to watch the passing scene. The streetlamps glowed in the darkness, circles of warm, golden safety. But just beyond the edge of each, shadows moved and shifted, and something dark and menacing walked those streets, I reminded myself.

"Have you brought arms?" I asked suddenly.

"In these trousers? I have only a few picklocks tucked into my sash." He lifted a brow towards the snug seams straining over his thighs and I gave him a consoling pat.

"Never mind. I have taken precautions."

"Veronica—" he began, his tone alarmed.

"Not now, Stoker," I said, putting my hand in my pocket to give Chester a quick pat. "We have arrived."

# CHAPTER

# 8

The club was a tall white house, elegant but unremarkable. It glowed from cellars to attics with the soft gleam of electric lights behind each window, and it took me a moment to realize that the absolute stillness of those lights meant that each window was carefully screened, blocking the interior from view. A discreet servant standing upon the curb waved the carriage around to the mews entrance, which had been sealed so that no one would overlook the comings and goings of the club.

Tiberius' coachman touched his hat and promised to keep the horses fresh and walking slowly about the square until we emerged.

"Never mind that," Stoker told him. "We shall be some time. Put the horses and yourself to bed and we will find our own way home."

The coachman gave him a knowing smile. "Aye, I've been with 'is lordship long enough to know the way of it."

He whistled to the horses to walk on and Stoker and I mounted the curb. The club was located just at the edge of respectability and privilege. Beyond the back garden lay the East End and all its attendant terrors; to the west was every bastion of wealth the capital could boast. At the intersection was this nondescript house of quiet gentility, the white stone façade punctuated with polished brass work and glossy black shutters. The door was black, set with a knocker sculpted into the shape of a star.

"Madame Aurore is nothing if not consistent," I murmured, remembering my Classical mythology. Aurora the dawn goddess rose each day from her couch just as the stars were beginning to dim, gathering them into her arms to festoon her hair and her robes with the last rays of their splendor.

Stoker did not lift the knocker. He instead flicked a glance to the porter, a slender figure in sober livery of black with tidy silver buttons stamped with stars. The porter sprang to attention, rapping a coded knock upon the door. With a start, I realized that the porter was in fact a young woman in masculine dress. Her hair was concealed under a powdered wig and her face was masked, no doubt to set the tone of the evening's entertainment, and as I looked closely at her, she bowed her head in a diffident gesture. Stoker did not look at her but flipped a coin deftly in her direction as I hurried to follow him. A new hauteur had come over him with his change in appearance. It was as if he had put on Tiberius' attitude with his clothes, and I both deplored it and found it deeply attractive.

The door swung back and another liveried person—this time male and possibly older than Methuselah—approached. His half mask fitted poorly, no doubt due to the elaborate condition of his moustaches and beard, which covered his face nearly to the cheekbones. He bobbed his head this way and that as he moved, never quite making eye contact. I admired his discretion.

"Good evening, sir, madam," he intoned in a low voice as he struggled into a low bow. Rheumatism, I suspected.

"I am Rev—"

The fellow flung up a hand, clearly aghast. "No names, sir, I beg you! The club is not famous for discretion because if we were famous, we would not be discreet." He smiled at his own little jest, baring a set of surprisingly good teeth. "This way, sir, madam."

He scuttled off, leading us into a small side parlor furnished in exquisite taste. The walls were hung with pale grey brocade woven with an abstract pattern of stars, and the upholstery was the same, a collection of armchairs grouped around a scattering of small, low tables. Porcelain, all of it pure white, was assembled in alcoves, and the effect was restful. The only color that broke the soothing grey was a massive vase of dawn-pink lilies on a sideboard and a painting hung above the fireplace—a portrait of a woman. Her face was in profile and she was dressed in Classical draperies of shifting shades of silver, blue, and rose, a lute propped at her feet. Low on her brow rested a starry diamond tiara.

"Wait here, please," the manservant instructed. He bowed his way out of the room, closing the double doors quietly behind.

"Surprisingly tasteful," I remarked.

"The best brothels are," Stoker said without trace of embarrassment.

"You and Tiberius seem well versed in the matter," I told him as I surveyed a narrow bookshelf. The volumes were all bound in grey kid and stamped with a single letter, "A," rendered in a severe, stark capital.

"I will admit to a misspent youth," Stoker allowed.

"I would hardly call it misspent if you learnt skills," I told him.

He blushed adorably, the tips of his ears turning pink.

"I suppose I ought to point out that this is not, strictly speaking, a brothel," said a low, melodious voice. There was the slightest trace of a French accent, and I knew our hostess had entered even before I turned around.

She was smiling in spite of my hasty attempts at an apology.

"Faugh! We must not be provincial about such things," she said, the smile broadening. "We know why we are here. My house is always open to people who understand what they desire."

There was good Gallic sense in what she said. She came forwards until I could smell her perfume, something dusky and heavy with only the slightest edge of rich, plummy darkness. She tipped her head, studying us. "I think I recognize a pirate when I see one, but who are you with your savage jewels, mademoiselle?"

"Boadicea," I told her.

"Ah! The Briton queen with the unpronounceable name. I shall not attempt it," she said gravely, but a light danced behind her eyes. I took the opportunity to return her scrutiny. She was wearing a gown very similar to the one in the painting—beautifully draped and heavy enough to bear the weight of a galaxy of diamond stars. The diamond tiara sat at her brow, darting sparks of light as she moved her head. Her extraordinary and elegant costume had been carefully chosen to make the most of her natural beauty. She had dark brows, strongly marked and arched, but her hair was the color of winter frost, varying shades of white and silver. It fell to her hips, a rippling river of ice.

So, this was the woman who had captured my half-brother's affections, I mused. I was not surprised; she was exquisite, with an air of mature worldliness that would no doubt appeal to many a younger man, especially one reared in the hothouse atmosphere of a royal court. I could well imagine any besotted youth showering her with jewels in a fervent attempt to earn her attention. Some mistresses kept their counsel, discretion being the better part of both valor and profit for them. Others blazoned their triumphs for the world to see, heedless of scandal or outrage. It remained to be seen which she would prove to be with regard to Eddy.

She extended her hand. "I am Madame Aurore, your hostess for the evening. I hope you will forgive the formality of a meeting, but I always make a point of greeting newcomers personally." She lifted one pale hand towards the open door in a gesture of command, and one of her army of pages trotted forwards with a tray and glasses.

"Champagne," she pronounced, insisting that we each take a glass. The fine crystal was like silk in my hand, and the wine was gently effervescent, the pale gold of new straw. We sipped, and she gestured towards the furniture grouped by the hearth, urging us to sit. The evening was warm enough that the fire had not been lit, but a pair of tall porcelain perfume burners stood upon the tiles, sending puffs of scented smoke into the air.

"I am always pleased to see new faces in my establishment," she began, "but you must understand the need for discretion."

"Naturally," Stoker said.

She gave him a look of approval as she made quick work of scrutinizing him with the eye of a practiced businesswoman, taking in the tailoring and the jewels. The overlong hair and the eye patch would make no difference to her. It was the aristocratic vowels and the gemstones that mattered.

"You have chosen an excellent night to pay a first visit to the club," she told us. "Tonight is our Wednesday *bal masqué*. I see you have brought masks," she added with a nod towards the black velvet dominos we each held. "The custom is that upon the stroke of ten, the entertainment begins. You have free rein of the house and the gardens, except for the suite on the third floor that is marked with a black velvet rope. That is my private apartment and not open to guests," she warned. "Should you lose your way or require anything at all, there are always pages to offer assistance. I pay them a generous wage, and it is for you to offer them whatever gratuity you feel appropriate. That is none of my concern." She paused, long enough for me to realize that the small army of black-liveried young people were there for more than just the opening of doors and serving of champagne.

"Oh. *Oh*," I managed.

She gave me an indulgent smile. "How refreshingly new you are, mademoiselle! I can see why monsieur has brought you tonight."

She went on. "I do not keep a record of my visitors, for your protection and my own. I cannot be compelled to reveal what I do not know and what cannot be proven. This is a private house and I am a private woman entertaining her friends—that is all the authorities need to know."

"Most appreciated," Stoker assured her. She gave a nod and continued.

"While the ball itself is underway, you may dance and consume all the food and drink that you wish. Converse, enjoy the entertainments. I take great pride in the originality of the themes and the generosity of my table. Should you have need, there are private rooms for more intimate activities. If the door is open, avail yourself of the apartment. You may shut the door for privacy if you wish. There is a silver ribbon tied to each doorknob. Leave it hanging outside if you are open to the prospect of company joining you. If you wish for complete privacy, take it into the room with you. When you depart the room, kindly ring the bell and a maid will come and freshen the amenities for future guests."

It seemed a most civilized arrangement, I decided. One might have a room entirely to one's own purposes or one might enjoy a bit of a crowd if tastes ran that way.

She went on. "At the stroke of two, the house will be gifted with darkness. The lights are extinguished and some guests take this as a signal to slip away. Others remain and the public rooms are given over to whatever the inclinations of my guests. You may find at that hour that invitations are presented to you—unexpected opportunities. It is, of course, your perfect right to refuse any overtures, but I suggest you accept them. Perhaps make a few of your own," she added, the edges of her mouth curling upwards. "Things you never imagined possible in the light become desirable in the dark."

I felt a shiver—a premonition?—shudder down my spine. Stoker, for his part, seemed entirely the man-about-town, raising his champagne coupe to his hostess. "To the powers of darkness," he said.

She smiled, a ripe, inviting smile, and lifted her own glass. They drank and I hastened to finish my own champagne. Madame Aurore offered a dish of tiny sugar pastilles flavored with mint. "To sweeten the breath after champagne," she told us. I took one—Stoker took seven—and rose as she clicked her fingers.

Instantly, one of her slender pages appeared, this one with dark skin and elegant ankles. He gestured for us to follow him as our hostess remained in her reception room.

"Have a good time," she called after us. "And I would remind you that Venus favors the bold." I turned back to see her smile, a thin, watchful smile that did not quite meet her eyes.

We followed the page from Madame Aurore's small parlor towards the sound of music.

"Would you care to join the *bal masqué* or would you prefer a more private setting?" the page inquired without the slightest trace of embarrassment.

"The *bal*," Stoker replied quickly.

The page inclined his head and led us through a series of corridors, each hung with rose or grey silk and a painting of the goddess of the dawn. In some she strode over hills, spreading the soft light of the morning over the landscape as she walked. In others, she was in the act of rising from her slumbers, the bedclothes tumbled suggestively. Sometimes she was accompanied by a battalion of maids strewing flowers and dewdrops, but at others she was depicted in the act of dressing—or undressing—with cherubs holding the ribbons of her sandals and stroking her delicate feet. There were nipples, so many of them, and blushing cheeks, rosy with effort or pleasure as she looked upon a sleeping youth. It was a glorious collection, with Auroras both fair and dark, some with blond tresses and some with black and every shade in between. Her skin was brown or pink or white, her features European or African or Asian. They were Aurora in every dimension, and I would have loved to have studied them at length.

But the page trotted on, leading us towards the sound of music, and a restless buzzing noise that I realized was the chatter of excited voices. I had expected languor from a crowd of undoubted sophisticates, but there was the underlying hum of anticipation, of needs yet to be met, clamoring in the blood.

We climbed a grand staircase carpeted in plush grey, with lavish sprays of hothouse peonies and roses spilling from urns at the foot. An enormous chandelier hung far overhead, the prisms scattering rainbows across the walls in glittering arcs. The page paused at the top of the stairs, just in front of a set of double doors that had been thrown open.

"Welcome," he said with an arch smile, "to the *bal masqué* of the Club de l'Étoile." He gestured widely and bowed, indicating we should enter. I darted a glance at Stoker, but the set of his jaw was impassive. Whatever he was thinking, he was disinclined to share.

I touched my mask to make certain it was secure. Stoker extended his arm and I took it. Together we stepped into a scene conjured out of myth. The room itself was a marvel, fashioned of grey marble with a ceiling painted in the style of Inigo Jones. It was delicate blue with drifting clouds, each circling the center, where Aurora held court, white hounds at her feet, a crown of stars adorning her brow. Below, grey velvet drapes covered the tall windows, and a series of electric chandeliers provided illumination. Between the windows were hung long mirrors, reflecting back each dazzling point of light again and again, multiplying them until the room seemed filled with endless golden stars.

At one end, a formally attired orchestra played a waltz, and at the other, a long table held a massive silver fountain that splashed with champagne. In between, dancers masked and garbed in every costume imaginable dipped and twirled to the music. A naked man dressed only in thick gold paint, shimmering from top to toe, partnered Anne Boleyn, elegant in black velvet with a slender, gruesome ribbon of scarlet at her neck. I recognized the central image of *Liberty Leading the People* with her red bonnet and bodice open to the waist; she was dancing with a French cardinal in crimson taffeta robes—Richelieu or Mazarin, I decided. And two women dressed as red-coated soldiers swayed together, not even bothering with the proper steps, their lips fixed upon one another as their hands clasped one another's buttocks beneath their uniforms.

Stoker swallowed hard. "Shall we dance?" he managed.

I nodded and he swept me into a waltz. For the first pass down the ballroom, I simply stared at him in astonishment, scarcely able to remember the steps. As we reached the dais and he guided me into a turn, he noticed my surprise.

"What? You are surprised I know how to waltz?"

"No, I am surprised that you are so skillful at it," I told him truthfully. He grinned at me then, and for a moment, the constraint that had settled over him ebbed a little. His arm tightened and he executed a series of complicated turns flawlessly, sweeping me along past the silvery lengths of the mirrors. The room was a riot of color and music and glamour, and for just this moment, I permitted myself to surrender to it. When the dance was finished, I should remind myself that we were there with a purpose, tasked with the impossible, and in danger of exposure. But not *this* moment, I told myself. For now, I would throw myself into the pleasure of the waltz, twirling and gliding until I was giddy with the motion. To hold my balance, I kept my eyes fixed upon his, my arms resting lightly where his clasped firmly. He was my anchor, my sole point of reference in a world that spun too fast, that would have thrown me off my balance if he had let go of me.

But he did not let go. He kept me upright, anchored, and that was the moment that I understood how he had changed me. I had been so long on my own, so apart from everyone, that I had not realized how he had pierced my solitude. I had finally acknowledged that I loved him, but it was not until that moment that I understood I needed him.

It was that revelation more than the physical exertion of the dance that threatened my equilibrium. The music drew to a close and we stopped, arms still held in a dancers' embrace. I stepped back sharply.

"Veronica?" he murmured.

"We will never find the right star if we keep getting distracted," I told him. "We should separate. Divide and conquer." My voice was firm, a good deal more decisive than I felt. His hand tightened at my waist.

"Veronica, this is not exactly the queen's drawing room. You cannot go haring off by yourself. You will invite trouble."

"Then let us see if trouble responds," I retorted. "Meet me on the staircase under the chandelier in an hour."

I turned on my heel and left him then. I think he started after me but thought better of it. His hand fell to his side, and I saw in the mirror a buxom Viking maiden sidle up to him. I strode away, feeling every inch the ancient Queen of the Britons, warlike and implacable.

Just then the orchestra struck up a new waltz, this one with a Gypsy lilt, demanding, insistent. The mood in the ballroom changed subtly. Invitations made with eyes and lips were accepted. Kisses and light caresses were freely exchanged, and the sounds of sighs and slightly tipsy laughter filled the air. As I made to leave the ballroom, my way was blocked by a young woman with gauzy skirts and a bared belly who was eating fire for a group of rapt gentlemen.

As I moved around them, one of the gentlemen stepped back—no doubt to avoid singeing his whiskers on her charms—and I nearly collided with him. From behind me, a strong arm slipped around my waist to draw me out of the path of danger. I whirled in surprise to see the face of my savior—the young porter who had admitted us to the house, blue eyes dancing behind her mask. Before I could thank her, she clasped me firmly and drew me into the dance, leading me expertly. Her gaze never left mine as we danced, the music urging us on, from a lazily sensual pace to something faster and more reckless. Her feet never faltered, and her grip never loosened. I matched her, turn for turn, my toes scarcely touching the ground at one point, my grand cape flowing behind us like a scarlet river.

At last, some breathless minutes after it began, the waltz ended in a climactic crash of cymbals and violins. My partner had guided me to the center of the room, dozens of couples pressed firmly around us. I opened my mouth to thank her for the dance, but before I could speak, she seized the moment.

She kissed me then, a light brush of the lips just at the corner of my mouth. She drew back her head, smiling. "Good night, Veronica Speedwell," she said in a hoarse whisper. Without another word, she set me back upon my feet and vanished into the crowd, gone as quickly and mysteriously as she had come.

One of the fire-eater's admirers jostled me then and I recollected myself, moving out of the frantic doings in the ballroom and thinking furiously. In spite of the house rules on anonymity, in spite of my mask, my enigmatic partner had called me by name. Someone in the Club de l'Étoile knew exactly who I was.

# CHAPTER

## 9

I left the ballroom, reeling a little at this latest development. There was no sign of Stoker, for which I was both grateful and annoyed. Grateful, as I did not particularly wish to face him until I had recovered my composure after both the hectic dance and the unsettling notion that someone had penetrated my disguise. And I was annoyed that he was not at hand when I needed him. (The fact that I had sent him away with some vehemence was entirely immaterial. He ought to have *known* to stay in the general vicinity, I thought, a touch irrationally.)

I made my way up the next flight of stairs without quite thinking the matter through. I had some vague idea of finding Madame Aurore's rooms and inspecting her collection of diamond stars. Surely the lady could not be wearing all of them, I reflected. If I were very lucky indeed, I might find the prince's offering sitting comfortably in her jewel box.

The gentle reader will no doubt be asking at this point if I had taken leave of my usual prodigious common sense. Surely it was sounder logic to attempt such an undertaking with my partner, particularly given his skill with lockpicking and weaponry. If nothing else, two pairs of eyes keeping watch would be more efficacious than one, and a couple bent upon wrongdoing can easily plead the demands of passion as an excuse for trespassing in a private space. I have no excuse. I am a scientist, seldom given to the vagaries of emotion, but that night my usual good sense had deserted me. The heightened atmosphere of the Club de l'Étoile was invigorating, and I was unsettled by my own response. I was accustomed to acknowledging and even encouraging my appetites; I had long believed that exercising a vigorous libido was a necessity for good mental health as well as physiological well-being.

And if I had examined my own heart more thoroughly, I would have found an even greater reason for my confusion. Less than a fortnight before, Stoker had risked his life to save mine in a daring and very nearly hopeless attempt to rescue me from peril. I had awakened the next morning with a conviction that I loved him as I had never loved anyone. The rest of our days in Cornwall had been passed in a delirious haze of anticipation, the memory of it tinged pink and dreamlike.

Yet now that we had returned to London, I had been aware of a creeping sensation of doubt. That a physical union between us would be gratifying I had no doubt. I was only too aware of Stoker's many attractions. But this new and burgeoning habit to rely upon him terrified me to my marrow. I had learnt not to be dependent through the harshest of circumstances. Could I now alter that practice? Could I really throw my hard-won independence to the wind and lean upon him?

It was a question that drove me to act that night with reckless bravado. I had to prove to myself that I was still the same explorer who packed her petticoats and her parasol and set off to see the world. I had to peer into the looking glass of my soul and see once more the intrepid spirit that burned within. If I lost her, who then would I be? A mere appendage of Stoker's?

Never! I vowed. I took up the tail of my queenly cape and set off to find Madame Aurore's private rooms. The corridors were full of people, some in couples, some in larger groups. Most were conversing, but a few were engaged in more obvious flirtations, whispering and giggling together, pressing fervent kisses to receptive throats. I passed them swiftly, calculating that I needed to climb up another floor to find Madame Aurore's sanctum, but no sooner had I darted down one corridor and around another than I became hopelessly lost. I could navigate the thickest rain forest with aplomb, but the Club de l'Étoile was a different thing altogether, designed to arouse and befuddle the senses. This floor was given over to the public reception rooms and Madame Aurore had evidently enjoyed planning out the most labyrinthine configuration. There was no grand corridor on this side of the house, only rooms opening one onto another in a long enfilade like pearls strung upon a chain. Each room had been furnished in a different style, setting an entirely different mood as one moved from chamber to chamber. I had just passed from a lush jungle habitat (created from an enormous number of potted palms and the odd caged tropical songbird) to an elegant if slightly hysterical interpretation of ancien régime Versailles hung with pink velvet and gilded furniture carved with ripe-breasted sphinxes. The air was thick with the signature scent of Madame Aurore's perfume, the same blend of sandalwood and vetiver and violet that pervaded the rest of the house. The effect was otherworldly, aided by clouds of incense smoking gently from jars upon the hearths. The smoke smelt of roses, and a deeper, muskier scent filled the air.

"It is chestnut," said a voice in my ear. I turned to see a tall, unlikely-looking woman standing beside me. She was dressed in an unflattering gown of harsh pink taffeta. A wig of lavish blond curls was topped by a lace veil, and enormous diamonds—paste, no doubt—glittered at her throat and ears and wrists. Perched atop the lace veil was a miniature crown, little bigger than a pudding dish and a perfect replica of the queen's tiny Jubilee diadem, sparkling with more false jewels. She wore a full mask of dark blue velvet, and this, coupled with the sooty kohl darkening her lids, brightened her eyes to the color of cornflowers.

"Is it?" I asked politely.

She nodded and the diamonds at her ears swung like chandeliers. "The flowers," she added, pointing with her fan towards the enormous vases of wide white blossoms. "Madame Aurore puts them out to remind us of why we are all here," she said with a little titter. "Because they smell of male effluvia."

I gave a sniff, recognizing a scent that had accompanied some of my most tender and pleasant recollections. Male ejaculation, once smelt, is never forgot. "Now that you have drawn my attention to it, the odor is *most* distinctive."

She gave me a long look from tiara to slipper tips. "I do not recall seeing you here before. Are you quite new?"

There was something appraising in that glance, but not unkind. "I am," I told her truthfully. "I am here with a companion. And yourself?"

I glanced around the room, where several dozen other guests were gathered, many of them women of various states of attractiveness. I had not expected to see so many ladies and I told my companion so. She laughed, and for the first time I noticed her Adam's apple, bobbing up and down above her diamond collar.

The kindly blue eyes met mine and she put out a long, very slender hand encased in pristine white kid and took mine in a gentle clasp. "You may call me Victoria."

"Veronica," I replied, seeing no need for pretense. "Are all the rest of the ladies like yourself?"

She smiled and I saw a tiny bit of lip rouge on one of her teeth, barely visible below the concealment of her mask. "Most. But a masquerade is the chance to become what one isn't," she said. "Besides, why should you ladies have all the joy of wearing something pretty?"

"Why indeed? Pardon me for the observation, but you have a little smeared lip rouge on your tooth."

She sucked her teeth vigorously before baring them at me. "Better?"

"No," I said. She reached into her bosom—padded, I realized—for a handkerchief, thrusting it into my hands.

"Be a dear and help me," she instructed with a touch of imperiousness.

I reached forwards with the handkerchief and wiped away the smudge of lip rouge from her tooth. "There, now. Much better." I showed her the stained handkerchief and she smiled.

"You are an angel," she said. I made to return the handkerchief but she waved me away, blowing a kiss as she went. I thrust the handkerchief into my pocket.

Having bade farewell to the charming if unorthodox Victoria, I made my way upstairs via another grand staircase. My costume excited only a little attention. A flash of thigh and a low scoop of décolletage were as nothing to this crowd, I reflected. My crown of fox teeth was possibly the most interesting thing about me. I fended off a not unreasonable number of invitations, most issued quite politely, and slipped up the stairs. As Madame Aurore had indicated, a black velvet rope marked the boundary between the public spaces and her own private apartments.

Unfortunately, she had not mentioned the guard. It was the same elderly fellow who had met us at the door earlier, but now I had the chance to look him over properly. He was so greyed and bewhiskered, I might have thought him a wizard out of a fairy story. An enormous nose protruded from the nest of hair upon his face, and above his half mask met two eyebrows of such enormity, they reminded me of a variety of particularly furry moth. He was sitting upon a chair, one stockinged foot in his hand as he massaged. His eyes were bright, sharply alert, and I fancied he rather enjoyed his employment.

He puffed out his shoulders and spoke in a rasping voice. "You'll not go a step further, madam, and that's the truth," he told me.

I fluttered my lashes. "Oh, have I wandered into someplace . . . forbidden?"

He leered a little at my neckline, his chubby cheeks puffing in and out furiously. "There's precious little forbidden in this house, and that's no lie," he informed me. "But you'll get nowhere with your feminine tricks. I'm immune."

"Feminine tricks?" I widened my eyes in apparent shock. "I wouldn't dream of such a thing. Besides, what tricks could I work upon such an experienced fellow as yourself?"

He made a bizarre little noise, halfway between a cough and a giggle. Then he doubled over, hacking deeply and unpleasantly. "You're a right minx, you are," he said, waggling his brows at me. He jerked his shoulder towards the closed doors behind him. "What you want with the mistress's rooms, then?"

"Oh, are these Madame Aurore's rooms?" I asked, innocent as a vestal virgin. "I was simply looking for a place to attend to lady's needs." I primmed my mouth and said nothing more, counting on the usual man's antipathy to anything related to a woman's personal requirements.

But he merely waggled his brows again. "Got your monthlies, then? That's inconvenient in this house. Although 'tis better than the alternative and that's God's own truth," he pronounced.

I gaped at him. For all my travels, for all my experience, it was the first time in the whole of my existence that a man had inquired about my monthly courses. "As it happens," I said tartly, "I am not, at the moment, experiencing my menses, but thank you very much for your kind inquiry. I merely wanted a place to powder my nose and tighten my garters."

He puffed his cheeks in and out, apparently thinking. Suddenly, he thrust his large foot in its grubby stocking towards me. "Rub me corns and I'll let you pass."

I looked at the noisome stocking. There was a hole in the seam and one malignant toenail was making an appearance. He wriggled the toes at me, and I reeled backwards from the odor.

"I think I shall decline your offer," I told him politely. "Perhaps a corn plaster from the chemist would help. And a nice soak in some salts with a little rub of castor oil."

He thrust out his lower lip. "What has the world come to, I ask myself, when a comely lass won't get her hands proper dirty for the sake of her elders?"

I tipped my head. He was being willfully outrageous. He might be my elder, but I was, by every possible measure of society's standards, his better, and I wondered if he might be intoxicated. I leant closer, in spite of the smell. There was, beneath the lowering odor of his feet, the slightest whiff of something sharp. Licorice, I decided.

His mouth worked a moment as he removed something he had tucked between cheek and gum. He spat into his palm, lifting it to offer me a half-sucked licorice drop.

"Want a suck, missus?"

"You must know better than to behave that way towards one of Madame Aurore's guests," I told him sternly. "Are you an ancient retainer of hers from her former life? Did you know her in Paris?"

His whiskered mouth worked furiously. "Maybe I did and maybe I didn't. Who are you to ask me such questions? Meddlesome jade," he muttered.

"You are a frightfully rude old man," I told him.

"And if you really needed the amenities, you would be back down those stairs, looking for the water closet," he informed me smugly, crossing one leg over the other and flapping that disgusting foot at me.

He was right enough there. I could not keep up the pretense of being a lost guest any longer, and further questions would only ensure that I was remembered, not an eventuality I desired when Madame Aurore discovered her diamond star was missing.

I bared my teeth in a smile. "Very well. I will withdraw. It was quite a diverting experience to make your acquaintance." I inclined my head and he flapped the foot again, imperious as a lord as he stared down his ridiculous nose at me.

I had just made up my mind to leave when a melodious voice sounded behind me.

"Robert, are you being tiresome to one of my guests?" I turned to see Madame Aurore smiling at us. She pronounced his name in the French fashion, and amusement twitched the corner of her mouth.

He muttered something, but she waved him off. "Send to the kitchens for a little refreshment. I would like to speak with my guest alone."

He hurried off with his peculiar crablike gait as Madame Aurore turned to me. "You must forgive him. He is a new acquisition and not entirely au courant with the ways of politeness."

"I am rather surprised you employ him in that case," I told her with a candor she mightn't have appreciated.

But to her credit, she smiled. "He was recommended by another member of my staff. Besides, I believe in giving everyone a first chance, mademoiselle. Won't you come and sit with me awhile? I should so like to speak with you, if your *compagnon de la nuit* can spare you?" she asked with a coaxing tilt of the head.

As Stoker was nowhere in evidence, I could not use him for an excuse. I inclined my head, smiling beneath my mask, and she opened the door to her sanctum. I followed her in, not surprised to find more of the elegant grey-and-pink color scheme used elsewhere in the house. She clicked her fingers and a giant hound rose from an enormous cushion and trotted over, rubbing its head against her hip.

"Good evening, my love," she crooned to the dog. She turned to me. "Sit," she urged. "Make yourself comfortable."

I did as she bade, wondering how to work the subject of her diamond stars into conversation. As I wrestled with the question, she seized the conversational reins, speaking in her low and musical voice about a variety of things—the décor, the excellence of the champagne that she poured. She opened a barrel of biscuits and fed a few to the dog, breaking them into bits and dropping the crumbs to the carpet, where the hound retrieved them happily.

"This is Vespertine."

"Named for the sweetest hour of the evening," I observed. "A lovely parallel to your own chosen name."

She gave me a long look. "He is my stalwart companion, are you not, my darling?" she said, scratching him behind the ears. He rolled his eyes ecstatically. "He has a Latinate name, but he is a very British dog," she told me.

"A Scottish deerhound?" I asked.

"Just so. He was given to me by an admirer who noticed a dog that looks just like this in one of my paintings of the dawn goddess. Every goddess should have a proper companion, he said." She scratched Vespertine again and he sighed. He was almost as enormous as Lord Rosemorran's Betony, but his form was much leaner, his legs long and elegant, as was his nose. Wide, expressive eyes stared at me from under a thicket of long, shaggy hair at his brow.

After a very few minutes, a scratch on the door heralded a page with a plate of confectionery from the kitchens. There were assorted pastries, each more delicate and elaborate than the next. Some were filled with cream, others robed in a sheen of chocolate.

"This is my favorite," Madame Aurore told me, gesturing towards a tiny puff wearing a candied violet at a rakish angle. I took one and bit into it, savoring the crisp pastry, the cream flavored with vanilla and honey.

"I order so many things with vanilla to be served that my chef imports more than any other household in London," she confided. "But it is an aphrodisiac."

"Is it indeed?" I darted out my tongue to catch the last crumb of pastry.

"Madame de Pompadour, the great mistress of Louis XV, used to dose herself with it in an effort to rouse her ardor."

"Was he so exacting?" I inquired. I surveyed the little plate and helped myself to a small bun decorated with a swirl of chocolate marbled to look like Florentine paper. Vespertine, sniffing deeply, rose from his mistress's side and came to sit beside me.

She gave a Gallic shrug. "No more than most men, I suspect. But La Pompadour suffered from the malady of coldness. Her passions could not be awakened sufficiently to satisfy her king. So she resorted to aphrodisiacs."

"Were they successful?" Vespertine dropped his head to my lap, the weight of his head crushing against my thigh.

She smiled, revealing tiny, pearly teeth. "Not entirely. But she was clever. She made herself a friend to her king, and whatever needs she could not satisfy personally, she satisfied by proxy."

I was intrigued in spite of myself. "How?" I dropped a hand to Vespertine's head, stroking his fur. It was coarser than I imagined, springy under my fingers. He gave another sigh and settled more comfortably.

"By establishing a house like this one. She kept it stocked with exactly the sort of maiden the king liked best, plump and rosy and eager for the pleasures of the flesh."

"She was a procuress."

"She was a businesswoman," she corrected swiftly.

"Like you." In spite of my determination to remain objective, I was beginning to like Madame Aurore. She harbored no illusions about who she was or what she did, and she would never apologize for either.

Again she shrugged. "I have been compared to many a worse woman, believe me. But I think you do not mean it as an insult?" She paused to smile at me before going on. "I am indeed a businesswoman, as you say. I see a need and I provide the remedy."

"And what is the need?" I asked, biting into the chocolate bun. It was less sweet than the vanilla confection, edged with something dark and almost bitter. Vespertine looked up at me with adoring eyes and Madame Aurore passed me one of his biscuits. He took it from me as gently as a lamb, lapping up the treat with his broad tongue.

Madame went on. "Pleasure, escape, satiety. Some people come here to remember, some to forget. My task is to provide the fantasy, to give them a place to play the game."

"The game?" I asked. I took up another bun, this one shaped like a horn filled with cream, and with madame's encouragement, I offered it to Vespertine. He ate the entire thing in one bite, licking his lips when he finished.

"The game," Aurore repeated. "Have you not considered what this place is? It is a nursery for grown-ups! This is what everyone wants—a return to the nursery."

"Do they?" I put in. Vespertine gave me another beseeching look but I shook my head at him. He settled at my feet and lay his head on his great paws.

"You look skeptical," she told me, her eyes crinkling at the edges as she smiled. "But consider life, my dear. It is dangerous and demanding, particularly in a city such as this. Every year more people crush into the capital. There are more trams and carts and carriages. The underground railway rumbles beneath us. Smoke belches out over the town, turning everything sooty and black. And in the streets, such noise! Such chaos! We must be warriors simply to cross the street." She painted a vivid picture, but she was not wrong. I had grown to love London, but there was much to be said for the occasional escape into the countryside. Green meadows and blue skies were infinitely preferable at times to the choking grey fogs and teeming pavements.

She went on. "Even in the privacy of one's home, there is always some responsibility, some new trouble. The maid has given notice or the drains are bad or the neighbors are unquiet. Where may a person refresh themselves? Give themselves up to the sheer joy of being cared for?"

"That is what you think this place is about?" I inquired. "Caring for the clients?"

"Guests," she corrected gently. "But of course it is! Here they are treated with all the love and tenderness of a favorite nursemaid. When they are hungry, they are fed, exquisite foods that are beautifully cooked. When they are tired, they repose themselves in the softest beds. There is music for the ear and the finest wines for the palate. Everything is done to gratify the senses."

"And when a guest wants more than a nice nap and a blancmange?" I asked.

"They are given what they desire. It is like being a child again and visiting your grandmama's house, where you are indulged in every whim. Only here, the whims are not so childish," she said with a meaningful gleam in her eye. It was the first real glimpse she had given me of a sense of humor, a lightness I found relatable.

"I had not considered it in that light," I told her. "But it makes a sort of sense."

She smiled. "I wish only to bring joy, mademoiselle. To help bring light and glamour and pleasure to people's lives. Such as you and your paramour."

I stuffed the last of the chocolate bun into my mouth and said nothing. At my feet, Vespertine had begun to snore, a gentle, rhythmic sound that was oddly soothing.

She gave me a reproachful look. "You think I have overstepped myself, but why should women have secrets among friends?"

"And we are friends?" I asked. "You do not even know my name." I paused deliberately, wondering if she would betray knowing my identity.

But if she did, she was more careful than her page. She merely smiled again. "I know your heart, mademoiselle. That is sufficient."

I sipped at my champagne before making a reply. "What do you know of my heart?"

"I know that you wish to give yourself fully to your companion but you are afraid."

There was challenge in her voice, but I could not deny what she said.

"Perhaps," I said slowly.

She made a dismissive gesture. "Let us be frank! You and this man are all but lovers. You move towards each other and back again, never quite succumbing to your passions."

"How can you tell?"

"Seduction has been my life's work, mademoiselle. I know how a man looks at a woman when he has had her. And I know how a man looks when he is suffering for want of her."

For reasons I would never understand, I blurted out the truth just then to this woman I hardly knew. "I wonder if we have missed our opportunity."

She nodded, her eyes warm with sympathy. "I know what you

mean. It is not good to wait. When you know what you want, you must move towards the culmination, but carefully," she warned. "These things must be done with delicacy, with grace. But there cannot be delay. A man will lose his nerve, and if his nerve is gone . . ." Her voice trailed off and she turned down the corners of her mouth.

"Yes, well. One would hate to see him lose his . . . nerve . . . as it were," I agreed.

She leant forward, her expression serious. "The time is ripe, my dear. You must not permit further delays to wreak the havoc upon your *amoureux*."

"What are you suggesting?"

"I suggest that you choose one of my private rooms, now, quickly. Before you succumb to doubts. A lovely woman has no need to perform, to seduce. She has only to offer herself," she counseled.

"And if he puts me off?"

"Then you must play the bull! You must seize him and be the dominant one."

I considered this. My attraction to Stoker was a complicated thing, not least because of the complexity of the man himself. His muscular masculinity concealed a gentle heart that throbbed to a poet's rhythm. He was sentimental, tender even, where I was pragmatic and logical. In spite of his prodigious scientist's brain, he was the most delightfully romantic soul I had ever known. Music could rouse him to passion or pity, and a few lines of Keats were as necessary as bread to him.

In contrast, my own emotions had so often to be buttoned and corseted and strapped into place, I hardly knew how to let them off the leading rein at times, preferring the tidy taxonomies of my work and robustly unsentimental couplings to unfettered feelings. It was not surprising that I was won over by a soul so different to my own in its expression and depth of affection.

But it was not his soul that kept me awake at nights, not his tenderness that drove me to chilly cold-water baths and vigorous exercise. No matter what I tried, there was a clamor in the blood that would not be quieted. Too often I had glimpsed that gorgeously developed physique, sculpted by the hand of Nature to perfectly suit my taste, I had no doubt. Every inch of him was firmly muscled and sleek, his thighs and shoulders beautifully molded, his flanks . . .

I dragged my thoughts away from Stoker's flanks with a great deal of effort and even more regret. There was no help for it. I desired him in every sense of the word, and it was his masculinity, so pronounced and defined, so opposite my own form, that enchanted me. And the power of that masculinity was no small part of its attraction. Stoker offered the delicious paradox of a man who could easily force submission but would never attempt it. With him, I could surrender every bit of the control I had fought so hard to achieve. I could unbuckle the clasps, unbind the ties; I could simply be. And that notion was the most seductive of all. So Madame Aurore's idea that the best way to resolve the situation was to play the aggressor was unsettling. I had my doubts it would work with Stoker—he could be maddeningly stubborn when he chose. And if it did work, did I even want him on those terms?

"You have given me much to think on," I told her. "Thank you."

She shrugged. "Of course."

I dragged my thoughts back to the reason for our visit to the club. My gaze fell to the diamonds scattered over her gown. "Your stars are very beautiful," I told her in a casual tone. "I have been admiring them."

She dimpled at me. "Gifts. From my generous admirers."

"They are all so similar, I wonder how you can tell them apart," I ventured, hoping she would invite me to look more closely at them.

But she merely smiled her inscrutable cat's smile. "Believe me, mademoiselle, I know them, each and every one. Of course," she went on,

"I cannot wear them all at one time. There are too many of them. I wear only a few tonight, and all of these are from an American gentleman I knew long ago." I remembered what Tiberius had told us about her American millionaire and felt a rush of satisfaction. The prince's Garrard star was not on display.

Madame Aurore gestured vaguely towards a closed door on the opposite wall. "My dressing room. The rest are all tucked away in a safe. One cannot be too careful with so many strangers about," she said sagely. Her expression was touched with sadness. "One cannot be too careful in any case as a woman in London these days."

"The murders in Whitechapel," I murmured.

"Horrifying. One thinks of those poor wretches . . ." Her voice trailed off.

"And one thinks how easily it mightn't be them," I finished. Her eyes locked with mine and I knew we understood one another. *How easily it might be us.*

"I am told you endured the siege of Paris," I said softly. "That must have held its own terrors."

She gave me a measured look. "I suspect you are acquainted with terror yourself, my dear."

I thought of the perils I had endured, the near tragedies I had survived, and for all my brushes with disaster, I could not number amongst them a fate as awful as what had befallen the women in Whitechapel.

"I have been lucky," I said simply.

"Yes," she said in a slow voice, "I think luck has a great deal to do with our fates. Our destiny lies in our stars." She traced one of her diamond stars with a fingertip. "But enough of this grim talk for the evening! You have come to enjoy yourself. We will not think of the sad ones just now."

She rose then, shaking the folds of her chiffon gown and passing a hand over her unbound hair. "I hope you have refreshed yourself, mademoiselle?"

She nodded towards the plate of tiny pastries. We had scarcely made an impression upon them, but I was conscious of the heavy sweetness left on my tongue. I rose, nudging Vespertine gently out of the way. He yawned, his jaws opening wide, and I gave him a pat of farewell.

"He likes you," she told me. "He does not take to everyone."

"I suspect not everyone gives him cream buns," I replied. "I have entirely enjoyed myself, madame. Thank you for your time."

She inclined her head and shook my hand before walking me to the door. "I am sorry to bring an end to our little tête-à-tête, but I have an appointment with a gentleman in half an hour's time and I must prepare to receive him," she told me with a meaningful look.

"Of course," I murmured. I was conscious then of a hope that had taken root during our conversation—a hope that Madame Aurore would not prove too great a villainess. That she had deliberately set out to seduce the prince, I had little doubt. One only had to glimpse her astoundingly expensive surroundings to know that guineas must run through her fingers like water. In an empire full of wealthy and illustrious prospects, a future king was the highest place to aim and she had been successful. I was not entirely happy at the idea of retrieving the star, by foul means or fair. It had been a gift, freely given and happily accepted, and I was conscious of a mulish determination rising within me to leave it with her. But I could not justify such a course of action unless I knew for certain she could be trusted not to use it against my half-brother.

Deep in such thoughts, I took my leave, noticing that the chair outside was once more occupied by the odiferous Robert.

"Learnt anything useful?" he asked with a waggle of his brows.

"What a nasty old devil you are," I told him, conscious once more of the strong odor of licorice, which clung to him with something else, a chemical note I could not place.

"I ain't nothing of the kind," he said, obviously affronted. His feet were plunged into a basin of hot soapy water and he flapped a hand at me. "Go on, then. Unless you want to watch an old man soak his feet, and if that's the sort of thing that lifts your skirts, I'll ask a shilling because nothing in this house is free."

I pulled a face at him and fled down the stairs, cape in hand.

# CHAPTER

## 10

I made my way down the staircase to the floor below. I wandered through the rooms in search of Stoker, eager to relate to him my minor triumph in discovering the general whereabouts of the star. I turned a corner and found myself in a long corridor, thickly carpeted in deep, plush grey, the walls hung with figured silk. It was quieter there, the music from the ballroom not even audible at this distance. A series of doors opened onto the corridor, all of them firmly closed and some sporting the silver ribbons Madame Aurore had spoken of—the sign that the couples within would welcome additions to their party.

I paused, thinking hard. Knowing Stoker as I did, I had little doubt he would have found himself either the kitchens or a library, and neither of those were likely on this floor. Before I could decide which way to proceed, a door a little distance down the corridor opened and a gentleman emerged. His dark auburn hair put me in mind of a fox's pelt. He paused when he saw me and gave me a long look as he came near.

"My goodness," he said in the drawling accents of an American from one of the southern states, "it appears Madame Aurore has been hiding the most alluring of her guests."

He reached a hand to touch something that no gentleman ought to touch without invitation. In a flash, he was flat against the wallpaper, his arm wrenched up hard behind his back, and gasping for breath as I gripped him hard in a place no polite memoir would name.

"Veronica, what in the name of seven hells are you doing?" Stoker inquired courteously from behind me.

"This gentleman caused me offense," I told him.

The man in question stirred, making noises of faint protest.

"What was that?" I asked. He made another sound, mewling almost as tears gathered in the corners of his eyes. I turned to Stoker. "He touched me. Without my consent."

"Most unmannerly," Stoker agreed.

"But it is an honest misunderstanding," the fellow whimpered into the wallpaper. "Most ladies in such an establishment are open to such direct overtures."

I blinked at him. "Are they indeed? How uncivilized." I raised up on tiptoes, tightening my grip slightly. "You really oughtn't go around grabbing unsuspecting women, you know. Even if they are open to erotic liberties. It isn't polite."

He nodded, the tears falling freely now, and I released him. He staggered, then dropped to his knees, giving a deep groan.

Stoker bent to look him in the face. "He seems all right. I suppose a few minutes on his knees won't do him much harm."

The man drew in a few deep, shuddering breaths before mopping his face with a handkerchief and staggering to his feet. His face had gone an alarming shade of puce.

I peered at him, then poked Stoker. "Are you quite certain he is all right? He looks as if he were about to have a fit."

The fellow waved his handkerchief. "Perfectly all right," he managed in a breathless voice. "I must offer my apologies, madam. Sir, is this lady in your keeping?"

Stoker leveled a narrow look at him. "As far as you are concerned she is. Although as you have just seen, she is more than capable of looking after herself."

The man winced, locking his knees together as his eyes rolled a little. "Indeed. I wonder if she might oblige me with a second round of castigation." He gave me a hopeful look.

"I beg your pardon?" I said.

"I have upon occasion found ladies here willing to engage in the disciplinary arts, but not one of them has proven as skilled as yourself," he told me. "You have a rare gift."

I flicked a glance to Stoker, who was barely managing to smother his laughter. I smiled politely. "That is very kind of you, I am sure. But I do not customarily engage in such practices, Mr. . . . ?

He retrieved his card case and extracted a calling card. "Francis Clay Hilliard, of the Charleston Hilliards. At your service, ma'am."

I took the proffered card and started to speak. "How do you do? I am Boadicea, Queen of the Britons."

We exchanged handshakes as civilly as if we had been introduced at a tea party, and Mr. Hilliard dusted off the knees of his trousers with his handkerchief.

"Am I to understand that you are here for the purposes of gratification, Mr. Hilliard? Physical gratification?" I asked.

"I am indeed, ma'am. A gentleman of esoteric tastes has, by definition, a limited number of opportunities for such indulgence, as I am sure you can appreciate."

"Certainly. And Madame Aurore's guests have been unable to assuage your desires?"

He held up his hands, light sparking off the signet ring on his little finger. Now that I had a proper peep at him, I could see he was thirty-ish, extremely prosperous-looking, and not unattractive.

"Now, ma'am, I would never like to imply such a thing. Madame Aurore has done her level best to supply my needs. I have been whipped, flogged, restrained, and ridden by half a dozen different beauties, and every one of them left bruises," he said in obvious appreciation. "But not one of them has your natural talents for bringing a man so quickly to the very edge of endurance. I did believe I was going to fall unconscious," he finished with an admiring nod.

Stoker had apparently had enough of Mr. Hilliard's praise. "Yes, her talents are legion," he agreed, taking me firmly by the elbow. "But unfortunately she is already spoken for. I am afraid we are otherwise engaged."

Without waiting for a reaction, Stoker propelled me firmly down the corridor and through a closed door, which he shut decisively behind us.

"That was not entirely necessary," I told him. "I did have the matter well in hand—Good gad, what *is* this place?" I demanded. We were in a private room, rather like a costly suite in an exuberantly overpriced hotel, but with a most unique décor.

"It is meant to be a garden in hell," Stoker informed me, pointing to a card pinned to the door: *Jardin d'Enfer.* I turned slowly, taking in the surroundings, mouth agape.

Every surface was upholstered in some shade of scarlet. Crimson hangings covered the walls; bloodred cushions softened the chairs. A wide bed had been made up with black satin sheets and a ruby satin coverlet. A thickly piled garnet carpet stretched from wall to wall, cocooning the room in color and softness. Even the marble fireplace was the color of good claret.

"It is extraordinary," I told him truthfully. I was suddenly quite aware of him standing just behind me, not touching me, but near enough to raise the hair on the back of my neck. I pulled off my mask and stepped into the room, towards fate, I decided.

"It will suit our purpose well enough," he told me. I marveled at the change in him. He was suddenly quite matter-of-fact about what we were about to do. I licked my lips as he removed his own mask and consulted his pocket watch.

"It is very nearly time," he said with some satisfaction. "He should be arriving at any moment."

"He?" I blinked. "I rather thought we would do this alone the first time."

He stared at me in mystification. "Veronica, what are you on about? I mean Madame Aurore's caller."

"What caller?"

He rolled his eyes. "There was a rather delectable little caramel tart in the supper room," he began.

"This is about *food*?"

"I was hungry," he put in pettishly. "I've had nothing but sandwiches since breakfast, if you will remember. I require sustenance. As it was, there was only one wee tart left, and a plateful of crumbs. I went belowstairs to see if there might be more on offer, and I overheard Madame Aurore direct a page to show a visitor up to her rooms as soon as he arrives."

"I had a tête-à-tête with her myself. She ushered me out on the same grounds. But if she means to entertain him in her private rooms, what are we doing here? We are on an entirely different floor."

Stoker preened a little. "By process of pacing out the interior architecture, I discovered that this suite, in particular the bathroom, is directly below her dressing room. I hoped we might overhear something through the ventilators," he added, pointing to the ornate rectangular grille set into the wall.

"Oh," I murmured, feeling a little deflated. I paused, then ventured to raise the doubts I had experienced after I had spoken with her. "Stoker, I am not entirely certain we ought to steal the star at all—" I began. But he had already darted into the bathroom, muttering about the likeliest listening post. "Later," I muttered.

It was just as well, I reflected. My usual decisiveness had deserted me, and I did not relish the notion of explaining my disordered thoughts to Stoker before I could make sense of them myself. Everything in my life seemed to have turned topsy-turvy in the past few days, and I had the strangest sensation of rowing after a sailboat that disappeared over the horizon. No matter how hard I pulled at the oars, I would never catch it, I thought in some dismay.

But this would never do! I gave myself a sharp mental shake and explored the suite. Between the door to the corridor and that to the bathroom stood a tall piece of chinoiserie lacquered in black. I opened it to find an assortment of accoutrements: whips, floggers, blindfolds, and restraints as neatly and tidily arranged as if they were no more exotic than a toast rack or stack of blotting paper.

I peered into the cabinet and extracted a dainty little whip of black suede, striking it smartly against my palm. It was exquisitely fashioned, leaving a stinging sensation but no mark.

A drawer in the cabinet held a collection of bottles, each carefully labeled in an elegant hand, unguents and aphrodisiacs, all crafted to heighten the sensations. The bottom drawer held various props—fans, feathers, and a gown large enough to accommodate Stoker should he be so inclined.

Like the rest of the house, the air here smelt of roses and vetiver and something darker, more sensual, simmering just beneath the surface. I gave a little sigh of pure delight, wondering if Stoker and I might arrange to have the room to ourselves for just a little while. The bed, I noted, was large and extremely sturdy.

"It's rather a nice house," I called to him.

"It bloody well is not," Stoker contradicted. "It might have escaped your notice, but it is Paddington Station for perverts out there."

"Perversion is in the eye of the beholder," I returned mildly. "These are adults free to choose their pastimes. Your judgments are both archaic and unkind."

Stoker gave an audible snort. "There are men roaming these rooms who pay extortionate amounts of money to have people do extraordinary things to them for purposes of sexual gratification and you are behaving as if it were nothing more than a Sunday picnic by the Serpentine."

"Prostitution is, not for nothing, the oldest profession, and you are behaving like a provincial. What difference does it make if a person is willing to pay for a service if another, quite obliging, person is agreeable to perform it? It is no different than buying the expertise of a chef or a tailor," I finished.

"Intimacy should not be transactional," Stoker said flatly.

"Provincial," I repeated in a mutter. I opened another drawer to find a series of heavy enameled eggs whose purpose I could only surmise.

"What was that?" Stoker called.

"Nothing," I called, slamming the drawer closed.

"Honestly, Veronica, what sort of woman are you? You can divest romance from the most intimate of connections and think nothing of it?"

"You are a romantic," I called back. "Of the incurable variety."

"You needn't make it sound as if it were a dread disease," Stoker retorted, coming to the door to give me a disapproving look. "It is a bloody nice thing that someone around here still believes in things like love and sentiment and—" He broke off, blushing furiously. "I do not know why in the name of Satan's seraphim I bother."

He turned on his heel and went back into the bathroom, leaving me to poke about the room, exploring its more esoteric delights. I was about to point out to him that half an hour's interruption to our investigative activities would not be entirely a dereliction of our duty, but before I could there was a noise from the corridor, a smothered giggle and the sound of a hand groping for the doorknob. I dove into the bathroom, closing the door swiftly behind me just as the door from the corridor opened.

Stoker, standing upright and fully clothed in the dry bathtub, his ear cocked to the ventilator in the wall, gave me a curious glance.

"I say—" he began, but he got no further. I hurled myself at him, clapping my hand firmly over his mouth. I jerked my head towards the bedroom and he gave a nod, taking my meaning at once.

Through the closed door we could hear the clink of champagne glasses and the rumble of voices, a man and a woman, I thought. There were merry laughs and a few groans and then the distinctive creak of bedsprings. I put my eye to the keyhole and saw our new acquaintance, Mr. Hilliard. He was undressed to his long underwear, flannel and striped. His moustaches were quivering with anticipation as a lady garbed as Helen of Troy strapped his hands together and picked up a small cat-o'-nine-tails. He gave a happy little sigh and turned himself over, derriere upwards, his face in the pillows.

I turned away before the first blow fell but I heard the singing of the little whip as it arced through the air and the sharp smack of the leather against the flannel-draped flesh. There was a happy sigh and his companion gave a brisk instruction. "Now, if ever it gets too much, you've only to say, love."

I pantomimed to Stoker the identity of the fellow being soundly disciplined in the next room and he rolled his eyes again. He gestured fiercely, suggesting we leave, but I shook my head. If he meant to eavesdrop on Madame Aurore's meeting, we would have to keep ourselves hid away in our porcelain prison. I removed my hand from his mouth, giving him a wary look.

He cocked his head, then put his lips to my ear, causing the pulse in my throat to quicken. "We might venture a whisper. They seem mightily distracted."

More blows and moans, louder now, along with Mr. Hilliard's cries of encouragement to his tormentor. I looked around the bathroom, admiring the porcelain fittings, the bright brass fixtures, beautifully modern and highly polished. Stoker made a brisk gesture with his fingers and I realized he was hearing something through the ventilator. I gathered up my cloak and joined him in the bath, pressing my cheek to the metal grille. The voices were muffled—and it was not easy to hear anything with the frankly exuberant noises coming from the adjoining bedroom—but I could just make them out. One of them—Madame Aurore, I surmised—spoke a few indistinct words. A male voice countered, speaking quickly and with some vigor.

"Whoever he is, he's angry," I murmured. I shifted a little, attempting to get more comfortable. The sides of the bath were angled, throwing us awkwardly together, with my back pressed to Stoker's front so that we could both listen through the ventilator.

Stoker nodded, his chin brushing my temple. From the other room, Mr. Hilliard had achieved some sort of resolution to his excitement, culminating in a series of high yelps, like the bark of a fox. I worried for a moment that he and his companion might avail themselves of the room where we were concealed, but after only a moment, distinctive noises resumed and I realized they were bent on another bout of congress.

Stoker and I returned our attention to the ventilator. The discussion upstairs continued for some minutes, the woman's voice even and calm as the man's voice continued to rage. I heard the pop of a cork and the sharp, bright clink of crystal.

"A toast," Stoker whispered, his mouth touching the edge of my ear.

I shifted uncomfortably, flexing my ankles to try to get the feeling back into my feet.

"Do stop that," he ordered in a harsh whisper, his hands suddenly firm on my hips as he gripped them, forcing me to stand still.

"I cannot help it," I protested. "I am half numb from the cold porcelain."

He made no reply but turned to listen again, shaking his head after a long moment.

"I think they have finished," he began.

It was my turn to fling up a hand. "They are still speaking," I hissed.

Their voices were pitched low and fast, as if they were pressed for time. Madame Aurore must have moved nearer to the ventilator at some point, for I heard her say, "He has sent word. We are to meet here in an hour so that I can hand over the star. Trust me." Then nothing for a long moment.

Afterwards, the unmistakable exchange of partings, the man's voice calmer now and even a little laugh from the woman. And then an odd little noise, half gasp, half moan, ending on an eldritch sigh. There was a long moment of quiet, then a few bumps and thumps. Finally, the slam of a door and silence.

"She is handing over the star to a fellow conspirator!" I murmured into Stoker's ear with suppressed rage. "She does mean to use it against Eddy! No doubt she has made arrangements with a newspaperman or some other unsavory type to sell it along with her story."

We exchanged meaningful looks. If Madame Aurore had a meeting in her dressing room in an hour, it would be necessary for us to enter, retrieve the jewel, and leave undetected before she returned. Stoker tapped his pocket watch to indicate how much time we had remaining and I rolled my eyes towards the bedroom, where our friends still disported themselves. It might have been possible to creep out of the bathroom and into the corridor without being apprehended, but the chance was slim, and a successful escape would depend largely on not being remembered after the jewel went missing.

We shrugged and silently agreed to make the best of it, settling in to wait until Mr. Hilliard and his companion concluded their activities. A few audibly exuberant minutes later, we were sitting in the bathtub, fully clothed, entirely dry, and very much put out with one another.

"This is the most absurd situation," I whispered.

Stoker held up a hand and whispered back to me. "If you wouldn't mind saving your disapprobation for another time, we have work."

"It is past midnight," I reminded him. Just then, our companions in the adjoining room reached a sort of crescendo, the various moans and shrieks and trills rising to a pitch that I greatly feared would offend the ears of any respectable dog in the vicinity. Poor Vespertine, I thought. Then a sort of exhausted silence fell. For several minutes more there was only that silence, and my toes began to prickle again with pins and needles.

"Do you think they have fallen asleep?" I ventured.

Stoker put a finger to his mouth and eased himself from the bathtub. He crept to the door and knelt, laying his eye to the keyhole.

He rose, smiling. "They have gone."

"Thank merciful heaven for that," I muttered. I was exultant, perhaps a trifle too much so. I went to jump from the bathtub, but my still-leaden legs would not quite support me. My knees buckled and I careered into Stoker, knocking him to the ground. I landed on top of him, legs akimbo, his hips settled neatly under mine.

"Well, this is not entirely how I expected this would begin," I said, his mouth a breath away from mine.

I paused and the world stood still. His bright sapphirine gaze held mine for a long moment and I felt the slow, steady drumbeat of his heart against my chest. His hands were tight on my arms, and I parted my lips, expectant.

"Oh well," he said brightly, thrusting me off of him and springing to his feet. "No harm done."

He bolted for the door and I followed, slowly, reflecting with some irritation that there was more than one mystery afoot at the Club de l'Étoile.

# CHAPTER

## 11

We made our way hastily downstairs to the more public rooms. It made sense to discover Madame Aurore's whereabouts before attempting to gain access to her private quarters, and we needed to compare notes without the possibility of another amorous interruption. Logic dictated to me that the later we made the attempt, the better. If we could effect our escape just as the guests were settling down to their most focused debaucheries, it would be almost impossible for anyone to follow us. In the meantime, we could conduct ourselves as any other guests at the club might—in a dance or a visit to the supper room.

As we made our way, I pondered Stoker's new zest for our detective like activities. He was often a willing participant in our investigations, but never as enthusiastic as *this*. To throw himself so fully into my little schemes was a new development, and one that I could not divorce from his obvious—and entirely new—shyness.

Stoker had never been bashful before. When he was not working in dishabille, he was disrobing entirely to take advantage of swimming in the pond or taking a dip in the heated plunge pool, and he was seldom careful about who saw him, least of all me. In fact, it had become apparent during our Cornish interlude that he sometimes deliberately undressed in front of me because he knew the sight of his naked, masculine, utterly delectable form . . .

My mind was wandering. I forced my attention back to the question of why, now that we had decided to take our relationship to a more intimate footing, he should play the wallflower.

"Oh, you silly cow!" I muttered. "He is bashful *because* he knows it means something now." The poor darling, I reflected with a smile. Madame Aurore had hit the proverbial nail squarely upon the head with her shrewd assessment that delay could bring only discomfort, but the sentiment applied not only to me. The attraction between us had been so strong for so long and this next step had been so long in the offing, it was little wonder he was finding himself suddenly reluctant. No doubt he was concerned about his ability to live up to my decidedly ambitious expectations. Of course, few men could, but that did not worry me in the slightest. I was, after all, a true daughter of Britannia, I reminded myself. I was the embodiment of the British spirit of putting one's shoulder to the grindstone and getting on with it. I would simply have to make this clear to Stoker. The sooner we bedded, the better. The last thing he needed was more time to fret himself about it.

Unaware of the direction of my thoughts, he guided me through the ballroom, gliding us through a series of turns until we emerged into the next room, the supper room, looking like any other couple in search of refreshment. The caramel tarts had been replenished and Stoker helped himself with a gusty sigh of pleasure. He heaped a plate with them and poured a rich pool of crème anglaise around them before finding us a curtained alcove, discreet but unremarkable, in which to sit and make our plans.

Hurriedly, I informed him of exactly where I believed the diamond star to be, explaining what I had learnt from Madame Aurore during our intimate conversation.

"Of course," I went on in a low voice, "we cannot be certain of how many we shall have to search before we discover the correct star. She might have dozens of the blasted things tucked away."

He shrugged. "The case will be scarlet leather."

"How in the name of seven hells do you know that?" I demanded.

He forked up a bit of tart with maddening calm. "My father always bought my mother something from Garrard after they quarreled. The boxes are scarlet."

I tipped my head. "Tiberius' safe is full of scarlet boxes."

"They quarreled rather a lot."

He continued to eat, placidly, intent upon the gustatory pleasure of the tarts. I watched his tongue dart out to claim a crumb from his lip and suppressed a moan.

"Veronica, are you quite all right?" he asked, peering at me in some concern.

"Entirely," I told him, making a mental note to visit Lord Rosemorran's cold plunge pool as soon as possible. "There is a point of difficulty in gaining access to Madame Aurore's private quarters. There is a footman outside her rooms—an elderly fellow who sits guard. We will have to make our way past him and any other servants who might be about."

Stoker considered this a moment. "There will be a servants' staircase. Let us attempt that and if necessary I suppose we could always garrote the old fellow and stuff him in a cupboard."

"He stinks of dirty feet and licorice. We would be doing Madame Aurore a favor," I replied.

I led the way, slowly so as not to betray we were anything other than ordinary guests. The entertainments had taken on a more forthright air, with men and women in various states of undress roaming the halls in search of partners. Lacy petticoats foamed at dimpled knees while the luscious curves of bared shoulders and half-revealed breasts rose over embroidered corset covers. The men were attired in various garments designed to show them to better advantage—Eastern robes, banyans, dressing gowns. I caught more than one glance of a bare, manly calf or a strong, supple pectoral muscle.

"If you would be so good as to focus on the situation at hand," Stoker said once, his consonants sharply clipped.

"I am an admirer of the male form," I replied with lofty disdain.

A narrow passageway led through a series of small bowers, little rooms fitted with couchettes where couples—and sometimes more—were draped, limbs intertwined as sighs filled the air. The lights were low and each bower was imperfectly concealed behind gauze draperies, giving the whole arrangement the feel of a unique theatrical entertainment. We charged past the lovers, making for the end of the corridor where a perfectly normal door led into the domestic offices of the house. We emerged, in fact, into the pages' hall, a large space with cubbyholes and benches and walls pegged for the hanging of livery. One fellow, with dark skin and a relaxed air, sat reading a newspaper and smoking a tiny cigarette that smelt of very good French manufacture.

He rose immediately. His jacket was draped over the arm of his chair, but his shirtsleeves were immaculate and his breeches and waistcoat beautifully tailored. He inclined his head, his voice accented with the lilt of Haitian vowels.

"I beg your pardon, sir, madam. This part of the house is not usually made available to guests, but if you wish, I suppose arrangements could be made," he began.

"No need," I told him. "We could use your help, though."

He did not bat an eyelash, and it occurred to me only later that he no doubt believed we were in search of the fellow for some immoderate purpose.

"We wish to know if there is a discreet way to the second floor," I told him.

He stroked his chin. "I suppose you mean the private staircase." He gestured towards a cupboard whose door stood open, revealing a narrow staircase snugged inside. "The servants' stairs."

I made towards them, but the page inserted himself neatly between my person and the open door. "I am afraid the servants' stairs are not permitted for guests." His tone was apologetic but his manner was decisive. We should not be gaining entrance through him. The page's pleasant expression never faltered. "Of course it is true that my duties require me to appear at all times at my best. This entails the most attentive brushing of my coat, and if I were engaged upon such a task, I should certainly do so with my back to the door. In which case I would be unable to see if anyone were to slip up the stairs."

I flicked a glance to Stoker, who sighed and extracted a notecase from his sash. He retrieved a banknote and held it up between two fingers.

The page clucked his tongue. "I regret, sir, that I do not feel able to turn my back just yet."

Stoker extracted a further two banknotes and put them carefully in the pocket of the page's coat.

"Naturally, I would only turn my back once," the page warned us. "If anyone were to return back this way, I should certainly feel obligated to remember such a thing."

Stoker gave him a sour smile and tucked two more notes into the pocket.

The page picked up his clothes brush. "Goodness, what smuts are on this fabric. I daresay I shall be busy brushing my coat for some full five minutes and completely oblivious to anything else that may happen in the house," he said. He applied himself to the tidying of his coat while Stoker grabbed my hand and hauled me towards the stairs.

"You oughtn't have given him so much," I hissed. "We could have come back another way and you can hardly spare such a sum."

"Do not worry," he instructed, grinning in the dim light of the stairs. "It was Tiberius' notecase."

We hurried up the stairs, mindful of the page's warning that his bribe had purchased us only five minutes' time. We climbed for ages, creeping swiftly on silent feet to the third floor. There was a narrow landing before the stairs wound further up—towards the servants' quarters, no doubt. We paused, waiting for any noise to betray a presence in the room beyond.

Silence surrounded us, pressing softly against us on all sides. I eased the door open and found only blackness. It took a moment to realize we were concealed behind one of the long grey velvet drapes. I edged the fabric aside with two fingers to find the room was empty.

I darted in, beckoning to Stoker. No sooner had we both entered than a movement from the sofa stopped us in our tracks. An enormous dark head rose from the other side and a low growl sounded.

"Hello, Vespertine," I crooned. "Stoker, give me something to eat. Hurry."

Without waiting for an explanation, Stoker stuffed something into my hand. I crept forwards, extending my palm to Vespertine. In it lay a crushed caramel tart.

"You really are the most impossible man," I muttered as the dog bent his head to lap up the treat in one motion.

"Yes, well, I seem to have saved you from being devoured by that hell beast," he retorted.

"Nonsense. Vespertine and I understand one another, don't we, darling?" I asked, scratching the hound gently behind the ears.

He rolled over on his back, waving his long legs into the air. "Not now," I told him firmly. He rolled back, his expression distinctly hurt as he returned to his position on the sofa.

"He looks distraught," I told Stoker.

"He is a dog," Stoker replied.

"You of all people should respect that animals have emotions," I began.

He held up a quelling hand. "This is not the time for a rousing discussion on the questionable practice of anthropomorphizing domesticated animals, Veronica," he reminded me. "Now, point me towards her dressing room so I can get on with playing the burglar."

I had no sooner lifted my arm than the knob of the outer door turned. We had just enough time to throw ourselves to the floor behind the sofa before the door opened. I landed on top of Stoker, and Vespertine, enormously confused, landed on top of me. If he had not been in search of more tarts, we might have remained hidden, but having sniffed out the location of Stoker's pocket, the hound applied himself to the vigorous investigation of its contents.

Stoker gave a muffled howl of pain and I heard a voice call out softly from the doorway. "I say, is anyone there?"

It was the note of fear that decided me. Whoever our visitor was, it was most definitely not Madame Aurore. It was someone more afraid of us than we were of them.

I pushed Vespertine off with some effort and rose. Just inside the closed door stood a familiar and hesitant figure.

"Victoria!" I cried.

I hastened to pull Stoker to his feet, dusting at the lavish display of crumbs that Vespertine had left on his shirt.

My friend from the supper room gave me a nervous smile. "Hello. I suppose you are wondering why I have come here."

I gave a gracious inclination of the head, grateful that it had not occurred to Victoria to question our presence. "Not at all. I suppose anyone might get lost in this house. It is so vast." I might have said more, but as I advanced towards Victoria, I saw her in the full glare of the gaslight. I had noted the Adam's apple before, but now, absent the mask, I could clearly see the bright blue of the protuberant eyes, the full curve of the generous mouth. And the moustaches that her mask had imperfectly concealed. I stood in mute shock as Stoker moved forwards, pausing to give a smart and correct bow of the head.

"Your Royal Highness," he said, "permit me to present Miss Veronica Speedwell. Veronica, this is His Royal Highness, Prince Albert Victor of Wales."

The pause after Stoker's words seemed to go on forever, and when I spoke it was with considerable effort. "Victoria," I corrected softly. "She introduced herself earlier to me as Victoria. It is impolite to penetrate a person's incognito."

Victoria peered at Stoker closely. "I know you."

"That depends, sir," Stoker replied evenly, "upon whether I am speaking with a lady named Victoria or Prince Albert Victor. I have indeed met the latter."

I stared at Stoker in some astonishment. He had failed to mention that interesting titbit, and I made a mental note to interrogate him thoroughly on the matter at a more propitious time.

The prince hesitated, then plucked off the crown and veil. "It appears I am discovered. I am indeed Albert Victor."

Immediately, the shoulders went square and the chin lifted, imperious as a future emperor.

"All part of the masquerade," he said, gesturing towards the ball gown. "I thought if I came as a woman, I mightn't be discovered, but you have unmasked me. Fair play to you, sir," he said, putting out his hand to Stoker.

I stared stupidly at the prince, at my half-brother. He was not looking at me. His attention was fixed upon Stoker. I could not speak. Standing scant feet from my own half-brother had dealt my composure a blow. Stoker evidenced no such distress. He shook the prince's hand and carried on as pleasantly as if we were having a conversation over a buffet supper.

"Now, where exactly did we meet—I have it! I went with my tutor to inspect the ship after the Battle of Alexandria, oh, what was her name, dash it?"

"The *Luna*, sir," Stoker replied quietly.

"Yes, of course! You were the surgeon's mate with the habit of taxidermy. I remember, you were working on stuffing a rather glamorous-looking macaw, and I quite took a fancy to it."

"You have an excellent memory, sir," Stoker said.

The prince smiled. "Well, one does rather remember a macaw. One of Lord Templeton-Vane's boys, are you not?"

"My father died last year," Stoker told him. "My eldest brother now holds the title."

"Ah, condolences and all," the prince said, obviously losing interest. He shifted his gaze to me. "Miss . . . Speedwell, was it?"

"Yes, Your Royal Highness," I acknowledged.

"But we have already met! Downstairs," he said with a puckish grin. "You were most helpful."

Stoker gave me a quizzical glance. "There was an incident with some lip rouge," I explained.

The clock on the mantel chimed the hour and the prince gave a start. "I do hope you will excuse me, but I am expected for a private meeting with Madame Aurore and the hour is upon us," he said, making a polite gesture of dismissal.

"We would leave you to it, sir," I replied boldly, "but we are here at the behest of the Princess of Wales."

The round eyes grew enormous and his mouth went slack in dismay. "Motherdear? What on earth do you mean?"

"She asked us to retrieve a gift you seem to have made to Madame Aurore," Stoker said.

He huffed a great sigh into his moustaches. "I cannot believe she did such a thing! Darling Motherdear. She must have been so upset," he murmured. "But how on earth did she—"

Conscious of the passing of time, I hurried on. "I rather think the details can be discussed at a later time, sir. The point is that Her Royal Highness was most insistent that we retrieve the jewel on your behalf."

"But that is why *I* am here," he protested. "I have dashed all the way down from Scotland on a decidedly uncomfortable train—have you any idea what third-class accommodations are like on a train from Scotland? I had a note from Aurore promising to return it." He gave a little laugh. "It appears Motherdear and I have been working at cross purposes."

I recalled the snippet of conversation Stoker and I had overheard through the ventilator, and we exchanged a quick glance. "It is possible, sir, that it was a ruse on her part to lure you here, for some as yet unknown purpose."

"It is *not* possible," he said with considerable hauteur. "I know well the quality of my friends, Miss Speedwell, and Madame Aurore is numbered among them. She would never betray my trust. She is a devout woman."

"Sir," Stoker began, but the prince held up an imperious hand.

"I will show you. Come," he ordered, leading the way towards the dressing room.

I said nothing, but a keen rebellious edge had sharpened itself on the whetstone of my resentment. He really was the most impossibly naïve creature, I decided. He had confided a scandalous secret on little more than the strength of my kindness in wiping away a little lip rouge. He had no real reason to trust us other than the fact that he knew of Stoker's family. Perched as he was on the top of the pyramid of privilege, he simply could not imagine that another soul from that world would harbor republican tendencies. Moreover, he had no notion that I was more closely connected to him than Stoker would ever be.

He passed me and I felt the brush of his lush pink skirts against mine, the whisper of a fragrance. Did he feel no strange kinship with me? No pull of blood to blood?

"Veronica," Stoker called softly from the doorway to Madame Aurore's sanctum. "Are you coming?"

"Of course," I said, hurrying to join them. The door was unlocked and Stoker pushed it wide. For an instant, we stood, grouped like a tableau, and no one spoke.

"It is not what I expected," I said quietly. It was as far from the luxurious elegance of the rest of the house as possible. Here no silk hung on the walls; no velvet upholstered the furniture. In fact, there was no furniture at all save a narrow bed made with a plain white linen coverlet. The only decoration was a simple painting of the Virgin Mary worked in heavy Renaissance oils. The room was curiously shaped, an imperfect octagon, and another door opened off of it.

"Its simplicity surprised me the first time she invited me here," the prince said. He nodded towards the closed doors. "That is her private exit," he explained. "It leads to the mews, so she can come and go with complete discretion. It is how I sometimes depart."

Stoker glanced at the small, nondescript room. "It's as tidy as a monk's cell," he observed.

"She was brought up in an orphanage outside Dieppe," the prince told him. "At least I think she was. She can be a trifle vague about her past."

We advanced towards the picture of the Virgin Mary. Beneath it were a candle, marked with the hours, and a small vase of flowers. None of the hothouse beauties from the public rooms; these were delphiniums and pinks, the blooms of a humble cottage garden. I was conscious then of a foul smell and wondered how long it had been since the water in the flowers had been changed. Apparently Madame

Aurore had greater trouble with her domestic staff than an insolent porter, I reflected.

"I am no churchman, but it seems a desecration to touch it," Stoker told me with a nod towards the makeshift altar.

I paused, considering. "It is supposed to. Most people are religious to some degree or another. They would hesitate to disturb something sacred."

"You, I presume, have no such qualms?" he challenged.

I pulled a face. "Neither do you. And if we are wrong, we can make God an apology."

I thrust the vase of flowers into the prince's startled hands, and Stoker removed the picture from its nail. Behind, set neatly into the wall, was a small safe.

"I say, what the devil do you think you are doing?" the prince demanded.

"Saving you from having a hand in your own destruction," I said, rounding on him in frustration. "If you are wrong about Madame Aurore, she can wreck your happy future with Alix of Hesse with her own two hands."

He seemed to settle at the mention of his beloved. "How do you know about Alix?"

"Your Motherdear told us," I snapped. "Now, do you happen to be in possession of the combination?" I inquired.

He blinked those wide, watery blue eyes at me. "You are the most impertinent young woman I have ever met. No, I certainly do not have the combination."

I turned to Stoker. "Can you manage it?"

He grinned and bent to the task at hand. "Father always kept us short of pocket money. By the time I was eleven I learnt how to break into his safe."

"A dubious talent," the prince remarked doubtfully.

"Wait and see," he replied. He leant towards the safe and began to spin the knob, listening intently. After a few minutes' effort, he made a series of swift motions and the safe responded with soft clicks. He pulled the narrow lever and the door slid open.

His Royal Highness gaped at Stoker. "You did it. You actually did it."

"My father's safe was twice as good as this bit of gimcrackery. I'll wager Madame Aurore has a proper bank vault and this is just to keep the servants from a bit of petty larceny," Stoker replied. "I could have opened it with a dessert spoon."

"You are the seventh wonder of the world," I told him, gripping his arm ecstatically.

He reeled backwards under the onslaught of praise. "Well, I don't know about that—"

"I do," I told him firmly. "Now, let us retrieve what we have come for and be on our way." I reached into the safe and extracted a series of leather boxes. The first two were blue but the third was scarlet kid. I opened it and was instantly dazzled by the brilliant glitter of diamonds. I almost could not bear to touch it, so luminous was its beauty. I turned it over and the engraving was exactly right: the initials AVCE and the mark of Garrard.

"This is the one," I breathed, cradling the blazing jewel in my palm. The diamonds sparkled even in the dim light. "It is the correct one, is it not, sir?" I asked the prince.

He regarded the jewel sullenly. "It is."

"Extraordinary," Stoker murmured as the diamonds sent a play of light across his face.

"And very nearly priceless," I reminded him. Stoker wrapped the star carefully in one of his handkerchiefs and tucked it into his pocket, the jewel making a rather obscene bulge in his trousers.

The prince raised himself to his full height. "I do believe that is my property, Templeton-Vane," he said, putting out a hand.

Stoker regarded him levelly. "We were asked by Her Royal Highness to retrieve the jewel and it is to the princess that it will be given."

"I really must insist upon having it," the prince said. A touch of frost edged his manner now, a tautness that betrayed his irritation at being thwarted.

"You shall not," I told him.

"Of all the cheeky nonsense," the prince protested. "Who the devil do you think you are to defy your future king?"

"Who the devil am I?" Four simple words would have revealed all. They trembled on my lips, but no sooner had I managed, "I am your—" than Vespertine appeared in the doorway, whimpering as he edged towards the bed. He bared his teeth, a growl rising from low in his throat. The dog had begun to tremble, badly, his warm brown gaze fixed upon the prince.

"Vespertine," the prince said, "whatever is the matter? We're old friends." Suddenly, Vespertine crept forwards, head low to the ground, the rasping growl turning from a threat to a sound of mourning.

"What the devil is wrong with him?" the prince demanded, looking up at us. "Is he ill?"

But I had followed the dog's attention, and I realized he was not looking at the prince at all; he was fixed upon the space beneath the bed. He stopped just short of the narrow cot, throwing himself to the floor and tipping up his great shaggy head to deliver a sound of such ululating sorrow that it pierced me to the marrow.

I knelt beside him, gathering my courage to peer beneath the bed because I knew only too well what I would find. Shoved beneath the mattress, barely visible behind the prince's billowing pink taffeta skirts, was the body of Madame Aurore.

# CHAPTER
## 12

The prince gave a low groan and covered his face with his hands. "Is there any chance—" I began, but Stoker, who had bent to see for himself, shook his head. "Cyanosis is setting in. She is quite dead. Her throat has been slashed." He did not mention the acrid odor of loosened bowels and bladder that attended death and which I had ascribed to stagnant water. That was an indignity too far for his sensibilities to remark upon.

The prince groaned again and I took his wrists in my hands, none too gently, a gross act of lèse-majesté that I did not pause to consider. "Your Royal Highness, this is not the time. We must get you quite away from here," I told him.

He lowered his hands, blinking furiously at me. "What?"

"You must not be found here," Stoker put in. "We have the star. For the love of Christ, let us *go*."

The prince nodded slowly. "We cannot simply leave her," he said, and I liked him better in that instant than I had yet. "She was my friend and we must see her properly attended to."

"And we will come back to make certain that happens," I assured him. "But Stoker is quite right, you must not be found here, particularly not in your present state," I added with a glance at his gown.

"Of course," he murmured. He gripped my hands suddenly. "You will come back? You will not let her remain there like, like . . ." His voice broke and I put my hand over his.

"I give you my word."

He nodded then. "Very well. We should take the back stairs, to the mews," he added, pointing towards the door opposite the one we had used. He held tightly to his veil, clasping it to his chest as a child will cling to a beloved blanket. Stoker tugged a little at the white linen coverlet, pulling it out just enough that it would touch the floor, shielding the sight of Madame Aurore's dead body from view. Vespertine settled near the corpse of his mistress, his long nose resting on his forepaws, his eyes deeply sad.

"We will return soon," I told the hound, patting him once.

"Come, quickly," Stoker ordered. He paused with his hand on the doorknob, and in that moment, pandemonium broke loose. The door opened, slamming hard into his face. He reeled back, blood pouring from his nose as he let loose a stream of profanity so filthy he could only have learnt it from an exclusive boys' school.

A hand, enormous and grasping, was reaching around the door, but Stoker flung himself forward, using his body weight to pin the arm into place as a howl of anguish filled the air. The arm was withdrawn just long enough for Stoker to slam the door closed, throwing the bolt.

"The other way," he ordered, shoving us towards the sitting room. We crossed it at a dead run. I led our little band, dragging the prince as Stoker brought up the rear. I eased open the door to Madame Aurore's rooms, expecting to see the aged porter sitting guard, but the corridor was deserted. I beckoned to the others and motioned for them to resume their masks, as I did mine. We hurried silently down the stairs. Just as my slippered foot touched the last step, I heard a cry.

"There!" A man dressed in one of the page's costumes pointed and two more dressed exactly the same looked our way. They made directly for us, and I realized we were now in flight, from whom I had not the faintest notion. But it was imperative that we remove the prince from the vicinity as quickly as possible. I slipped my dagger from my girdle, prepared to fight our way out, if necessary, but just then the house was plunged into darkness.

"They've dimmed the lights early!" a giggling voice proclaimed, and there was a responding moan of pleasure.

I would have said it was a happy coincidence that the lights should have been extinguished just as we required an escape, but I do not believe in coincidence. Still, I am not one to quibble when a rescue is in order, and Stoker and I were determined to see the prince got safely away. I linked one of the prince's arms with mine; Stoker took the other. In the pitch black of the hall, I relied upon Stoker to guide us. He had a cat's sense for darkness, and navigated us swiftly along. Our progress was inelegant. We bumped into furniture, got ourselves tangled in draperies and tassels more than once, and tripped over a hassock that seemed to be providing support to three people engaged in languorous lovemaking. I fell into one receptive pair of arms, shoving myself free at the cost of the Templeton-Vane tiara, which toppled off as I fled. I cursed, wondering how on earth I would explain its loss to Tiberius, but we had more urgent business to attend.

We descended the stairs, twisting and turning through various rooms and corridors. I became quite disoriented until I caught a sudden whiff of chestnut and stopped, causing the prince to slam into me, protesting.

"I do say—" he began.

I prodded him to silence just as I heard a delighted voice from a few feet away. "Yes, twist it just like that, only *hard.*"

"Stoker, not that direction," I muttered, shoving him away from the direction of Mr. Hilliard and his latest inamorata.

"Through the gardens," he whispered back, tugging us forwards. We moved then in a peculiar little crocodile, Stoker in the lead, me in the rear, and the prince tucked snugly between. We crossed the ballroom, dark as it was and echoing with the occasional groan of some well-timed caress. The door to the gardens was unlocked, and we passed through quickly. The gardens themselves were chilly, illuminated only by starlight and the thinnest waning crescent of a moon surrounded by a scattering of stars, Madame Aurore's emblems blazing out like the tiniest of diamonds on a bolt of black velvet. A faint breeze stirred the trees, making menace of their withering branches. In the summer, this would be a fair place for disporting oneself in a handy bower. Now, with autumn creeping onwards, it was full of shadows and a faint air of peril.

Stoker led on, never slackening his pace, until we reached a wall.

"What now?" I demanded.

"We climb," he said shortly. Without waiting for a consensus, he levered himself onto the wall, fitting the toes of his boots and his fingertips into the little crevices between the crumbling bricks. In a matter of seconds he was sitting astride the top of the wall, reaching down.

"Sir?" he urged.

The prince turned back to me. "I am hardly dressed for this," he started to protest.

"Think of it as an adventure," I instructed. "Now, take his hands and I will boost you from behind. Or we can leave you here and you may look to save yourself."

He gave a start—either at the notion of being discovered or the brazenness of being spoken to in such a fashion—and did as I ordered.

Stoker grasped him around his long wrists and hauled him upwards. The prince scarcely had time to put his feet to the wall before Stoker had him up and over, rosy skirts billowing as he descended. I had already launched myself upwards, swinging nimbly to the top and over, dropping to the pavement below.

"That was splendidly done," the prince told me as he landed next to me. Stoker had dropped him none too gently, but he took it like a proper man of spirit. "What now?"

Stoker landed next to him, his boots striking with a thud. "Did you come with a carriage?"

"My good man, I hardly think so," the prince told him with a touch of reproof. "I hired a hackney and sent it away when I arrived."

"Hell and damnation," Stoker muttered. "We shall have to find another. Come on, then."

We hurried around the outside of the wall, skirting it until we came to the corner, where Stoker lifted his middle finger and thumb to his mouth, giving the sort of sharp, distinctive whistle known to drivers around the city. As we waited, Stoker stripped off his vast black cloak.

"You cannot go abroad in that," he advised the prince. His Royal Highness quickly removed the pink gown, thrusting it into my arms. He wore trousers underneath but no shirt. Its absence was quickly concealed by Stoker's enveloping cloak. Somewhere in our flight, the prince had dropped his tiny paste crown, and now he flung away the earrings that matched it. He tugged off his blond wig and pitched it into the bushes, using the veil to wipe away the worst of the face paint.

"Not respectable enough by half, but it will have to do," I said. "At least now you are not likely to be arrested by any passing bobby."

A hackney clattered up to the curb with a driver perched atop, muffled to the cheeks against the rising chill.

"Thank God," I muttered.

No sooner had the words left my mouth than I heard footsteps approaching, quickly, pounding hard on the pavement. They came at us from two sides. I half turned to look, and as I did so, my arm was clasped tightly. I felt a prick in the soft flesh inside my elbow. I cried out—more in rage than in pain—just as I saw another figure bring a hand to Stoker's upraised arm, plunging a hypodermic into his shoulder. The prince gave a cry, but he crumpled at once as one of our assailants drove a needle into his arm. I saw the driver of the hackney leap down to open the door and shove the prince inside as my knees felt suddenly boneless, unable to hold me up, folding like paper.

My eyes rolled heavenwards and darkness gathered at the edges of my vision, clouding closer until all I saw was a tiny pinprick of light and at the center several dark shapes.

"At last," a voice said. And that was the last I heard for many hours.

I woke not with a start but with a gradual lightening of the darkness pressing against me. There was a sense of coming back into my own body, as if my consciousness had flown elsewhere whilst my body remained tethered to the earth, but try as I might, I could retrieve no memory, form no impressions of where I had been or what had been done to me.

After several minutes, I was able to determine that I was sitting upright. There was an odd floating quality to my awareness, as though my head were only nominally attached to my body and might drift away if I let it. I could not yet open my eyes, so I merely sat, composing myself and stretching out my consciousness like the quivering antennae of an Atlas moth to learn about my surroundings.

I felt a dampness in the air, the cold chill just before dawn, I thought. And I smelt something riparian, not the fresh river water of the countryside but the heavy, muddy musk of the Thames. I shifted slightly, scraping my slipper on the floor. It was stone, and cold through the satin of my shoe. The tiny noise echoed for a moment—a large room, then, situated not far from the waterside. A warehouse? There was no sense of anything near to my head, so I guessed the ceiling was high, the floor obviously uncovered, the damp stone giving off a particular scent of its own.

My arms and legs were bound, and a blindfold had been secured imperfectly over my eyes. The fabric was soft, a handkerchief perhaps. There was a mildly sore spot on my arm where the needle had penetrated, but otherwise my only complaint was the woolly feeling in my head. I assessed my circumstances with some relief. My clothing felt intact, and there was no telltale soreness about my person to indicate that I had been abused or violated in any fashion save the means of sedation administered by the needle.

The chair upon which I sat was wooden and sturdy, and I realized after a moment that it was situated with its back to another chair. I pulled forwards slightly and felt the ropes about my chest catch. A deep groan answered, and I was seized by a rush of joy so heady I very nearly collapsed.

"Stoker," I said, testing out my voice.

For an agonizing moment, there was no reply. At last, an answering growl.

"What in the name of the oozing wounds of Christ is happening?"

"It appears," I said slowly, "we have been abducted. Are you injured?"

"My head feels as though I were on the third day of shore leave," he said bluntly. "You?"

"I am perfectly fine except for a curious lightheadedness."

"The sedative," he told me. "The effects should wear off soon. Faster if we had a stimulant."

"You mean like coffee or brandy?"

"Or a nice solution of cocaine," he said, reminding me that he had once before roused me from a stupor using just such a method.

I turned my head and scraped my face along the shoulder of my gauzy dress. The gesture was enough to catch the handkerchief, dragging it free. I shook my head and the handkerchief dropped to the ground. I blinked against the sudden glaring light, but a moment's respite showed that the light was feeble, a single oil lamp situated in the corner, far away from where we were. A narrow bed stood next to it, and atop it, the slender form of the prince, his mouth open and emitting gentle snores. The fact that we had played a role in the abduction of the future king was a good deal more than I could readily comprehend at present, so I made a note of his presence and his regular, even breathing and decided to worry about him later.

Stoker and I were sitting on wooden chairs, back to back, each of us bound individually and then roped together to keep us upright. If I turned my head as far as possible, I could just make out the edge of Stoker's body, clothed in his trousers and shirt, his boots gone along with his weapons, I had no doubt. I wriggled a little before letting out one of Stoker's oaths under my breath.

"Weapons?" Stoker asked.

"They've taken them," I replied. "Yours?"

He paused a moment, shifting in his chair. "I had only the picklocks in my sash," he reminded me. "Gone, as best I can tell."

"And the jewel?" I asked. But I already knew the answer.

"Also gone." He gave a little sigh that might have been resignation.

"Well, it will require all of our ingenuity to escape from this," I said firmly.

"You needn't sound so uplifted by the notion," Stoker told me.

"Why not? Have we ever yet been in a situation we could not master? It requires only a little careful consideration and a bit of imagination," I informed him.

"Veronica. We have been abducted. Our weapons are gone. My boots and all of our outer garments have been taken. This bloody room is freezing and we will no doubt die of exposure in a very few hours if they do not return to finish us off before that."

"Warehouse," I corrected.

"I beg your pardon?"

"Loose your blindfold and see for yourself."

The next few minutes passed uncomfortably as Stoker wrestled with his limitations to remove his blindfold. But at last he did, and he raised his head, no doubt blinking against the dim light as I had done.

"It is indeed a warehouse," he said.

"Thameside?" I suggested.

"From the odor, not far," he said. He lifted his chin and sniffed deeply. He had the olfactory sense of a bloodhound, and I trusted his observations in that regard far more than my own. "But it smells more like Whitechapel. Tobacco. Cotton," he added. When I met him, Stoker had been living on the premises of his taxidermy studio, a vast and decrepit warehouse on the banks of the Thames that was in the late stages of decay. It had been destroyed in a fire, taking the remnants of his life's work with it. There were dozens of such buildings between the riverside and the crowded dens of Whitechapel.

"The prince is here as well," I told him.

Stoker stiffened. "Bloody hell. Where? How is he?"

"There is a bed on the other side of the room. He is sleeping peacefully, no doubt still under the effects of whatever they used to render us unconscious. I suspect he will be coming round soon enough," I finished, more to persuade myself than him. I could not begin to contemplate the fate that would befall us for this misadventure involving the heir to the throne.

Just then the door opened and a tall, deceptively pleasant-looking fellow entered, bearing a large basin of what appeared to be porridge.

He did not seem troubled that I had pushed aside my blindfold, and I blinked up at him. He was enormous, well over six and a half feet in height, with the docile demeanor of a man content never to ask questions or have a complicated thought.

He carried a pewter mug, and when he lifted it to my lips, I smelt sour beer. I had no thirst for it, but I knew the importance of nutrition and hydration and I forced myself to drink. He spooned a few bites of porridge into my mouth, messily, and I studied him as he moved, noting the slow, resolute motions, the placid expression on his face. This was no mastermind. This was the dogsbody, tasked with menial duties and nothing more. Questioning him would be a waste of breath, but it would be helpful, perhaps, to establish some sort of rapport or at least gain some information.

I gave him a soft look from beneath my lashes. "Thank you, you're very kind," I murmured.

He grunted and spooned in another bite of porridge. I swallowed it hastily. "What is your name? I should like to know to whom I should be grateful for such courteous treatment."

Behind me, Stoker shook once convulsively in what might have been a suppressed oath or a laugh. It was impossible to tell.

Our captor took a long moment to think of a suitable reply, but at length he managed to utter a few words. "Quiet Dan."

His voice had an unmistakable Irish lilt, and a creeping certainty stole over me as Quiet Dan moved to offer Stoker a bit of sustenance. When he had finished, he looked to the prince. Eddy was still sleeping peacefully, emitting tiny snores. He shuffled out again, taking his nasty porridge bowl with him.

"That porridge was beyond burnt," Stoker grumbled. "He might at least have put a bit of honey in it."

"I think our problems might be of a more generous magnitude

than the state of the refreshments," I replied. "You realize our captor is only a henchman?"

"I do. That is the sort of fellow who couldn't plot his way into his own shoes in the morning," Stoker said.

"And you detected he is Irish?"

"The accent is unmistakable. Between Dublin and Limerick, I should think."

"How on earth have you deduced that?" I demanded.

"When Merryweather was born, his wet nurse was from the County Offaly. She used to tell me stories while she fed the little brat," he said, but there was a fondness, albeit reluctant, when he referred to his youngest brother. "I was quite mesmerized by the size of her bosoms," he went on.

"Yes, well, if you can possibly tear yourself from a sail down the river of nostalgia, you might realize that an Irish captor raises one most unwelcome possibility as to the author of this little misadventure," I said.

He sighed again. "Uncle de Clare."

"Uncle de Clare."

The last time we had seen Edmund de Clare, he had thrown himself out the window of Stoker's riverside workroom, his flesh aflame as he plunged into the filthy waters of the Thames. His corpse had not been recovered, but I had been assured that there was nothing terribly unusual in that. The vagaries of the river meant that there was no way of knowing for certain where a body would emerge, if at all. It was so easy to think of Edmund being swept out to sea and the whole wretched ordeal being finished. Too easy, it seemed.

"I thought he was dead," Stoker said. "When a fellow has the flamboyance to catch on fire and plunge out of a window into a filthy river, he ought to have the courtesy to be dead."

"You would think," I replied in a tone of authentic bitterness. "But I always had my doubts. It would be just like him to survive such an escapade only to resurrect himself in order to vex me."

"Be easy," Stoker counseled cheerfully. "It may be an entirely different villain. After all," he added with a jerk of his head towards Eddy, "he has a fair few enemies. This mayn't have anything to do with you. Or me."

Before I could reply, the door opened again and a man stood silhouetted in the doorway. I had not met him in two years, but I knew him at once.

"Hello, Uncle," I said pleasantly. "The last time I saw you, you were on fire. I see you have been extinguished."

He came forward, into the light, leaning heavily on a walking stick of Malacca. He had been a handsome man—once. He made his way slowly into the room. One leg seemed twisted and he moved it with great effort; one arm was tied up in a silken sling, the hand covered with a glove. The fire had wrought its damage, but those scars were honest, the twisting of flesh by flame. I had met dozens such men upon my travels—former soldiers, fishermen, explorers. Accidents were common in the realm of natural history. Stoker himself bore the relics of a voyage gone disastrously awry. But this was different. This was a man whose very spirit was damaged, and that was nothing to do with the physical ravages of his ordeal.

"Your mother used to brazen out her troubles as well," he said, a glint in his eye. "Or at least she did before she killed herself."

"Well, that was uncivil," I told him, striving to keep the tremble from my voice. "But I suppose I have only myself to blame. Should I have greeted you with open arms? A thank-you for the delicious supper? Or a kiss on the cheek and a compliment on your skills as a kidnapper? You seem to have got so much better at abduction since our last meeting."

"God, you've a tongue like an adder," de Clare said. He signaled to Quiet Dan, who came forwards with a small chair. De Clare settled himself carefully, like a man well accustomed to the grip of pain.

"The years," I said slowly and with some pleasure, "have not been kind."

"No," he agreed more pleasantly than I would have expected. "They have not."

He paused a long moment, studying me. "You are so very like her. It is not enjoyable to converse with a ghost, Niece."

"I am not my mother," I said, my hands curling into fists beneath my bonds. "I am my own person."

"That you are," he said, settling back expansively in his chair. "You have the look of her but none of her gentleness. She was bendable as a willow, our Lily. Beautiful as a faery and twice as wild, but she was weak."

"I think you will find that the willow is considered one of the strongest trees in nature," Stoker offered. "The genus *Salicaceae*—"

"Enough," de Clare said, beckoning Quiet Dan forwards once more. "Another word from you and I shall let him beat your head against the floor until it is soft as a boiled apple."

Stoker bristled but said nothing more.

De Clare turned his attention back to me. "When the Prince of Wales abandoned her, Lily allowed her emotions to get the better of her. She gave way to her despair instead of rising above it. She took her life because she was too weak to live."

"Perhaps," I said, struggling to keep my voice calm, "she was too mired in that despair to see another way."

He gave me a narrow look. "Aye, there was another way. She could have made her claim public, forced the prince to do his duty by her."

I gave a short laugh. "Do you really think that would have been permitted? She would have been silenced and well you know it. The advisers and lawyers and ministers would have seen to it that her story never became public. She would have been pensioned off and sent abroad with me."

*Sent by someone like Lady Wellie,* came the disloyal thought. And not for the first time, I wondered what Lady Wellie would have done if confronted with the truth of my existence when I was still young enough to be made to go away.

De Clare leant towards me a little. "Or she would have rocked the monarchy, brought it to its knees. Given us a new queen," he said with a mocking little bow of the head.

"So, it is the same plot as last time?" I asked. "You mean to use my quasi-legitimate status as the daughter of the Prince of Wales to call the succession into question and light a scandal that will burn down the English monarchy?"

"More or less," he acknowledged.

"I thought you might have given up, considering you almost died the last time," I pointed out.

"Almost is not dead," he returned. "I survived that ordeal because it was meant."

I rolled my eyes heavenwards. "You cannot be serious. You survived through sheer bloody luck and the fact that the window offered a straight drop down into the river to quench the flames. Nothing more."

"You see only coincidence and I see the hand of God," he murmured.

"If you really believe that God preserved you in order to see this scheme to fruition, you are even more delusional than I first thought," I said in considerable exasperation. "It is impossible to argue with a mind that does not admit scientific fact and relies instead upon dogma delivered by the hand of an invisible author."

"It is a scientific fact that I survived," he replied, his mouth twisting into a rictus of a smile. "Just as you have. I made a study of your travels, Niece. I know what you have survived. Shipwrecks, volcanoes, landslides. If you cannot see the will of God unfolding there, I pity you."

"So, it is the will of God when you get what you want, but you refuse to accept when it crosses your purpose?" I challenged. "How do you know my mother's suicide was not the intention of God? The succession of the heirs of the current queen? The subjugation of Ireland? To attribute anything to the whims of a capricious deity is the refuge of a limited mind, Uncle."

He regarded me a long moment. "You will see it for yourself in time."

I glanced to the bed where the prince still slept. "Were you responsible for Madame Aurore's murder?"

"In fact," he said slowly, "I was not."

In spite of myself, I believed him. My immediate concern was escaping de Clare's clutches with both of my companions. A rush of guilt had engulfed me when I spied Eddy's slender form stretched out upon the narrow bed. My uncle had abducted him in the course of snatching me. The responsibility of that nearly knocked me to my knees, but before I could nurture the hope that de Clare had taken him without knowing his identity, it was dashed.

"I see the prince is sleeping like a babe, although he is not half so innocent, given his choice of pursuits," my uncle mused.

"What do you mean?" I demanded. "Why is he here?"

"You will see that in due course as well," he promised.

"I have no interest in a crown," I said evenly. "I thought I made that clear when last we spoke, Uncle."

"You might have no interest for yourself, and that is a good thing. A woman should not have ambition for herself."

"I am so glad to have met with your approval." I bared my teeth in a semblance of a smile.

He went on as if I had not spoken. "But you must have some consideration for your kin, for your faith, for your country."

"By kin, you mean the de Clares, whom I have never met save yourself. By faith, you mean Roman Catholicism, a religion I have never practiced. And by country, you mean Ireland, an island where I have never set foot."

He blinked at that. "Never set foot? All your gadabout ways, galloping about the world, and you have never seen Ireland, your motherland?"

I shrugged. "The butterfly population is poor."

He swore under his breath. "You have no proper feeling for your heritage," he thundered.

"My heritage is my choice," I replied. "And I choose England."

He thrust himself uneasily to his feet with the aid of his walking stick. "You will revisit that decision, Niece, before all is said and done."

He cast a quick look at the prince, still lying peacefully asleep. "You might want to get to know your brother a little while there is still time."

With those ominous words, he left us. Quiet Dan closed the door behind him, and I sagged a little against Stoker's back.

"Well, it appears Uncle de Clare has not relinquished his dream to see you sitting on a throne," he said dryly.

"He is mad," I began, but just then I glanced to where Eddy was lying, eyes wide open as he stared at me in astonishment.

# CHAPTER

# 13

The prince sat up slowly, shaking his head from side to side. "Templeton-Vane," he said, focusing his gaze on Stoker.

"Yes, Your Royal Highness. And Miss Speedwell."

Eddy blinked several times as he looked at me. "Are you both *tied* to those chairs?"

"As you are to the bed," I replied helpfully.

His gaze dropped to the iron cuff at his ankle, securing him to the bed by a length of chain. "Who the devil would have the effrontery to do such a thing?" he demanded, sitting bolt upright.

"It is rather complicated," I began.

"Try," he ordered.

"Very well. The man who has taken us captive is an Irishman by the name of Edmund de Clare. He is a relation of mine and it was my abduction he intended to effect."

Interest kindled in his eyes. "I say, what did you do? Did you steal his money? Run off with an unsuitable man?" He flicked a glance to Stoker and had the grace to blush slightly.

"Oh, I am as unsuitable as they come," Stoker said blandly, "but de Clare was intent upon abducting Veronica long before she met me."

I threw him a repressive glance over my shoulder. "That is not helpful."

He shrugged and I went on. "Nothing like that," I assured the prince.

"What was all that palaver about you and a throne?" he inquired.

"My uncle is rather strongly in favor of Home Rule. He thinks Ireland should be for the Irish," I explained.

"Oh, one of those," Eddy remarked, punctuating his comment with a jaw-cracking yawn. "I say, is there food?"

"Only a little porridge they brought round earlier, but it was thoroughly nasty," Stoker said.

"Is there any left?" Eddy asked, his nose quivering like a hopeful rabbit's.

"None," Stoker replied.

"Are you quite certain—" Eddy began.

"Will you stop talking about the bloody porridge!" I demanded, blazing him to silence. He reared back, clearly astonished.

"No one except my papa ever speaks to me like that," he said, his tone decidedly sullen.

"It is your papa I mean to talk about," I said coldly. I took a deep breath and expelled it slowly. "He is my papa as well."

Eddy looked at me a long moment. "Are you certain? I mean, you're much better-looking than my other sisters."

"Quite," I said, cutting off the word sharply.

His expression softened. "Papa has not been stingy with his affections. I daresay there are more of you born on the wrong side of the blanket than the rest of us know about."

"I was not born on the wrong side of the blanket, not entirely."

He blinked rapidly. "Whatever do you mean? Papa cannot take a second wife. Motherdear is his wife and he is not a Mussulman. The Church of England would never allow it."

From behind me, Stoker's fingers stole into mine, clasping, warming, lending me his strength and his support. I gripped them back with all the strength of a drowning woman, never more grateful for his presence.

But he said not a word, knowing this tale was mine to tell.

"My mother was an actress called Lily Ashbourne," I began.

"I know her!" Eddy exclaimed. Animation lent a childlike air to his usual languid expression. "I have seen photographs of her—oh, she was a beauty. You do indeed look like her."

"They met in 1860 in North America, and it was over her that the Prince of Wales quarreled with his father."

"Yes, I remember that story," Eddy said excitedly. "Papa had behaved very badly and Grandpapa came to scold him. They went for a long walk in a cold rain and Grandpapa took a chill from which he never recovered." He dropped his voice confidingly. "Grandmama still blames Papa for that, you know. She has never entirely forgiven him for the love affair."

"Yes, well, it was not a mere love affair," I explained. "My parents were married. And it is the fact of that marriage that your grandfather confronted our father with when he came to see him."

Eddy began to shake his head again, as if the act could tidy his disordered thoughts, bringing them into some sort of sense. "But that cannot be. Grandmama would never give her permission."

"And so the marriage would not be legal in England," I agreed. "But they were married in Ireland. By a priest."

He reared back. "A *Catholic*?"

"My mother was a member of the Roman Church and it was a clergyman of that faith who joined them in marriage and presided at my christening."

"Then you are a Catholic as well?" he asked doubtfully.

"Only in the most technical sense," I replied. "I have never been confirmed and have no desire to be."

"But you were baptized," he persisted. "Surely that must count for something."

I said nothing, giving him a long moment to work out the implications. I began to number the butterflies in the gossamer-wing family, Lycaenidae, starting with the subfamily Curetinae, the sunbeam butterflies.

I had just progressed to the hairstreaks of Theclinae when he gave a sudden sharp intake of breath. "But the throne—your uncle! That is what he meant, the old devil. If you were born in Ireland to parents whose marriage is recognized by the Roman Church, the pope himself could proclaim you queen in Ireland when my father is dead," he said, his eyes fairly popping from his head.

"That is the essence of his plan," I admitted. I saw no purpose to explaining the worst of it—that my uncle clearly intended to hedge his bets by taking the actual heir to the throne into his keeping to ensure that he would never wear the crown.

"Your Royal Highness," I began gently, but Eddy merely raised a hand.

"No more just now," he said, and it was not a command but a plea. I nodded and he lay down on the narrow bed. He put his hand into his trouser pocket and drew out a small object. When he saw me looking at him, he gave a rueful smile. "I know it's frightfully childish, but it gives me comfort."

He opened his palm to show me a tiny grey velvet mouse. "He was a gift from my father upon the occasion of my birth," he explained. "His name is Chester."

# CHAPTER 14

The prince slept then, or at least pretended to, and Stoker and I, who ought to have applied ourselves to securing our freedom, instead fell suddenly into an uncomfortable doze. I awoke with a jerk, vaguely aware of the passing of time.

"Good," Stoker said. "I was beginning to think you were going to sleep right through your own escape."

He wriggled, causing the bonds connecting us to tighten. "Stoker, I do not know what you are about, but I must ask you to refrain from doing calisthenics. It is most vexing."

"What I am doing is working my way free," he said, slipping out of the ropes that held us. In one swift motion he came around and knelt in front of me to work the knots at my ankles.

"How on earth did you manage it?"

"Veronica, I spent the better part of two decades either in the circus or Her Majesty's Navy. There has yet to be invented a knot that I do not know." To prove his point, he tossed aside the ropes that had bound my ankles and started on my wrists. The dim light fell upon his face and I saw the rivers of dried blood upon his skin, the deep violet of a bruise on his cheekbone, and the unnatural swelling.

"Yes, it is broken, and do not make a fuss," he instructed. "I am more concerned about what that villain might have done to you."

"I told you I was fine," I reminded him. "And you told me you were uninjured as well."

"No, I didn't. I said my head hurt," he told me.

"You lied by omission."

"I did not want you to be as concerned about my well-being as I was for yours," he said simply.

I bent forwards and took his face in my hands, pressing a petal-soft kiss to his broken cheekbone. "Do not play the great protector with me," I told him. "I can avenge my own injuries."

"And mine as well," he answered with a sudden grin. I felt a constriction in my chest ease. I had feared, almost without knowing it, that something had changed, that one of us would shoulder too much blame for this and shatter the fragile thing we had nurtured between us. But the smile that lightened his expression was familiar, and it promised that we would get our own back before this adventure was finished.

"Where do you think they put the drugs?" I asked. "The porridge or the beer?"

Stoker shrugged. "Either. Both. Little matter. They no doubt wanted to keep us quiet for a period of time and heavy sedation was the simplest way to do it."

"Very possibly," I agreed. I toured the perimeter of the space, realizing that there was only one door—the one my uncle and his villain, Quiet Dan, had used. The windows were high and small and the floor was swept clean with no remnants, no discarded tools that might help us fashion a weapon. We talked in whispers as Eddy still slept.

"Do you think we should free him?" I ventured.

Stoker shook his head. "Let the poor devil sleep for now whilst we form a plan."

"Have you anything upon your person that we might use?" I asked.

Stoker patted himself thoroughly. "No, and you will remember someone has taken the precaution of removing my boots."

I shrugged. "Can you pick the lock? Even if we must escape with you in stocking feet, we should at least attempt to get out of this room."

During my tour of the room he had been applying himself to an examination of the lock. He rose, shaking his head.

"Not a chance without tools. There are two heavy locks, quite new."

"New? Installed on our behalf?" I wondered.

"Quite possibly." He straightened and stretched a little, wincing as he straightened his arm. A dark crimson stain had settled on the white cotton of his sleeve. "Those bollocking stitches have burst again," he said in some annoyance. He had sustained a light stabbing—Tiberius' handiwork—during our foray in Cornwall, and the stitches—my contribution—had been repeated after the first attempt had failed during the exertions of an unexpected swim. It was yet another indication that my uncle and his fiends had been none too gentle in their efforts to convey us to our present location. I added a new hash mark to the tally against them as Stoker settled himself back onto his chair.

"What are you doing?" I demanded as he folded his arms over his chest and closed his eyes.

"Resting."

"Resting? Stoker, we are meant to be escaping!" I remonstrated.

He opened one blazing blue eye—the other was swollen nearly shut—and regarded me. "We have no means. We have been fed drugs, and judging from the angle of the sun through that beggarly little window, we have gone without food or water for the entire day. My head hurts. My arm hurts. My cheek hurts. When de Clare deigns to make another appearance, I will dismember him with my goddamned teeth if I must, but until then, I mean to marshal my strength. I suggest you do the same."

"How you can sit so calmly right now is beyond me," I fretted.

The eye took on a roguish look. "Can you think of anything else to occupy our time?"

"You cannot seriously be attempting to seduce me into physical congress at such a moment," I said in an appalled whisper.

"No, but I have distracted you enough to stop your infernal pacing around." He closed the eye and sat, brooding or sleeping, I could not have said which. I drifted off myself after a while, and was just enjoying a rather pleasurable dream involving Stoker and a picnic hamper in a rowboat on a glittering sea when the key scraped in the lock. The noise roused all of us as Quiet Dan entered, this time with a companion. Stoker jerked awake with a growl while Eddy came to slowly, blinking and yawning until he spotted the revolver clutched in Quiet Dan's hand.

"Are you pointing that at *me*, sir?" Eddy asked, his indignation unmistakable.

Quiet Dan said nothing but kept the pistol aimed at Eddy while his companion carried in a tray laden with dishes. Whatever advantage our being loose from our bonds might have won, it was lost with the precaution of keeping the prince under the beady eye of the gun's barrel. De Clare had clearly anticipated the fact that we would liberate ourselves at the first opportunity and had taken no chances that we might escape.

Quiet Dan remained just inside the doorway, never taking his eyes from the prince as his colleague set the tray down upon the floor with a resounding clatter. He disappeared through the door and returned with a porcelain pot for hygienic purposes. He placed it wordlessly in the corner and gave a jerk of the head to make certain we saw what he had left for us. He paused long enough to unlock Eddy's chain to permit his use of the hygienic equipment and left us as silently as he had come, Quiet Dan keeping the gun trained upon Eddy to ensure his safe departure.

"And they say the Irish are talkative," Stoker said, coming forwards to inspect the tray with a connoisseur's sniff. "There's no pudding."

"Don't be such a child," I scolded fondly. "Look, there is an overripe pear. You can have that for your sweet."

For the rest, there was a watery-looking but not entirely unappetizing stew, fresh bread rolls, a wedge of cheese, and some apples, soft and a little bruised but otherwise wholesome enough. I held one out to Eddy. "Eat," I instructed. "We will need all our strength if we mean to fight our way out of here."

He took it with fingers that trembled slightly. "That fellow had a revolver," he said slowly. "Pointed at *me*."

"Yes," I said, as kindly as I could.

"Do you think they mean to kill me?" he asked, drawing up his chin with all the lofty courage of his station.

"Probably," Stoker said through a mouthful of stew.

"Stoker, do repress the instinct to be quite so frank, I beg you." I turned to the prince. "It is possible, but I think if they meant to do such a thing quickly, it would already have been done. I think it far likelier they mean to hold you for ransom."

"Do you really believe so?" Eddy brightened perceptibly. The notion of being kidnapped instead of murdered outright roused his appetite and he came to sit on the floor with us, helping himself to a bowl of stew and a bread roll. He poked a spoon gingerly at the stew, but finding it unexpectedly tasty, he dug in with ravenous vigor.

When he had scraped the last of the meaty juices from the bottom, he looked to us with a shy smile. "I say, this is almost enjoyable. I mean, one naturally doesn't *like* to be abducted, but if one must be, there are worse companions."

"Thank you," Stoker said, his tone dry as a Mongolian desert.

"You seem to have adapted remarkably well," I observed as I helped myself to another bread roll.

Eddy nodded. "Yes, well, one is prepared for this sort of thing."

Stoker choked on a crumb. "Prepared?"

"Of course. There has been the possibility of abduction or assassination since the day I was born. Grandmama's life has been attempted eight times," he said with obvious pride. "Mostly by the Irish." His expression turned pensive. "Come to think of it, my uncle Alfred was shot by an Irishman in Australia. But he recovered and they hanged the fellow," he finished cheerfully.

He chewed thoughtfully a moment. "Of course, it isn't always the Irish one must be careful of. The anarchists have become dreadfully bold in recent years, particularly after their success in Russia."

The assassination of the Russian tsar had been a bloody affair, with bombs as the weapon of choice. At the time, I had just embarked upon a voyage to the Solomon Islands in search for some rather spectacular specimens of Papilioninae, and the violent aftermath of the assassination was front-page news for some months. The fact that the chief architect of the plot had been a young and attractive woman had only proved fuel for the flames, and her hanging had been both swift and public.

"Were they anarchists?" Stoker asked, applying himself with appreciation to his pear. "I thought they were Russian reformers."

Eddy waved a hand in an airy gesture of dismissal. "Reformers, revolutionaries, anarchists. They are all cut from the same cloth, are they not? They would tear down our world and rebuild it to their own ends."

"Well, we have had a chance," Stoker pointed out. "Perhaps they could do a better job of it."

The prince dropped an apple from nerveless fingers. "Are you in sympathy with these devils, Templeton-Vane?"

"No," Stoker said flatly. "Having witnessed it at close quarters, I am no friend of violence to achieve one's ends. But neither am I persuaded that our current system is fair or just. My brother inherited thousands of acres of land, a home that money could not build today, and privileges encompassing the ability to make laws and the right to be hanged with a silken rope should he ever commit a capital crime. And why? Is he more able than any of his brothers? Than a sister might have been? No. He has no claim to any virtue beyond punctuality—he was the first to be born—and that of a male appendage. It seems precious little justification upon which to build a society."

Eddy nibbled at his apple, then gave a slow nod. "I do understand what you say, Templeton-Vane. My aunt Vicky was born first, you know. She is quite different to Papa. She is sharp as a new pin, clever and good with words. She can grasp an idea before Papa can even open a book. I do not speak ill of him, you understand," he added with a hasty glance behind him, as though the Prince of Wales were eavesdropping upon his son's intemperate words. "But I know she was my grandfather's favorite child, his eldest. Perhaps she would make a better queen than Papa would a king," he finished in a thrilled whisper. It was clearly a daring line of conversation for him. He turned to me with a curious look.

"Of course, people might say the same of us," he mused. "You are the elder, and in some people's eyes, you would have a better claim."

"I do not want the throne," I told him firmly. "I am the very last person who would appreciate a crown."

He broke a bread roll apart in his fingers, dropping crumbs to the floor. "Can I tell you a very great secret? I feel as though I might."

He looked from me to Stoker eagerly, and Stoker gestured in encouragement. "These are extraordinary circumstances."

Eddy's expression was one of frank relief. "Yes, you feel it too, don't you? That one might say anything here and be understood. It is quite apart from the world outside, most unreal." He fell silent a moment, pushing the crumbs together into a pile with his finger. "I am sometimes, just very occasionally, rather afraid of it all."

"You should be," I said.

He jerked his head up, making a little moue of surprise. "Do you think so?"

"Yes. The man who does not fear power is a man who ought not have it," I replied. "It is a great deal of responsibility—too much for one person, in my opinion. But it is the system we have and it is for you to make of the role what you will."

"But what shall that be?" he asked softly.

"What do you care about?" Stoker put in.

Eddy considered a long moment. "I do like horses. I am very fond of polo." He thought some more. "I like Alix of Hesse, my cousin," he added with a blush. "She is a lovely girl, just what a queen ought to be."

"Very nice," I said encouragingly. "But what of politics? What change would you like to see in the world?"

He stared at me as if he were hearing the question for the first time, and I realized with a start it was entirely possible it was. A prince in the direct line of succession would not be so much asked his opinions as given them, and I had little doubt what reactionary views he had been fed with his daily bread.

To my everlasting astonishment, he spoke with sudden authority. "I should like to see Ireland free."

Stoker dropped his pear. "You support Home Rule?"

"I do," Eddy said with even more conviction. "I do not know how it may be achieved, one must consult ministers and men of learning for that, I suppose. But there seems no good reason to me that they should not be able to govern themselves under supervision from London."

I suppressed a smile. It was not the complete and free Home Rule that the Irish themselves wanted, but he was a good deal more amenable than any other member of the royal family, I suspected.

The mood had turned companionable; perhaps our shared captivity had created a sort of attachment that is possible only in times of peril. I had often found it to be so during the course of my travels. (A forced interlude with a Corsican bandit of great charm had ended with him vowing to give up his errant life of villainy and take holy orders. He still sent me regular missives from the monastery where he devoted himself to the making of pungent cheeses.) As I looked at this kindly, charming, and slightly moronic young man, it occurred to me that our shared blood might account just a little for our sympathy with one another.

He turned to me suddenly, as if intuiting my thoughts. "Would you mind if I were frightfully rude? Just a little?"

I brushed the crumbs from my fingers and sat back. "What would you like to know?"

"How long have you known? About Papa. That he is your father, I mean."

"The week of the queen's Jubilee," I told him. "My mother died when I was very young and I was reared by friends of hers. When the second of them died, I discovered the truth about my birth. Some people had already known of it."

"Your uncle de Clare?" he guessed.

"Among others," I temporized, not wanting to invoke the names of Lady Wellie or Sir Hugo just yet. "In any event, my uncle had devised a ridiculous plot to produce proof of my parentage and put me forward as a sort of alternative queen. He thought the pope might like it," I added with a smile, but Eddy's expression remained sober.

"And you refused?"

"Naturally. I am answerable to no one," I told him gently. "If I were queen, even a puppet, pretender queen, I should have no life of my own."

"As I do not," he finished, the full mouth curving into a rueful smile. He sobered suddenly. "Wait a dashed minute—what proofs?"

"There were documents," Stoker explained. "A marriage contract, registry page, baptismal certificate. That sort of thing."

"Yes, that would be enough to put a good deal of doubt in the right quarters," Eddy agreed.

"But we burnt them," Stoker told him. I did not betray the lie by looking at him. We had, in point of fact, burnt a packet of forgeries created by Stoker to serve as a facsimile of the originals. Unbeknownst to me at the time, he had switched the documents, allowing me to make a public and convincing show of burning the pages in front of my uncle while still retaining the proof of my identity. I turned to Stoker in puzzlement.

"Uncle de Clare saw me burn what he believed were the original papers. How on earth can he expect to carry out such a ludicrous scheme without them?" I asked.

Stoker shrugged. "No doubt he has some fresh deviltry in mind."

Eddy cleared his throat gently. "I was wondering, have you ever met Papa?"

"I have not. I met your aunt Louise last year, and your mother— when was it? Yesterday? The day before? I have lost track of time now," I told him.

I did not mention the tiny jewel our father had sent me at the conclusion of a particularly challenging investigation. It was the nearest I had come to a gesture of acknowledgment from him, and I was not certain if I wanted more. My feelings towards my father were ambivalent in the extreme. I vacillated between craving his attention and hoping never again to hear his name. Love and hate are not incompatible emotions, I reflected. And while I neither loved nor hated him, I would never be indifferent to the man who had sired me.

Eddy spoke again. "I will make certain you meet him when this is finished. I give you my word."

I resisted the urge to smile. It was the promise of a child and I would not hurt his dignity for the world. "Thank you, sir."

"I think perhaps, just as long as we are all captives together," he said with a matey smile, "we should be familiar. You may call me Eddy. And you are Veronica, are you not?"

I nodded, my throat too tight for speech.

Stoker liberated the last apple from the tray. "Excellent. Now that we are refreshed and acquainted, let us create a plan."

"For what?" Eddy blinked at him, the slow blink I was beginning to understand meant that he was struggling to understand or anticipate a line of conversation.

"For escape," I told him with a grin. "For escape."

It will never work," I told Stoker flatly.

He folded his arms over the breadth of his chest and stared at me with challenge in his gaze. "Have you a better idea?"

"No, but I suspect Huxley could conjure a better scheme," I protested. After finishing our simple meal, we had worked together to arrange as much privacy as possible for visits to the porcelain apparatus in the corner—another circumstance that leads to greater intimacy in friendship, I have discovered—and then proceeded to create and discard twelve different plans for escape. The last was, in my opinion, entirely the worst.

Upon searching our garments for possible tools or weapons, Stoker had unearthed the paper twist of sedative he had originally thought to administer to the porter at the Club de L'Étoile. He had hit upon the notion of putting it into the dregs of the beer in his cup and giving it to Quiet Dan when next he appeared.

"To what end?" I demanded. "It will get us past this one door, if we are lucky. There is no way of anticipating what further obstacles lie on the other side."

"And we cannot discover them until we are *on* the other side," Stoker pointed out with maddening calm.

"You know as well as I that getting him to drink the stuff will be nigh on impossible, and even if you manage it, how will you ensure that he collapses whilst he is still on this side of the door? And what of his companion?"

He ticked off the replies on his fingers. "We shall simply have to be more clever than Quiet Dan, which I am quite certain I would be even were I in a thorough coma. As far as the timing, if I put all of the wretched stuff in at one time, it will work swiftly and we will simply have to hope that it will be swift enough. And with regards to his companion, Quiet Dan is armed and we will avail ourselves of his weapon in order to secure our release."

I again protested that there was no point in securing our release from the room until we knew what lay on the other side.

"This door stands between us and freedom no matter how many others there are," Stoker retorted. "And if we get on the other side, then there is one fewer obstacle to our release."

"Unless we walk directly into a nest of them," I reminded him. "We have seen my uncle de Clare and two of his henchmen, but I counted more at the time of our abduction, and for all we know, they may be lurking just outside and prepared for such an eventuality. Quiet Dan will no doubt have told them that we loosed our own bonds."

"They would have done that in any event when they fed us," Stoker said.

While we argued, Eddy's gaze bounced from one of us to the other, as if at a tennis match.

"I say we are not men if we do not try," he put in suddenly. "With apologies to your sex, Veronica. Although I daresay you are the match of any man in courage," he added gallantly.

I resisted the urge to remind him that men did not have a monopoly on bravery. It would only confuse him.

Before we could agree on a plan, the door opened suddenly and Quiet Dan appeared, once more holding out a revolver to ensure our compliance. He gestured for us to move towards the bed, sitting side by side like laundry pegged out on a line. When we had arranged ourselves, he stepped aside.

I expected my uncle to visit us again; abductors, in my experience, do love to come and chat with their captives. After the previous discussion, I was rather looking forward to it. My uncle was no great wit, but it passed the time, and I straightened my tunic, anticipating an amusing few minutes whilst I sparred with de Clare over the deluded and melodramatic plot he was intent upon pursuing.

But the figure that moved out of the shadow of the doorway and into the light was not my uncle at all. And as I looked at the familiar face, I realized we were in far more danger than I had ever imagined.

# CHAPTER

## 15

Inspector Archibond!" Eddy exclaimed, attempting to rise, relief limned on his features. I grabbed at the cloak he wore wrapped about his person and tugged him back down as Quiet Dan lifted his gun.

"Sit down, Eddy. I do not believe Inspector Archibond is in any way being a friend to us."

Archibond came forward. "Shall I apologize, Miss Speedwell? I realize these conditions are primitive, but I do hope you understand they are only temporary."

From the other side of me, Stoker made a low, menacing sound.

"Mornaday told me he was like that when challenged," Archibond said to me. "A thoroughly uncivilized fellow."

"I suppose that depends upon one's notion of civility," I remarked.

He laughed. "I must say, I very much respect your bravado. You have a stout heart, Miss Speedwell."

He knelt, bringing his face on a level with mine. "I must say, I am deeply intrigued by the possibilities you present. I think we are going to get to know one another quite well in the coming weeks. These fellows will ensure you do not attempt anything unwise," he added with a jerk of the head towards Quiet Dan and his companion, who had slipped into the room behind Archibond.

"Wherever did you find them?" I asked sweetly. "Judging from their noses and ears, they are all former boxers. And, judging from their aroma, they are also unfamiliar with soap."

Archibond gave me a rueful shrug. "They belong to your uncle, my dear."

"I cannot believe you have thrown in your lot with such a madman," I told him. "I never much cared for you, but I at least thought you were of sound intelligence. I see I was mistaken."

Eddy spoke up. "I must insist that you release us at once, Inspector," he said. I marveled at how he managed to give the impression of looking down his nose at a man who was on eye level with us, but it was bravely done.

Archibond shook his head. "I am afraid that is simply not possible, sir. Not at present."

"Have you sent the ransom note to my family?" Eddy demanded.

Archibond's expression was inscrutable. "No."

"Well, get on with it, man!" Eddy exploded. "You cannot expect us to stay here forever."

"I assure you, that is not at all my expectation," Archibond said evenly.

"What exactly *is* your expectation?" I inquired politely. "Please do tell us if this is a personal kidnapping or if your motives are political in nature. You have attached yourself to my uncle's plan, so I can only assume you are in sympathy with the Irish cause."

Archibond shuddered visibly. "Heaven forbid."

"Then you are simply anti-monarchist," I guessed. "Casting your lot with the Irish to topple the throne entirely and let us reinvent ourselves in England as a republic?"

Archibond smiled. "Not even close, I'm afraid. But you are correct in that the present incumbent has entirely overstayed her welcome. We, all right-thinking Englishmen—and Irishmen," he added at a low grumble from one of his ruffians, "are quite finished with being ruled over by a German hausfrau and her band of inbred ne'er-do-wells. It is high time that they were replaced. It is high time all of you," he said with a significant glance at Stoker and Eddy, "were replaced."

"I told you," Eddy muttered. "Anarchists."

"Near enough," Archibond allowed. "Our current systems make a show of serving men of merit, but they are a lie. Without the proper connections, without the proper name, the proper schools, a man cannot make his way in the world according to his abilities. It is time for that to change."

"You ought to try America," I suggested. "They are quite enthusiastic about self-made men there."

Archibond gave me a thin smile. "I would far rather reshape my own country, thank you."

I shook my head. "You complain you are not making your way in the world, yet your ascent through the ranks at the Yard has been meteoric, I am told."

"Not through my own merit," he said in real bitterness. "I was given advancement upon the recommendation of my godfather, who was Home Secretary at the time."

I remembered hearing something of the sort when we had first made Archibond's acquaintance. Something else niggled at the corner of my memory, a bit of scandal from the English newspapers when I had been abroad in Madeira.

"The Home Secretary? The one who was forced to resign after his wife sued for divorce claiming he had another family tucked away in—where was it?"

"Barnstaple," he supplied. His expression was grim. "His fall affected all of us. My sister's fiancé broke off the engagement and she has been forced to come and keep house for me instead. My own career at the Yard has been effectively ruined. I will never climb higher because I have no patron to smooth the way. Sir Hugo has made it perfectly apparent that I have achieved all I may ever hope for under his aegis."

"Still, to be second at Special Branch is no mean feat. Why is that not enough for you?"

"Because everything I have worked for has been ruined by the peccadilloes of another!" he protested. "And what of the thousands of others, trammeled under the boot of tyranny, without prospect or hope of improvement? You could step one foot outside this door and meet dozens, nay, *hundreds* of men who will live and die in the station to which they were born, never knowing what they might have been with the proper education, with training and opportunity."

I gave him a pitying look. "You cast yourself as a benefactor and yet I suspect your largesse will begin and end with you, Inspector."

"I would see this country refashioned for the good of all," he countered coldly.

"It is the dream of an adolescent," I told him. "I have met one or two anarchists on my travels, and without fail they are exceedingly childish. Anarchy is the sort of idea one may embrace at university, but one would be very ill-advised to take it home and marry it. Their plots have frequently been catastrophic failures," I added. "No one yet has brought down civilization as we know it to remake the world."

"It is only a matter of time before someone succeeds," he insisted. "And I intend to be that man."

"So you have abducted the future king and entered into a conspiracy with an unrepentant Irish radical who would install a puppet queen? Hardly a marriage of like minds," Stoker pointed out.

Archibond's gaze slid away and he did not answer.

"How does murdering Madame Aurore fit into your scheme?" I asked.

He did not flinch. "A necessary casualty and not a particularly regrettable one. Any further questions?"

"I can think of a few dozen," Stoker said amiably. "To begin with, how did de Clare find you?"

"I found him," Archibond said. "He very nearly died the last time he encountered the pair of you, but he dragged himself out of the Thames and his henchmen spirited him back to Ireland to recover and to brood on his losses. When I learnt of Miss Speedwell's true identity, it was an easy enough matter to track him down."

"How did you discover my birth?" I demanded.

He shrugged. "The files at Special Branch hold all sorts of secrets and Sir Hugo is often too busy to notice where I have been wandering. I studied the files in hopes of discovering something, anything, I could use to leverage myself into a better position. Those file drawers are full of nasty little scandals—adultery and profiteering and cheating at cards and gambling. But imagine my delight when I learnt your secret, Miss Speedwell. It cast all the others into gloom, I assure you."

"And de Clare was only too happy to have someone new to recruit to his cause," Stoker guessed.

"My dear fellow, the matter was settled over a bottle of good Irish whisky and a handshake."

"He is an unrepentant lunatic," I said succinctly.

"What a very hurtful thing to say about one's blood relation," he said thoughtfully. "I prefer to think of him as dogged in his pursuits." He paused. "He rails quite a lot—gets into these dark moods where he sits up all night, nursing a bottle of rather fine, peaty whisky and saying decidedly unkind things about you. He has spent the last months in a fever of frustration because he had no idea where you were. He had a dozen plots to kidnap this one and torture him into talking," he said with a jerk of his head towards Stoker, "and you can thank me for putting him off that idea." He paused, but when no sign of gratitude was forthcoming from Stoker, he shrugged and went on. "He was ripe as a plum when I found him, ready to fall in with my plans at the first approach."

He rose then, rubbing his hands together briskly. "Now then, I merely wanted to look in and make certain our charges were of good cheer. I will return later."

He edged towards the door, and that was when they made their mistake. Quiet Dan and his companion withdrew first, leaving Archibond exposed.

Stoker surged up from the bed in a single, fluid motion, taking up one of the chairs and smashing it in a single blow so that he held a piece in each hand, brandishing them like a lion tamer. He started forwards, making straight for Archibond. The inspector stepped back swiftly, letting Quiet Dan move to the fore. The Irishman raised his gun but Archibond gave a shout of alarm.

"Don't shoot, you cretin! If you miss it will ricochet," he protested. Quiet Dan resorted to his fists, swinging wildly, but Stoker never paused in his implacable advance. He dropped to his knees, slashing with the spindles at the Irishman's knees, bringing him down hard. Quiet Dan howled, but the noise was cut off as Stoker slammed one spindle into his solar plexus. The fellow pitched forward, and Stoker cut up sharply, putting all of his strength into a blow that snapped the fellow's head back so hard, I could feel the crack of it in my bones.

From the doorway, Archibond raised his own revolver, aiming carefully at me and stopping Stoker squarely in his tracks. "On your knees, Templeton-Vane," he said through gritted teeth.

Stoker hesitated and Archibond cocked the pistol. "I am not de Clare," he said, his voice cold as a winter wind. "Believe me when I tell you that you care far more than I do if she dies. On your knees."

Stoker complied this time, lacing his fingers behind his head.

"Now on your face," Archibond instructed.

Stoker lay facedown and gave me a long look of resignation. I gave him a nod in return to show that I understood, and before he could respond, Archibond circled around and lifted his boot to aim a careful kick at Stoker's jaw. His eyes rolled back in his head but Archibond kicked him once more for good measure. Thoroughly and obviously shaken, Archibond signaled angrily to a staggering Quiet Dan and his companion. Together they scooped Stoker up under the armpits and dragged him from the room.

"Where are you taking him?" I demanded.

Archibond gave a thin smile as he left, banging the door behind him.

I slid back down to the bed as the key turned in the lock.

Eddy made a sympathetic noise. "Poor brave fellow. God only knows what they will do to him. He oughtn't to have gone for them. It was a foolish thing to do."

I turned to him, torn between pride in Stoker and scorn for Eddy's lack of perception. "Foolish? He has just got himself out of this room without picking a lock. While he is gone, he will assess the conditions outside and will know the best course of action when he returns. To my way of thinking, we have just doubled our odds of escaping," I informed him.

His expression was pitying. "He mayn't even survive. We don't know them, Veronica."

I twisted my hands into fists, stubbornly clinging to my optimism. "You don't know Stoker."

Without Stoker's reassuring presence the next few hours dragged. Eddy and I did our best to pass the time, but I was preoccupied with the nuances of Archibond's visit and what they implied. He had not answered when Stoker inquired about the finer points of the plot, but it was not difficult to imagine the broad strokes. Archibond, with his mission to burn down the world he knew, had searched long for just the right match to put to the tinder. In me, he had found it, knowing the scandal that erupted from my story would sweep the Empire. Using my uncle's scheme as a starting point, he could disgrace the current royal family and set off a crisis of confidence in the monarchy, to expose them as disreputable and amoral, the antithesis of the virtuous and Christian model of propriety they had so often claimed to be.

Then, when the Empire was still reeling from the shock, he would allow de Clare to present me with my credentials to the world, proclaiming me queen. That would plunge Ireland into chaos, with the Roman Church and its thousands of adherents across the globe taking the position that I was the legitimate queen. The Empire would fracture, and other lands would seize the chance to shape their own destinies, breaking with London in order to strike out for independence.

As soon as that happened, stronger nations like Germany and America would involve themselves, swooping like birds of prey to pluck the vulnerable and promising pickings, quarrelling amongst themselves to divide the spoils. In the end, Archibond would get what he wanted: anarchy. A world on fire where a man's birth meant nothing compared to what he could do.

And as the architect of the chaos, Archibond would be perfectly poised to catapult himself into power. He might rail about the downtrodden and the disadvantaged, but I had traversed the globe and met few saints upon the way. Archibond was like every other fanatic I had encountered: fixed upon his own ambitions while cloaking them in a mantle of beneficence. The slender compensations of life in public service, even if he rose to the pinnacle of Special Branch, would never satisfy his aspirations. He, like so many other greater men before him, longed to leave his mark upon the world, and he cared nothing for the devastation that might ensue.

As I pondered the unthinkable, Eddy managed to piece together the implications of one rather chilling omission on Archibond's part.

"They haven't sent a ransom note," he said quietly. "That means they intend to kill me."

"You cannot know that," I told him in a harsher tone than I meant. "Besides, you are not going to die here. I forbid it."

"You are a very managing sort of person," he said with a courageous attempt at a smile. "I would fear to disobey you."

"See that you don't," I told him.

His smile faltered then. "I can't believe they really murdered her. She was a lovely woman," he lamented. "Kind and generous, well-read, witty."

"You were fond of Madame Aurore."

He gave a little shrug. "I suppose. I was not in love with her," he said quickly. "You must not think we were more than friends."

"Most gentlemen of her acquaintance were more than just friends of hers," I observed.

He blushed a little. "I know. And I spent time in her rooms, private time. But only for conversation! She was very easy to talk to."

I raised a skeptical brow. "Is that really the extent of your endeavors there?"

"It is!" he insisted. "At least, that is all I did with Aurore. One couldn't very well go to such a place and not have a sporting time," he added seriously.

"I wonder what your Princess Alix would make of such activities," I jibed.

He drew himself up. "It is a gentleman's obligation to be experienced in the marriage bed. Naturally, I would not continue such activities once we were wed."

"Then you would be a distinct departure from the rest of your family," I told him. I returned to the subject of Madame Aurore. "What kinds of things did you talk about?"

He laced his long fingers together. "Mostly Alix. She was advising me on how to woo her properly. She was very kind."

"I rather liked her myself," I told him. "We were not so very different."

"We used to play cards," he confessed. "Usually two-handed whist. For ha'pence a point. I owed her rather a lot of money at the end."

"If you were only friends, why did you give her the star?" I asked.

He shrugged. "She needed money, she said. Running her establishment is terribly expensive. Only I couldn't give her money outright because I haven't any, not enough to help her, at least. Papa keeps me on a bit of a short lead," he said, his moustaches quivering a little.

"How did you expect to pay for the diamond star?"

"Oh, well, Motherdear has an account at Garrard. I thought if I just ordered a trinket there, then Aurore could sell it at her discretion and they would send the bill along and Motherdear's solicitor would see it paid."

He seemed so cheerfully unaware of how ridiculous it was to expect his mother to pay for a jewel for his friend that I did not have the heart to mock him for it. Instead I smiled by way of consolation. "You have a generous heart, Eddy."

He blushed again, this time in pleasure, I think. "Motherdear often says so. Papa has a less flattering opinion of me."

"Do you not get on with him?"

He struggled to find the words. "I'm not sure anyone really gets on with Papa. He's frightfully intimidating in person." I had only seen my father once, from a distance, but it was enough to know that Eddy's assessment was correct. "Of course, one of his lady friends has nicknamed him Prince Tum-Tum," Eddy confided with a grin. "And when I think of that, it makes him less terrifying."

"I am sure he does not mean to terrify you," I assured him.

"Oh, I don't know. He is petrified of his own mama, and I think he has some idea that is how things are supposed to be. Even George is frightened of him and he isn't frightened of anyone."

"George? Your brother?"

"And my best friend," he said swiftly. "He's a good chap, our George. He is cleverer than I am, better at his studies and things. He is quite popular too. People always like him," he added with a wistful look. I felt a rush of sympathy for this kindly young man, sandwiched as he was between a dynamic father and an outgoing younger brother.

"People don't always see me, you know. Not really. They see the Prince of Wales' son, the future king. Most people don't see Eddy."

"I do," I assured him.

"Yes, well, we are locked up together, so it makes it rather easy," he returned with a self-deprecating little grin. He sobered again. "If they do mean to kill me, I hope you will tell the family that I faced it like a gentleman," he said.

"Eddy—"

"I mean it," he told me, seizing my hand in his. His palm was warm and broad, the fingers long and graceful where they curved over mine. "I have made no mark on the world, Veronica. If I die, how I face it will be the only story I have. I will endeavor to make it a good one."

I gripped his hand in reply. "We will not permit that to happen, Eddy. You have my word."

# CHAPTER

## 16

Some hours later, the door opened and Quiet Dan and his compatriot returned, an unconscious Stoker slung between them. They dropped him to the floor and carried in a tray of food.

I went to where Stoker lay bleeding. He was breathing evenly, but there was a nasty lump on his head and the stitches on his arm had torn further asunder. I rounded on them in fury. "You might at least bring some water and bandages, you wretches," I said in icy tones.

Quiet Dan had the grace to look abashed, and although he left, he returned quickly with a pitcher of water. He drew a nasty-looking handkerchief from his pocket and offered it.

"Thank you, but I would rather not give him septicemia," I replied. "Go away now."

He did as he was bade, shuffling away and locking the door behind him as Eddy stared at me in disbelief.

"He did what you told him," he said in awed tones.

"A woman who knows her mind is a surprise to a certain type of man. They do not know how to react to it, so they generally obey," I said in some distraction as I examined Stoker for further injuries.

"If this is your idea of seduction, I am doomed," he murmured.

"You are conscious, then?" I asked, nearly light-headed from relief.

"I am unlikely to be anything else with your ham-fisted poking," he complained. "I would have enjoyed a few more minutes of sense-lessness, you know."

"I know," I said, my eyes suddenly awash. I had time to dash away the unshed tears and compose myself before he looked at me.

Eddy crept near. "Do you require anything, Templeton-Vane?"

"A bit of morphia and a nice single malt would be just the thing," Stoker replied. "And some cake."

My laugh was mirthless and brittle. "Well, we haven't any of those, but once we are out of here, I promise you a plateful of cakes, the best Julien d'Orlande can bake."

"I shall hold you to that," he said, slipping away again.

"Stoker," I called softly.

He opened his good eye and held my gaze with visible effort.

"What have you discovered? Is escape possible through the rest of the warehouse?"

He shook his head slowly and gave a low growl of pain. "No. At least four locked doors between us and the street. Find another way."

He gave a deep groan and rolled onto all fours and was lavishly sick. I put out my hand for the cloak Stoker had given Eddy and he handed it over without a word.

"Empty the food from one of the bowls and bring it here," I instructed. Eddy obeyed with alacrity, and it occurred to me that, for all his lofty position, he was accustomed to following orders. Grandmother, father, tutors, commanding officers in army and navy—all would have dictated to him.

"Wrap the bowl in the cloak and then break it," I said. He blinked.

"The cloak will muffle the sounds of the breakage," I explained in some exasperation. "We do not want them to know we have fashioned a possible weapon."

"Oh, that is clever," he said. He did as he was told, with excessive enthusiasm, I reflected, as he presented me with a pile of shards. He had broken the bowl so comprehensively that only a few pieces large enough to be of use remained. He gave me an eager look, like a puppy that has just sat upon command.

"Very good, Eddy," I said. I plucked the largest piece from the cloak. The remaining splinters of china were embedded in the fabric.

"That was silk," he said mournfully. "And the only thing I had for warmth."

"I don't care if it was woven by virgin nuns sitting on the pope's lap," I told him. "He needs it more than you. Give me that water." My handkerchief had disappeared somewhere during the evening's adventures, and so I used the shard of broken bowl to start a rip in the fabric, then tore a long strip free. I wetted it and wiped away the worst of the blood and the sick.

Stoker roused himself then and quietly cataloged his injuries, supervising our basic treatment. We had little to work with, and no doubt to him our efforts were almost as unpleasant as the beating itself. He looked even worse when we had finished, bruises and rivulets of dried blood festooning his face.

Stoker lay quite still when we had completed our acts of ungentle mercy. His eyes were closed, but his breathing was even.

"Is he unconscious now?" Eddy asked curiously.

"I do not know. Better for him if he is since we've nothing for the pain," I pointed out.

Stoker's head was heavy in my lap, but I would not move it for all the world.

Eddy settled near us, shivering a little, his slender chest mottled with cold. I noticed then the tattoo upon his arm, and he held it out for inspection. The image was a Jerusalem cross, a central equilateral cross with four smaller ones set in each quadrant. Surmounting the arrangement were three crowns.

"George and I got them in Jerusalem. Papa got the same on his tour of the Holy Land so we thought it would be a lark to have them done." The notion of both of my half-brothers choosing to adorn themselves with the same tattoo our father had was oddly moving. I had little doubt that Eddy struggled to find approbation in our father's eyes. Had he hoped this gesture would help?

He turned, displaying his back. "George and I had these done in Japan," he told me. Inked across his skin was a large red and blue dragon embellished with fire.

"Very handsome," I said.

He turned back, his expression wary. "Mind you don't tell Motherdear. She doesn't know, you see, and she mightn't approve."

I did not bother to explain to Eddy that my opportunities for conversation with Her Royal Highness were limited in the extreme. He shivered then, and I held up my arm, opening my cloak. "There is room enough for you to warm yourself here if you don't mind sitting quite close."

He moved to my side, settling himself under my arm as I wrapped the cloak around us both, Stoker's head still on my lap. We were still sitting thus when Archibond appeared, looking a trifle haggard.

"You seem discomposed, Inspector," I said coolly. "But I expect managing a madman must be a bit tiring."

His smile was thin. "Miss Speedwell. I see you and your companions have made yourselves comfortable."

"As comfortable as possible under the circumstances, although you must admit these are hardly fitting surroundings for a future queen. Oughtn't there to be silk sheets and roasted duck on gilded plates?"

He ignored my jibe. His gaze was restless, and there was a new wariness about him. I wondered if he was losing his nerve for the enterprise. Perhaps he was discovering for himself how difficult it was to work with someone so devilishly bent upon his grandiose ideals.

"Tell me, Inspector, how precisely do you anticipate being able to prove my claim? I am quasi-legitimate at best," I said in a deliberately pleasant tone.

"Your grandmother de Clare passed away earlier this year. In going through her effects, your uncle discovered a letter from your mother communicating the details of her marriage as well as your conception and birth." He twitched a little, his manner one of acute discomfort. "In the letter, she entrusted your care to your grandmother. She made it quite clear that she intended to destroy herself."

"You have my mother's suicide note?" I demanded.

"We do," he affirmed.

"If I was to be given to my grandmother to rear, then why did I stay with the aunts?"

He shrugged. "Apparently your grandmother de Clare was a good Catholic. She never forgave your mother for her act of self-destruction. In spite of your uncle de Clare's best efforts, she could not be made to see the potential benefit to keeping you in her custody. She was content to let your mother's friends have the charge of you. By the time your uncle managed to discover their names and whereabouts, they had changed their names and taken you to England."

"They wanted me," I said, hardly able to comprehend that the aunts—a courtesy title, for they were no kin to me, having been my mother's dressers during her time in the theatre—had gone to such lengths to keep me with them.

"They were, by all accounts, devoted to your mother," Archibond said quietly. "It was most likely a moment of weakness that caused her to write to your grandmother. No doubt she repented it, urged them to take you before any of the de Clares could find you."

I could well imagine it. My mother, beautiful and broken when my father betrayed their marriage in order to marry his Danish princess, had turned to her dearest friends to help her. What misery, what despair she must have felt! And in a moment of anguish, she had reached out to her blood family, hoping they would give me the understanding and love they had never offered her.

What had caused her to regret her appeal? It must have been a deed borne of desperation. Had she acted in a moment of despair and only realized the seriousness of her plea in the cold light of morning? Had she succumbed to a moment of madness? Had she been so sunk in misery that her lonely existence in that austere family had been transformed, in her mind, to security—the kind of stability she wished for her only child?

In the end, she had opted for the found family of her friends to rear me. We had moved often, always eluding something. I never understood the specter that stalked my childhood. A rumor, a whisper, a glimpse of a familiar face, and the aunts would be off again, packing up whatever cottage or modest flat we had taken, and striking out for parts unknown. But theatre people have a wide acquaintance, and we were often forced to slip quietly away from those who might have exposed the aunts for who they really were, who might have seen a familiar profile as he lingered backstage, waiting for his adored to slip behind the footlights, who might have seen a child and done the maths and realized whose child I was.

They were affectionate enough, the aunts. There were stories at bedtime and my first ring net for butterflying and doses of castor oil when I was ill. But there was always a sort of wariness about them as well. Once whilst hunting in Costa Rica, I had discovered a unique golden chrysalis, the most unusual thing I had ever seen on my travels. I had nurtured it carefully and eventually witnessed the birth of *Tithorea tarricina*, one of the most exotic and beautiful specimens I had ever handled. I ought to have netted it; such a find would be worth half a year's salary. I could have named my price with any aurelian collector in Europe. But I could not bring myself to interfere with something so beautiful, so wild. It belonged to nature and not to humankind. So I watched it testing its damp and trembling wings, trying them on the soft breeze that ruffled my hair. It ought to have lurched and listed, but instead it rose in one great flap of those enormous wings and lifted itself above my head, out of reach and beyond the horizon before I realized what was happening. It was like watching a miracle of creation, and I felt no loss at its passing away from me but only joy that I had been, for however fleeting a time, connected with it.

It was only much later that I realized this was the attitude I sometimes detected in the aunts. They could be occasionally at their ease with me, instructing me on how to roast a chicken or make a bed or turn a seam, but then I would catch a glimpse of something watchful in them, as if they had invited a tiger to tea and were surprised and unnerved at how it lolled upon the hearthrug. I was part of them and none of them, and as soon as I could, I made my way in the world, net in hand, to find others like me. I had met a few in the course of my travels—most were base metal and counterfeit in their charms. But one or two had been like Stoker, bright gold and pure through and through. I had no doubt, for all her failings, my mother was the same. It was no use attempting to explain such things to men like Archibond or—worse—my uncle. What is unrefined can never appreciate what is tempered.

And so I did not try. De Clare was a lost soul; I had seen too clearly the glint of obsession in his eyes. It was the expression worn by fanatics and evangelists the world over, the dogged determination to see only one point of view and entertain no truths but the fantasy in one's own mind. He would see this thing through to the end, no matter how many people it destroyed. I wondered if Archibond's cool detachment would prove more amenable to persuasion.

The more I pondered it, the less unlikely it seemed. Archibond had, upon our previous meetings, struck me as dissatisfied with his lot, pricked bloody by the thorns of thwarted ambition. He knew he was a clever man—perhaps more clever than most—but he had not the humility to recognize his own limitations. He feared them, but he could not perceive them, and what might occasionally haunt his wakeful nights was the terror that the world would never understand exactly how clever he was. His progress at the Yard had been stalled; there were few opportunities for him to advance to greatness. I could smell the stink of longing upon him. In spite of his protestations of egalitarian ideals, he yearned for accolades, for a knighthood or a baronetcy, a title to set him above those who were currently his betters but never his equals.

This then was his roll of the dice, as reckless and determined as any wager any gambler had made. I saw the faintest trickle of perspiration at his hairline and I realized he was desperately afraid but he had come too far to back out now. That feeling of being cornered would make him ruthless. He could not go back, so he must go forwards, whatever the price.

I considered all of this in the space of a few seconds before speaking. "That letter is no proof," I told Archibond gently. "My mother might have been delusional. She did, after all, take her own life shortly thereafter. And you, above anyone, must know the necessity of corroboration."

His hands curled into fists at his sides. "I cannot speak to your mother's state of mind, but de Clare will. He will swear to it."

"He was not there," I pointed out.

"Yes, but who knows that?" Archibond retorted.

"The Prince of Wales will deny it all," I told him.

"The Prince of Wales? Who the devil will believe him after it comes out what his family have been up to?" Archibond countered with a flick of the finger towards Eddy.

But I saw the flicker of doubt in Archibond's eyes. He had planned this scheme in exacting detail, but execution was a different matter. Now that he was in the thick of it, he could see the flaws, I was certain. He still believed he could carry out his plot, but the more doubt I sowed, the longer he might hesitate to press forward, purchasing a little time for us. And time was opportunity—opportunity for us to find a way of escape, for someone to discover us, for the hue and cry to be raised about Eddy's disappearance.

I forced my voice to lightness. "I am curious, Inspector. How do you mean to continue the charade that I am queen in my own right unless I am periodically trotted out to make speeches or open Parliament or even to be crowned? I must be seen by the people. And how can you ever guarantee that I will do so without appealing to them to free me from my pretty gilded cage?"

"Your uncle believes," he said slowly, "that you will be persuaded to come around." He did not glance to where Stoker lay, but we both understood his meaning precisely.

"I have seen my uncle's methods of persuasion," I said candidly. "Did he tell you he had me abducted once before? Hauled onto a boat to be carried off to Ireland, only I jumped into the Thames rather than let him sail away with me. My uncle has no intention of attempting to persuade me to serve as his puppet queen," I added. "He has a rather low opinion of me, if you have not yet detected it."

In spite of himself, Archibond gave a small smile. "He might have mentioned your intransigence a time or two."

"Exactly. I expect he will establish a government in my name and then have me declared incapacitated in some fashion—perhaps I will be drugged, that is the simplest way. A little prick of a hypodermic and your new queen would be sitting in a corner, talking to herself and wearing a flowerpot on her head, completely incapable of governing. How easy then to have her own uncle established as regent to keep a firm grasp of the government during her incapacity."

"A plausible enough scenario," Archibond allowed.

"And one you have discussed?" I guessed.

"It might have been talked of."

"What is to be your role when my uncle is regent and has control of the entire Empire? There will be no office higher than his. Do you really mean to take orders from that Bedlamite?"

Archibond canted his head to the side. "My dear Miss Speedwell, you persist in believing that your uncle and I are playing the same game, but I can assure you, I am executing a perfect gambit in the chess match of my life whilst he is still sketching naughts and crosses with a fingernail."

His smile turned suddenly savage. "Do you really believe I would be taken in by his ridiculous Irish sentiment? He drinks and weeps as he talks of a de Clare being Queen of Ireland, did you know that? Do you realize how many bloody songs about Brian Boru I have had to endure? But do give me a little credit, I beg you. I know exactly what your uncle is going to do, and moreover, I know exactly what I will do—not in response to him, but to make him do what I want in the first place. I understand your hope, that I might be open to an appeal based upon our shared sensibility and logic, and I applaud you for it. I would have done the same in your circumstances. But you must understand, my dear. I am far more dangerous than your uncle. He wishes to harm you because he has a grudge for the ills you have done him. I will harm you because it will teach you to obey."

He accompanied the words with the caress of a fingertip drawn slowly down my cheek. "I will bruise you where no one can see. I will make scars that will never heal. Do not oppose me. Do not challenge me. And above all, do not underestimate me."

With that, he wrapped a loose tendril of hair about his finger, curling it slowly, drawing me closer as he tugged gently upon it. I could smell the fragrance of his hair oil, and I knew I should never forget it as long as I lived.

"I say, turn loose of my sister," Eddy ordered, drawing himself up with the stiff precision of his training as an officer of the Tenth Hussars.

Archibond regarded him with amusement. Suddenly, he tucked the hair behind my ear and patted my cheek gently. "Be a good girl, Veronica. Whatever happens to you—and to them," he added with a nod towards my two companions, "is entirely your choice."

He left us and I turned to Eddy. "Well done, Eddy."

He bristled. "One does not like to threaten another gentleman with violence, but I will not let any man bully my sister." He deflated a little then. "Although I must say, he is a chilling sort of monster, isn't he? I rather thought you were going to be able to twist him round your little finger at first."

I shook my head slowly. "No. Not a man like Archibond. That was never going to be possible."

"Then why did you play up to him, behaving as if he were the only true gentleman and your Uncle de Clare was a dangerous madman who must be stopped?"

"He *is* a dangerous madman who must be stopped," I pointed out. "But Archibond is the true devil in the deal. He is far more cunning and ruthless than Edmund de Clare. Uncle has the old Irish grudge of hating the English coupled with the same sort of monomania one sees in those of very low intellect."

"What makes you say that?"

"I daresay you have never met a butterfly collector, Eddy," I told him. "Not a proper one. Most folks are content with a broad collection, amassing as many different types as they can. A true fanatic wants *every* specimen, dozens of a singular species, and the quality does not matter. They will pay almost as much for a moldering old wreck that's crumbling to dust as they will something freshly netted and still smelling of the meadow. They want everything because they cannot bear another collector to have anything. They might make coherent conversation or present themselves as normal, but scratch the surface and you will find an absolute fiend, incapable of sharing or empathy or rational understanding. They are driven by one desire only and that is to amass more than anyone else has."

"But how does that translate to low intellect?"

"To be of truly high intelligence, one must have an understanding and appreciation of other people, an ability to empathize and relate."

"I suppose he does," he said with a nod towards Stoker.

I paused. "Revelstoke Templeton-Vane could be beaten senseless, drugged, and half out of his wits and he would still be twice the man Archibond is on the best day of his life."

After a moment, Eddy nodded. "I can see that. So what now?"

"We wait," I told him. "Archibond will no doubt speak with my uncle and with any luck they will quarrel and give us some time."

"Time enough for what?" he persisted.

"Time to make a miracle."

# CHAPTER

## 17

I do not mind admitting that the next hours were the darkest I had yet spent in that place. Stoker exhibited alarming signs of needing proper medical attention—the most alarming of which was agreeing when I suggested such a thing.

"You never think you require a physician," I pointed out.

He gave me a small smile. "Perhaps just this once."

My mind whipped back to a similar situation when he had been shot for my sake and we sat for hours, waiting for help that might never have come. This time there was no bullet to blame, only the booted feet of those ruffians who had broken his ribs and likely punctured a lung. He spat up blood from time to time and his breathing was labored, and when he smiled, it was a ghost of the smile I knew so well. Only the feel of his hand in mine was the same.

I used the last of the water in the pitcher to bathe his brow.

"I was going to drink that," Eddy protested feebly. "But I daresay his necessity is the greater," he added swiftly at the murderous expression on my face.

He had obviously been thinking, for when he spoke again, he ventured a question. "What do you suppose they mean to do to disgrace me? How will they blacken my name?"

I considered giving him a comfortable lie, but he had already risen to the occasion more than once during our ordeal, and I thought it best to pay him the compliment of the truth.

"I expect it all began with Madame Aurore and the star. You gave her an expensive trinket that could easily be traced back to you."

"But she was going to return it," he protested. "As soon as I told her I had had second thoughts on account of Alix, she swore she was going to give it over."

"Was she?" I asked, giving him a moment to think.

"Well," he said slowly, "she *said* she was, but I suppose she might have been telling an untruth."

"Let us presume she was," I said kindly. "Did she ask for the jewel in the first place?"

"Oh yes, down to the exact engraving on the back," he affirmed.

"The engraving that connected the gift definitively to you," I pointed out.

"Dash! You're quite right," he said unhappily. "It didn't occur to me then, you see. I just wanted to help out a friend. But once I gave it to her, I realized unscrupulous persons might use it to make a scandal, and I was worried it might get to Alix's ears. My family are no strangers to gossip," he added darkly.

"I'm certain," I murmured. "In any event, that was when you asked for the jewel's return, is that correct?"

"Yes, and she never came out and refused, but she put me off. Said she had it laid away for safekeeping and it would take some trouble to retrieve it."

"Madame Aurore kept all of her jewels in her personal safe," I reminded him.

"So she did! I ought to have recollected that," he said, tugging at the ends of his moustaches.

"When did she send word that she would return the star to you?"

"Oh, the day of the masquerade. She sent a coded wire to me at Balmoral and said if I wanted the star I had to come to her and she gave a time, saying it was quite urgent and if I didn't retrieve it then, she could not be held responsible for what became of it."

"And you did not view that as a threat?" I demanded.

"How could I?" His expression was frankly dumbfounded. "She said she was returning the jewel. I thought she was simply in some sort of trouble. So I went to Louise, my sister, and told her I needed gear for a masquerade. She fitted me out with a gown and some paste jewels and face paint in a bag and I dashed for the express train down to London. I made it only just."

"When did the wire come from Madame Aurore?"

He shrugged. "Just before luncheon."

I calculated swiftly. Shortly after Stoker and I had decided to attend the masquerade, the wire had been sent to Eddy, luring him to the evening's entertainment. I did not believe in coincidences. I thought of Archibond's careful maneuvering. We had been invited to sleuth on the princess's behalf, but when we had refused, it was Archibond's oblique hints as to Lady Wellie's distress that had prompted us to investigate her desk, unearthing the diary and the notes she had made regarding Eddy's whereabouts during the Ripper murder.

"I believe Inspector Archibond has been making a good deal of this up as he goes along," I said slowly. "The original intention was no doubt to implicate you in a scandal of a most sordid nature at Madame Aurore's. But the Ripper murders gave him an opportunity to do something far more devious."

"The Ripper murders? What on earth have they to do with me?"

I explained swiftly about the anonymous note and Lady Wellie's attempts to establish his alibi.

"Poor Lady Wellie," he said softly. "How horrified she must have been."

"You don't blame her for even entertaining the notion?" I asked.

"How could I? She has looked after us all of her life. She was looking after me still. She made it her business to put me quite in the clear," he said firmly. "If she had not fallen ill, she would have made it perfectly apparent that I was nowhere near Whitechapel during those terrible crimes."

I did not disabuse him of his illusions. Lady Wellie's proof of his innocence would hold in a court of law but not the court of public opinion. One whisper attaching his name to the murders and he would go down in history as an homicidal maniac.

I went on. "The Ripper murders have been a stroke of luck for Archibond," I mused. "Nothing else could keep Special Branch so preoccupied that he could work out his schemes undetected. He has no doubt kept careful records of your visits to Madame Aurore's house with an eye to presenting them once you were implicated in her murder."

"You think that was his plan?" Eddy paled in horror.

"I do. That was why you had to be lured back to her house at a specific time, to ensure that Archibond and his men were there to do the deed. And the time was set for an evening when Stoker and I were there as well so that Archibond could kill three very particular birds with one stone."

Eddy ticked them off on his fingers. "Eliminating a co-conspirator in Aurore, establishing my presence at the house at the time of her murder, and giving them an opportunity to abduct you and me, so that we would be in their power."

"Precisely."

"I cannot approve such actions, but they were efficiently done," he observed.

"I think it is as much a lack of manpower as efficiency driving their actions," I pointed out. "We have seen my uncle de Clare, Archibond, Quiet Dan, and one other. I think they have chosen to keep their little plot as quiet as possible in order to avoid word getting out."

"That would be a reasonable precaution," Eddy agreed.

Just then the door opened and my uncle de Clare appeared, leaning on his walking stick, with his minion, Quiet Dan, lurking behind.

"Good evening, Niece," he said amiably.

I inclined my head. "Uncle. How kind of you to visit. It was gracious of Inspector Archibond to permit it."

He thrust himself upwards. "What's that?"

I opened my eyes wide. "Well, obviously he is the mastermind of this little endeavor. The kingmaker, as it were. Or I suppose we would call him a queenmaker, although it doesn't have quite the same ring, does it?"

Eddy was watching de Clare closely but said nothing, letting me prattle on, goading my uncle in ways I knew he would never accept from a woman.

"It is understandable," I remarked. "After all, you are merely an Irish countryman and he is an inspector at Scotland Yard, a member of Special Branch, no less. It was very wise of you to put someone cleverer than yourself in charge."

He came forwards, his lips stretched in a thin line.

"You think I would play second fiddle to that arse-faced Englishman?" he demanded.

I shrugged. "He seems to be making all of the decisions," I pointed out. "And why shouldn't he? You are superfluous to his requirements."

His eyes goggled. "Superfluous! Damn your insolence, girl. This entire plan is *mine*."

"Is it? It might have been when you began. But you have given him too much rein and he has slipped the traces. He has no need of you now, does he? He knows what you intend and he has me. What use are you?"

I paused to let that sift through the murky waters of his thoughts. "It is not true," he muttered.

"Perhaps not," I said graciously. "He might intend for the pair of you to be partners to the very end. But if you are willing to take the risk, then you are a greater gambler than even I realized."

"'Tis no risk," he said mulishly. "We work together and he takes his orders from me."

"Do I, now?" Archibond's voice was silken. De Clare had not seen him approach, but I had noticed the shadow falling over the doorway as I framed my last remark. De Clare whirled, his expression dark.

Archibond entered, clearly intent upon placating him. "Are you listening to her? She's an artful woman, I will give her that. She is trying to divide us by sowing discord, de Clare. Surely you can see that."

His tone was reasonable, but the expression in his eyes was watchful. And with good reason. Quiet Dan and his companion stood at the ready. If they were prepared to abduct the prince and assault the brother of a peer, heaven knew they would not scruple to bludgeon an officer of the law if de Clare ordered it.

De Clare nodded slowly. "Aye. She is a canny bitch and no doubt about it. Her mother was another just as like." He smiled a mirthless smile. "All the same, she has a point."

Archibond's mouth tightened. "Does she indeed?"

"She does. Who is to say that you won't cut my throat for my trouble when you've got what you want?"

Archibond gave a patient sigh. "De Clare, we have been through this. We each have a role to play in our little drama. This is no time to give up the faith."

"Faith! That's a lot to ask of a man when his life is on the line," de Clare pointed out. "We could all of us hang for this if it goes awry. And even if it don't. Why should you see me right at the end and not come over greedy? You might have character flaws I had not anticipated."

"Character flaws? Good God, man. Do you hear yourself?" Archibond demanded. "We are conspiring to commit treason and you have decided that this is the time to worry about character flaws? Of course I have character flaws! I agreed to the cutting of a woman's throat for this endeavor. Does that not prove my commitment?"

"You agreed to it," de Clare allowed. "But 'twas Danny who did the slicing," he added with a jerk of the head towards Quiet Dan. "There's no blood on your hands, Mr. Archibond. Lily-white, they are."

Archibond shot me a look of purest loathing. "If you attempt to stir up trouble between us one more time, I will have you gagged, do you understand me?"

I looked to my uncle. "You notice he does not ask your permission?"

De Clare curled a lip. "She is my niece, Archibond. Touch a hair on that pretty head and I will give her your balls to keep in her pocket."

Archibond winced. "My dear de Clare, must we descend to crude threats of violence?"

"If an Irishman has learnt violence, he has learnt it at the hands of the English, so you will spare me the lectures, Inspector," de Clare told him in a tone of chill finality. "Now, she is a twisty little bitch, and there's no doubt about that, but she is right. I've no reason to trust you. And I shall be keeping an eye on you. Mind yourself."

With that he stalked out, leaving Archibond to give me a slow smile. "Well, it appears I have underestimated you, Miss Speedwell. I shall not make the same mistake again. Your uncle and I have a gentlemen's agreement and we will abide by it."

He turned, whistling a little tune as he left. The others followed, and I heard him whistling still as the door closed behind them. It was not until I heard the rasp of the key in the lock that I realized what he was whistling. "God Save the Queen."

I took a seat on the floor, resting my head against the wall.

"Thank God. I thought those chattering bastards would never leave," Stoker said.

I looked down to find him grinning at me. He moved slowly to stand.

"I thought you were dying," Eddy told him in obvious relief.

"It would take more than those Irish hooligans to kill a Templeton-Vane. I've been hurt worse by Tiberius just for taking his horse without permission. But they were enjoying it rather too much, and I have no fondness for pain. I thought if I pretended to swoon they might lose interest, and they did. They have no imagination," he added. "They only like administering a beating if they can hear you scream."

"That is quite enough," I told him, shuddering

Stoker rubbed his hands together briskly. "All right, then. I want to get out of this bloody place and put an end to this madness once and for all."

"Agreed," I said, more briskly than I felt. "What do you suggest?"

He stared at me. "Suggest?"

I gaped at him. "Really, Stoker. You are the only one of us to have the lay of the land, a crucial bit of intelligence if we are to effect an escape. And what else were you doing when you were lying around with all the feverish activity of a pygmy sloth? You might have been developing a scheme for our liberation."

"My scheme was to try to get out through the door and that did not end in success," he returned coolly. "The least you two might have done is develop another plan. I don't know what you think my life has been up until this point, Veronica, but until I met you, there was very little call for me to elude abductors and murderous thugs."

"Feathers," I said in some irritation at his sudden lackadaisical attitude. "You're just being difficult because you are in pain. I know for a fact that you were engaged in actual warfare."

"If you are referring to the Siege of Alexandria, might I remind you that I stood on the deck of a ship as it lobbed cannon fire ashore? I was not exactly vaulting through the rigging with a cutlass in my teeth," he replied.

"Still, this is child's play compared to that."

"It bloody well is not! I had the might of Her Majesty's Navy, which included some rather ferocious guns and a few thousand sailors at my side. Here I have—"

"You have me," I told him, lifting my chin.

He broke off and grinned again. "Well, I daresay the Egyptians would have been a damned sight more cowed by you than the navy's guns."

"And me," Eddy said, drawing himself up with visible effort at regaining his courage. I knew then what Stoker had been playing at. By refusing to take the mantle of leadership, he forced Eddy to put aside his fears and step into the breach. Necessity will always triumph over nerve in a person of character, I reflected.

Stoker gave him a look of quiet approval. "Very well, what do you propose?"

Eddy paced the room slowly, studying it from every angle. It was excruciating in its slowness, but he got there in the end, and when he pointed to the clerestory windows, I nearly gave a shout of triumph.

"The windows?" he said in a hesitant voice.

Stoker and I exchanged glances. "It is possible," Stoker said finally.

"Can you climb?" I asked Eddy.

He nodded. "Six years on Royal Navy ships. Although those were ropes, not stones," he added doubtfully.

"It is a beginning." Stoker's tone would brook no hesitation now. "Shall I go first?"

"It must be me," I insisted.

"I am a better climber," he objected.

I looked at the windows again, marking the slender dividers between them, and then eyed Stoker's broad torso. "Your shoulders will never fit through," I said.

"Dash, I hadn't thought of that," Eddy said, his moustaches turning down in dejection.

"That is a problem for later," Stoker said. "For now, we will worry only about how to get there."

I bent and unlaced the slippers on my feet, tying them securely together and slinging them about my neck. I looped up the modest knee-length skirts of my tunic, knotting them high on my thighs.

Stoker was making his own preparations, stripping off the shirt that strained across the breadth of his shoulders. I caught my breath at the sight of the bruises, dark violet and enormous, blossoming over his ribs. Here and there the skin was lacerated, the blood sticky and dark.

"This is going to hurt," I told him.

"No doubt," he said, and he smiled at me, a smile of such dazzling devotion and good humor that I vowed to myself whatever happened in the whole of my life I would never forget that moment when, in spite of everything—my insistence upon involving us in yet another perilous undertaking, my murderous relations—he threw himself into this adventure with the whole of his heart. And I vowed then that whatever became of that night's work, I would endeavor to meet him in the same spirit, headlong into what life threw at us.

He handed his soiled shirt to Eddy. "It isn't very nice, but there is a chill tonight and I daresay I will not feel the cold as acutely as you." It was the truth, but not the whole truth. None of us wanted to think about the fact that we would, if successful, shortly be traversing insalubrious streets of the capital with the future king looking as disreputable as if he had just committed a series of felonious assaults. At least Stoker's ragged shirt would conceal the prince's distinctive tattoos as well as keep him that tiny bit warmer.

Eddy did not hesitate. He, who was accustomed to the finest linen and cleanest garments, took the shirt streaked with blood and sweat and donned it gratefully.

Stoker put himself into position and braced his thigh, slapping it once as he looked at me. "Up you go."

I stepped on his leg and his hands came around my waist, vaulting me upwards until I could find a handhold. I pushed upwards with my feet, clinging to the stone like a limpet. I put my hand out and groped blindly for a place to grip.

"There is no handhold," I protested. Stoker had climbed up next to me, spreading his arms and legs across the corner to hold him fixed into place.

"There is me," he said. "Use me to get where you must."

And I did. Even now I cannot bear to think of the exquisite pain he must have endured as I climbed with his help, moving ever higher, perched precariously above the stone floor of the warehouse. Eddy watched us from below, eyes fixed upon our slow and steady ascent.

We progressed in this fashion, Stoker using himself as a human bulwark, until we neared the window and I no longer looked down, preferring instead to keep my eyes on the goal, the small clerestory window above us. Just then I realized our efforts would be for naught. A narrow beam ran from the wall just under the window, an ideal means of approach. But the window was set a good seven feet above the beam, tantalizingly, heartbreakingly out of reach.

"It is too high," I told him. "I cannot reach it."

"I have a plan for that," he assured me.

Stoker edged himself out onto the beam, his feet placed just so, his legs taut with effort. He stretched out a hand. "Come on, then."

"I haven't room to pass you," I said.

"I will take care of that," he promised. I edged out to meet him. I have a good head for heights—butterflying demands the occasional foray onto rocky outcropping or jungle cliff—but that was a singularly unnerving experience. We were perhaps thirty feet above the stone floor, our lives suspended by a beam no larger than the span of Stoker's palm. He knelt as I approached and braced his hands.

"Onto my back," he ordered. "It is the only way to reach the window."

I did not hesitate. I did as he instructed, climbing carefully onto his back, wrapping my legs about his waist and grasping his shoulders with both hands. He paused, letting my weight settle onto him, then began to rise, pushing through his thighs to lift us both into the air.

For just a moment, I had the most curious sensation of flight, like a butterfly raising itself upon the wind for the first time. I had no connection to the earth except through him; he was an extension of me, and my life was wholly in his hands.

I stretched out my arms and grasped the edge of the window. Stoker was standing, but I was still not quite able to shift myself all the way out of the aperture. Slowly, and with infinite, sweat-inducing care, I climbed him, moving my weight from his back to his shoulders, placing my hands on the window glass, pushing it open. I felt his palms beneath my feet, as solid as the earth below, and then he gave one fluid shove and I was up and out, through the window and perched on the roof.

I paused only long enough to catch my breath before maneuvering around to look back. Stoker was already halfway down again, swarming with the agility of a jungle creature. He positioned himself as before and instructed Eddy how to begin. Their progress was slow, achingly so, and every second that passed felt an eternity, perched as I was on the roof.

Eddy faltered halfway up and Stoker half pushed, half hauled him onto the beam. What followed was one of the most harrowing experiences of my life: the heir to the throne dangling a heart-stopping distance from the stone floor, dependent completely upon us for his safety. Stoker swore with a new vigor as Eddy climbed his back for the last part of the endeavor.

"I am sorry," Eddy muttered as he reached up to grasp my hands. I leaned back, bracing my feet on a handy ledge and pushing through my legs to pull him free. He came out with a pop like a champagne cork, bouncing onto the roof with a gasp of surprise.

Below, I heard a muted roar, and I peered through the window, expecting to see Stoker still on the beam, but it was empty. Entirely and heartbreakingly empty.

# CHAPTER

## 18

M y God!" Eddy exclaimed. "Stoker!"

I shushed him ruthlessly. "We must not draw attention to ourselves," I reminded him. "Look there!"

I spied Stoker's hands, wrapped around the beam. I peered into the gloom and saw him, hanging underneath, supported only by his bruised wrists. I said nothing else and I gripped Eddy's hands, warning him to silence. Stoker could afford no distraction.

Using his body weight, he began to swing, gathering momentum until he was able to fling himself onto the beam. It was a maneuver that would have come easily to one of the great apes, but I had not realized Stoker's talent for brachiation. He looked supple and athletic as a monkey as he swung—or at least he might have if it were not for the soreness of his ribs. At the last moment, one of them must have taken him by surprise, robbing him of breath and momentum just as he swung up onto the beam. He flew too far, launching over the beam and almost down again, catching himself by one arm and one leg. By sheer force of will he corrected his position, regaining the beam and lying flat, heaving hard. He looked up and saw me then and grinned, giving me a brisk nod.

"Thank God," Eddy whispered from behind my shoulder. He waved at Stoker. "I say," he called in an exaggerated whisper, "how precisely do you mean to get from there to here?"

"Give me one minute," I said to him. I motioned for Stoker to wait quietly, which he seemed perfectly content to do, as it provided him a chance to catch his breath and compose his nerve for the last ascent.

I turned to take stock of our surroundings as I tied on my slippers. The roof was rather flat, for which I was entirely grateful, and edged with a small parapet. A hasty survey revealed a cache of building supplies, among them a rope.

I handed one end to Eddy. "Make this fast around that chimney stack with one of your sailor's knots," I instructed. He seemed grateful to have a task and he moved swiftly to obey, whisking the rope through a series of intricate maneuvers until it was secure. Upon further direction, he made a series of simple knots along its length and I dropped it through the window, dangling it in front of Stoker. He grasped it and looked up, his expression thoughtful.

"I said earlier that we would solve the problem of my fitting through the window when the time presented itself. I believe that time is now," he observed. But I had already considered the predicament and developed a solution.

"Look away," I instructed both of them. I took up a broken brick, and—wrapping my hand in the edge of my tunic's overskirt—I used it to shatter the other pane of the clerestory. The dividing lead was rusted nearly through and a smart tap with the piece of brick brought it clattering down.

"If you would care to make a little more noise, I think perhaps the folk down in Gravesend haven't quite heard you," Stoker said politely.

"Save your breath to cool your porridge," I ordered. I was nearly giddy with relief that we had a plan, and one that would work.

But I exulted too soon. Perhaps the sound of breaking glass had alerted them, or perhaps it was simply very bad timing, but just then the door below bounced back on its hinges and Quiet Dan and his fellow villain appeared. The smaller wretch took out a pistol and fired wildly, the bullet chipping a bit of the beam near Stoker's foot. He did not tarry after that. He swarmed up the rope, swift as a gibbon, thrusting his torso through the window just as another shot went wide.

Without waiting for a third, I thrust my arms under Stoker's shoulders and heaved with all my might, eliciting a roar of pain from him. But he burst through the window like a devil out of hell, rolling me onto my back and landing flat atop me, knocking the breath from my lungs.

I lay, dazed, until he hauled me to my feet with one hand and Eddy with the other. We took to our heels, vaulting the stacks of bricks and racing towards the parapet. It was a foot or so from the edge of the warehouse roof to that of the adjoining house, and we launched ourselves over the parapet and across the gap at a dead run, never hesitating. We landed safely, but this roof was much more steeply pitched, and we each lost our footing more than once. I dared to glance down a single time but pulled back just as Quiet Dan fired his weapon, drawing screams from the people in the street. It looked to be a quarter of the city I seldom frequented, populated by seamen and beggars and ragpickers. There were lights glimmering below us, but a shifting mist from the direction of the river obscured the view, for which I was fervently grateful. If we could not easily see them, they could not easily see us.

But they could hear us, and my slippers thudded dully, revealing our whereabouts as we ran. Stoker was still in his stocking feet, silent but wheezing like an asthmatic donkey thanks to the damage to his rib, and Eddy was emitting little gasps of either excitement or pain, I could not be certain.

Far beneath us, I heard our pursuers and another voice—Archibond. He was shouting, arguing sharply, pointing out to Quiet Dan that shooting at me would hardly win him praise from my uncle. From that point on, the shots ceased. But still they marked our progress, down the street and across another alley. We paused to catch our breath, resting against a chimney stack as we heaved great lungfuls of sooty night air. Stoker dared a peek over the edge of the roof and immediately I heard the cry of one of the Irish, "There he is!"

We waited a moment more, and then came the unmistakable sound of boots, hobnailed and heavy, climbing the outside stairs attached to the building. It was the shorter of my uncle's henchmen.

Eddy stood bent double, his narrow chest heaving as he tried to catch his breath. He could not run much longer, I realized.

"Shall we make a stand?" I asked, squaring my shoulders and ready to stand back to back with my stalwart companions.

"God no," Stoker said fervently, grabbing my hand once more. He beckoned to Eddy and we scrambled and leapt to the next building, just managing to land in safety. Our pursuer was not so lucky. I saw the wild light in his eyes as his hands scrabbled at the empty air and he fell. A moment later, I heard a dull thud and a deep groan. Eddy would have paused, but Stoker urged him on, around the chimney stacks and through a narrow wooden door that led to a precariously pitched staircase. We descended the steps at a dead run, bursting through doors and out into the yard behind. For just a moment, Eddy's delay and the confusion we had created obscured our progress, and we used that chance to disappear down the alley behind, keeping to the shadows until we emerged into a wider street.

"Where the devil are we?" I muttered. Eddy looked around as if astonished that such a filthy and insalubrious place could exist in his capital.

"This cannot be right," he managed.

Stoker glanced up and grinned. "I know exactly where we are— and I know exactly where to go."

We were content to let him lead, myself as much for my own chance to rest as the opportunity for him to set the pace. Running over rooftops with a collection of injured ribs is no feat for the faint of heart, and Stoker had risen to the challenge like a warrior. But such a pace would only draw attention to us now, and it was far better to blend with the people in the street, at least as much as we were able with Stoker half-naked and bare of foot and Eddy dressed in a blood-stained shirt. I was the most reputable looking of our little band, and even I resembled an escapee from the nearest asylum. But we limped along, content for now to seek refuge in this unwholesome quarter.

It was, as I had imagined, a poor part of the city, where a pipe of opium might be had as cheaply as a woman's virtue or a length of silk. If there was silk to be had, I reflected. The women I saw were dressed in cheap trumpery, proud of their hard-won frills and meager joys. Their faces were hectic with gin and recklessness, but beneath it I saw the narrow, pinched look of those who have known poverty as a close companion for all of their lives. The men were much the same, leering into their glasses of beer and bragging to one another about their imagined triumphs.

Stoker guided me through with the air of a man staking a claim to his property, and I knew enough to let him. The rules were different here; a woman alone might easily be expected to be on the game, earning her keep by lifting her skirts, and there was little safety to be found. I chafed against the notion that I required protection, but I con-soled myself that I could best look after Stoker by keeping my head down and studying those around us in search of our pursuers. Eddy followed silently in our wake, and I had little doubt anyone would con-nect him with the dashing young man whose photograph graced the windows of so many establishments. We attracted a little comment—some ribald jests, for the oddity of our costumes—but Stoker's expression soon put an end to anything more. Strength was respected here, and the bruises on his face showed he was not a man to shy from a fight. Few would have been ready to challenge him, and those who might have been were so far into their cups that we avoided trouble by the expedient of walking hastily away.

After several dizzying turns and a labyrinthine half an hour that I could never have retraced on a map, we came to a small establishment on a corner, brilliant with light and loud with conversation and scraps of music. It seemed convivial, although marginally less so when the doors flung open and two women, each holding the other by the hair, tumbled into the street. Other patrons stumbled out after them, calling good-natured wagers on the fisticuffs that ensued.

A series of accusations were larded in between the blows, and it soon became clear that they were quarreling over a job and the fact that one of them had poached an opportunity from the other.

"I'll not get another place half as good, you gammy-handed bitch!" roared the smaller of the two. I worried for her slight figure, but she gave as good as she got, better even, because she emerged the victor, knocking her opponent out flat into the gutter. She accepted the accolades of the crowd, which roared its approval as coins exchanged hands and someone thrust a glass of gin into her hands.

She went to sip from it and caught sight of us. "Mr. Stoker!" she cried. "Fancy seeing you here!"

"Hullo, Elsie," he said, putting out his hand.

She shook it with pride as several of the assembled crowd gaped. "Would you look at that?" I heard one onlooker murmur. "Shaking hands with the likes of our Elsie. She's up amongst the toffs now, in't she?"

Elsie lifted her chin. "Keep civil tongues, the lot of you. It's good to see you, Mr. Stoker. You too, miss," she added, bobbing her head at me.

I recognized her then—a brief acquaintance from months before, encountered outside Karnak Hall. The last and only time I had met her she had been servicing a gentleman in an alley. She had been quite taken with Stoker, although our encounter with her had been fleeting at best.

"Elsie. It has been some time," I said politely. "I hope you are keeping well."

"Better than you by the look of it," she said. "Who's yer friend?"

Eddy's expression was frantic and I had the most dreadful premonition that he was about to blurt out his true identity.

"This is Eddy," I cut in, stepping neatly on his instep. "He is mute, so he will not be saying a word," I added. "Not a single word," I finished with a warning look at the prince.

He nodded vigorously.

Elsie smiled warmly. "Any friend of Mr. Stoker's is welcome here."

"That is very kind of you, Elsie. I am afraid we have run into a spot of trouble this evening," Stoker began.

She gave us a narrow-eyed gaze. "I know someone on the run when I see 'em. Let's get the lot of you inside and away from prying eyes."

Elsie shepherded us into the drinking establishment and whisked us to a table in a corner. The others filtered in, resuming places at tables and in front of the long bar. Our hostess raised her voice to the man tending the clientele. "Mind you close that door, Tom. We don't want strangers about."

He did as she bade him, and she settled us with all the concern of a mother hen for her chicks. "Now, then, my ducks. I will go and fetch us a bottle. You make yourselves comfortable. I shall be back in a tick."

She bustled off and I turned a curious eye to Stoker, aware that Eddy was watching us with avid attention.

"It is not what you think," Stoker began.

"I think that whilst I was in Madeira, you made it your business to find Elsie and make certain she suffered no ill effects from assisting us with our last investigation," I said calmly.

He blinked rapidly. "You realize in earlier days you'd have been burnt as a witch?"

"Oh, no doubt," I agreed. "Was it difficult to find her?"

He shrugged. "Not terribly. I started asking around Karnak Hall and eventually ran her to ground not far from here. I bought her a hot meal and we talked for a long time. I returned a few weeks later, and we fell into a sort of friendship, although she would never call it that."

He broke off as she returned, a skinny barmaid trotting in her wake with a fresh bottle of gin and four clean glasses. "Here we are, my dears. Have a tot. To your health," Elsie urged, lifting her glass.

The spirits were not unwelcome, I had to admit. Eddy drank with some enthusiasm, and I found the beverage reviving after our ordeal. I hoped as well it would have an anesthetizing effect upon Stoker's many injuries. Elsie surveyed him with a knowing eye.

"Been in a donnybrook, have you, Mr. Stoker? I know the signs. Well, you've no call to worry here. You're among friends," she said warmly. She nodded towards me. "You too, miss."

"Speedwell," I informed her. "Although you may call me Veronica."

She drew herself up so that the cluster of silk violets on her hat bobbed indignantly. "I should think *not*," she told me, her mouth in a firm line. "That would not be fitting. I will say 'Miss Veronica,' but that is as far as I will go."

"Very well," I told her, chastened. Eddy put out his hand to pour another measure of gin, grinning a little witlessly as he drank the second down in gulps.

"You'll want to slow yourself, lad," Elsie told him kindly. "That is no drink for gentlemen and I daresay you've no head for it."

Eddy blinked and clutched the empty glass to his chest, weaving a little in his chair. He had drunk too quickly and the misadventures we had suffered were beginning to take their toll. When I turned to Elsie, I saw Eddy's hand snake out for the bottle and I moved to slap it away, but Stoker spoke up.

"Eddy has had a long and tiring day, Veronica," he reminded me obliquely. "Perhaps it is better for everyone if he drinks himself to sleep."

Eddy nodded vigorously and poured another measure of gin, nursing it as tenderly as if it were a newborn babe. I shrugged. Perhaps Stoker was right. If Eddy drank himself to the point of unconsciousness, it would at least remove the possibility of him revealing his identity in public.

I turned to Elsie. "Stoker tells me that the pair of you have been meeting since last spring."

She pinked with pleasure. "That we have, miss. He's a good man."

"He is a good man who wouldn't mind a visit upstairs," Stoker said, rising from his seat. Elsie directed him to the nearest water closet with careful instructions on the vagaries of the temperamental plumbing. When he had gone, she settled back, regarding him with a fond leer.

"I do love to watch him go," she said, keeping a practiced eye upon his backside until he was up the stairs. She looked to Eddy, who was slumped in his chair, his fingers slack around his glass, then turned back to me. "You must know that I never saw Mr. Stoker in a professional sense," she said, suddenly earnest. "He has never laid a finger on me."

"I know."

She nodded and refilled my glass. "So long as we're clear on that. He's a good lad, innocent as a lamb, and I'd not have him any other way."

I coughed, choking a little on my gin and more on her assessment of his character.

"You think him innocent?"

She widened her eyes. "Lord love you, miss. If there's one thing I know, it's men. And that one is good as gold. He'd never lift a hand against a woman and he would never think the worst of one. Puts us on a pedestal, he does."

I considered this and decided she was more correct in her assessment than otherwise.

She went on. "He's made me an allowance, you know. 'Tis anonymous and I'm not meant to know the identity of my benefactor, but he's not half so clever as he thinks. He sends it through a temperance worker and she brings it, twenty shillings, every time. He wants to make certain I have money enough for a bed and a hot meal, bless him."

"He could find you employment," I pointed out. "Better work than what you have."

She blinked. "I don't mind my work, miss. I make silk flowers when I can get the materials. I made these," she added, touching a fingertip to her little bouquet of silk violets. Each one was elegantly shaped with a tiny golden bead at the heart and a leaf of green velvet. The whole affair was bound in ribbon of green and violet silk and added a touch of elegance to her black hat.

"Very pretty," I told her truthfully. "Mightn't you get work with a milliner?"

She flapped a hand. "No, miss. That's for girls, and I am no spring chicken. I make my flowers the old-fashioned way, my gran taught me. But the fashion nowadays is for great bloody birds, and I'll not stuff a *bird* to put on my head. It's unnatural, that is," she said vehemently.

I had to agree. The fashion for befeathered millinery including heads was a ghoulish one.

She went on. "No, miss. This suits me well enough. I make flowers for some of the less expensive suppliers when my hands are nimble. When the wind is out of the east, they swell up like Cumberland sausages, they do, and it's all I can do to button my boots." She thrust out her hands and I saw they were swollen across the knuckles, marked with rheumatism, one of the innumerable disadvantages of the life of the poor—sketchy nutrition, damp beds, and chilly nights spent in fogbound streets.

"That's when I find myself a fellow for the evening and make a little coin that way," she said, as if it were as natural as anything.

Stoker returned, subsiding heavily into his seat as Elsie signaled for another bottle. We sipped the vile stuff as if it were vintage champagne. It would never do to insult our hostess, and Stoker's innate courtesy was the stuff of legend.

He glanced down at her hands and touched one knuckle lightly with a fingertip. "Rheumatism. November is coming along, Elsie. You need to sleep inside."

She bristled. "That don't always happen, Mr. Stoker," she told him, her mouth slightly mulish.

"What about the allowance from the temperance worker you told me about?" he asked gently. Elsie and I exchanged quick glances, neither of us willing to reveal to Stoker that his little fiction had been exposed. (It has long been my experience that men are confused and sometimes upset by the truth. It is a kindness to let them go on believing what they like in such circumstances.)

"Sometimes I helps a few of the other girls out," she told him, raising her chin. "Long Bet needed new boots last week, and Mary Jane lacked a few shillings to renting her own room. She's got a snug little place of her own, just around the corner," she added. The dreams in this part of the city were as small and pinched as the faces. Four walls to call one's own. A hot meal, a pair of shoes with sound soles.

I thought of the little Gothic temple that Lord Rosemorran had given over to me to use as my own, a bolt-hole where I was snug and safe. I had meals cooked in his kitchens, a generous wage. Elsie would be mistaken by many for a drab, and I might be taken often for a lady, but neither of these was entirely the truth. We were, both of us, women who worked, making our own way in the world. I had expertise and knowledge, but my greatest advantage had been the sheer luck of being born into a gentler class. I might fall a little, but Elsie, whatever she did, could never climb.

Stoker went on, careful not to scold. "Where do you sleep when you've given your coin away?"

She shrugged one bony shoulder. "The corner of a yard, sometimes. A quiet doorway."

"Sleeping rough is dangerous," Stoker told her. "Particularly now."

He did not say the fiend's name; there was no need. Everyone in London knew of the murderous devil who stalked Whitechapel, exercising his brutality upon the women who lived there.

Elsie gave him a fond look and patted his hand. "Lord love you, I can take care of myself, Mr. Stoker. Don't you worry."

But a line had etched itself between his brows, and I knew he would think of Elsie, stubborn, incorrigible, generous Elsie, sharing her meager bounty with her friends.

She rose suddenly. "Come on, then, ducks. You cannot go haring about the city dressed as you are. I've spoken to a few of my friends. We've had a whip-round to see the lot of you dressed decently and a bite to eat."

She led the way upstairs and showed us into her accommodation for the night—a small room fitted with a narrow bed and a washstand with a cracked bowl. Eddy managed the stairs under Stoker's ungentle coaxing and flopped onto the bed.

Elsie gave him a fond look. "He's a pretty sort of lad, isn't he? I imagine he has a mother what loves him dearly. Just look at those moustaches!" She shook her head. "But he cannot hold his drink and that's God's own truth."

He burbled out a snore just then, and Elsie left to find us clothes while Stoker and I took turns washing with a pitcher of cold water, shivering but happy to be at least marginally cleaner than we were. I stripped off the robes of Boadicea at last as Stoker peeled away the shirt he had lent Eddy, the fine cotton stiff and crackling with dried blood.

Elsie appeared, her arms full of garments, and clucked over Stoker's injured flesh. "I brought something for those bruises. Seen it often enough with the sailors who fall to brawling," she added. She produced strips of bandages and a bottle of ferociously pungent liniment. "This will help." Without waiting for permission, she bent to her task, pouring a palmful of liniment into her hand and slapping it onto his skin.

He howled in protest, but she would not let him squirm away, holding him firmly until the nasty stuff had penetrated his flesh. "Now, isn't that just like a man?" she demanded. "Kicking up such a fuss over a little good horse liniment. I made less noise when I was in labor."

"You have children?" I asked as I shook out the petticoats she had brought for me.

"Aye, miss. A pair of them. Molly is in service with a wine merchant and Jemmy is a deckhand on one of them great ships with Cunard," she said with unmistakable pride.

"Do you see them often?" I stepped into the petticoats and tied them firmly about my waist.

"Heavens no, miss. That would never do," she said with no trace of regret. "They're my flesh and blood and I love them, but I'll not have them living a life like mine. They need better, and if I catch them in this part of the city, I'd tan them properly." I did not doubt it. Most mothers in her situation were content to let their children follow in their footsteps, their future bound by the limitations of poverty and lack of imagination. But Elsie had glimpsed a bigger world, and I marveled that she had managed to launch her children into it.

She bossed Stoker into a set of borrowed clothes, down to the boots. "Got those off Tom from the bar," she said proudly. "He reckons he can sell them to you for three shillings."

Stoker handed her Tiberius' empty notecase, a fine affair of bottle green leather set in silver. "It hasn't a tuppence in it, but I can promise Tom will get far more than three shillings in pawn for it."

She hurried away to make the trade whilst Stoker wrestled Eddy into a moderately clean shirt of striped cotton, tying a jaunty scarf around his neck for warmth. He dropped the slumbering prince back onto the bed as Elsie returned several minutes later with word that Tom had accepted the barter, and just then another figure appeared, a young woman, blond, with her hair piled high in an attempt at glamour.

"This is my friend," Elsie said, "Mary Jane."

The girl thrust out her hand. "I prefer Marie Jeanette," she said with a touch of reproof. Elsie gave her a light push.

"You're Mary Jane Kelly, and don't you go putting on airs, my love," she said in an indulgent voice.

The girl thrust a dress at me. "Elsie said as you needed something to wear. It's my second best," she told me.

"That is very kind of you," I began, but she waved me off.

"Any friend of Elsie's. If it weren't for her, I wouldn't have my room," she said proudly. The dress she had brought was rather too short and in a virulent green hue found only in the more lavish jungles. But it was a far sight better than anything I could call my own at the moment, and I thanked her again.

Mary Jane busied herself buttoning me up the back as Elsie plucked the violet-strewn hat from her own head and pinned it firmly into place. "There you are, miss. Proper dressed you are now, although I cannot like those boots with that dress. You ought to have had black kid."

I peeped down at the audacious scarlet boots she had found for me. "Never mind. I am very grateful to you, Elsie. And you, Mary Jane. You must let us pay for the clothes."

She waved me off. "Never you mind, miss. We were happy to do it, all of us."

I was deeply touched. The people who made their living in Whitechapel had little enough, but they shared it willingly. It was the sort of place where tea leaves once brewed would be gladly handed to a friend for a second go. I knew better than to insult her by speaking again of money, but I gave Stoker a significant look and he nodded almost imperceptibly. He understood, as did I, that nothing makes a person feel so rich as the ability to give to another, and to rob Elsie of her generosity would be no kindness. In time, Stoker would ensure Elsie received some little sum more and she would share her bounty, we had no doubt. Clothes were a commodity in that quarter and might be sold or pawned for the price of a meal or a bed. To have been given such riches was a testament to how generous Elsie had been with her friends in their own times of need.

But the clothes were the least of what we were given that night. Elsie sent a boy to the cookshop in the next street and he brought back two covered plates, still steaming.

"I got none for your man Ed," she said, nodding in satisfaction as she presented the plates, a delectable smell wafting from the thick gravy bubbling through vents in crusts of golden pastry. "He'll not want food for a while, I'm thinking, but the pair of you should eat up now."

Stoker stuck a fork into the pastry, sending a river of rich gravy spilling onto the plate.

"Eel pie," he said happily, falling on the food with gusto.

I ate mine almost as swiftly—as much from hunger as from the fear that Stoker would help himself to it if I did not. We had a little bowl for spitting out the bones, and as we ate, Elsie bustled about, neatly folding our own clothes into a basket.

"Mind you," she fussed, "I would rather have had the chance to wash them properly, but I think that tunic of yours is fit for nothing but the rag basket," she warned me.

"I cannot think of when I would possibly have need of it," I assured her. "Keep them to sell to the ragpicker." The items were hired and Tiberius had given surety for them, but they were little better than remnants at this point and the tiara was rolling around somewhere in the darkness of the Club de l'Étoile. At least I would be able to return the armillae, I reflected grimly.

Elsie clucked and fretted, as fastidious as a spinster as we mopped up the last of the eel gravy with the bread she had brought. The meal was filling and hot, and that was all that may be said in its favor. In spite of its delicious aroma, the eel pie was greasy and even the bread was unsavory, with a strange, gritty quality.

"That's the plaster of Paris," Elsie said when I remarked upon it, pronouncing it "Paree."

"Plaster?" I asked.

"The bakers add it to the flour to make it stretch further," she said with a matter-of-factness that told me she expected nothing better.

"They adulterate the bread?"

"And the milk and the meat and the preserves," Stoker put in. "There's not a pail of milk between here and Guernsey that doesn't have chalk mixed in."

"Lord only knows how I managed to keep my little ones alive on it," Elsie agreed.

"Unconscionable," I said firmly, making a note to send her a loaf of the good white bread always at our table in Marylebone. There were many things I took for granted, living in an earl's household. We ate few meals with his lordship, but his kitchens provided our food, and it was beneath Cook's dignity to send out anything less than first-rate, even to his lordship's employees.

Elsie shrugged. "'Tis the way it has always been, miss. No need to get into a bother over it. Now, Mr. Stoker, you eat up the last of that pie and I will take you down the back stairs."

Stoker shoved the last bite of pie into his mouth and got to his feet. The borrowed boots were clearly too small and painful, but at least he no longer had to traverse London in his stocking feet. He roused Eddy by the expedient of an application of cold water to his face.

Eddy came to with a start, blinking furiously, but he caught sight of Elsie and smothered his protests in the nick of time, contenting himself with a scowl until he noticed his clean shirt. He smoothed it appreciatively and Elsie gave him a smile.

"You're welcome, lad. That stripe suits you, it does."

He inclined his head with all the graciousness his breeding had instilled. Elsie hurried us down a narrow staircase clearly meant for the maidservants. A single guttering candle illuminated the dingy enclosed space, and we groped our way carefully down to the bottom, stopping at a small door. Elsie turned to Stoker. She reached beneath her skirts and drew out a long, slender blade. "You'll want a weapon, Mr. Stoker," she said flatly.

He shook his head. "Keep it. If you insist on sleeping rough, you will need some means to defend yourself."

"Lord love you, sir, I've got one better," she said with a grin, producing a wicked-looking knife with sharp serrations. She tucked it away again and gestured.

"Now, this passage leads to the yard. Cross it and in the back wall you will see a door opening onto Flower and Dean Street. Close the door firmly behind you, mind, and turn hard to the left to take you to Brick Lane. Follow that towards the river to Whitechapel High Street.

There will be plenty of folk still about so you shouldn't attract much attention, but keep to the shadows just the same."

We promised we would and with many thanks on our side and many protestations of embarrassment on hers, we were away, moving into the darkness. We followed her instructions, crossing the yard of the gin palace and finding the little door set into the wall. We slipped through it, into the street. It was a small thoroughfare, scarcely more than an alley, connecting two larger roads, and here and there it was pierced with a pool of warm yellow light from a lamppost. The lamps flickered and I saw that a soft, veiling mist was rising off the river on the cooling night air. It swirled and thickened as we walked, muffling some noises and bringing others startlingly close.

Wordlessly, I joined hands with Stoker and Eddy. It was an eerie walk through the London streets that night, moving from shadow into golden light and back again, the fog rolling in, obscuring faces and figures of those we passed. The changing weather had driven some folk inside. It was quieter than I would have expected, with footsteps sounding only occasionally near us. Ours clipped sharply against the pavement, Stoker's reassuring and solid next to my quicker, lighter step, Eddy's almost silent in his evening shoes. I began to identify those who passed us by the sound of their stride. The hesitant, birdlike noises belonged to an old woman, bent with age and rheumatism, while the slow and ponderous stride that came after was a hefty fellow, well into his cups but not entirely drunk, stepping with the exaggerated care of one who is certain only of his uncertainty.

They walked by, the mist parting only long enough for us to glimpse a snippet of a lined face or a portly figure, and we were alone again in the darkness, ears pricked like a pointer's, straining for any sound of pursuers.

We made another turn but must have got it wrong, for instead of the broad main road of Whitechapel High Street, we found ourselves in a narrow and evil-looking alley, its broken curbstones and filthy gutters barely visible in the light of the single streetlamp.

"Stoker," I began. I did not have to finish.

"I know. We had better retrace our footsteps," he said. His tone was one of thorough annoyance, but I knew better than to imagine it was with me. "I wasn't paying careful enough attention," he told me. "These bloody boots are strangling my feet. Give me a minute."

He stepped to the side, bending double to tug them from his feet. He withdrew the knife that Elsie had given him, turning the blade to the boots to slash the insteps. Eddy chose that moment to be lavishly sick in the gutter, heaving out the remainder of the cheap gin he had imbibed. I moved a little distance away and waited, standing alone under the light of the guttering streetlamp.

I felt his presence before I saw him, just another shadow in the darkness. But he detached himself from the gloom, moving towards me, a deeper blackness than the nothingness behind him. His height was unremarkable, his coat black as a raven's wing. His hat was pulled low over his features and a muffler wound tightly about the lower half of his face concealed the rest. He moved with purpose, coming closer as I turned to see him.

I realized how it must look—a lone female figure, standing under a streetlamp in that particular quarter. I wore a conspicuous dress, cut low and edged in cheap lace, fashioned to draw the eye. My face still bore traces of paint from the costume ball, and the hat upon my head was gaudy with violets meant also to draw the eye.

For many years I have thought of that moment. I have been menaced countless times, faced death upon more occasions than I care to number. But never in the whole of my life have I felt a presence as predatory as that one. He made no motion to harm me; said nothing; threatened nothing. I did not even sense violence in him; that was not what made my marrow cold. I sensed only anticipation, rising excitement in the quickening of his step, the sharp intake of breath.

Just then, Stoker straightened from behind me. "There, that ought to take care of the bloody things," he said, his voice ringing through the mist. Eddy joined us, wiping his mouth on the back of his hand.

"I do apologize," he said, sounding haggard. "I think perhaps that bottle of spirits may not have been of the highest quality."

The shadowy man did not slacken his progress. He merely changed his course, turning swiftly aside, but still coming so near to me that his hand brushed my skirts as he passed. And as his glove lingered on the tawdry fabric, there was a breath, a single slow, moaning exhalation that ruffled the hair at my cheek.

And then he was gone, moving into the shadows. Stoker and Eddy had not even noticed him passing, so subtle and quiet were his movements. But I would never forget him for as long as I lived, and I knew that evil had touched me that night.

His boots no longer a problem and Eddy recovered, Stoker applied himself with a clear head to the issue of navigation and soon had us on the correct course. He shepherded us through the dark streets until we reached Whitechapel High Street and the long road towards home.

# CHAPTER

# 19

We moved slowly, as much from the blanketing fog as from Stoker's injuries and Eddy's inebriated fatigue. Now that the excitement of the flight had ebbed, stiffness had settled into our bones. Our footsteps flushed a few pairs of lovers trysting in alleyways and the occasional transient settled for the night under a bit of accommodating shrubbery. More than one bobby gave us a penetrating glance, but no one stopped us, and as we crossed by, the bells of the Church of the Immaculate Conception in Mayfair struck the hour of four in the morning.

"I quite forgot," Eddy said sleepily, "where are we bound?"

"My brother's house," Stoker told him.

"Oh, indeed?" Eddy blinked to wakefulness. "And why are we going there? Is Lord Templeton-Vane expecting us?"

"Not that brother," he said shortly.

He led us to a peaceful square a few streets from Tiberius' address, where the houses were a little more modest but no less expensive. Keeping to the shadows, we slipped down the area stairs to the small, discreet entrance for domestic endeavors, waiting whilst Stoker rapped softly at the door. After a long moment, a butler appeared, dressing gown rigidly tied and nightcap so tidy I wondered if he slept standing up. He opened the door with a scowl, but at the sight of Stoker, he reared back in astonishment.

"Mr. Stoker! Good evening, sir," he said with a bow from the neck. "Is everything quite all right?"

"It will be, Dearsley. Would you please rouse Sir Rupert and let him know I am here."

"Certainly, sir, but would you and your party not be more comfortable in the drawing room?" he asked.

A small smile played about Stoker's lips. "I rather think a bit of discretion is in order," he said in a conspiratorial whisper.

Dearsley bowed again. "As you wish, sir. I will be but a moment. May I offer you or your companions refreshment?" He eyed Eddy, who was weaving conspicuously on his feet. "Perhaps a little strong black coffee?"

"After you've wakened my brother," Stoker told him.

"Very good." Dearsley hurried away and Stoker and I went through to the kitchen, settling Eddy on a chair, where he promptly nodded off again.

It was only a moment or two later before the master of the house appeared, Dearsley close behind.

"Stoker, what the devil—oh, I do say, pardon me, Miss Speedwell. I did not see you there." In contrast to his butler, Rupert looked decidedly askew, his dressing gown obviously tied in some haste and his silvering chestnut hair disordered. He smoothed it down as he spoke, and tugged his dressing gown closed over his bare shins, but not before I noticed that he—like Tiberius and Stoker—had rather fine legs.

"Good evening, Sir Rupert—or should I say good morning?" I asked pleasantly.

He eyed my costume with its rather exuberant display of bosom and immediately jerked his gaze away, blushing furiously. "Stoker, I do hope you have an excellent reason for keeping Miss Speedwell out and about at such an hour," he said.

Stoker's only reply was to point to Eddy, slumped and slumbering in his chair. Sir Rupert looked once, then gave a start, peering closely at the sleeping prince.

"Is that—"

"Yes," Stoker told him.

Rupert sniffed deeply. "Has he been—"

"Yes, to excess, but it was entirely understandable under the circumstances," I assured him.

Sir Rupert's expression was pained. He gestured for Dearsley to close the kitchen door and set to making the coffee before turning once more to us. "I do not mean to be insulting, you understand, but I do hope you will forgive the indelicacy of the question: did you, by any chance, abduct this young person?"

"We did not," Stoker assured him.

"Although he *was* abducted," I pointed out. "But not by us."

"We liberated him," Stoker added.

"It was the least we could do," I put in. "He was at least partially abducted because of us."

"I don't know about that," Stoker argued. "I think they would have taken him if we hadn't been there, although it certainly played perfectly into their scheme to kidnap us together."

"Oh yes," I agreed as Rupert pinched the bridge of his nose.

"Would you care to start at the beginning?" he encouraged.

"Certainly," Stoker said. By unspoken agreement, we all fell silent until Dearsley finished brewing the coffee. He set the pot and various impedimenta on the table and discreetly withdrew, leaving us to convene our council of war, as it were. I played mother, pouring out a steaming cup for the brothers and another for Eddy, putting it to the side to cool just a little as he rested.

"Nothing to eat?" Stoker asked his brother hopefully.

Sir Rupert spread his hands. "There are bananas on that sideboard, but otherwise, I am afraid I cannot help you. I do not know where the key to the larder is kept."

I was not surprised; few gentlemen even knew where their kitchens were. Stoker had just opened his mouth—no doubt to offer to pick the larder lock—when the kitchen door opened and a tall, statuesque figure appeared. Her dressing gown was exceptionally fine violet silk and her nightcap was Belgian lace and neatly tied under her chin, and she carried herself with as much dignity as if she were wearing Court dress.

"Stoker!" she exclaimed in genuine pleasure. She came forwards, extending her hands, and Stoker jumped to his feet.

"Hullo, Lavinia. I am sorry to have woken the household," he said. She put up her cheek to be kissed and he obliged.

"Think nothing of it, dear boy. We don't see half enough of you," she assured him in a low and musical voice. She caught sight of me then and smiled. "You must be Miss Speedwell. Tiberius has spoken of you with the highest admiration," she told me.

"That's very kind of you, Lady Templeton-Vane," I said.

She glanced around the table. "I see Dearsley has managed coffee, but there ought to be food, and if I know Stoker, it ought to be sweet." She drew a key from her pocket and opened the larder, carrying out a large fruitcake, cheese, a small cold ham, and some chutney. She made quick work of carving the ham and putting out plates. "There now, eat up. And perhaps when you are finished you will explain why the future King of England is intoxicated in my kitchen," she finished in the same pleasant tone.

Rupert sighed. "I suppose it is not worth asking you to go back to bed and pretend you haven't seen him?"

"It is not," she acknowledged. "Stoker, I presume there is a story to tell?"

"There is, Lavinia." With admirable clarity he apprised his brother and sister-in-law of the situation, omitting only my identity as the semi-legitimate daughter of the Prince of Wales.

"You say your uncle is involved?" Sir Rupert asked. As a party to our first encounter with de Clare, Rupert already knew my secret, but as a barrister, he would consider himself bound to secrecy, and the shrewd look he gave me as he listened to Stoker's tale conveyed that he understood the purpose of the abduction plot perfectly.

"He is," I confirmed. "Has there been any word of the prince's disappearance?"

Lady Templeton-Vane shook her head, setting her lace ruffles to waving. "Nothing in the newspapers and I daresay we would have heard a whisper or two."

"It has only been twenty-four hours since he was taken from Madame Aurore's establishment," Rupert pointed out. "It may well be that his sister has been thorough enough in concocting a story that no one at Balmoral has missed him."

"Then we must return him to Balmoral before they do," she said serenely.

Sir Rupert goggled at her. "I beg your pardon, Lavinia." It was not a question. Sir Rupert was clearly and completely appalled.

But his wife of twenty years was unruffled. "Rupert, it is quite simple. The prince is here, in our kitchen. What is easier than smuggling him out into the mews into our carriage and taking him to the station? He would be conspicuous in our company in those tradesman's clothes," she went on, "but Lucius left several suits of clothes in his wardrobe before he went off to Cambridge and I daresay something of his will come near enough to fitting the prince."

"I am not concerned with the sartorial practicalities," Sir Rupert began.

"You ought to be," Lavinia Templeton-Vane said calmly. "Stoker, do have another piece of fruitcake. I know how much you like this receipt. Grated apple is the secret."

Sir Rupert cleared his throat. "My dear—"

"Oh, don't 'my dear' me!" his wife erupted, startling us all. "I am always hearing from you and Tiberius about the grand adventures Stoker and Miss Speedwell are getting up to. Did it never occur to you that I might like a grand adventure myself?" she challenged, lifting her chin.

Sir Rupert opened his mouth, then closed it again, wordlessly.

Lady Templeton-Vane went on, putting an imploring hand to her husband's sleeve. "We are not too old for an escapade, Rip," she said gently. "I will order Dearsley to pack a hamper while we dress. We will give His Royal Highness plenty of coffee and food and a proper suit of clothes, and then we will take him to the station and board the first train for Scotland."

"And what then?" Sir Rupert asked in a dazed tone.

She shrugged. "We have hours on the train with the prince to concoct a reasonable story in the event he has been missed. If there is any storm at all, it will be a tempest in a teacup if he returns in the company of a sober middle-aged couple of respectable reputation. You are one of the nation's most distinguished barristers, Rupert, and I am the patroness of seven charities. No one would believe the prince has been carrying on in a scandalous fashion if he has been in our company."

"She does have a point," Stoker put in. "Several of them, actually."

"I am well aware," Rupert replied in a mild tone. "I have long said the only person who has ever bested me in an argument is my wife. She would have made a far better barrister than I."

"Do not talk about her as if she were not here," his wife instructed, smiling as she poured another cup of coffee for Stoker. She gave me a glance. "I do wonder, Miss Speedwell, if that frock is entirely to your taste?"

"It is not," I assured her.

"Then we will find you something more suitable as well," she promised.

"I think it best if we give them the loan of the carriage instead," Sir Rupert put in. "It will have them to Marylebone and back by the time we have need of it, and at least we will spare ourselves the possibility of them being arrested for vagrancy from wandering the streets at this hour."

To my surprise, Stoker agreed, and Rupert sent Dearsley to rouse the coachman. It was some minutes until the carriage was standing ready in the mews, and we passed the time in finishing the impromptu meal and exchanging pleasantries. Lady Templeton-Vane trod a fine line between her natural curiosity and her innate courtesy, asking questions of me but taking great care not to pry.

When the soft knock came at the kitchen door to signal the carriage's arrival, she put out her hand to me. "It has been a very great pleasure to meet you, my dear. I hope you will come for tea so that we may get better acquainted."

"I would like that," I told her and was rather surprised to find that I meant it.

Stoker kissed her soundly on the cheek as I shook hands with Sir Rupert. "Miss Speedwell, it is, as ever, a most interesting encounter."

I grinned. "I do hope, Sir Rupert, that someday we will meet when we are not obliged to depend upon you for a service."

"Do not distress yourself, Miss Speedwell," his wife assured me. "He is never happier than when he is of use."

They exchanged a smile of long familiarity and fell to talking with Stoker as I went to wake Eddy. I touched him gently on the shoulder and he roused himself with a start. I handed him the coffee and explained where he was and what would happen next.

"So the Templeton-Vanes will see you safely back to Balmoral and that should be an end of the matter," I told him.

"And Archibond?" he demanded.

I shrugged. "Without either of us in his power, there is precious little he can do. No doubt as soon as we were lost to him, he took to his heels. A man like that would never leave his survival to chance. I have every confidence that he had an escape plan in place, and that de Clare has scuttled back to his hole in Ireland or perhaps even abroad this time. Still, to make certain their misdeeds are known to the authorities, Stoker and I will explain everything to Sir Hugo Montgomerie. If either ever sets foot in this country, or attempts to use the diamond star against you, he will be held accountable, Your Royal Highness," I promised.

His moustaches drooped a little. "You were calling me Eddy, but I suppose the time for that is past."

"It is."

He took my hand in his. "I do not know if we will meet again, Veronica. Papa—" He broke off, struggling for words.

"Your papa mightn't like it," I finished for him. "I have to go now, Eddy. The carriage is here."

He walked with us as far as the door, holding my hand the whole while. As I moved away, he suddenly clasped me to him, putting his long arms around me and holding me close, his head ducked against my neck. I hesitated, then returned his embrace for a fierce moment. He was spoilt and sometimes silly, thoughtless and young for his age. But there was a sweetness to him, a childlike candor that touched me, and I realized it might be the only time in the whole of my life that I would have the chance to hold a younger brother in my arms.

After a long minute, I moved away. I stepped into the carriage and heard Stoker slam the door behind us, knocking once upon the roof. The wheels turned slowly, rolling us away from the quiet mews and the people we left behind. I did not look back.

# CHAPTER

## 20

It was nearly dawn by the time we reached Lord Rosemorran's estate at Bishop's Folly. We had passed exhaustion many hours back, but we took precautions, aware that there was a slender chance that de Clare and Archibond had anticipated our returning home. We left the carriage in the next street and walked around the estate, entering by means of a hidden door in the far side of the walled property.

No sooner had we set foot on the grounds than the dogs rushed us, Huxley and Bet and Nut flinging themselves at us in an ecstasy of welcome. Stoker fell to his knees from a particularly ill-placed thrust of Bet's head, and I occupied myself with scratching Huxley and Nut lavishly about the ears.

"They would have alerted anyone to strangers on the premises," I told Stoker, and he, too weary to speak, merely nodded. I helped him to his feet and, his arm draped over my shoulders, guided him to my little Gothic chapel. I drew off the borrowed boots, now falling to tatters, but did not help him undress further. He had fallen backwards onto the bed as soon as I began to tug and was completely asleep by the time the second boot hit the floor. The dogs arranged themselves around him protectively, and I covered him with a quilt pieced together from bits of clerical vestments. I pulled off my borrowed feathers—dress, hat, and boots—and did not bother with the rest, merely wrapping myself in my dressing gown and curling into a question mark on the little red sofa that had once graced an archbishop's palace. It was chilly in the chapel, and my last thought was how nice it would be to light a fire . . .

I awoke to sunlight streaming over my face, the night's fog burned away in a blaze of autumnal gold. I looked at once to the bed. Stoker was sitting up, leaving traces of blood and soot on the sheets along with copious amounts of dog hair.

"You are up early," I said cheerfully.

He gave me a sour look. "If you dare to be merry, I will filet you like a haddock. I had a ghastly night's sleep and I feel like something death might have forgotten."

"You will end up with forty kinds of blood poisoning if we don't attend to those wounds," I told him. "Let me just—"

"I am off to have a wash," he said shortly. "I can manage."

He was gone, taking the dogs with him, before I could form a suitable reply.

I made a lengthy and thorough toilette, scrubbing off every vestige of the past few days and dressing myself in my favorite ensemble, my hunting costume. Designed for chasing butterflies, it had proven eminently suitable for our work as well. It consisted of a fitted white shirtwaist buttoned under a waistcoat of black and violet tweed. A narrow tweed skirt concealed slim trousers and long boots, laced to the knee. Topping it all was a jacket, cut severely but cleverly so that there was no extra fabric but plenty of range of movement. The skirt had an arrangement of buttons enabling it to be tucked out of the way in any number of configurations. I slid a handful of minuten—the tiny headless pins used by lepidopterists to secure their prey—into my cuffs, and tucked my favorite knife into my boot. I had no intention of being caught unawares again, I reflected grimly.

Dressed and clean, I presented myself at Lady Wellie's rooms to find Lord Rosemorran just emerging. He wore his usual expression of vague benignity as he stopped to speak.

"How is Lady Wellie?" I asked.

"No appreciable change. She drifts in and out of consciousness, but seems comfortable."

"I am glad to know she is no worse," I told him.

He blinked as though just seeing me properly. "Were you and Stoker absent? I went to speak to you yesterday, but you were not in the Belvedere."

"I apologize, my lord. We were assessing a possible acquisition for the collection," I lied smoothly.

"Ah, no matter. I can't remember now what I wanted. Something to do with a delivery, I think."

"I am sure it will come to you," I said. I thought of de Clare and Archibond. It was narrowly possible that they might attempt to gain entry to the estate, and with the earl's children about, it was an eventuality that chilled me to the marrow. But I saw no need to raise fears where they might be unfounded, so I temporized. "It occurred to me, my lord, to ask about security arrangements. The collection is rather valuable, after all, and there ought to be some protection for it."

His brows rose again. "My dear, did you not know? There is always a guard about the place. Two of the gardeners, one of the drivers, and the underbutler are all former members of the Yard on secondment for Aunt Wellie's security."

I blinked at him. "Are you quite serious?"

"They take it in turn to patrol the property at night. It was Aunt Wellie's idea. She thought it might be a good notion to have a few sturdy lads about the place."

"How long ago did she bring them into the household?" I asked, suddenly suspicious.

The earl tipped his head, calculating. "Heavens, when was it? Right about the time of the Jubilee, I should think. When you and Stoker came to live here."

I said nothing for a long moment. *That impossible old woman,* I thought. She had lived decades in the shadow of danger and never set a watch for her own protection. It was not until I had come to live at Bishop's Folly that she had ordered a guard. I thought of how many times Stoker and I had slipped out, nodding towards a vigilant gardener or making use of a driver, certain we were being discreet. And now to learn they had been keeping her apprised of our comings and goings all the while! It was equal measures annoying and touching.

"Very wise of her," I told him.

I took my leave of his lordship and made my way to the Belvedere. Stoker was already there, looking more disreputable than I had ever seen him. His shirt was fresh, but he had neglected to shave, no doubt due to the various cuts and bruises decorating his face. He wore his eye patch, and when he moved, it was with great care.

"Not entirely decomposed, then?" I asked sweetly. It was apparent he had no wish to discuss our adventures yet. It was ever thus. In the heat of danger, he was a warrior, brave to the point of recklessness. But when it was finished and the peril had passed, a bleakness seemed to settle on him, a thorny dissatisfaction with the mundanity of life, I thought.

I considered forcing the issue, but in the end, I took refuge in our usual banter.

His only reply was a growl. I waved a hand. "You need a good breakfast and movement to stretch out those muscles," I advised. I made my way straight to the sarcophagus, where breakfast was laid out. Our plates, heaped with eggs and mushrooms, deviled kidneys and sausages, were covered with domes. Pots of tea and racks of toast stood shoulder to shoulder with jams and butter and even a small crock of porridge. I lavishly buttered a piece of toast and drizzled it with honey, waving it in front of him like a red cape to a bull.

"Come and eat," I ordered, handing over the toast. He took a bite and canted his head.

"What in the name of seven hells is that smell?"

I tipped my nose in the air. "You smell it too? I rather thought the sausages had gone off." I poked one experimentally.

Stoker picked it up in his bare fingers and bit off a hearty piece. He chewed, his expression thoughtful. "It's just a good Cumberland sausage. Nothing but pork and herbs."

I took a bite for myself. "The kidneys?" I suggested. Kidneys were never my favorite food, but Stoker shook his head.

"I already ate one. They are quite wholesome."

I shrugged. "Then no doubt it is one of your vile specimens."

He folded his arms over his chest, carefully, since his ribs were damaged. "I will have you know that my specimens are impeccable. I keep a perfectly clean workshop."

"Of all the mendacity," I began.

I broke off, watching as Nut began to sniff the sarcophagus, pressing her elegant little nose to the seam between the lid and the body of the coffin.

I looked at Stoker, whose expression had turned wary. "There is no mummy in that sarcophagus," I said. "It is full of antique prosthetics, the collection of the fourth earl."

"I took those out whilst you were away in Madeira," he informed me. "His lordship received an offer on them from an American, some eccentric millionaire who wanted them for his museum in a state whose name escapes me."

"Then it ought to be empty?" I asked.

He nodded, but his face was doubtful. Nut's inquisitiveness had turned to eagerness; she rose on her hind legs, scrabbling at the coffin, marking the paint with her toenails. It was a shabby thing, a Greco-Roman copy of a much older design, but it was still an artifact, and I nudged her away with difficulty.

Stoker sighed and without another word retrieved the pry bar whilst I cleared the breakfast things off of the sarcophagus. I put out my hand for the tool. "Give it to me. You cannot manage with your ribs."

It was an indication of how badly he was injured that he did not argue. I removed my jacket and folded it neatly, taking a few moments before I had to tackle the distasteful task.

"You can put it off as long as you like, but you will still have to do it," he said.

"Don't be brutal." I fitted the narrow end of the bar into the crack between the lid and the coffin and pushed, wedging the two pieces apart. Immediately, a cloud of foul air rolled out, causing me to drop the bar. Nut gave a great whine and ducked her tail between her legs. Huxley and Bet were hiding behind a caryatid, far too wise to investigate. They had learnt that lesson when a set of Wardian cases holding badly preserved amphibian specimens had leaked formalin onto them both and they were forcibly bathed to remove chemicals and bits of frog.

"Cowards," Stoker said. They stayed where they were and I fitted the bar into place once more. I pushed twice and made no headway.

"For the love of God's grace, put your back into it," Stoker ordered.

I did so, giving one great shove, and the lid moved, sliding halfway off, exposing the interior of the sarcophagus. For a moment, we went no further. Neither of us was really keen to look inside. But of course, we did not have to. We already knew.

Inside the sarcophagus lay the body of Madame Aurore.

# CHAPTER

## 21

"Bloody bollocking hell," Stoker said softly. Nut rose on her hind legs, peering into the sarcophagus. "For God's sake, get down, you hellhound."

I gave him a level look. "A little something to drink, I believe."

"This is hardly the time for a tea party," he remonstrated.

I reached under my skirt for the flask of aguardiente I habitually strapped there. "I should have thought you would know better by now," I said. I took a hearty draft and passed it to him. When he had drunk, I capped the flask and replaced it, the little gestures bringing a sense of normality to a situation that was most provoking.

"Do you suppose that"—I gestured towards what was left of Madame Aurore—"has been placed here as a warning?"

He shrugged. "Possibly. Or it is a plot to incriminate us. Should the authorities be alerted, we are in possession of the body of a murder victim." He studied the body, and I steeled myself to do the same, refusing to look away, as I considered it my duty to be fully informed. I noted at once a change in the corpse from how we had originally found her.

"They have made an attempt to cover the wound," I remarked,

pointing to where a narrow piece of linen had been wound about her throat, almost but not quite concealing the gaping slash. It was crusted with blood, although some effort had clearly been made to tidy her. Her face had been wiped, but streaks of scarlet still stained her skin, and her dress had not been changed although the stars had been ripped from the fabric, leaving wounds in the silk.

"This was all done in haste," Stoker observed. "She has not been properly prepared—hence the odor. And she has not even been thoroughly washed. Disgraceful."

In spite of his work with dead creatures—or perhaps because of it—Stoker was always keen to find dignity in death. Hence his distaste for Mr. Pennybaker's collection of coronation kittens.

I peered into the sarcophagus and gave a gusty sigh. "At least whoever brought her to us was kind enough to bring the Templeton-Vane tiara," I said, pointing to where it lay. "I can return it to Tiberius."

"You will want to clean it first," Stoker said mildly. "That blood won't come off easily."

"Well, one more thing to explain to Sir Hugo," I said in resignation. I moved towards the caryatid where my hat hung, but Stoker grasped my hand.

"Not just yet, I beg you."

"You want to delay telling Sir Hugo that we have a murder victim lying around? What if the children find her? Or worse, the dogs?"

"The dogs want nothing to do with her, and I am not suggesting we keep her indefinitely," he protested. "But Sir Hugo is going to be extremely tiresome about this, I have no doubt. And if we could provide him with at least a little information to exculpate ourselves, it might go a great deal better for us."

I pondered that and could not fault his logic. We had occasionally been on the receiving end of Sir Hugo's temper, and it was not an experience I cared to repeat if I could possibly avoid it. If nothing else, it might spare Stoker the indignity of another comprehensive search of his person and lengthy questioning, as well as eloquent lectures on our ethics, intelligence, and priorities. Sir Hugo would be enraged enough to discover that we had spent twenty-four hours in captivity with the prince without rushing to inform him of the matter. I consoled myself with the thought that the prince's security had been of paramount importance and that the Ripper investigation would take precedence over a pair of miscreants and their thugs who had no doubt fled the moment we eluded them. Sir Hugo would be empurpled with emotion, and I was content to put off such a confrontation for as long as possible.

I turned again to the corpse and pulled a face. "I wonder how they were able to bring her here," I ventured. I explained about Lady Wellie's guards, watching as Stoker's face turned increasingly interesting shades of puce. "You knew!" I accused.

"Not until recently," he said, holding up his hands. "I became suspicious when I asked one of the undergardeners for a bit of milkweed for some butterfly larvae and he brought me verbena. I started paying closer attention and I identified four men who had not been very long in his lordship's employ and whose tasks were quite often carried out by others. I asked a few discreet questions and finally, one night when Lady Wellie and I were rather deep in our cups, she admitted it. She has been concerned for your safety, and with good reason," he added.

"Her guards have not been terribly effective," I argued. "We have had all manner of strange callers, one or two bent upon mischief."

He shrugged. "It is an imperfect system. She did not want you to know, so she has ordered them to be unobtrusive above all. Your comings and goings are far too varied for any discreet efforts to be completely effective."

He had a point. I nodded towards the corpse. "It still does not answer how this was brought in without attracting attention."

He thought, running a hand over his whisker-roughened chin. After a moment, he pressed a bell, summoning the boot boy, George. Once a winsome little fellow, George had shot up to a gangling height whilst I was in Madeira. An Adam's apple bobbed in his throat, and his voice frequently broke in the middle of a syllable.

"New story about the Ripper, miss," he said, brandishing the latest edition of the *Daily Harbinger.* I looked at the lurid picture on the front page and shuddered, imagining what they would say if His Royal Highness were implicated.

"I shall read it later," I assured him. "Whilst we were away, did anything curious happen? Visitors? Deliveries?"

He nodded, eyes fixed upon Stoker's tin of treacle fudge. I handed it over, ignoring Stoker's muffled noise of protest.

"Help yourself to a grand piece—no, have another. You are a growing boy," I told George, smiling.

"Fank you, miff," he managed through a mouthful of sticky fudge.

Stoker took the tin back with bad grace, plucking several pieces for himself. George continued to chew happily, pausing only to pet Nut, who nuzzled up to him in hopes of a titbit.

"George," I prodded gently. "Visitors?"

"Oh, yes, miss." He swallowed the last of his fudge. "A bloody great—sorry, miss, I mean a rather large crate came first thing yesterday morning."

Stoker glanced around the orderly chaos of the Belvedere. "Where, precisely, is it?"

George looked left and right, forwards and backwards, scratching his head. "I dunno, sir. The fellow had a sack barrow and wheeled the crate in himself."

"And was he ever alone?" I inquired.

George flushed. "It weren't my fault. I know I was supposed to stay with him, but Lady Rose set to hollering, and you know what she's like," he said darkly. I did indeed. Lord Rosemorran's youngest child was a tiny force of nature. When she bellowed, all activity on the estate came to a halt.

"What was the trouble with Lady Rose?" Stoker asked.

George shrugged. "Devil take her if I know," he said in some disgust. "She just wailed for the better part of ten minutes, loud as a shrike. Everyone crowded around, but she wouldn't say what the matter was. She screamed until Lady Cordelia came."

"And then what?"

He shrugged. "Lady C. promised to dose her with castor oil if she didn't give over, and she quieted down quick enough after that. She just tossed her head and went about her business saying she was sure she didn't know what all the fuss were about." He pulled a face. "Women."

"Indeed," I agreed. I wrested the tin away from Stoker and handed it to George. "Thank you, George. Do finish this off if you like."

"If I like?" He gave a guffaw. "I should think so, miss." He cradled the tin under his arm as tenderly as a babe as he left, the dogs snuffling happily behind him.

Stoker gave me a dark look. "That was all the treacle fudge I had."

"I will buy you another tin and better," I soothed. "But it is important to pay one's informants."

"Informants," he said, curling a lip.

"Informants," I confirmed. "George is shaping up quite nicely."

"I don't see how you can possibly say that—" He broke off suddenly. "You don't really think that Lady Rose would—"

"Don't I?" I said grimly. "Come along, Stoker. We have to beard the little lioness in her den."

We ran Lady Rose to earth in her tiny playhouse. She might have chosen any of the diminutive pavilions scattered about the estate—a miniature French château, a Japanese pagoda, a longhouse of the Eastern Algonquin peoples. But she had selected instead a de-cidedly grubby hermit hut from Gloucestershire. It had once housed a recluse of great renown, a fellow who entered his solitary life during the reign of George II and had not died until the fall of the Bastille. The present earl's father had purchased it for a farthing and had it brought to London to adorn his grounds at Bishop's Folly, to limited success. Most visitors mistook it for a compost heap. It was woven of willow, arched to the height of a middling-aged child, and embellished with leaves and vines that played host to a riotous assortment of insect life. Lady Rose loved it because no one else ever dared enter, either from mild claustrophobia or fear of infestation.

Stoker had no such qualms. Lady Rose entertained him occasion-ally to tea there, although I was seldom afforded such hospitality. She had taken against me during our first meeting, and it was not difficult to determine the source of her hostility. Her misleadingly cherubic face lit at the sight of Stoker entering her little domain. Her greeting to me was decidedly less warm.

"Oh, it's *you*." She had been scolded repeatedly for rudeness to her inferiors, but the lesson had not yet taken hold. For my part, I ignored her jibes, as I had long ago formed the opinion that it is best never to notice children at all in any capacity lest they take a simple greeting as an overture for discussion—or worse yet, touching by grubby, sweet-sticky fingers.

I made an exception this time. I gave her my most winsome smile. "Good morning, Lady Rose. I see you have a new tea service."

The stump that formed her table was spread with a dingy linen cloth—no doubt pristine until she had got her grimy little paws on it—and set with a miniature collection of Wedgwood. She pulled a face and poured out a cup of tea for herself and for Stoker. I raised a brow and she sighed theatrically before pouring a thimbleful of ap-palling russet brown liquid into my cup.

Stoker took a manful sip, then set the cup down, choking. "What an unusual and original flavor," he managed, his eyes streaming.

"I took the slop leaves from yesterday's tea," she said matter-of-factly.

"And added?" Stoker prompted.

"A little cinnamon and ground clove."

"And?" Stoker pressed.

She shrugged. "Mustard seed."

"There it is," he said, wiping his brow with one of his enormous handkerchiefs. Lady Rose slanted me an artful look.

"You aren't drinking."

"Perhaps later," I said, pushing the cup a little distance away.

She fixed her gaze upon the cup and stared hard, her expression one I had seen only too often.

"Very well." I sighed. I took up the cup and drained it, putting it carefully back onto the saucer. I held her gaze with my own, betraying no reaction whatever to her vile concoction.

She poured out the rest of the noxious brew. "I need something stronger, then," she grumbled.

"Why? Are you trying to poison someone?" I asked pleasantly.

"Not exactly *poison*," she answered, her brow puckered in thought. "But a little discomfort wouldn't go amiss."

"Whose discomfort?" I inquired.

"Charles'," she said, giving the syllables dark emphasis. Charles was his lordship's second son, and as devious a creature as I had ever encountered. The trouble was, he had the looks of a Botticelli saint, so very few people ever believed him capable of real mischief. I had a fondness for the boy myself, but I could easily see how his tricks could irritate a younger sister beyond endurance.

"Now, Lady Rose," Stoker began firmly.

I nudged him with my foot. "Stoker, I rather think that Lady Rose and I might like a few minutes of conversation. Just us women."

Lady Rose opened her mouth, no doubt to protest, but the sound of the word "women" brought her up sharply. She gave me a look of grudging respect. "Yes, please, Stoker." Her eyes followed him as he left. She regretted letting him leave, but I could tell she was mightily curious about what I wanted.

I came directly to the point. "Yesterday, I believe a crate was delivered to the Belvedere."

Her eyes slid from mine. She was an adroit liar when she wanted to be, but she had not expected this. I settled back on my stump, arranging my skirt smoothly over my trousers as I waited.

"Was there?" she asked.

I huffed a sigh at her. "Come now, Lady Rose. You are a better liar than that and we both know it. Your delivery was a beat too late, and your voice has gone high."

She thrust out her bottom lip a little. "Very well. There was a crate."

"A large crate, taken into the Belvedere."

She said nothing, but a tiny nod acknowledged what I said was true.

"Now, George or another member of staff is supposed to remain with all deliverymen until they have left the premises, but George was drawn away from his duty—as was everyone else—by what I am given to understand was a rather spectacular display of temper on your part."

"I may have fussed a little," she said begrudgingly.

"Lady Rose," I said, allowing a note of warning to creep into my voice. She tossed her pretty curls.

"Do you think to frighten me?" she demanded. "You dare not strike me."

I gave her a thin smile. "My sweet Rose, I don't have to strike you to make you suffer. Now, tell me what you know and I will tell you exactly what to put into your brother's tea to make him purge his guts up."

A smile of dazzling radiance broke over her face as she spat into her hand and thrust it towards me. "Word of honor?"

I spat into my own palm and shook firmly. "Word of honor."

# CHAPTER

## 22

A quarter of an hour later, I quitted the hermitage, in full posses-sion of what I wanted to know and having explained to Lady Rose the precise dosage of rhubarb to dispense to Charles with instructions to administer it in a double-steeped pot of tea for the maximum effect.

Stoker was resting in the snuggery, the little area at the top of the gallery stairs in the Belvedere. It was furnished for comfort, not glam-our, and it was the one spot where we often went to brood or rest as we worked out a particularly knotty problem. He was draped long on the sofa, reading the *Daily Harbinger*, the very copy George had brought that morning.

"Anything of relevance?" I asked as I took a seat in the large arm-chair that leaked stuffing and provided a haven for a very polite family of mice.

He tossed the newspaper aside, steepling his fingers under his chin as he swung his feet onto the floor, moving gingerly and wincing a little at his injuries. "Just the same old tripe." He flicked me a glance. "When does it end? These poor souls, living on scraps at the edge of civilized existence. They suffer more than the worst wretch in our prisons, and yet what crime have they committed except to be born poor and forgotten?"

It was a familiar refrain. Stoker had been a child of privilege and wealth, but he had run away in his youth. His father always had him found and dragged home again, yet those boyish adventures had shaped the man he had become. He had lived cheek by jowl with every variety of person, taking in their knowledge, studying their ways. Some philosophies—most, in fact—he had rejected. He was no respecter of institutions simply because they boasted antiquity. He believed, like all good radicals, that everything ought to be examined anew by each generation. What served society should be retained, and what did not should be discarded without sentiment or reserve. He was a very modern man, his guiding principles in complete accord with my own. We might occasionally quibble about the specifics, but together we wanted nothing more than to leave a world better than the one into which we had been delivered.

I picked up the discarded newspaper and skimmed it quickly. "They have no real sympathy for the victims," I observed. "No understanding of what would drive a woman to sell herself for a few coppers. They do not care that people are born into the vilest slums and must live the whole of their lives bound by its limitations. For all their faults, I do envy the Americans that," I told him. "They permit a man to make himself and do not hold it against him. A woman as well."

He was silent a long moment before asking, "What did Lady Rose say?"

"She was paid to stage her little act, just as we expected."

He sat forwards. "Paid? By whom?"

"By a man with a great deal of facial hair and a strong smell of licorice," I told him.

His eyes lit. "That bloody old porter at the club."

"No doubt," I agreed.

"And if he was able to manage a crate containing Madame Aurore's body without assistance, I think we may presume that he is significantly more able of body than he pretends. What do you know about him?"

I shrugged. "We spoke twice. He was outrageous to the point of insult both times, overly familiar and appalling. I wanted nothing more than to get away—" I broke off and Stoker waited whilst I puzzled it out. "But of course. His maladroit behavior was as much a masquerade as his pretended infirmity. If he infiltrated the club in order to spy or to wreak some harm upon Aurore, what better way to ensure he was left to his own devices than to act like a tiresome old ruffian?"

"The only question is why she would ever permit someone like that in her club," Stoker mused. "She was elegant and refined, as were her surroundings."

"I mentioned something of the sort to her and her response was that he was new, a sort of charity case, I gathered. She said words to the effect that she believed in giving everyone a first chance."

I fell silent again, thinking hard. "There was something else. An odor besides the licorice that I could not place. It was decidedly chemical in nature."

"And you do not know what it was?"

I shook my head, frustrated. "No, it was elusive, only a whiff because the licorice was so strong, almost as if he were using it to mask the other. If only I could place it!"

"When did you notice it?" Stoker asked.

"I caught a first sniff of it when I spoke with him before entering her rooms," I said slowly, "but I did not really smell it until afterwards, when I stopped to talk to him again."

"What did you think of?"

I closed my eyes. "Sheep shearing."

"Lanolin?" he suggested.

I shook my head again, eyes still closed. "Not that. The tufts of wool that lie in little drifts when one is shearing sheep. And dressing-up boxes."

I opened my eyes to find Stoker grinning at me and I groaned. "The odor was spirit gum. He was wearing a false beard and eyebrows."

"And the bushy whiteness of it made you think of sheep being sheared."

"And the spirit gum put me in mind of dressing-up boxes because one is always sticking on beards or moustaches," I finished. "Extraordinary. However did you work that out?"

"When I was learning Latin, I had the devil's own time memorizing declensions," he told me. "I used to read aloud as I walked, and I was always more interested in the birds and plants than the words. I discovered if I recalled what I had been looking at or smelling at the time, I could often remember what I had read."

"How very curious. You ought to write a paper," I suggested.

He shuddered visibly. "You know my opinions on the social sciences. And, in case it has escaped your attention, we have the problem of a corpse to dispose of."

"But why bring her here?" I asked.

He rubbed his chin thoughtfully. "She was delivered here before we escaped. Matters would have been going according to plan for your uncle and Archibond at that point. With Archibond in Special Branch, it would have been an easy enough matter for him to arrange for the body to be discovered here. But it makes no sense."

"Because they would have had no reason then to discredit *us*," I said, picking up the thread of his thoughts. "She needed to be discovered at the club in order to implicate Eddy in her murder. Archibond indicated as much. And if Eddy were thought to have murdered a courtesan so near to Whitechapel, it would be a very short leap to laying suspicion of the Ripper's crimes at his door. Imagine the furor!

There is not a newspaper in the Empire or abroad that would not shriek the scandal from the headlines. Even if he were proven innocent, he would never escape the stain of it. I am persuaded Madame Aurore was brought into the plot as a means of luring Eddy into indiscretion, and at some point, Archibond or Uncle de Clare decided it was not enough for her to play the role of courtesan, she must play the role of victim as well."

Stoker broke in. "So, she was murdered by Quiet Dan and left for Eddy to find at the appointed hour. Remember, they were in the mews stairs, ready to burst in and discover him standing over her bloodied body."

"But we fled and they lost time in chasing us down, just enough time for someone else to nip in and retrieve her body," I reasoned.

"Someone who had been watching her closely and was on hand, ready to act swiftly and decisively to foil as much of the plot as possible," Stoker added. "They not only chased us down but abducted us from the pavement outside the club and had to take us to the warehouse in Whitechapel. No doubt it was some time before they could return to the club and then discover their corpse had disappeared."

"What a nasty shock for them," I mused. "To have set up such an elaborate scene only to have it ruined, first by our running away and then by someone else whisking her body away."

"But why bring it *here*?" Stoker demanded. "And furthermore, who outside of the original plot even knew we were there?"

There was the sensation of whirling, as if I were dancing, and I remembered the strong grasp of the female porter who had partnered me. *Good night, Veronica Speedwell.*

"There was someone," I said slowly. "The female porter who admitted us."

Stoker shook his head. "We gave no names, there was no list."

"But she knew me," I told him. "Later that evening we danced."

One brow quirked upwards. "You danced?"

"Waltzed, actually. She is quite a good partner, a little lighter in the turns than you are," I explained. "And when the dance was finished, she said, 'Good night, Veronica Speedwell.'"

"And you are only just now telling me this?" he asked in a voice that was murderously calm.

"I have been a little busy since," I returned coldly. "You will forgive me if an abduction rather pushed such a trifling incident out of my mind."

"It is hardly a trifling incident, Veronica," he replied. "Our identities were known by at least two porters at that club, one who danced with you and one who hauled Aurore's corpse into our home. I do not much care for the possibilities."

"I understand," I said, humbling myself a little. "But perhaps the possibilities are not as bad as you fear. As you say, if we were meant to be implicated in Aurore's murder, someone need only send an anonymous note to Scotland Yard and her body would be discovered in our possession. But that has not happened. I think someone brought her here for safekeeping."

"Have you quite taken leave of your senses?"

"I have not. It is perfectly logical, if you would only stop to consider it. The porters knew some of what was transpiring at the club. Perhaps Madame Aurore took them into her confidence. Perhaps they eavesdropped for pleasure or money. In any event, they knew who we were, and when they discovered their mistress's dead body, they brought her here, entrusting her, as it were."

"That is the most far-fetched, fantastical—"

"Have you a better theory?" I challenged.

He fell silent, gnawing on his lower lip. "I have not," he said finally. "It is logical."

"Thank you."

"I still do not like it," he growled. "It puts us in the path of danger."

"In the path of danger?" I was frankly incredulous. "My dear Stoker, in the past two days, we have been abducted, held against our will, chased, shot at, and—in your case—thoroughly beaten. We have not been so much in the path of danger as standing in the middle of it, surrounded on all sides."

"Hence my irritation," he finished glumly.

"That and a lack of sustenance," I told him in a firm tone. "We have missed luncheon, but I will order a full tea and then you will rest. It will be some time before you recover your strength."

It was a mark of his fatigue that he argued with me for only a quarter of an hour before giving in. "What about Sir Hugo?" he asked as he finished off the last of the scones some time later, licking cream and jam from his fingers in contentment.

"I will send a note requesting an audience as soon as he can spare us the time," I promised. "I think it best if we speak in person. If nothing else, he will be pleased enough to see the bruises on your face and might take pity on us."

"Then perhaps we ought to show him my ribs," he said sleepily. He gave a great cracking yawn and settled into the sofa. A moth-eaten old coverlet lay along the back and I drew it over him, tucking it neatly under him. I usually resisted all impulses to nurture—it is never a good idea to let people get accustomed to one's servitude—but Stoker had earned a little kindness, I reflected.

And whilst he slept, I penned a brief note to Sir Hugo, stating only that we requested an audience at his convenience and dispatching it with a coin for George. Afterwards, I settled to labeling a case of *Papilio buddha*—Malabar Banded Peacock butterflies—whose notes had gone astray. I had just removed a sweet little imposter nestling amongst them (Common Bluebottles, *Graphium sarpedon*, are often mistaken for the more elusive Banded Peacocks) when Stoker appeared, looking a little better for his rest.

"Has the post come?" he demanded, helping himself to a cup of tea from the stone-cold pot.

"A telegram from Rupert in elaborate code," I told him. "The parcel has been safely delivered to Scotland with no troubles. That is an end to that," I said, clearing my throat. It had been a hectic twenty-four hours in Eddy's company, and I was glad he had been speedily returned to the bosom of his family. Apparently his sister's prevarications had roused no suspicions, and he was happily ensconced once more at our grandmother's castle, no doubt spending his days tramping upon moors spread with heather and harebells, returning late to a cozy tea by the fire, butter dripping from toasted crumpets as they shared inside jokes and titbits of gossip about other members of the family.

"Veronica?" Stoker said softly.

I roused myself and waved a hand to the rest of the post, returning to position my little Bluebottle in a more appropriate collection. Stoker flicked through the pile of letters and circulars that had accumulated during our absence, throwing most of them onto the floor with his customary nonchalance. He plucked one letter from the pile, tearing open the envelope and skimming the contents in a fury.

"Bloody bollocking hell," he muttered.

"Trouble?"

"It's Pennybaker," he fumed. "He claims there is a problem with the quagga. *My* quagga."

"What sort of problem?" I asked, attempting to sound interested. Frankly, I was far more excited by the discovery of a dysmorphic specimen in the collection of Banded Peacocks. To encounter one with male and female characteristics in such good condition was a rare find indeed, and I envied the collector who had netted it.

"He says the glue has proven inadequate," he said, jaw clenching furiously.

"It is possible to have a bad batch of glue," I pointed out. My calmness only incited his fury further.

"I make each batch of glue myself," he reminded me. "You know that. My formula is precise, my methods exacting. I have never, *never* returned a specimen to a collector in imperfect condition. He is threatening legal action."

"Legal action!" I turned at last from my butterflies. "That sweet little man? Feathers. He drank champagne from my slipper. I don't believe it for a moment."

"Well, he is," Stoker insisted, waving the letter like a flag. "And I will not stand for it. Are you coming with me?"

"Coming? You mean to visit him?"

"He invites me. Says that we can settle this like gentlemen because he is not unreasonable and expects that with a few modest repairs we can put this behind us. Modest repairs," he repeated, muttering a few other choice phrases that have no place in a polite memoir.

I sighed and put away my collection of Banded Peacocks. Stoker was in no fit state to traipse about the city, particularly not in a mood of effervescent rage. I reached for my hat and pinned it securely to my head.

"Very well, I will come. It has turned chill again, but we can hail a hackney at the corner," I said.

"We are taking one of his lordship's carts," he said, raking his hands through his tumbled hair. "If Pennybaker does not appreciate my work, I will take the quagga back."

"I will not be accomplice to stealing an ass," I warned him.

"Never say 'never,' Veronica."

# CHAPTER

## 23

I t took us the better part of an hour to reach the Pennybaker home, and I resigned myself to the possibility of participating in a felonious theft as Stoker's accomplice. It would, if I am honest, not be the worst thing I had done. Stoker sat in a tense and silent fury—nothing kindled his ire so much as a perceived insult to his work—and so I set myself instead to reciting the butterfly genus Papilio in order of discovery.

As we drove, a storm began to brew, blotting out the lovely autumnal sunlight, dimming its gold to pewter. A brisk breeze whipped up across the heath, bending the late grasses and causing the cow parsnip seed heads to nod heavily as the last of the hawthorn fruits shimmered like jewels against their leafy cloaks of dark green.

I had just reached *Papilio laglaizei*—a relatively new specimen, identified in only 1877—when at last we came to the address. The driver gave a light tug to the reins and the horse eased to a crawl. Stoker and I alighted before it even stopped, vaulting through the narrow gate and through the overgrown shrubbery. I opened my mouth to suggest a measured and conciliatory approach, but Stoker was already lifting the great brass door knocker, rapping sharply.

"Mr. Pennybaker!" he called, pressing his ear to the stout door. "Mr. Pennybaker, are you there?"

The door swung open on its ancient hinges and the quizzical face of Mr. Pennybaker peered out through his round lenses.

"Is that you, Mr. Templeton-Vane?" I was not surprised to see his expression was one of acute distress. The little man was obviously attached to his trophies, and to have a failure in the mounting of the quagga so soon after its delivery was an aggrieving development.

"It is," Stoker said in a tone of arctic hauteur. "I received your note and have come as requested to investigate the quagga."

"That is not necessary," Mr. Pennybaker said with unexpected firmness. "In fact, I would like you to leave at once. I have decided I want nothing whatsoever to do with such shoddy work. You are a *charlatan*, sir," he said, his brows trembling with emotion as he gave us an imploring look.

Stoker drew himself up, towering over the little fellow as he moved past. "I will accept no criticism of my work until I can inspect it for myself," he replied over his shoulder. "I am entirely certain there is no fault in the glue . . ." He continued on in this vein as Mr. Pennybaker tottered in his wake towards the gallery.

"Sir," Pennybaker said, tugging at his coat, "I really must *insist—*"

"Calm yourself, man," Stoker directed. "Whatever is wrong with the quagga, I will put right, you have my word upon it." His mood was softening at Pennybaker's obvious anguish, but he would not be deterred. The integrity of his work had been called into question, and that was a situation not to be borne.

"Best to let him get on with it, Mr. Pennybaker," I soothed as we came to the gallery.

He attempted once to bodily position himself between Stoker and the door, but Stoker picked him up gently by the shoulders and set him aside. He opened the door and stopped dead in his tracks as Penny-baker gave a low moan of protest.

"What is it?" I demanded, wondering what sort of damage the quagga could possibly have sustained, when I saw them.

Archibond stood in front of the painted ass.

"I am sorry," murmured Mr. Pennybaker. "I did try to warn you."

"What the devil—" Stoker stared at Archibond in frank aston-ishment.

I gave our erstwhile abductor a look of frankest loathing. "Mr. Pen-nybaker, I can only presume that this man prevailed upon you to send that note through some threat of bodily injury?"

"Worse," the kindly fellow said miserably, "he threatened to burn the quagga."

He gestured towards the painted ass, which stood in splendid and perfect condition.

"I knew there was nothing wrong with my mount," Stoker said in satisfaction.

"I thought you would never come," said Archibond pleasantly as he leveled his revolver.

It took a moment for Mr. Pennybaker to understand the implica-tions. "Is that a revolver?"

"It is," I told him.

"Why is that chap pointing it at us?"

"Because he wants us to do exactly as he says, which is rather a good idea," Stoker told him.

I gave Archibond my most severe look. "Do stop waving that around," I ordered. "You will frighten poor Mr. Pennybaker."

"On the contrary, it was the waiting that proved distressing. Now that things are happening, I find it rather thrilling," said the gentle-man in question, blinking rapidly.

Archibond's smile was thin. "Thank you for your prompt arrival. I have trespassed upon our host's hospitality for a far shorter time than I would have expected."

The curtains had not been drawn and the bushes outside the window rustled. It would have been a cozy room with the draperies closed and the fire burning merrily, but under the present circumstances it seemed unwelcoming. Trophies stood in every corner, their eyes glowing in the shadows, giving the atmosphere an otherworldly air. A superstitious soul might have felt we were being watched.

But such fancies were of little practical use, and I realized the longer we could keep Archibond talking, the greater the chance one of us could disarm him. Of course, it also increased the risk that dear Mr. Pennybaker might be injured. We must tread with exquisite care, I decided.

"You anticipated that Stoker would respond to any suggestion of his work being inferior," I said, drawing Archibond's attention.

"Naturally. Of course, it would have been easier to take the pair of you from Bishop's Folly, but abducting you from under the nose of Lady Wellie's hired surveillance is no easy matter. It seemed far simpler to lure you here and finish the business well out from under prying eyes," he explained.

"But how did you even know about Mr. Pennybaker?" Stoker asked, shifting almost imperceptibly to the side, widening the possible arc of fire should Archibond attempt to shoot one or all of us.

Archibond's smile was thin and humorless. "A few careful inquiries in the right quarters about your latest commissions were an easy matter."

"Where is my uncle? And those ruffians he employs?" I inched away from Stoker, broadening the arc further still.

"Gone," was the tight reply. "Fled, either back to Ireland or some other benighted place. You will appreciate it is rather difficult to trace him without the resources usually at my disposal."

"Leaving the responsibility of the crimes you committed together to fall squarely on your shoulders," Stoker pointed out. "You would have done better to have run with him."

A muscle in Archibond's jaw twitched. "There is no proof of any crime," he said evenly. "There is no body."

"*Body?*" came Pennybaker's squeak of a reply.

"Never mind," I consoled him. "And the inspector is quite wrong. There is a body and therefore evidence of a crime, but he has misplaced it."

"I did not misplace it," Archibond said sternly. "It was stolen."

"From under your nose," I pointed out. "Careless of you."

He swung the gun towards me. "Enough, Miss Speedwell. Your commentary is not required."

"But it was careless," Stoker said, drawing Archibond's attention back to himself. "I mean, you went to all the trouble to have Madame Aurore murdered and yet you failed to keep account of what became of her. I call that careless."

Archibond steadied his weapon. "I think we are quite finished here," he said in a tone of forbidding finality.

I took a deliberate step in front of Stoker. "Do not even think of shooting him."

I felt the warmth of Stoker at my back, his calm presence so relaxed as to be almost unnerving in such a heightened atmosphere. Really, did *nothing* disturb his sangfroid?

Archibond gave me a frankly incredulous look. "I have a revolver, Miss Speedwell. I rather think that puts me in charge of what happens here."

"Do you indeed?" came a voice from the long casement windows, the accent a familiar Irish burr. My uncle shoved the casement fully open, careful to let his henchman precede him into the room, weapon at the ready. He came to stand, braced by his walking stick, glowering at Archibond. "Do you think you are the man pulling the strings, my good lad?"

Archibond sighed. "I thought you were gone, de Clare."

"Not without seeing this business through to the end," my uncle told him, glowering.

"In that case, go back to the warehouse and wait for me," Archibond directed.

"Oh, you'd like that, I suppose, with the police sniffing around, ready to arrest whoever sets foot on that property," de Clare snarled.

Archibond pricked like a pointer. "What the devil do you mean?"

"I mean, the police have been there. You think I don't know a fellow in plainclothes even when he has the stink of Scotland Yard about him? I know what I saw. And I had one of my lads keeping watch on you. As soon as he told me you were bound for Hampstead Heath, I knew what you were about. You meant to get your hands on these two and cut me right out of the plot," he accused.

"I thought you had fled," Archibond pointed out calmly. "And if you had not, taking these two back into my own custody assures I am not circumvented."

"Circumvented! And what put that thought into your head?" jeered de Clare.

"Perhaps the fact that you took Madame Aurore's body off the premises," Archibond returned.

De Clare flushed, a deep mottled red. "Do not play games with me, you English prick. I know you took her, and I know why. You mean to frame me for her murder and keep the girl under your control," he said, jerking his chin at me.

Archibond's tone was arctic. "I would hardly need to frame you for murdering Aurore since your man slashed her throat on your orders. And as for playing games, you are scarcely in a position to talk after what you did with the body."

They had squared off, each man's temper flaring, Archibond's cold and de Clare's blazing. It made for an interesting study. I glanced back at Stoker and he shrugged. I knew him well enough to interpret the gesture. He would do nothing so long as the two of them were at loggerheads. If the quarrel played out and they did violence to each other, so much the better for us. We might well escape in the confusion. Along with poor Mr. Pennybaker, I thought. But the gentleman was staring at the pair of combatants, eyes wide with interest as he took in their contretemps with all the avid interest of a spectator who has wagered his last guinea at a horse race. Stoker moved, angling his body in front of Pennybaker so the man would be shielded from any possible violence.

De Clare was fairly leaping at Archibond's accusation. "I tell you, I did nothing with the body! It was you who spirited her off to God knows where."

Archibond rolled his eyes heavenwards. "And when, precisely, would I have had an opportunity to do that? I was with you, or have you—in your paranoiac fantasies—forgot that? It is perfectly apparent that you must know where the body is."

"I do not!" De Clare was fairly vibrating with rage at this point. He raised his pistol to Archibond, who countered by leveling his own revolver at de Clare, and there were quite enough guns in that room for my taste. I decided to step in, holding my hands up.

"Stop this brangling at once," I instructed. "I know where the body is. So I suggest you both calm down and discuss this rationally before gunfire breaks out."

Archibond gave me a suspicious look. "You know where the body is?"

"Yes, someone left her for us to find," I told him. "We rather thought it was the pair of you, intending to notify the police and have us arrested on suspicion of murder."

Archibond's tone was one of chilled scorn. "Why the devil would we want you accused of murder when you are the linchpin of this whole endeavor?"

I shrugged. "You might have intended to catch Stoker in your little trap," I pointed out. "It is one way of eliminating him from the equation."

"There are other ways," he said.

And before I understood what he meant to do, he shifted his stance, turned to Stoker, and pulled the trigger.

Time stood still as the scarlet bloomed across Stoker's shirtfront and he slid to his knees. He looked up to me, an expression of disbelief on his face. "Not again," he said, half laughing. "I don't bloody well believe this."

And then he collapsed onto the carpet at my feet.

# CHAPTER

## 24

The instant Stoker fell, several things happened. De Clare, believing Archibond had shot at me, immediately fired at Archibond. His aim was not as true and he merely caught the inspector in the arm. Archibond lifted his other arm to return fire, but before he could, a form vaulted through the window.

"Mornaday!" I cried as our old acquaintance entered, his own revolver drawn.

"Inspector, surrender yourself," he instructed. "The rest of you are under arrest, except for Miss Speedwell."

Archibond did not lower his weapon. "I don't know what you think you are playing at, Mornaday, but that is enough. As your superior, I order you to lower your weapon and take these people into custody."

"I am afraid not, sir," Mornaday said evenly. "I have my own orders and they come from higher than you."

Archibond's features twisted into a snarl, but before he could pull the trigger, a shot rang out. He pitched forward, surprise registering on his face. De Clare and Mornaday had not moved, and neither had Quiet Dan. But behind Archibond, his wide eyes as stunned as the rest of us, a smoking musket of some antiquity in his hand, stood Mr. Pennybaker.

"Oh dear," he said, dropping the musket to the ground. "I seem to have hit him in the posterior vena cava. I do believe that will be a fatal wound."

"Christ in chains," Mornaday muttered. He swung his revolver to de Clare. "You and your man. Drop your weapons and against the wall."

De Clare grinned. "I think not, lad. There's one of you and two of us."

The little clock on the mantel began to chime, but I could not make sense of it, for time had frozen. We were a tableau: Pennybaker, horrified at his own actions, standing in rigid disbelief; De Clare and Quiet Dan opposite Mornaday, alone and outnumbered and attempting to hold them off.

And most significant of all, Stoker, lying on the hearthrug, his life's blood pooling beneath him.

It was easy to see what would happen next. De Clare and his minion would open fire on Mornaday first, then Pennybaker. They would finish off Stoker and take me prisoner and that would be the end—the end of my life as I had known it, the end of my love.

I bent as if to look at Stoker, but I came up almost immediately. The gesture was simply a way to shield my movements as I slipped the knife from my boot. Once before, Stoker had lain bleeding from a bullet and I had thrown a knife straight into the heart of his attacker. This time, I did not throw it. I surged forward, blade in hand, and my aim was true. I buried the knife where I intended, in my uncle's torso, pulling it up and sharply to the left as he stared at me, his expression one of complete disbelief. For a long moment we were locked together, his arms coming up to grip mine, almost in an embrace. And then he eased his hold on me, slipping from my grasp with a little shudder that gave way to perfect and final stillness.

Quiet Dan fired once, hitting Mornaday in the shoulder, dropping him to the floor. Beyond where Mornaday had stood, framed in the windows, was my dance partner, the female liveried and masked porter from Madame Aurore's, the deerhound Vespertine at her heels, a rifle hefted to her shoulder. Without breaking stride, she fired twice in quick succession, taking out Quiet Dan. Mornaday slumped on the carpet, grasping his bleeding shoulder.

He gazed in disbelief at the porter, who surveyed the room, rifle still at the ready.

"I told you to wait in the carriage," Mornaday sputtered.

"And I told you this was my story," said the porter, removing the powdered wig and her mask. She bowed in my direction. "Miss Speedwell, how nice to make your acquaintance once more," said J. J. Butterworth. She peered at Stoker. "Mr. Templeton-Vane does not look at all well."

"He must have a doctor," I said, falling to my knees.

Mr. Pennybaker roused himself. "Let me see."

He pushed me gently aside and began to probe the wound. "What the devil do you think you're doing?" I demanded. "He needs a doctor."

His gaze was placid as a millpond as he began to order J. J. Butterworth about, fetching instruments and implements. I continued to stare at him, my hands streaked with Stoker's blood. After a moment, he glanced up at me. "Did I not tell you, my dear? I am a retired professor of surgery from Edinburgh University. I learnt my trade on the battlefields of Crimea. I am rather familiar with this sort of thing."

I sagged in relief then. Guiltily, my attention settled on Mornaday, still clutching his bloodied shoulder. "You are wounded as well. You should have treatment."

"It is a flesh wound," he assured me. "Bloody bullet went right through." He glanced down at the recumbent form of my uncle. "More than I can say for him. One of the Ripper's victims wasn't cut as badly as that," he said, his expression one of mingled distaste and approval.

"I wanted him to know that I meant it," I said dully.

He put a heavy hand to my shoulder and for the first time I realized his brows were white, heavy and unnatural. The odor of spirit gum and licorice still clung to him. "Of all the fiendish stratagems," I breathed. "You were the porter outside Madame Aurore's rooms. You are the one who brought her body to the Belvedere."

He nodded. "There is much to tell. But later. When he can hear it too," he added with a nod towards Stoker.

I returned the nod and went to help Mr. Pennybaker, mastering my shaking hands and the dull certainty that if anything were to happen to Stoker, life would not be worth living.

The next hours were not ones I remember with any great fondness. There was blood—a great deal of it—and copious swearing, both on Stoker's part. He came to once or twice before Mr. Pennybaker, a gifted and courageous surgeon, managed to employ the necessary anesthetics. He administered ether with a liberal hand and Stoker finally slept, a calm and motionless sleep that mimicked death. Mr. Pennybaker, having received his training on the battlefield during the Crimean War, was just as comfortable performing surgery on his dining room table as he would have been in hospital, he said.

"And a man is as likely to die of dysentery or typhoid as his wounds in such a place," he added calmly. "We will attend to him here so long as you can provide me with a steady hand and a strong nerve."

I did as I was told, handing over instruments newly boiled and still hot from the pan, wiping his brow as he worked, never asking questions or daring to look beyond the ends of my own arms. I moved like an automaton, at his bidding, with no mind of my own save what he needed of me.

Mornaday was there, patiently waiting his turn, and J. J. Butterworth as well. We worked, this curious band, as one unit, with the surprising Mr. Pennybaker as our leader, giving orders in a calm, authoritative manner. He was patient with us, and because he displayed no nerves, we were able to do things we could not have even imagined. J. J. was quietly sick into a potted palm in the corner at one point, but she rallied and returned, and in that moment, I realized we were destined to be allies for the rest of our lives. Mornaday, whose loyalties had so often been tested, was the greatest help of all. Before Stoker was thoroughly sedated, he was in a mind to fight, and it was Mornaday who sat on his legs and held him down, even as the wound in his own shoulder opened and the blood flowed freely.

When it was finished and the last bandage had been tied and the last pool of blood had been mopped, Stoker lay, pale and unresponsive, as immobile as one of Madame Tussaud's own creations. Ether, that glorious insensate elixir, was slowly being pumped from a bottle through a rubber mask over his face. It was J. J.'s task to squeeze the balloon on the bottle at regular intervals to ensure the anesthesia's delivery.

I looked at Stoker's face, a curious marble cast to it that I had never seen before.

"It is the ether," J. J. said knowledgeably. "He will come around soon enough when Mr. Pennybaker removes the mask."

"How do you know that?"

She shrugged. "I have nursing experience."

I did not ask and she did not elaborate, but it occurred to me that our lives had perhaps not been so very different after all. Both of us were women of the world, forced to make our way without help from others. And I made up my mind then that if ever I were to tell my story, it would be to her.

Mornaday's injuries were dealt with swiftly—a mere matter of a few stitches and a bandage that he sported with considerable pride as his superior from Scotland Yard arrived.

"Sir Hugo," I said, greeting the head of Special Branch when he entered with a few of his juniors.

"Miss Speedwell," he replied dryly. "Why am I not surprised to find you in the midst of this debacle." He turned his penetrating gaze upon Mornaday. "And you have managed to get yourself shot, I see."

"Only a little," Mornaday replied with a winsome smile.

Sir Hugo was not impressed. "A few minutes in private, Mornaday. You will brief me and then I will give orders."

Mr. Pennybaker hastened to show them into a small study, where they remained locked away whilst one of Sir Hugo's juniors stood watch and the other was dispatched to the gallery to investigate the scene. When his investigation was concluded, he slipped into the room with Sir Hugo and Mornaday, and after a moment, the trio emerged, sober of face and manner. Sir Hugo turned to his men. "There are three consequences in the gallery. Inspector Mornaday will show you where."

Mornaday looked to Sir Hugo, his face alight. "*Inspector* Mornaday?"

"Yes, well. If you haven't earned it yet, you will with this night's work," Sir Hugo said, adding a grim smile for emphasis.

"Yes, sir." Mornaday saluted smartly.

Mr. Pennybaker spoke up. "I must protest, sir," he told Sir Hugo. "This man has been injured and is in need of rest."

"I will rest when the job is finished," Mornaday said, earning him an approving nod from Sir Hugo.

Mornaday escorted the others out, J. J. trailing discreetly in their wake—no doubt to sniff around for whatever gleanings she could find to print.

Mr. Pennybaker excused himself to fetch more hot water and clean bandages, leaving me alone with Sir Hugo. The head of Special Branch fixed me with an impassive stare. His eyes were deeply shadowed and there were new hollows beneath his cheeks, new silver threads in his dark hair. The Ripper case was clearly wearing hard upon him, and I knew he felt the failure of bringing it to a close every moment.

"I wish I could say you looked well," I began.

His smile was slow in coming. "It would be ungentlemanly of me to remark that you are looking less than bandbox perfection yourself, Miss Speedwell."

"Most ungentlemanly," I agreed. "Did you receive my note?"

"I did. It arrived concurrent with Mornaday's urgent summons to this location. Providentially, I was in the office at the time. I should like to point out that you omitted to relate several key pieces of information," he said with his customary severity.

"I thought you rather had your hands full with the Ripper investigation. This seemed less important." I gave him a grin, which he did not return.

"Your consideration does you credit," he told me.

"What will happen now?" I inquired.

He sighed. "What do you think?"

"That you cannot risk opening an investigation," I said simply. "A public inquest would bring it all to light—my uncle's plans, my identity. It would accomplish almost what de Clare intended in the first place, would it not?" I did not wait for him to reply. "And, perhaps more damning, it would expose Archibond, a member of your own force, as an anarchist just when you cannot afford the disapprobation of the public."

"They already hate and fear us for not bringing this monster to justice," he said, clearly reluctant to speak the fiend's name. "They call us incompetent and corrupt and brand us as failures because we cannot solve the insoluble. If we permit this case to become public, it would indeed prove a blow from which the dignity of the royal family—indeed the Empire itself—could not recover."

"Did Archibond have family?" I asked.

He shrugged. "A sister who kept house for him. She is the only one who will care when he does not come home."

"What will you tell her?"

"The same as we will tell the rest of the Yard—that Archibond was in pursuit of a criminal and died in the attempt. The criminal escaped. The doctors at the Yard will certify Archibond's death as a fall, and he will be given a quiet hero's funeral. It is better than he deserves."

"And de Clare and his man?"

Sir Hugo considered this. "The Thames carries all sorts of refuse out to sea," he said after a moment. "And what is carried away does not come back."

I nodded. "It is a kindness to preserve the fiction of Archibond's respectability for his sister's sake."

"It is more for the sake of my men," he said with more candor than I expected. "Their morale is at low ebb at present. I could not countenance breaking it further. Those who are here today are my most trusted juniors. They will die before they reveal what he was. And it is a good secret to die with."

He gave me a tired smile. "And you will go on about your life," he said firmly. "Without meddling in matters you oughtn't."

"Certainly," I said in a milky tone whose blandness did not fool him for a moment. His expression turned severe.

"You have had enough lucky escapes to do credit to a cat," he told me. "One might even say you were born under a lucky star."

He reached into his pocket and drew out the diamond star that had been the source of all our troubles. He held it out to me and I took it, marveling at the heft. Illumination broke across the surface, glittering in the gaslight.

"Where did you find it?"

"Archibond had it in his pocket. My man turned it over when Mornaday and I were in conference."

I handed it back to him. He regarded me in obvious surprise. "I thought you might like to return it yourself."

"No, thank you," I said firmly. "I have had quite enough adventure for the moment."

He gave me an enigmatic look. "I am glad to hear it, although I think I shall believe it when I see it, Miss Speedwell."

He shook hands and left me then, just as Mornaday returned, looking a little green for his recent exertions. Mr. Pennybaker entered with a fresh can of hot water, his eyes shadowed with fatigue, but he would not rest with unfinished business.

"What about you now, Miss Speedwell?"

"What about me?" I inquired.

He looked at my arm. "My dear, didn't you realize? You have been shot."

I glanced down at the sleeve of my jacket where a neat hole formed the black heart of a rose of blood. "Mornaday," I said distinctly. "I do hope you won't hurt yourself when you catch me."

And before he could respond, I pitched headlong into blackness.

When I awoke, the first exquisite sensation was one of floating, just resting gently upon a golden cloud that drifted on a golden sea. I shifted slightly and a shaft of pain ripped through my arm.

"Mind you move slowly," said a familiar voice. "If you tear out those stitches, Pennybaker will have my guts for garters. He told me to watch over you."

I opened my eyes to find J. J. Butterworth sitting on a chair, her eyes deeply shadowed, but her mouth curved into a smile. A line of sunlight fell upon the carpet at her feet.

"Stoker," I said, barely forming the words through lips so parched I could scarcely speak.

"Awake before you, and now out again," she told me. She rose and put a cup to my lips. Water, that most precious, most delicious libation. I drank greedily until she took the cup away. "Not so fast. You will heave it all up again if you aren't careful. It is the ether making you thirsty. I will give you another drink in ten minutes if you stay awake."

I forced my eyes wider. I turned my head, that strange and floating balloon that seemed oddly detached from my body. I tried to move, but my legs refused to answer, weighted and dead.

"I am paralyzed," I murmured, closing my eyes.

J. J. snorted. "You are not paralyzed. Vespertine is lying on your legs."

I opened my eyes again to see the great shaggy beast draped over my lower limbs, head heavy upon my stomach, eyes gazing up at me in anxious adoration.

"He refused to leave you," she told me, ruffling his ears fondly. "I wanted to keep him for myself, but he has attached himself to you."

"I do not want a dog," I said, forming the words slowly and distinctly. My tongue still felt not entirely under my command.

"Well, you have one," she said firmly. "Deerhounds are a frightfully loyal breed, and he has already lost one mistress this week."

I lifted one hand and put it onto Vespertine's head. He gave a deep sigh and settled further, closing his eyes as I did mine. Perhaps owning a dog was not such an unthinkable proposition after all.

After a moment, I opened my eyes again and inspected my surroundings. I lay on a narrow bed, tucked firmly beneath a coverlet printed with elephants. I blinked hard and then closed my eyes again.

"Do you see elephants or am I having an hallucination?" I demanded in a hoarse croak.

"They are on the walls as well," she informed me. "You have been put to bed in the night nursery at the top of the house."

"For God's sake, why?"

"Because with three beds already in one room, it was almost a makeshift ward. Far better for looking after the lot of you," she told me.

I opened my eyes again and looked to my left. Mornaday occupied a narrow bed identical to mine, save that his coverlet was printed with dancing bears. A nightcap was perched at a quizzical angle on his head, and his mouth was open as he delivered lusty snores. With great care for my aching head, I turned to the right. Stoker.

I thrust myself up onto my elbow and paused as the room spun like a carousel. My other arm was bound to my side by a sling. I pushed gently at Vespertine and he leapt gracefully from the bed, landing noiselessly on his feet.

J. J. swore but came to me, helping me up. "Go slowly," she admonished. "You've had nothing to eat and you were under the ether for rather a long time. Your arm will be fine, by the way. Pennybaker probed the wound thoroughly and found a piece or two of bullet that must have chipped off, but the rest passed through. He stitched you up and it looks rather like the constellation Orion now."

"I don't care if he cut the bloody thing off," I muttered as I tottered across the few yards of carpet to Stoker's bed. He lay just as I had seen him last, pale and still. The only change was a darkening of the beard at his jaw.

"You said he was awake," I told her, my tone more than a little accusatory.

"Was," she emphasized. "And I said he was out again. He needs the rest. As do you," she added. I looked down at him for a long time before I allowed her to coax me back to my bed. I tumbled down onto it and into sleep. Just as I drifted off, I mumbled my thanks.

"You are welcome, Princess," she said with a note of amusement.

It was not until the next time I woke that the little barb stuck. I awoke and immediately realized what she had meant.

"Bloody bollocking hell," I said, opening my eyes.

"Well, that is one patient clearly feeling better," Mr. Pennybaker said in his mild voice. He applied a finger to my pulse as I struggled to rise.

"A moment, if you please, Miss Speedwell."

"How are the others?"

"Mr. Mornaday is in the grip of a fever. Nothing serious, but he did quite overexert himself and I should like to keep an eye on him for a day or so more. You are free to get up and move about as you like, my dear. I have examined the wound. There is no sign of infection, but I am afraid it will leave a series of small scars. You will have a story to tell when you wear an evening gown."

I pushed Pennybaker aside. Stoker sat up in bed, his beard frankly disreputable now, but he was smiling. That beautiful, inimitable smile. His torso was lavishly bandaged and bruised every color imaginable, but his coloring was good.

I flew at him, landing on his bed with a thump and heedless of Pennybaker's admonitions. I cupped his face in my hands, my voice tender and deceptively sweet. "Stoker, I hope that you will mark me well when I say, if you ever do such a thing again, I will shoot you myself and save the villains the trouble."

Several days later, Mornaday and J. J. Butterworth joined us for a sort of postmortem, bringing word of the doings abroad. J. J. was illuminated like a faery light as she bore her latest endeavors in the *Daily Harbinger* in triumph.

"The Ripper has struck again," she pronounced. "And they let me have the front page," she added, pointing to the byline.

But my gaze had fallen to the name of his latest victim. "Mary Jane Kelly," I said slowly, remembering the pert girl with the pretty blond hair and the cheap dress I had not returned.

I forced myself to read the piece as J. J. went on. "This one was killed in her room in Miller's Court," she told Stoker, whose face was ashen against his pillow. I remembered the man who had passed us in the street the night we wandered in the fog in search of Whitechapel High Street, the sense of foreboding that had leeched from him.

I thrust the newspaper back at J. J. "It is very well written," I told her truthfully. "It is as if I were there." The details of the crime turned my stomach.

"I hope that this will finally prove to those toffee-nosed prigs in Parliament that something must be done for the poor and indigent," she said, her color high.

Mornaday was watching her with a gleam of emotion in his eyes, and I wondered if he knew his feelings would never be reciprocated. J. J. Butterworth would make no man a wife. She was wedded to her career, her calling to expose the truth to the harsh light of day. She was a crusader, and crusaders were always touched with a bit of the fanatical. There was also the matter of the waltz we had shared and the tiny kiss she had bestowed upon me at the end of it. I looked at her and saw she was watching me, a small, inscrutable smile playing about her mouth. I knew that some women had Sapphic inclinations, and of course it was possible J. J. was one of their number. But I suspected she was more enchanted with the fact of her own outrageousness, calculated little stratagems designed to keep everyone she met slightly off-balance. She had faced many trials in her quest to become a journalist of renown, and I did not doubt she would use any weapon at her disposal in the pursuit.

Stoker put out his hand for the newspaper. He read in silence, and when he had finished, his jaw was set. "Would you be interested in interviewing a woman who knew her? Someone who could tell you what it is like to live on the streets? To sleep rough and to earn your bread on your back?"

She leant forwards eagerly. "Would I indeed!"

Mornaday looked affronted. "It is far too dangerous," he began.

J. J. rounded on him. "What I do is not your concern," she told him, her tone biting. I had little doubt this was a conversation they had had on more than one occasion. "Besides," she went on, "you had no objections when I wanted to work for Madame Aurore to write an exposé on the doings at her club."

"I had the most strenuous objections," he reminded her coldly.

"And look where that got you," she jeered. "I did it anyway. You would never have got your own post there without me."

"Is that how you came to be on hand?" I asked him. "We were grateful for the assistance, but you might have told us."

He had the grace to look a little abashed. "I could not be sure. I heard snippets of the inspector's plots, and I kept my ear to the ground. I trailed him a time or two and discovered he was meeting with de Clare. That put me immediately in mind of the last time that particular fellow came to our attention. Archibond was spending a good deal of his time at Madame Aurore's—too much for a man merely bent upon a bit of rumpy-pumpy," he added with a leer that would have done credit to a satyr. "I deduced the Club de l'Étoile was more than a spot for debauchery. It was a meeting place, a focus for some dastardly plan. So I prevailed upon J. J. to help me gain employment since she already had a post there," he acknowledged grudgingly.

I turned to J. J. "How does it happen that you were already in Madame Aurore's employ?"

"Mornaday," she said smoothly. "He was kind enough to volunteer the information that the club was a rich source of material for a story with all the comings and goings of the great and good."

"Volunteer!" Mornaday snorted. "You got that out of me with your feminine *wiles*."

J. J. blinked at him, wide-eyed and feigning innocence. "I haven't the faintest idea what you mean."

Mornaday grumbled under his breath. "She had been sniffing around the club for some weeks, making notes for a story she intended to write. When I asked her to secure a position there for me, it was the least she could do."

"I think what Mornaday *means* to say," she put in coldly, "is that he extorted a reference from me on the grounds that he would tell Madame Aurore exactly what my purpose was in taking employment in the club and ruin my story if I did not help him."

Mornaday's smile was smug. "Sauce for the goose, my dear." He turned back to me.

"I went in disguise so that Archibond should not know me."

"And kept your disguise even when speaking with friends," I put in.

"I could not know you were not a part of the plot," he returned. "I had to be certain. I even came round and gave you tickets to the theatre to test you, which you bloody well failed. Innocent people would have used them."

"I do not care for Gilbert and Sullivan," Stoker reminded him.

Mornaday scoffed. "What sort of Englishman doesn't care for Gilbert and Sullivan? They are national treasures, they are. In any event, your turning up at the club that night roused my suspicions. I had given you the perfect outing if you were innocent, but instead you appeared, just in the thick of the most damnable conspiracy I have seen since the last time de Clare darkened these shores. It was very difficult to entertain any possibility of your innocence after that."

"What persuaded you?" Stoker demanded.

Mornaday shifted in his seat. "I discovered Madame Aurore's body, just after the deed was done. I had seen de Clare and one of his men go into the dressing room, and I heard voices, raised. When they came out, de Clare's lad was putting a gore-stained handkerchief back into his pocket. I slipped into her room and found her there. I heard someone coming and hared into her bathroom, hiding behind the door."

"So you heard everything when we entered with the prince?" I guessed.

"Most of it," he affirmed. "Enough to realize none of you had a bloody thing to do with the conspiracy. So I decided to help."

"Help?" Stoker's expression was frankly skeptical.

Mornaday colored deeply. "Yes, as it happens. I did you a very great service. I scuttled down to the generator house and cut the electricity so you could get away in darkness. I meant to find you and lead you out of the place myself, but . . ." He trailed off, clearly uncomfortable.

"But?" I pressed.

"But he fell down," J. J. said, scarcely suppressing her mirth. "He tripped over a leg in the darkness and fell headlong into the punch bowl. He came out festooned with liquored fruits."

He scowled at her, no doubt deploring the less than romantic picture she had painted. He wanted to believe himself a swashbuckling hero, and yet to J. J. he would only ever be Mornaday, the bungling charmer of Scotland Yard.

I reached over and pressed a kiss to his cheek. "Well done, Mornaday. You always come through in the end. In spite of yourself."

He brightened considerably at that and Stoker folded the newspaper with maddening precision. "Yes, indeed. I suppose I ought to thank you for arriving when you did. A few minutes later and I might have been dangerously injured," he said, giving a significant look to the bandages still swathing his torso.

Mornaday's smile faded. "Yes, well. I did my best, didn't I? I spent half the night clearing up after you, carting corpses around to keep the prince from being implicated."

Stoker opened his mouth to argue, but I held up a hand. "If the pair of you mean to brawl, kindly wait until both of you are fit and do it properly, with pistols at dawn. Miss Butterworth and I will serve as your seconds."

"Speak for yourself, Miss Speedwell," J. J. said. "I rather think we should let them get on with killing one another. It would save us all a great deal of time and bother."

"I have had quite enough of pistols," Stoker said dryly. He gave Mornaday a long, level gaze. "I suppose we really do owe you a debt of thanks. Not just for a timely arrival, but for protecting the prince."

"I am still not persuaded he is worth it," Mornaday said with a ghost of a smile. "But you are welcome." A moment of understanding, perfect and amicable, hung between them. I might have known it would not last long.

"Still, you did leave our rescue rather late," Stoker said.

Mornaday thrust his hands into his hair. "Do you know how hard it was to find you? You vanished from the club in the middle of the night and I had no notion of where Archibond might have taken you nor where you might have disappeared after."

"We were at Bishop's Folly," I told him unhelpfully.

"You. Went. Home," he managed, biting off each syllable.

"Well, we got the prince to safety and then assumed Archibond was far too intelligent and de Clare too unnerved to stay in England. It seemed a safe enough proposition," I said by way of defending us.

Mornaday shook his head. "If only I had gone to you then," he said, his tone frankly mournful.

"But then you might not have had the opportunity to apprehend the conspirators," J. J. pointed out with infallible logic. She turned to me and to Stoker. "Poor Mornaday was at a loss once you disappeared from the club. There were records connecting Archibond with the warehouse in Whitechapel, but it took more than a day to put the pieces together, and by that time you had escaped him and he had fled. Mornaday and I could not unravel the next bit of the plot until we compared what we knew and were able to anticipate Archibond's last desperate gambit—luring you here." She smiled in obvious satisfaction. "Whilst Mornaday was haring around town in pursuit of Archibond, I was following you. I suspected you were the key to the whole scheme, as much as Mornaday tried to keep your name out of it. And when I recognized you at the club, I knew I had only to go to Bishop's Folly anytime I wanted to pick up your trail."

I gave her an even stare. "And you know the purpose of the plot."

She nodded. "I do. They meant to use a series of scandals to throw this lot off the throne and install you in their place."

"You are no respecter of institutions," I commented mildly. "And yet you are willing to protect them. You have not written about this in your newspaper. An ambitious reporter, sitting quietly on the story of the century. It beggars belief."

She curled her hands into fists. "I am ambitious, and I mean to make a name for myself," she vowed. "But I will not do it that way, not with that sort of destruction. The cost would be too high. The world is not ready for such anarchy."

"You are a royalist after all," I said softly.

"I am a pragmatist," she corrected. "I want to write stories that will do real good, accomplish some purposeful change. Like speaking with the women who live in Whitechapel," she said with a nod towards Stoker.

"I will arrange it," he promised.

"And you will keep my secret?" I asked.

She gave me an assessing look. "Let me be a part of your adventures whenever possible, and I will keep it to the grave, Miss Speedwell," she said, extending her hand to shake mine.

"That is a bargain, Miss Butterworth."

. . .

S toker remained in Pennybaker's care for more than a fortnight before he was permitted to leave. I stayed with him, sleeping in my narrow elephant-bedecked bed next to his in the night nursery. I left him only once—to retrieve clothing from Bishop's Folly and make our excuses to the earl. I sketched a vague story about an accident, and his lordship, distracted by the new arrival of a set of cameos of polished Vesuvian lava, made suitable noises of sympathy and told us to take as long as we needed before returning. I was delighted to find Lady Wellie on the mend, and took tea with her before I left.

"Well," she said, eyeing my sling disapprovingly, "I see you have been up to mischief whilst I have been incommoded."

"A bit," I conceded. Over tea from her Wedgwood crocodile service, I told her the whole story, including our harrowing adventure with Eddy and his secret return to Scotland.

"I know," she said calmly.

I blinked, pausing in the act of dolloping a bit of strawberry jam on a muffin.

"You do?"

She smiled, her old bird-of-prey smile that never changed. "My dear child, I have had regular visits from most members of the family."

She did not need to specify which family. My heart beat faster, thudding dully against my ribs as I put the spoon aside with careful hands.

"Was—"

"Your father? No. But the Princess of Wales came. And Eddy." She gave me a close look. "You liked him, didn't you?"

"I did. In spite of myself. There is an unexpected sweetness to him."

She paused, nodding gravely. Her gaze drifted and her expression was inscrutable.

She poured out a fresh cup of tea, stirring with deliberate calm. "By the way, you might return my diary when you have a moment. That is how you and Stoker discovered my state of mind, is it not?"

I did not bother to deny it. "We were concerned, and Archibond played upon those worries expertly."

"As he did my own," she said. "The anonymous note and the cuttings were his, planting that monstrous suggestion."

"It was unkind of him," I began.

"Unkind! It was diabolical," she said with real venom. "But once the idea had been raised, I saw how easily our enemies might make political capital of it, true or not."

"He is not responsible, you know," I told her firmly. "Eddy could never have committed the murders in Whitechapel."

A flicker of emotion crossed her face. In another, I might have called it guilt. But I was entirely certain Lady Wellie was unacquainted with such a feeling.

"I did not believe it," she told me. "Not really. But all possibilities, no matter how distasteful, must be investigated, if only to rule them out. I did not believe it."

I might have believed her if she had not repeated herself. For whatever reason—ill health, fatigue, distraction—she had permitted her imagination to get the better of her, doubting a man she had known since birth, whose every flaw and virtue were as familiar to her as her own face. She would not forgive herself easily, and she would never forget.

I did not have the heart to prod her further. I returned my attention to my muffin and she said suddenly, her eyes bright, "I am glad you had a chance to spend time with him."

"So am I.

"You might have told us of your suspicions before the princess appealed to us to retrieve the jewel. It would have saved a great deal of trouble."

She put her cup into the saucer, rattling it only a little. "Do not think I am unaware of how badly I mishandled matters this time. That Archibond should—" She broke off, composing herself after a moment. "I have decided to take a sabbatical. The weather is not good for my neuralgia, and I need the sun. I am leaving next week for Egypt."

"You will be missed," I told her.

"Yes, well, it will give me a chance to complete my recovery and contemplate my sins," she said crisply.

"It does not matter now," I said. "It is finished."

Her smile was pitying. "My dear child, it is never finished. Our enemies are cunning and careful. And they are legion."

"And this time they have lost," I assured her. "Mornaday and Sir Hugo will never reveal my patrimony."

"And that reporter?" she asked, her lips thinning with displeasure.

"Miss Butterworth and I have come to an understanding," I said coolly.

"Indeed?"

"Yes, we have shaken hands upon the matter and I trust her."

Her mouth curled. "A gentlemen's agreement?"

"No," I told her. "Better than that. It is a ladies' agreement."

# CHAPTER

## 25

The other order of business at Bishop's Folly was not nearly so pleasant. It transpired that, during his interview with Sir Hugo, Mornaday had omitted one significant detail—the murder of Madame Aurore.

"Why on earth would you fail to tell him about that?" J. J. demanded.

Mornaday looked frankly mulish. "I couldn't very well tell my superior that I had been haring about London with a corpse in tow, now, could I? There are laws about such things."

"Why not?" she asked disdainfully. "You were covering up a crime, something Sir Hugo seems entirely comfortable with."

"I was never supposed to be working in the Club de L'Étoile in the first place," he reminded her stiffly. "Archibond was my superior. If Sir Hugo discovered I had spied upon him and trailed him on the strength of nothing more than a suspicion, he would drum me out of the Yard, and my new promotion would go hang on a washing line. Besides, Sir Hugo did what he did out of necessity for the good of the nation—nay, for the good of the Empire."

She snorted. "You mean for the good of his own arse. If anyone knew an anarchist had carried out an abduction of a senior royal under the very nose of the people tasked with their protection, he would be out of a post before you could snap your fingers," she said, clicking her fingers for emphasis.

Mornaday flushed hotly. "Sir Hugo Montgomerie would *never* put himself first in such a situation, and if you think he would, you are the most cynical—"

I held up a hand. "Pax, children. Now, regardless of *why* we have a corpse on our hands, the point is that we do. And she must be dealt with."

In a late-night whispered council of war in the night nursery—now Stoker's recovery ward—we decided amongst ourselves that she ought to be laid to rest quietly. She had no family to mourn her, no close friends, we discovered. Mornaday went to make discreet inquiries at the club, but it was shuttered, the staff dispersed, and her solicitor could offer no further information. Madame Aurore had built a career on secrets and she took them to her grave.

Following Stoker's careful instructions, Mornaday and J. J. and I disposed of Madame Aurore. We returned to Bishop's Folly late one night to finish the sordid task. We tied strips of cloth soaked in camphor over our mouths and noses to counter the stench, but J. J. was sick again when Mornaday removed the lid of the sarcophagus. I retrieved the Templeton-Vane tiara, cleaning it carefully before wrapping it in a piece of velvet and putting it with the armillae into a rusted biscuit box for safekeeping. Only Stoker would look there, I reflected, and so long as there were no biscuits to be found, the tiara would remain undisturbed.

"Best dispose of this while we're about it," Mornaday said, tugging an armful of pink taffeta from a bundle near the corpse's feet.

"That is the gown the prince was wearing," I said at once. I retrieved the bundle, only a little soiled from its proximity to decomposition. "How did you come to find this?" I demanded.

He pulled himself up, puffing a little with pride. "I was following you that night. Not near enough to stop them snatching you off the curb," he said, clearly irritated with his own failures. "But I managed to recover that. I still had it when I went to collect madame's body," he added with a jerk of the chin towards his former employer. "I stuffed it into the box with her so it wouldn't fall into the wrong hands. Between that and that bloody awful tiara, I did nothing but clear up after the pair of you all evening," he added with a grin.

Together, the three of us removed Madame Aurore from the sarcophagus, carefully covering her with a linen shroud. Mornaday retrieved the crate he had used to transport her, a simple box of suitable dimensions, and we placed her within it, cushioning her with reams of linen. A lavish application of quicklime drove back the worst of the odor, and Mornaday nailed the lid into place. He pasted a label on the top with the direction of the nearest mortuary.

"I have a doctor who will sign a death certificate of natural causes for a few pounds," he said, sighing heavily. "She will be buried as a Jane Doe."

"A wretched end for such a glamorous creature," J. J. put in.

"At least it is a Christian burial." Mornaday bristled. "We have discovered that she met Archibond some months ago and he brought her into the plot with de Clare. Archibond was surveilling the prince in order to find some snippet of scandal to use against him. When he realized the prince was frequenting the Club de l'Étoile, he made a point of cultivating her, of discovering her vulnerability."

"Which was?" I asked.

"Money," was J. J.'s succinct response. "She lived lavishly, and she was generous to her friends and servants, more generous than she could afford. She had exhausted her credit in this country and was beginning to feel the press of her debts. Archibond promised her a fresh start in the Argentine if she helped him. She was not a bad woman," she said, her expression wistful. "I like to think that she might have refused to hand Eddy over to them in the end."

Mornaday's lips tightened. "She ended a pawn in Archibond's schemes, but let us not forget, she conspired to overthrow the monarchy. It is no worse than she deserves."

J. J. and I exchanged glances. How like a man not to understand.

Before we left, I collected the post that had come in our absence. Amidst the bills and circulars and begging letters, there was one envelope, larger than the rest. It was stiff and crested, with my name on the front but no address. It had been delivered by hand. There was no note, only a photograph. It was His Royal Highness, Prince Albert Victor, resplendent in the uniform of the Tenth Hussars, moustaches waxed and curled, gaze steady as he looked to the middle distance. Our future king, I mused. I turned it over to find an inscription.

*To Veronica Speedwell, the bravest woman of my acquaintance. If you have need of me, you have only to ask. Eddy*

On a whim, I went to the bookshelves in the snuggery, dusty and sagging with the weight of the volumes stacked there. It took only a moment to find the one I wanted. It was a guide to the royal and imperial families of Europe, complete with subsidiary titles. I flicked through the pages until I came to His Royal Highness, Albert Edward, Prince of Wales. I traced the lesser titles with a fingertip. Duke of Cornwall. Duke of Rothesay.

*Earl of Chester.*

I slipped my hand into my pocket and retrieved my little velvet murine companion. Eddy might have been given a Chester of his own, but his would always be the second, I reflected. I replaced the book and went back downstairs, tucking Chester the First away in safety. I smiled to myself and propped Eddy's photograph on my desk where I could look at it from time to time as I worked. Our paths would take us very different places, but they had crossed once. And that was enough.

It was a cool and windy day in November when we decided to return the Templeton-Vane jewels to Tiberius' house. The fox-tooth tiara had been cleaned, albeit with a broken fang or two, but the armillae shone as brightly as ever. We had both of us enjoyed our time at Mr. Pennybaker's house. It had been a holiday of sorts, a respite from the real world and all its attendant horrors. We had rested in comfort and security as our wounds healed. Stoker had taken up a needlework project, and I had read aloud to him from the latest natural history journals, although to be entirely honest, these were often cast aside in favor of Stoker's favorite French novels. Mr. Pennybaker spent a good deal of time with us, telling entertaining tales of his own adventures—most of them *quite* unexpected for such a diffident little man. (And one or two so delightfully salacious that I was sent out of the room on an errand during the telling. I prevailed upon Stoker to relate them later, which he did in lurid detail.)

We left him with a pang of regret, but it was time. The wind had risen, sharp and laced with the first frost of the season. The spiderwebs in the hedgerows were dotted with pearls of ice, and each lovely ruby berry was sheathed in a thin, diamond-hard layer of the stuff. The whole world sparkled that morning, and we returned to the Belvedere with a sense of homecoming.

Of course, the place was absolute bedlam. The dogs—Vespertine included—were outraged at the fact that Cook's cat had escaped the kitchens and was sitting on top of Lady Rose's hermitage, scolding them all as she sat, just out of reach of their most determined efforts to drag her from her perch.

Patricia the tortoise, whose wedding day had arrived at last, was destined for disappointment when the crate bearing her bridegroom had finally been released from Customs. Procured at great trouble and expense by his lordship, the male tortoise proved much more youthful—and smaller—than his fearsome wife. She outweighed him by some sixteen stone and he was so tiny as yet she might have worn him for a hat.

She moaned her disapproval and lumbered away just before Lady Rose's efforts with her brother's tea bore fruit of the most noxious variety. Charles was busy being sick in the shrubbery amidst the howling dogs and the moaning tortoise and the sound of the earl remonstrating with his youngest child when Stoker took me firmly by the hand. He retrieved the biscuit tin with the tiara and the armillae and whistled up a hackney, giving the driver Tiberius' address.

We arrived to find the house shrouded in darkness.

"Locked up tight as a drum, she is," the driver said shrewdly. "Won't be no one to look after you, it seems."

"No matter," Stoker said, handing me from the carriage. "I have a key." He paid the fellow and sent him off. I followed Stoker not to the front door, which was heavily barred and bolted, but down the stairs to the area door. He fitted his key to the lock and in a moment we were inside the sleeping house, the very air muffled.

"Hungry?" he asked as we passed through the kitchens.

"It would not do much good if I were," I observed, peeking into the pantry. "The larders are bare. Tiberius must have given orders to clear them out to avoid mice whilst he is away."

Stoker grinned. "But I'll wager the wine cellar is full." He vanished down a narrow stairway to a little cellar where Tiberius stored his prized vintages. He emerged with a dusty bottle of great antiquity.

"Chambertin, 1803," he said with a flourish.

"Is that good?"

"I haven't the faintest idea. But he kept it locked up, so I know it must be valuable."

"You seem intent upon robbing Tiberius blind," I pointed out.

He tipped his head. "I think, after our escapade in Cornwall, he rather owes us."

"I quite agree," I said as he retrieved his knife. In a moment, he had sliced through the wax seal and pulled the cork. He poured us each a measure of wine, and it ran red as rubies and smelling of berries and smoke.

"To another successful adventure," he proposed. We touched glasses and sipped, and that wine was like nothing I had ever tasted. There was a silken quality to it, and a ripeness that beat like wings in my blood, and I looked at him over the rim of the glass and realized we were alone, entirely alone, with no prospect of interruption, no duty, no obligation.

He drained his glass and picked up the bottle. I said nothing, but there was no need. I followed him as he made his way through the house, the town home he had known since boyhood. He needed no illumination to find his path, and it was not until we reached Tiberius' guest suite that he lit a candle.

"Tiberius always orders the gas to be restricted whilst he is away," he explained. "But there are plenty of candles and the water will be hot if you want a bath." The plumbing at the Roman baths at Bishop's Folly had still not been repaired, and I longed for a proper soak, but Stoker was playing for time. He was a little nervous, as I was. We had no excuses save fatigue to keep us apart. This then was the moment we must choose to move forwards together—or remain forever divided, friends but nothing more.

I, too, played for time. I went into the bathroom, a luxuriously tiled little chamber where a massive copper bath stood in splendor. It filled quickly and I hurled in great handfuls of salts with trembling hands. I was aware of a new wakefulness, an urgency that caused my limbs to shake. I stepped out of my clothes, noting the fresh pink scars like tiny stars on my shoulder, marks of a warrior, I decided. Great clouds of steam rolled through the room as I unpinned my hair, letting it fall until the ends trailed in the foaming water.

I lay back in the bath, the water lapping my shoulders as I closed my eyes. I thought of all the dark times Stoker and I had both endured. I thought of the risks we had taken for one another, the bullets and knives and near drownings, the fires and furies we had faced down because we would always stand, back to back, against the world. If I ever lost that stalwart devotion, I did not think I could survive it. I had never in the whole of my life known such perfect companionship, the quarrels and the laughs, the moments of complete and unspoken understanding. He was not another half, for I was whole unto myself. But he was my mirror, and in him I saw reflected all that I liked best in me. I saw honesty and pride, loyalty, and a willingness to stand, however difficult, in service of one's principles. He was a twin soul to my own, and if I had not loved him so much, I would never have feared so much losing him.

My cheeks were damp with steam and tears, and I took up a washcloth to wipe them. This would never do. I had gained nothing I valued in life from sitting back, I told myself firmly. I had never shrunk from a challenge; I throve on it. I thrust myself to my feet, water cascading over the sides of the bathtub and onto the floor. There would be no more waiting, no more hesitation. From this moment forwards, I vowed, we would be together in all things. We belonged to each other.

I reached for a towel, but before I could grasp it, the door opened. Through the clouds of steam, I could see him, mother-naked and the most glorious thing I had ever beheld. I knew, as I so often did, that the course of his thoughts had brought him to the same conclusion as mine. The time for questioning and doubt was past. We had chosen.

He said not a word; there was nothing to be said. He simply strode across the marble floor, certain as a king, and came for me.

The well-informed reader will already be aware of the practices of the lion of the African savannahs. These noble beasts, when mated, will consummate their union numerous times in the course of several hours, until the male is thoroughly exhausted and the female is content. I say, with all possible modesty, that *Panthera leo* might have learnt a thing or two from us. I had always experienced a certain hectic pleasure when Stoker and I kissed, but that was the merest prelude to what we achieved that night. We began in the bathroom, where the steaming tub and its attendant luxuries provided several opportunities for amatory investigations. When the water cooled we meant to remove ourselves to the guest bed, but we had to pass through the dressing room, where a lushly upholstered black velvet chaise proved eminently worth our diversion. Then I think there was a chair, at just the right height for a particularly pleasurable activity that even now draws a blush to my cheek. We finished in the bed, having wrought a path of modest destruction from the bathroom—water flooding the floor—to the writing table, where the blotter betrayed a thoroughly salacious imprint of someone's backside, and on to the great four-poster bed itself, the tester knocked askew and the slats weakened.

We lay, entwined, hearts beating against one another, one of his hands wrapped in my hair as the dawning sun gilded the edges of the draperies.

"It's morning," he murmured sleepily. "The first morning."

He said nothing else, but I understood him. This was the first morning we had awakened in each other's arms, but it was more than that. This was the first morning ever, the beginning of all creation as far as I was concerned. A new life for us had begun, hand in hand, arm in arm, facing down the rest of the world. What adventures would await us!

We lazed like leopards, my fingertips tracing his scars old and new like contours on a map. "But this is an end, Veronica," Stoker said severely. "No more exploits, no more bullets, no more investigations. A man can only stand being shot or stabbed or half-drowned so many times before he begins to take it rather personally. Now, promise me, this is an end to it."

I opened my eyes very wide. "I promise."

He narrowed his gaze. "Are your fingers crossed behind your back?"

I grinned. "Of course they are."

He sighed. "Very well, then. I suppose I must surrender to my fate. Because you are clearly destined for adventure. And I am destined for you."

I kissed him then, properly and with real gratitude for his understanding. Ours would never be a small and staid existence. Wherever we went, we would go together, making our way side by side, as equals in every adventure. Excelsior!

# AUTHOR'S NOTE

Mary Ann Nichols. Annie Chapman. Elizabeth Stride. Catherine Eddowes. Mary Jane Kelly. These are the names of the five canonical victims of Jack the Ripper. In the fascination with one of the world's most notorious serial killers, the names of these women are often lost, and there are many misconceptions about them, most notably that they were prostitutes. Women at the poorest levels of society often engaged in periodic sex work in order to make up the price of a bed or meal, without identifying themselves as prostitutes by trade— Scotland Yard's own criterion for determining who was a sex worker. These women used sex work to supplement their meager earnings in a system that was designed to crush the poor. Their lives were far too complicated and nuanced to be explained in a short author's note or a few scenes depicting their reality. History is reclaiming the stories of the women of Whitechapel as more than victims of heinous crimes, and anyone interested in reading more about them cannot do better than Hallie Rubenhold's groundbreaking collective biography of them, entitled *The Five*.

The mention of London homeless sleeping rough or setting up tent cities in 1888 in Trafalgar Square is factual. The hysteria surrounding the Ripper murders focused attention and resentment on a variety of targets: immigrants, the poor, the rich, the mentally ill, the Jewish community. Newspapers were flooded with letters demanding social reform, urging the wealthy to admit their responsibility in creating a system that disadvantaged the poor and kept them trapped in a cycle of want, ignorance, and—far too often—violence.

The idea that His Royal Highness, Prince Albert Victor, was a possible suspect in the murders did not appear in the annals of Ripperology until the 1970s. There are still those who entertain this notion, but it has been proven that the prince had an alibi during the killings. The prince was guilty of being spoiled and perhaps not terribly bright, but he was not homicidal by any stretch of the imagination. He was most often described as charming and sweet and disinclined to exert himself mentally or socially, leading some to believe he had a learning disability or shared his mother's deafness, although there is no concrete evidence for either.

Two other rumors that have also persisted for decades are that the prince was involved in the Cleveland Street scandal in 1889 that exposed an establishment at that address as a brothel specializing in homosexual activity and that he was a transvestite, dressing in drag for parties during which he answered to the name "Victoria." Unable to trace a reliable source for the latter story, I have used female dress solely as a masquerade costume for the prince rather than as a means of personal expression. As to his sexual orientation, it remains a complicated—and perhaps unanswerable—question at this date.

From letters written by Eddy to family members in the autumn of 1888, we know he was deeply in love with his cousin Princess Alix of Hesse—the first of at least two strong heterosexual romantic attachments in his life. He was created Duke of Clarence in 1890 and died in January of 1892 of complications from influenza at the age of twenty-eight, plunging his mother into profound mourning although many newspapers abroad were unflinching in their editorial relief that he would never reign. His fiancée at the time of his death, Princess Mary of Teck, went on to marry his brother, George, and together they guided the United Kingdom through the dark days of World War I as King George V and Queen Mary. For the most recent and exhaustive inquiry into the prince's connection to the Cleveland Street scandal as well as a thorough biography, *Prince Eddy: The King Britain Never Had* by Andrew Cook is highly recommended.

Eddy's first love, Princess Alix of Hesse and by Rhine, refused his advances on the grounds that she had already fallen in love with Tsarevitch Nicholas of Russia, later Tsar Nicholas II. Upon her marriage, Alix changed her name to Alexandra Feodorovna, and she and Nicholas—along with their five children—were executed in 1918 during the Russian Revolution. She was canonized as Saint Alexandra Romanova in 2000 by the Russian Orthodox Church.

Her Royal Highness, the Princess of Wales—later Queen Alexandra—did have a collection of diamond stars from Garrard. They are believed to remain in the collection of the British royal family today.

While Victorians referred to the ancient British queen as Boadicea of the Iceni, scholars today prefer Boudica of the Eceni.

# ACKNOWLEDGMENTS

Heartfelt and most profound thanks to everyone at Berkley/Penguin who works so hard to make Veronica happen, especially Craig Burke, Loren Jaggers, Claire Zion, Jeanne-Marie Hudson, Jin Yu, Jessica Mangicaro, Jennifer Snyder, Ivan Held, Christine Ball, and Tara O'Connor. I am indebted to every department—sales, marketing, publicity, editorial—for their dedication, and I am, as ever, awed by the immensely talented art department and their determination to make these books so beautiful.

If I had diamond stars of my own to hand out, they would go to Pam Hopkins (my savvy agent of twenty years), Danielle Perez (my gifted and generous editor), Ellen Edwards (my inspired acquiring editor), and Eileen Chetti (my deft copyeditor).

Another galaxy of stars would be presented with thanks to the booksellers, reviewers, bloggers, readers, librarians, and bookstagrammers who have taken Veronica to their hearts and made her their own. Diamonds also for Jomie Wilding, the Writerspace team, and the many friends and writers who have given so generously to Veronica and to me: Blake Leyers, Ali Trotta, Delilah Dawson, Ariel

Lawhon, Joshilyn Jackson, Lauren Willig, Susan Elia MacNeal, Robyn Carr, Alan Bradley, David Bell, Rhys Bowen, and the Blanket Fort.

For Mom, Dad, and Caitlin—you are my everything.

For Phil. Forever. For always. Thank you.